The Golden Road

by

Celia Hayes

Geron GA *& Associates*

San Antonio, 2016

Notes from the Author

Thanks, acknowledgements and appreciation are due to a great number of people who contributed advice and support to the writer of this novel. I should begin with thanks to those who volunteered as beta-readers: Bernadette Durbin and Mike White, and to the readers of various websites where I posted selected chapters as I wrote them.

This book is also dedicated to my parents, my original alpha readers, and to my daughter Jeanne – who offered much serious plotting advice.

Celia Hayes
San Antonio, Texas
September 2015

The Golden Road

Chapter 1 – Two Boys

Spring came to the lowlands around San Antonio de Bexar as it did in every year – springs of clear water flowing clear and ice-cold, with meadows of flowers splashed in swaths of yellow, pink and the deep rich blue of buffalo clover as if a reckless artist had chosen to go mad with the paint. Young Friedrich Steinmetz, whom most everyone called Fredi, came with his brother-in-law's herd of cattle and three hired buckaroos to sell the cattle in the market-plaza in Bexar. Carl Becker's ranch spanned a stretch of the hills that defined the valley of the upper Guadalupe, where he had built a tall stone house and brought Fredi's older sister to it some eight years before. The Hill Country – ranges of limestone hills quilted with oak trees, formed the wall between the grassy and well-watered lowlands, long-settled by white men and Mexicans, and the Comanche-haunted plains of the Llano country. For more than half his life, it had been home to Fredi and his twin brother Johann. They were alike in form, being wiry of build, hazel-eyed and with light-brown hair, but different in character. Fredi was the scapegrace, impulsive and bold. Johann was the clever one; this very spring he was to sail away and study medicine in the Old Country, that country where the twins had been born sixteen and a half years before.

"I want to go and see Johann off when the cattle are sold," Fredi said, that night when they were less than a day's journey to Bexar. The sun had already faded to a deep apricot blush in the western sky, and the stars to glimmer pale in the sky overhead. The herd was pastured in a meadow on the bank of Salado Creek, running deep and cold at this time of year. The cattle drank from it eagerly, after a warm afternoon of being chivvied across a dry stretch. Fredi's brother-in-law Carl Becker helped himself to another piece of journey-bread, and answered through a mouthful. "You're gonna have to travel on your own, then. I can't stay long enough from the place to see you to Indianola and back an' I sure as Hell can't pay your way on the stage."

"That's what I planned on," Fredi answered. "An' … if I run out of money, I'll work my way back."

"That's the spirit," Carl Becker grinned. He was a big young man, Saxon-fair and soft-spoken, some fifteen years older than Fredi. They spoke together in German, that language which Carl had from his family, who had been settled in America some three or four generations longer than the Steinmetzes. "But you better get yourself back as soon as you can – I don't want to explain to Magda and Vati that I've let you loose on the world, all on your own."

"If Johann is old enough to go study medicine in Germany," Fredi answered. "Then I don't see how anyone would mind me making my way in the world. You told me that you enlisted in a Ranger company when you were the age I am in now."

"That was different," Carl answered, but didn't offer any explanation as to why that would be. "And if something happens to you, your sister will skin me alive."

"She's all taken up with the baby," Fredi answered, carelessly. "But I won't see Johann for years and years, Carl – we're brothers! I want to see him one more time … we can hurrah in Indianola for all the times we won't be there with each other." He fixed Carl with pleading eyes. "I promise I'll come straight back to the ranch."

"Promises like that are nut-shells, made to be broken," Carl answered, with a touch of wry cynicism. "You and Johann are as thick as thieves and I always like to think that he keeps you out of trouble … Go and see him away – but if you do get into a ruction on your own, I promise I will come down and skin you myself. Especially if I have to bail you out of the *cabildo*."

"Excellent!" Fredi exclaimed, joyfully relieved. "As soon as you sell the cattle, then – I'll take the road toward the coast. Johann and Mr. Coreth are to take passage on the steamer to New Orleans in three weeks. I'll be back well before mid-summer. You can count on me!"

"I can count on you to be a handful – and that's what worries me," Carl answered.

The cattle sold readily; long-horned piebald creatures for the most, only a little less wild than the deer that roamed the hills. Three mornings later, Fredi rose early and went to the stable around in back of the rambling old-fashioned adobe brick mansion on Soledad Street. The chimes from San Fernando Cathedral faintly sounded the hour for daily Mass, but crickets and frogs in the rushes at the river-edge sounded yet louder. In the quiet of dawn, Fredi saddled his own horse, a tough little paint-pony from the borderlands, where his and Carl's host owned several leagues of land straddling the Rio Grande. It was time to get started; Fredi was aware of a sense of breathless anticipation, the same as he had felt on that day when his family set out from Albeck, near Ulm in Bavaria. That was almost ten years ago, when Fredi and Johann were barely seven years of age. Almost two-thirds of their lives since had been lived in Texas.

"I'd not want to go back to Germany," Fredi confided to his pony. "I can't even remember much; and of that I do, I don't even want to think about. You'd never get me to cross an ocean again, not if you gave me the whole of Gillespie County." This was something that he and Johann had argued about – practically the only thing over which they disagreed.

"You sound as if you have made up your mind," Carl remarked from the stable doorway and Fredi started a little. His brother-in-law moved as noiselessly as an Indian; Fredi had never become accustomed to that.

"I have," he replied. "And I wasn't just going to sneak away. It's just that … I guess I want to see the elephant, like in the story. Vati says it's like in one of his books, about folk longing to make a pilgrimage. But he says that it's not where you're going that matters – it's just the journey. Johann has always been the one with all the brains and book-learning. He wants to be a doctor; everyone thinks that is the greatest thing. I don't know what I want to do," Fredi added, in a burst of candor. "Except be as rich as a First. Maybe I should go to California and look for gold. When you were my age, Carl, what did you want to do?"

"Live to grow old," answered Carl, with a dry and completely un-humorous chuckle. "But I take your meaning, hoss; I didn't want much else, back then. My sister often told me that my lack of ambition was terribly exasperating."

"Well, I can work cattle, tame horses, drive a wagon, and dig ditches," Fredi answered. "Likely I won't starve. I can read and write, as well. Maybe something will come up in Indianola."

"Maybe it will," Carl said. "Give Johann my best wishes, when you see him."

"I will," Fredi's heart rose within him; it seemed like he had been given permission.

The sun was just barely up in the eastern sky, sending erratic fingers of light across Main Plaza, when Fredi rode out of Soledad Street. All around the edge of the Plaza, the day was beginning for the market vendors, for the Mexican women bringing heavy kettles of spicy meat and bean stew from their homes, to sell to the hungry of all races as the day wore on. Fredi gazed upon it all, with a sigh of happiness. All the world lay before him. The last thing Carl had done for him was to draw out a map on a piece of paper, showing the road toward Victoria, and thence to Indianola on the coast, on the shores of Matagorda Bay. He had written out the landmarks along the way, and now the folded paper was tucked into Fredi's the pocket of his round jacket, jacket buttoned to his chin against the morning chill. Carl had also given him a little roll of paper notes, which Fredi had accepted reluctantly – this was a quarter of the profits from the sale of the cattle, and Fredi knew very well that Carl and his sister Magda had plans for every penny.

"It's your share, for the work you have done," Carl said finally and Fredi acquiesced.

The road south called to him. It was time.

The first few days of it went very well; Fredi was well-familiar with the out of doors, of rolling up in a blanket or two, and sleeping on a bed of last years' leaves, or begging hospitality at a farmstead in exchange for splitting firewood. He had begun to think that this adventure into the world was going very well ... but a very few miles from the town of Victoria, his pony began to limp. Fredi dismounted immediately, fearing the worst, and discovered that it was only a thrown shoe. This was good, since it was only that and not a worse injury to the pony, but the unfortunate aspect of the matter was that the shoe itself was nowhere to be found. Fredi led his pony back along the pair of beaten tracks which constituted the road for half a mile or so, before concluding that the shoe was gone. He would have to find a blacksmith in Victoria to forge a new shoe.

There were two blacksmiths in Victoria, and a wheelwright as well, but the sun was already setting, and evening shadows were already creeping out from the tall trees around the blacksmith's forge.

"Can't do 'er until morning, Dutch," said the first smith, a burly fellow whose leather apron was smudged and scorched with the marks of his profession. He was already closing up his enterprise for the day. "Leave your horse in my corral, though – I'll do it first thing in the morning, after breakfast. Go ahead and pay me now." He contorted his soot-blackened countenance into an expression which Fredi realized must be a wink. "Guarantee – you're first in line, o' course."

"Then I can resume traveling, first thing," Fredi answered, with relief. He brought out his roll of notes, paid from it the sum required, and returned it to his pocket. The smith looked at him, replying,

"Aye, if you are looking for a place to spend the night, Miz Pratt takes in travelers for a night or so, just down the street. Two bits for supper and a bed for the night. You may have to sleep on the verandah, though."

"I don't mind," Fredi answered with relief. "I'm hungry and tired – anything will suit me."

"Good attitude to have, Dutch," the smith said. Fredi shouldered saddle-bags and blanket, still wondering why everyone was calling him 'Dutch.'

The streets of Victoria were crowded with wagons, horsemen and now and again the occasional foraging pig. Fredi sniffed in appreciation at the good smells of bread, and roasting meats which wafted from those houses along the way toward the one which the smith had directed him toward. It looked as if there were a great many other travelers staying at the Pratt boarding house, to judge from the wagons lined up along the road, and team animals corralled nearby.

The woman of the house – presumably Mrs. Pratt agreed, unenthusiastically, to set another plate at the table for him. She had a harassed and unhappy expression on her face, a greasy meat fork in one hand, and brown smears of an unidentifiable substance on her apron. Fredi moved a little aside; she also smelled most revoltingly of stale sweat and wood-smoke and wished that he had chanced his luck almost anyplace else.

"Yew kin spread yer blanket in the parlor, if ye don't mind them as are leaving early," she said; Fredi barely grasped what she said. He was not used to English spoken with such a barbarous accent. "And for five cents extry, hot breakfast in the mawnin'." She looked at him with a mildly curious expression. "Yer one of these furrin fellows, ain't cha? Yew talk funny."

"I was born in Albeck in Bavaria," Fredi answered, at least as baffled by the question as much as he was by her speech. "But I have been working for my sister's husband – he has a ranch in the Hills."

"A Dutchman – so I thought," Mrs. Pratt answered, as Fredi took out his roll of money, and some small coins. He counted them carefully and put two bits and a nickel in her hand, thinking that a hot meal would be good, but that Mrs. Pratt probably didn't set near as good a table as his sister Magda did.

No, she didn't. When the household and guests set down at table that evening, Fredi looked upon the dishes set out; a dish of pork chops *(overdone to the point of being as leathery as his belt)*, a bowl of cooked potatoes *(underdone and still unpleasantly crisp in the center)* drizzled in rendered fat from the pork and what might have been chopped grass, some boiled turnips and carrots, also drizzled in fat, but cooked to tastelessness *(a mercy, all else considered)* and a plate of cornbread, which against the odds had the welcome quality of being hot, tasty and crisp on the edges. There was also a glutinous jar of preserved sweet something to go with it, but Fredi let the preserves go from him without comment – although he did wish that he had the nerve to say out loud what he thought of in his head; which was that this board did not groan, but merely whimpered faintly in alarm – an English witticism of which he was rather proud of having thought. A glance at the other boarders, most eating as heartily as if they were starving convinced him of the wisdom of discretion. But two of them had resigned expressions on their own faces as they ate of the meager bounty with distinct un-enthusiasm. Fredi divined from the general conversation around the table that they were true Yankees, all the way from New York. It interested him, as it seemed they were brothers and traveling on horseback in Texas for interest and pleasure – not for business, as was the motivation of the others. He heard their name as Homestead; the older named Frederick, the same as his own name, only in English.

"You should go to Neu Braunfels … Friedrichsburg, even," he assured the two Homesteads with all the earnestness at his command. "Funny that it has the same name as we two – but it was named for Prince Friedrich of Prussia as a leading member of the Verein. We are all German folk there – and I do not know of any woman among us who does not set a good table… at least as good as this," he added, as he caught a suddenly-suspicious glance from his hostess, bringing another dish of leather-tough chops to the table.

"We live for promises," murmured the younger Homestead brother. Fredi thought that he had better hold his tongue. His sister had often chastised him for being offensively brash – and in this place, he knew no one and no one knew him.

But the older brother remarked, thoughtfully, "I did not know there were so many Germans settled in Texas, until someone gave me a copy of the *San Antonio Zeitung* – all in German, it was. Could have knocked me over with a feather."

"Oh, yah – there are many here who came with the Verein," Fredi was happy to have drawn their interest. "There are many German businesses in San Antonio – and in Indianola, too. My father is a friend of Professor Lindheimer – do you know of him? He has discovered many new plants here in Texas?"

"He has?" Frederick Homestead asked, with very real interest lighting his face; thereafter the rest of the evening passed congenially as far as Fredi was concerned. He sat outside after supper, with the Homestead brothers smoking their pipes, in idle conversation with each other and Fredi, regarding curious plants of Texas, what kind of industries had drawn the German settlers and the road toward Austin which would afford the most leisurely tour of the countryside. Exhausted by the days' journey, Fredi wished most desperately to roll himself in his blankets and get some sleep, but the other guests seemed more willing to stay and talk – and drink from a surreptitiously-passed bottle until almost midnight. He found a corner of the verandah, and fell into restless sleep, with his head pillowed on his rolled-up jacket. In the middle of the night, he thought he dreamed that someone was shaking his shoulder,

"*Geh weg, Johann, ich bin schläfrig,*" he mumbled in protest. *Go away. Johann – I'm sleepy.* The person that he thought was Johann fumbled at the coat, at his shoulder again, and then withdrew.

Of course, it couldn't possibly have been Johann, he realized in the morning, when he struggled out of the blanket, and began to put on his coat against the morning chill. With a sense of mounting dismay, he realized that his money had vanished – the small roll of bills was gone, all of his jacket pockets were empty. Empty of paper money, that is; there were some small coins remaining, so he knew that he had not dreamed that Carl gave it to him.

He had been robbed in the night, likely by one of the other guests. There was little he could do, Fredi realized with a certain sense of sinking disappointment in the unfairness of the world. This was not a place where he was known, no one would have reason to take his word, and of course he could point no fingers. Looking around the parlor where the boarders sat at breakfast, he could see clearly that there were many fewer for breakfast than there had been for supper the night before. Likely the thief had already departed. The friendly Homestead brothers were already gone. Carl would also be disappointed in him, Fredi was certain. He could not hold onto his money for a week, without being robbed.

'At least – I have already paid the blacksmith,' he told himself; the one cheerful thought among this wreckage of plans. He fished out the small coinage in the pocket, and decided that as he was hungry, he would spend a substantial portion of what remained to him on breakfast. Not a good breakfast, if the boardinghouse supper of the previous night indicated – but at least a breakfast. Hope triumphing over brief experience, he went and paid his five cents to Mrs. Pratt – and settled onto an empty chair at the table. Breakfast as served was slightly less appetizing than supper; fried salt pork, more bread made from cornmeal, and dark-black and bitter coffee, sweetened with molasses and no cream to be seen. The same gummy jar of unidentifiable preserves went around the table – also a dish of somewhat rancid butter. Fredi helped himself to the first, passed on the second without comment, and announced to the table at large,

"I've no more money than what I've spent for this meal, and I'm looking for paid work."

"Oh?" ventured one of the other lingering guests. "Turns out I need someone to drive a wagon for me, as far as Indianola."

"Indianola is where I am going," Fredi answered. "How much?" He had noted him the night before; a slight, dark-haired young teamster, who talked like an educated Yankee but had the courtly manners of a Southren gentleman. His wagons stood outside the boarding house, and Fredi was pretty certain that his cattle – tamed eastern cattle with small, curving horns and obedient manners – were among those pastured in the corral. But the Yankee teamster had been one of those especially merry with the bottle going around; soft-spoken and polite when sober but loud, even obnoxious, after the bottle had passed him several times.

"Three dollars and board along the way," the teamster answered. "And promise of further employment after Indianola. That suit you?"

"Fine," Fredi answered, and reached his hand across the stained and crumb-scattered tablecloth. "Friedrich Steinmetz, at your service, sir."

"No sir about it. Alfred James Slade; Jack, to all and sundry." They shook hands solemnly. Fredi looked with distaste on the remains of breakfast, a distaste fleetingly mirrored in the expression of his new employer. "I'm not hungry anymore," said Jack Slade. "So let's get on the road, Fred. Time's a'wasting."

"It is," Fredi agreed, bolting the last slice of corn bread on his plate. "But I must get my horse from the blacksmith, first."

"Five minutes, Fred." Jack consulted a silver pocket-watch that he pulled from his waistcoat pocket. "Time waits for no man."

Fredi joyfully hitched his limping cow-pony to the back of the wagon by a lead-rope. His father was right; something always came up, he thought. And the slovenly Mrs. Pratt averred that Jack Slade was an upright and honest man, although Fredi wondered if he should put any trust in the word of a woman who cooked so badly and yet kept an open table. Jack himself told Fredi that he had been a soldier away out in Santa Fe during the war with Mexico and hauled freight on the overland trails. Fredi's respect for him rose immensely, more for having traveled that far into the west, than for having been a soldier.

"I came this way once before," he said to Jack one evening. "But there wasn't a regular road then, or even a city. We lived in a cave in the sand cliffs for a couple of weeks."

"You won't know the place now," Jack chuckled. He lit his pipe with a twig. "There's a ruddy long wharf for the Morgan Company steamships to tie up at, three more for ordinary shipping, more houses and mercantile establishments than you can shake a stick at – and a lighthouse at the point of Pass Cavallo that folk can see the light of for almost twenty miles. There's even a regular toll-bridge over Powderhorn Bayou." He puffed at his pipe thoughtfully for some minutes. At the edge of the circle of light cast by the campfire, the draft oxen and Fredi's pony cropped new grass with a faint crunching sound which hinted at the relish with which they grazed. "So, what are you going to do, once you've seen your brother off? Go off home, or look for another job?"

"I haven't thought about it," Fredi answered, although he had thought of practically nothing else. *How could he face up to Carl and his sister, after having lost the money they had given to him?* "But you know what I would like to do, Jack? I'd like to go to California and prospect for gold, but I'd have to work my way there."

"If I get the right sort of Army contract, I'd hire you on as a teamster," Jack mused, laying back on his elbow and looking at the stars coming out overhead. "It might get you almost there; Salt Lake City, maybe."

"I'd rather not walk all the way," Fredi said. "I'm a regular buckaroo, now – I've got my pride."

The coastal plain was as flat as the ocean itself, Fredi thought, the next day; a waving sea of grass or tall cane, with cloud-shadows ripping across it as the clouds themselves were driven by the wind in the blue sky overhead. The road bent around the edge of Powderhorn Bayou, and there was the bridge; more of a long causeway, of planks laid over cypress pilings driven deep into the bed of the lake. Ahead of them, beyond the far end of the bridge, a smudge of smoke hung in the air. In the lead with his wagon, Jack paid the toll for them both, and Fredi's team followed his out onto the bridge.

Waterfowl skimmed across the surface of the water, calling intermittently to each other. The hooves of the team and the iron-shod wheels rolled over the plants with a different sound, a loud and hollow noise, rather than the muted clumping they made on the dusty road. Fredi could already smell the salt-tang of the sea, although he could see nothing yet but the marshy bayou. He would have hurried on, save for Jack's wagon in front. His impatience communicated itself to the oxen or perhaps it was their own nervous temper at being out on a narrow plank bridge across water as far as their limited vision could see.

There – there was the end of it, and the town beyond; a sea-coast town, of tall pastel-painted houses and storefronts, with wooden sidewalks elevated slightly above the shell-sand road, tight-packed by constant traffic. Filmy white curtains billowed from tall windows upstairs from the shops on the ground floor, and the seagulls mewed overhead, soaring on near-to-motionless wings. The nearer their wagons got to the shore, the more crowded the streets, which ran in parallel to the coast. As the wagons plodded through a cross-street running down to the beach, Fredi caught a glimpse of blue-gray sea, ruffled with lines of white-capped wavelets and glittering with a sequin-sprinkle of tiny reflections of the sun. At a certain intersection, Jack called "Whoa!" to his team and walked back to speak with Fredi.

"The cargo is for Runge and Company," he said. "Down this way – they have a warehouse and a wagon-park, so I'll consider your duty to me fulfilled as soon as we are there. Go seek out your brother, as soon as we have unharnessed these brutes, and if you are looking for me afterwards, I'll be at the American Hotel. The Widow Eberly – the good lady of the house sets a better table than Mrs. Pratt in Victoria, but if it is too expensive for your pocket, I'll stake you a meal."

"Thank you, Jack," Fredi answered. It was true, as Vati always said; something always came up. He and Jack saw the wagons to the back of Runge and Company. To Fredi's abundant joy, the clerk at Runge was another German, a boy about his own age. He saw the team unharnessed from the wagon, bid a farewell to Jack, collected his pay for the work, and headed on his pony toward the Morgan dock

– which headed out into Matagorda Bay nearly the length of the bridge across Powderhorn. The dock was a huge and expansive structure, as wide and sturdy as a paved avenue raised above the shifting waters of the bay. The salt-sea air blew fresh in his face. Such an invigorating change – but Fredi did not relish it all that much. There were things and memories brought back to him, borne by the odor of saltwater and sea-spray; of the open sea, a rocking wooden deck, and the dark nightmare of a violent storm at sea, with all the passengers puking in their bunks for days. When his older sister Magda spoke of that journey it was always to insist that she would remain in Texas for the rest of her natural days, rather than to suffer again another journey such as they all had endured.

Fredi sought out the steamship booking office, a structure of sawn planks still smelling faintly of new wood, overlaid with the odor of tobacco smoke, salt air and tar. Beside the dock, rocking slightly at anchor was a steamship, with a pair of side paddle-wheels taller than the height of two men put together. There seemed to be a great deal of activity about it; Fredi didn't see anyone among those who might be passengers who looked like his brother or Mr. Coreth. Perhaps they would know in the steamship office. The man behind the desk looked over his spectacles.

"Mr. Coreth and young Mr. Steinmetz? They've gone on the *James Day*, lad. Yesterday it was."

"But … they were supposed to go on the *United States*!" Fredi was horrified – a day too late! "I had a letter …that is, my father had a letter from Mr. Coreth, outlining their schedule. They weren't supposed to sail until tomorrow." The ticket agent looked at him sympathetically.

"Ah, but the *United States* was scheduled to carry a full cargo of cattle on the lower deck, intended for New Orleans. Travelers don't much like enduring the smell of it, y'know. The *Day* carries passengers and regular cargo only. They came in early and Mr. Coreth was happy to exchange a cabin and depart two days earlier."

"That was my brother, with Mr. Coreth," Fredi felt as numb as if he had been struck. All for nothing! If he had not had to hire to Jack, if his pony had not thrown a shoe, if he had not boarded for the night at Mrs. Pratt in Victoria … all the horrible 'ifs' accumulated. The journey was wasted; his money was gone. Failure tasted in his mouth like ashes and vinegar. How could he go back to Carl's ranch and confess such a failure? "He was returning to Germany – my brother. This was my last chance to see him for… I don't know how many years."

"The *James Day* is well out into the bay now," the agent replied, not without a little sympathy. "Two days toward New Orleans, if running to schedule. You can send a letter with the next mail, I reckon. It might catch up before your brother departs from there."

"I will do that," Fredi answered, without any enthusiasm. "Thank you, sir."

His heart heavy within him, Fredi walked back along the dock to where he had left his horse, tethered to a handy rail at the side of a warehouse. Now he recollected Jack Slade's promise to spot him a meal at the American Hotel. Well – Jack was the only person he knew in the whole town. "I just don't think I can go back," he confided to his pony. "I'll look like a fool. But if I come back with enough money to pay back Carl…"

The sun danced on the sparkling waters of Matagorda Bay; the sky was as blue as the heart of a sapphire, and Fredi's spirits rose. Hadn't Vati always said that something would come up?

Chapter 2 – Thirty Men and Four Hundred Cattle

It was coming on to noon; a helpful passerby directed Fredi to that part of town called Brown's Addition. The sun beat down, unimpeded by any speck of shade from trees, glaring almost painfully on the trampled white shell-sand that composed the streets of Indianola. There had not been much in the way of trees, as far as Fredi recalled from his first stay in Indianola; Karlshaven as it had been called then. He remembered with the erratic clarity of a child; spindly oaks and fields of low-growing scrub with roots that barely clung to the sand around the marshes and bayous, the smell of human waste, and of rotting wood furniture abandoned in the space between high and low tide. Now Indianola spread out her brightly-painted houses, shops and warehouses as far as he could see. It might well have been an entirely different world.

The American Hotel was one of the biggest; tall windows opened onto the sidewalk into the public rooms, and the rooms upstairs onto two rows of wide wooden galleries. From outside, Fredi could hear the sound of agreeable conversation, the clink of metal against china – and better yet, the smell of good cooking, wafting in a most enticing manner, doing combat with the odor of horse dung and wood-smoke and winning.

"I'm looking for my friend, Jack – Jack Slade," he said to the woman who stood behind a tall desk in the main hall of the American. "He said he would be here and that he'd treat me to supper."

"Aye, he's one of my guests at present," the woman replied. She was an older lady, dumpy and dressed in unflattering black; the Widow Eberly, or so Fredi presumed. Her countenance was unbeautiful but shrewd. "In the dining room, back in a corner with the other bachelors – an' I should warn you, young whipper-snapper, this here is a respectable family place. I don' hold with men getting' rowdy and breaking up the place; it's hard on the furniture an' hard on my account ledgers." She bent an especially severe look upon him – but a look mixed with a certain degree of matronly affection which quite removed the sting of the warning.

"I quite understand," Fredi answered, tendering a brief and respectful bow, at which the lady proprietor appeared to be mollified. "My parents – my sister and brother-in-law too – they have always insisted on manners in a public place…"

"Good for them, I say," the proprietress beamed approval. "Young people these days need for their elders to set a good example. You sound like one of those Dutch folk hereabouts; like the Runges and the Schmidts. You wouldn't be kin to them, by chance?"

"No, ma'am," Fredi answered. "My father has a shop in Fredericksburg and I have worked at the ranch that my sister's husband owns on the upper Guadalupe near Comfort. Carl Becker; everyone knows him."

"Bless my soul, indeed I do," exclaimed Widow Eberly. "Mrs. Williamson's young brother the Ranger! Mrs. Vining that was. She had a boarding house in Austin, just as I did for a good few years. He visited her now and again; brings back memories, it does! So he has a good property now, married and settled down! That was good, for I know Mrs. Williams worried about him a good deal."

"I guess so," Fredi shifted uneasily. Now his guilt over loosing Carl's money was rekindled. "He and my sister, they have two little boys … but I am setting out on my own now. My friend Mr. Slade, he said he would help me find work."

"That's a good kind thing for him to do," the Widow Eberly agreed. "You go right on through. The gentlemen by themselves are at the round table in the corner. Your Mr. Slade would be there, I am certain. Such a nice, polite young man, too, even if he is a Yankee," she added. "There ain't no gentleman quite like a Southren gentleman I always say."

The dining room was as full of tables and chairs and people as it was of the smell of good food and conversation. Such a change from the dismal board at Mrs. Pratt's, Fredi thought, his crushed spirits reviving. He threaded his way to the corner, where four or five men sat alone, the other tables seeming to be the reserve of families – well-dressed and prosperous families in the main, like the richer folk of Bexar. Maids in plain dresses and white aprons moved among the tables with dish-laden trays. The platters of roasted or boiled meats, temptingly sauced vegetables and fresh-baked breads set his mouth to watering in anticipation. Oh, yes; much more appetizing than Mrs. Pratt's inedible chops and tortured potatoes.

Jack looked up from his plate, which he was emptying with dispatch and apparent delight, exclaiming, "Fredi, I didn't think to see you so soon, but nothing like a good dinner at someone else's expense! Sit down, lad – did you find your brother?"

"I did not," Fredi replied, momentarily despondent. "The steamship they were on cast off two days early. I was too late."

"Sorry about that," Jack sounded genuinely sympathetic. "A pity; I have brothers – fond of 'em, too. Sit down, sit down. I promised you a good meal, at least. What do you plan to do now? Go home to your brother-in-law's ranch, or work your way to California?"

Fredi drew in a deep breath, having come to the point of decision. "California it is," he answered, feeling a most sudden sense of relief at having decided. Now it seemed as if the very journey were inevitable.

"Good for you, Dutch. You're at the right age for a young man to go adventuring. I s'pose you'll be looking for work to take you in that direction." Jack looked up and caught the eye of the nearest serving-maid, who came at his beckon and set a plate and a knife and fork in front of Fredi. "Tell Mrs. Eberly this young gent is my guest. So, what can you do besides work cattle and drive a wagon?"

"Tend and tame horses," Fredi replied, aware that at least one of the other gentlemen at the table was looking at him with a speculative eye. "Plant potatoes, minister to apple trees ... track game over rough land, and find water by watching the mud-daubers. I can read and write also."

The man across the table from him barked a short laugh. "You're ahead of the game with that, boy. Say, Jack, going to introduce us? I'm always looking for literate hands. Trouble is, they mayn't last very long, but they don't do much damage while they're with me."

"Friedrich Artur Steinmetz," Fredi half-rose and extended his hand over the table to the other man.

"Pleased to make the acquaintance," the man replied, around a mouthful. He was stocky and dark-tanned, with a square jaw, and a direct look, about the same age as Jack. Straight dark hair clipped short stood up on his head like curry-comb bristles. "Gilbert Fabreaux. Sorry, don't have a middle moniker. The family was too poor to provide one when I was born. Don't hold it against me, though. I'm hiring drovers and wranglers."

"Gil is looking to take a herd of cattle to California," Jack interposed. "He has intelligence that miners in the gold camps are an excellent market for beeves. They're paying more than a hundred dollars a head – in gold ..."

Fredi whistled in astonishment. Carl had barely gotten a fifth of that, for each of his own herd, sold in the market in San Antonio, and Fredi suspected that most of that value was in the hides, rather than the meat. "How much are you offering for a day's work, Mr. Fabreaux?"

"Call me Gil," the other man replied. "The usual; fifty cents a day, plus meals, paid when the herd is delivered to buyers in California. I figure to start next month."

"He's planning on taking the southern trail," Jack explained. "Starting from the Fabreaux place on the lower San Antonio south of Goliad with a herd of four hundred, and three wagons full of supplies. How long do you think it will take, Gil?"

"Should be there no later than Christmas," Gil Fabreaux answered, while Fredi mentally began tallying the pay which he would have accumulated by then. More than a hundred and twenty American dollars if he started today and then he would go to the gold mines and earn even more!

"Count me in, Gil," he said. "I have my own horse and saddle. And my brother-in-law can vouch for me, just as Jack can...If you will," he added, looking toward Jack, who grinned.

"My pleasure, Dutch. It's a pity I've already contracted to shift a wagon of dry goods to Fort Belknap, else I'd come with you to the gold mines."

"I can always use a good man," Gil sounded regretful, "But you've given your word to Mr. Torrey, so I don't 's'pose you can't walk it back now."

On the following morning, Fredi and Gil Fabreaux headed north, on the road toward Agua Dulce, waving goodbye at the edge of town to Jack, leaning against one of the porch posts at the American Hotel. It had rained the night before, but now the sky was washed clean of clouds, and every blade of brilliant green new grass seemed edged with a beading of tiny crystal drops. The rain made the road muddier than usual, though. Fredi thought of how his horse had thrown a shoe, and what he must write in a letter to Carl. He had already posted a letter to his father, with the last pennies in his pocket. It turned out

that Gil Fabreaux knew Carl; they had served for a time together in
Captain Jack Hays' Ranger company. Sometimes Fredi wondered if
there were any fit men of a certain age in Texas who had not done so.

The Fabreaux home-place turned out to be a sprawling house of
logs; a bachelor establishment for the Fabreaux brothers, of whom
where were five. Gil was the middle brother. There was a cook for the
place though; a tall free Negro woman named Eppie who reigned over
the detached kitchen with a rule of iron, her hair covered with a crisp
white turban. There were also already gathered a dozen hired hands,
most of them little older than Fredi. They bunked in the shabby
quarters in the oldest part of the house, and worked at assembling
Fabreaux cattle from the gentle rolling meadows and creek-beds in
the district around, branding the calves and sorting out which were
best-suited for the long journey. It was flatter, richer country than in
the stony hills on either side of the Guadalupe; Fredi found it a change
for the better, although the wildflowers weren't a patch on what they
were around the Becker place. And if Eppie didn't set quite as good a
table as his sister Magda did, the meals provided for the hands were
miles and away better than Mrs. Pratt's, now established in Fredi's
young mind as the very nadir of abominable cooking.

"None of the heifers with new calves," Gil explained wearily for
the twentieth time, as a new calf scampered bawling away from the
fire built to heat the brands, to rejoin its anxious mother in the open
pasture. "Only yearlings and older; keep back the best-looking
heifers, too. Don't want to waste good breeding stock in a gold-
miner's stew-pot." They worked all of that early spring day in the
shadow of a spreading oak at the edge of the fenced pastures; Gil with
Fredi and another hand, a lanky nineteen-year old from Illinois named
Charlie Goodnight who could neither read nor write, but knew all
about tending cattle and driving freight wagons. Charlie's stepfather,
the preacher Adam Sheek, had a fine holding on the Upper Brazos –

but Charlie had younger brothers and sisters, and was determined to set out on his own. He and Fredi were well on the way to being good friends, from their first meeting when Fredi admired Charlie's long rifle, and read the verse engraved upon it – a verse which Charlie said was a favorite of his stepfather, and which he could not himself read. *"Seek ye first the kingdom of God and his righteousness, and all these things shall be added unto you."*

"Also good," Fredi answered, as he coiled up his lariat. He felt good, that day – able and competent. A week at working for the Fabreaux brothers, and anticipation of an adventurous journey along the southern trail had restored his confidence in no small degree. "We are almost done, yes?"

"We are, Dutch. Another twenty good steers for the herd and then we'll start moving. O'course, I'm waiting on another teamster, with that last load of salt-junk, flour and beans. Three wagons of supplies, the remainder we don't use to be sold at a profit in California. I've contracted for some more horses, from the Doyle place on Banquete Creek. Ma'am Doyle should be bringing them here on her way to Louisiana next week some time." Gil set the branding iron head back into the fire and came to lean against the split-pole fence around the pasture which held the California herd. "They look fine, don't they, Dutch? Imagine every one of those longhorns as a sack of gold nuggets. We have to get 'em there, o'course."

"That's what I'm hired for," Fredi answered, and Charlie grinned. They both quite liked Gil, a liking tempered with respect. This Fabreaux brother had his mind fixed on work, expenses, and profits ... and cattle; a thoughtful, sober-spoken person, especially for so young a man. The venture to California was a thing agreed to by the other brothers, and Gil had even made a brief exploring trip with another cattle drover the year before. If it worked out to profit them, they would venture into sending more herds over the southern trail –

they would repeat it. If not, they would return to driving their herds over the Opelousas Trace to New Orleans, or north to the markets serving the northern emigrant trail at jumping-off places along the Missouri River.

"It's a gamble," was how Gil explained it to Fredi as two more heifers with calves were brought from the grazing grounds. "But one where I believe that I have made the odds in my favor; after all, the trail is established, the Federal Army has soldiers posted all the way and on the southern trail there is no hazard of being caught in the mountains in winter and starving to death."

"But are there dangerous Indians?" Fredi persisted. "I know that our Mr. Meusebach, he made a peace with the Comanche ... but those others?"

"Apache, mostly." Gil replied. "Fierce, but not so much inclined to raid as freely as the Comanche do. You ought to get yourself a good sidearm, anyway. If you can't raise the cost of one by the time we hit the trail, I'll ask my brothers. Ransom is always after buying the newest and best. He might trade for one of his old ones and I'll take it from your wages."

"Thanks, Gil," It relieved Fredi enormously; Carl hardly went anywhere outside the farmyard without his brace of old-fashioned patent Colts. The one thing Fredi miss-liked about going to California was the thought of going there un-armed.

It took them another week to complete the herd for California: all healthy four and five-year-old steers and heifers, most them only a little tamer than deer and buffalo. Piebald, brown, red and black, each crowned with a sweep of horns stretching to the height of a man, sometimes jittery in the presence of men and horses; Fredi tried seeing them as Gil did; a bag of gold for every single one, and failed utterly. They were just cattle; he could not imagine a place where they were so scarce as to each command the price of two-thirds of his wages for the best part of a year.

Two enormous freight wagons stood in the yard of the Fabreaux home-place, each heavy-laden with supplies and gear for the long journey; wagons with a box slightly bowed and with a cover which flared out front and aft. Each wagon would be pulled by no less than four teams of tame oxen, as they carried at least two tons of goods and foodstuffs each. Two days before departure, the third wagon arrived; a lighter wagon pulled by mules; this was to hold the drover's bedrolls and baggage, and being on springs intended to carry any who might fall injured or ill. The mule wagon was driven by a scarecrow of a man. He was of indeterminate years and put together in an untidy gangle of limbs, topped with a thatch of fading ginger hair. Fredi gawked at him, as he hopped nimbly down from the wagon-seat, for he was dressed in clothing which had once been fine, yet appeared to have been intended for a much shorter man. The sleeves of his coat, and the threadbare shirt underneath it barely covered his knobby wrists. He was also accompanied by a small black dog, which followed his master with equal agility; a short-furred dog with upright ears and tail, and what looked like a comical set of grizzled chin-whiskers fringing its sharp little muzzle. The dog promptly cocked a leg and pissed against the wagon-wheel. The driver looked around – at the ramble of the house, the packed wagons with their covers put back so that more could be added to their loads, at Fredi.

"Good day to you indeed," the ginger-haired man said, sweeping off his battered top-hat with an air of burlesque courtesy which just escaped giving offense as the amiable expression on his face was transparently sincere. "Have I the honor of addressing the honorable Mr. Gilbert Fabreaux? If I have no', will you kindly convey me respects to him, and say that Polydore Aloysius O'Malley is arrived and is ready, willing an' able at his service, as agreed to when we met in Indianola on the 15th instant of last month?"

"Yes … er, no," Fredi replied. The man's accent was a strange and oddly musical one to him; English, but not like any English that Fredi had learned from Vati, or Carl, or the accents of Jack Slade or Gil Fabreaux. He barely grasped the gist at first hearing. "I am not Gil – Herr Fabreaux. He is around here – working. There is much to do with the cattle…"

"Understand perfectly, boyo." O'Malley replied, adding in a chiding tone of voice. "Nipper, behave yourself, now." The little black dog had trotted over to the stoop to baptize it in a brief sprinkle. "He's no' such a bad dog, but this is a strange place. If ye can tell Mr. Fabreaux that I am arrived and at his disposal, young mister …?"

"Freidrich Artur Steinmetz," Fredi answered. "But everyone calls me Freddy – or Dutch Fred, although I am not a Hollander."

"Understand all too well, Freddy. 'Tis here that I have always to explain that I am not a damned John Bull, but an exile from lovely Erin, that blessed green isle. Through no fault o' me own," O'Malley added, with an air of righteous certitude. "Are you an exile from your own lands, Freddy, over the late unpleasantness of revolution?'

"No," Fredi answered, although he didn't quite understand the reference. "My father sold his house and fields, and came here on the promise of a bigger house and more land."

"Ah, the promises they use to lure the poor deluded fools to emigrate," O'Malley exclaimed, deeply sympathetic. "And then live like poor beggars, when all those promises turn out to be trumpery stuff." The little black dog, Nipper, came and sniffed at Fredi's boots. Then he stood on hind legs and rested his forepaws on Fredi's knee, his pointed ears both up, and sharp brown eyes looking at him interrogatively. Fredi liked dogs and Nipper seemed a most particularly friendly one, if a little odd-looking. Fredi let Nipper sniff at his hand, before he petted him.

"No sir," Fredi shook his head at O'Malley's words. "My father and my sister's husband all received more lands than they could dream of and my father's house is finer than the one we left in Ulm. Everyone says so. Although," Fredi allowed, somewhat grudgingly. "The Verein did not full-fill all of their promises to us. Still, we are all well-content. It is a grand country, but I would wish to see more of it. And to strike it rich in the gold-fields of California. I am hired to herd cattle there for Herr Fabreaux."

"Then we will be comrades of the road, Freddy," O'Malley beamed all over his face, and extended his hand. "I have – I had a little brother named Freddy, away back in Ballycastle. Good to know that America has been good t'ye, and mayhap the gold mines will be even more generous. Now, take me to Mr. Fabreaux, if ye would be so kind, for here I was worried that I would be late, for one of the mules threw a shoe on the road and I must take mesel' to the nearest blacksmith."

"That happened to me, too," Fredi shook hands with this odd and talkative character, feeling some kinship to him on account of this shared misfortune. "On the road outside Victoria. But you were not late, for Mr. Fabreaux is still waiting for the horse herd."

"Saints be praised," O'Malley exclaimed in considerable relief. "I did fear that I would be late! Such a lovely country this is, now that spring is here. Reminds me of where I was born, so it does. Ballycastle in Antrim … forgive me, Freddy-boyo. 'Tis a small place and dear to me, but you would not know it, one great ocean and half the Americas away!"

"I was born in Albeck, near Ulm in Bavaria," Fredi answered stoutly, "and I am not offended at all. No one we ever met in Texas has heard of it either. Mr. Fabreaux is in the study and if he is not, then one of his brothers will know where he is."

"Thank you, boyo," O'Malley whistled to Nipper, and snapped his fingers. As if he had been given a command, the little dog sprang from the ground to the footrest of the wagon-seat and from there to the seat, where he curled himself up into a neat black and grizzled ball. He looked as if he would sleep, but the sharp little ears remained pricked upwards and his eyes followed after his master.

To Fredi's vague astonishment, Mr. O'Malley joined the other hands in the bunkhouse that evening. He would have thought that O'Malley, a gentleman of parts and quality, despite his eccentric appearance and dress, would have been accommodated in one of the guest rooms. No; O'Malley carried in a battered carpetbag and an old-fashioned many-caped coachman's overcoat, and claimed a simple pallet bed upon which Nipper promptly made himself at home, burrowing underneath his master's coat as if he felt a chill. It turned out that O'Malley had brought with him several recent newspapers, which made him enormously popular with those hired men and boys interested in the latest news.

The following morning brought another odd visitor to the Fabreaux place, a visit heralded by a shout from the road which ran by the farmyard, some distance from the house.

"Hello the house! Fabreaux! Come out and get your damned horses!"

Fredi was helping O'Malley shift some of the food supplies from the mule wagon to the ox-drawn Santa Fe wagons, under Gil's direction. The harsh voice brought them out from the far side where they had been working.

"Saints above," O'Malley breathed. "It sounds like a…"

"A woman," Fredi supplied. "Madame Doyle, I think."

"If you say so, boyo," O'Malley replied, although he sounded as if he did not believe the evidence of his eyes. "Left to me, I'd have to see her without her shift before I'd swear to it. So she would be the woman they tell such tales of!"

"Keep a civil tongue in your thick head, O'Malley," Gil chided him from the corner of his mouth, before striding out into the farmyard to meet the woman. "Sally, we were beginning to worry."

"I don't know why," Sally Doyle replied. She was tall and straight-backed as a soldier on parade. She might have been forty but looked older, for her face was weathered and tanned, in spite of her plain calico sunbonnet. She had pale eyes, the color of a blued steel knife and every bit as piercing. To Fredi's amazement, she rode astride like a man, wearing a wide split skirt of fine leather, and a man's round jacket. She also wore a belt around her waist with two pistols depending from it and completely ignored the assistance which Fredi and O'Malley had leaped to offer her in dismounting. Her horse was very fine, almost the largest and best-blooded that Fredi had ever seen. A herd of horses, of a quality a little less fine, followed her on the road, chivvying by a dozen Mexican buckaroos. Sally Doyle handed her reins to Fredi without looking at him, adding, "Look after him, boy. I have business to do."

"You don't waste time, Sally." Gil Fabreaux observed, in admiration.

"No, I don't." Sally Doyle finally cracked a smile. Just for a moment, her countenance softened, and there was a sparkle in in her eyes. Fredi could well believe that a man of certain qualities – and an utterly fearless one to boot – might be charmed. "You wanted thirty of the best, Gil, and I was able to oblige." She waved at the nearest vaquero, who tipped the brim of his hat to her. The horses began to be chivvied into the holding pen in which Fredi and the others had been branding cattle for weeks before.

"For the usual exorbitant amount, I presume," Gil Fabreaux laughed, so Fredi knew he wasn't being serious. Sally Doyle took down the canvas nosebag which hung from her saddle-horn. It seemed heavy from the way she held it, and jingled as if it held coins within.

"I don't fill this with gold money every trip by being cheap," she answered. "Time's a 'wasting, Gil; let my boys put them in your pasture, and line them up, one by one. You tell me which ones you favor, then we'll dicker about the price for them all."

Fredi and O'Malley watched for a moment, holding the reins of Madame Doyle's horse. She and Gil went up into the wing of the house which held the room that the Fabreaux brothers used as an office. O'Malley shook his head, as if he pitied Gil Fabreaux.

"Jesus, Mary and Joseph, what a woman! Now it comes to me mind what I have heard of her. Freddy-boyo, she is not a woman, not as we poor mortals know them and blessed creations that kind are, indade. This one is an elemental spirit, as above the ordinary kind as angels are above men. Although not in the same way, ye will understand. Best water her horse, Freddy."

"But who is she?" Fredi asked, much puzzled. "Do you know her?"

"I do not know her, but I know of her," O'Malley answered, as Gil Fabreaux called from the verandah.

"See to Sally's horse, and then go back to shifting the supplies – just as I told you, O'Malley."

"My pleasure, Sirrah!" O'Malley called back, touching his hand to the brim of his battered top-hat in salute.

"What do you know of her, then?" Fredi asked. The tall fine-blooded horse followed him, clumping obediently after in the direction of the water trough, fed by a smaller trough from the well-house for the convenience of horses and mules in the farmyard.

"Aye, well she wasn't always Mrs. Doyle," O'Malley answered. "I'll tell the rest when you finish watering Her Ladyships' fine-blood gelding."

Fredi tended to the horse and left it tied to a handy porch-post. He could hear Gil's voice and that of several Fabreaux brothers inside, chiming with that of the awe-inspiring Madame Doyle. "So, tell me, O'Malley; this Madame Not-Always-Doyle. Is she famous?"

O'Malley chuckled. "She is that, Freddy-boyo. She has a fine establishment to the south of here, near to the foine city of Corpus Christi it is. On the old King's Highway, which runs all between Louisiana and Mexico; she deals in horses and other fine goods. Very profitably, for her word is bond, and that nosebag of hers is full of gold, which I would not have believed until I saw her. She is from one of the old families, as they are reckoned in this new country – which wouldn't be over fifty years." O'Malley fetched up a deep sigh from the wellspring of his being. "Where I am from, Freddy-boyo, an old family is one of those who have the blood of the nobility an' high kings of Tara in their ancestry."

"Where I am from," answered Fredi sturdily, "My ancestors were spreading dung on their fields or the fields possessed by a First for as long as we remember. My father says that in America we may rise by our own merits; not through the blood of a robber with a suit of iron and a sword, or a courtesan who spread her legs to the right man."

"Aye, so you are acquainted with the concept, Freddy-boyo!" O'Malley said with a quick grin, although Fredi wondered exactly which concept O'Malley meant. He decided not to think about it.

"This new kind of old family will suit us very well," Fredi answered. "So this Madame Doyle came here as a child with her parents; as my brother-in-law come with his, in the time when this was a holding of Mexico. And then what?"

"Well, she married to a landholder named Robinson while still a girl and settled down to a family hearth and home and children. Until she and he parted ways. I canno' be unsympathetic, entirely," O'Malley added generously. "For he was a soldier also, and spent time in the field ranging with a company. It grieves a woman sore, to have a husband more away about his patriotic duty then tending to his own. And ye see how she is; she could no' have been very welcoming when he did return, after having been accustomed to managing by herself. In the end she went to the magistrates and divorced Robinson. She took the property she had from her father; cattle and land, mostly – and then went and married another man." O'Malley scratched his bristly jaw, and Fredi listened, fascinated. "A man named Scull; sounds a Dutch name, like your own kin, Freddy-boyo. He had no need to travel, being a gunsmith with a settled trade. But it did not work out, so they say."

"What happened to Mr. Scull?" Fredi asked and O'Malley lowered his voice, as if about to vouchsafe a mystery.

"He died, so they say … some have it that she shot him herself. Others say he drowned crossing a flooded river on horseback; swept away in the flood, him and the horse alike. When they asked his good lady, did she want to send out men to search for Scull's remains for proper burial, she answered, 'no, she did not care anything for the body, but that she would like to have gotten the money in the belt around his waist.' Oh, boyo, she is a perilous woman indade." O'Malley sighed, very deep. "And so she married again; to Doyle, but I am thinking he will not last long. The good lady is too much a woman for any one mortal man."

Chapter 3 – Dead Man Well

The Fabreaux herd set off on the long trail drive to California late in April; four hundred cattle, thirty drovers, twice that many horses and three wagons. The night before they left, Gil Fabreaux and his brothers hosted a fandango at the ranch-house; they roasted a whole pig, and the local Mexican-made whiskey flowed fairly liberally among the hired drovers, the Fabreaux boys and their kin and neighbors. They ate, drank and danced with the few women among them, ate some more, boasted of their own prowess with knives, guns and women, drank a little more and told wild tales of the Indians and the deserts beyond Fort Thorn. O'Malley's little dog, Nipper, capered on his hind legs, appearing to dance at the bidding of his master, who brought out a tin penny-whistle and played a merry Irish tune which Fredi did not recognize. At close to midnight, when two of the other hired hands challenged each other to a contest of marksmanship with their patent revolving pistols by shooting the flame from a lighted candle at forty paces, Fredi prudently withdrew to the bunkhouse. Gil Fabreaux had repeatedly said how they should get an early start – and he would be stubborn enough to insist on it, no matter how many aching heads there were.

O'Malley had already done so himself, but he was not asleep yet, lying on his bunk fully-dressed, but with his boots side-by-side underneath, and Nipper curled into a tight brindle ball at his feet. "Freddy-boyo, are you out of humor with celebration so soon? It is not near eleven of the clock, now. You're just a young sprout an' likely this is the last bit of merriment until California. I thought you'd be up with the larks at dawn."

"They are drinking," Fredi answered, sitting down on his pallet to take off his own boots and work trousers. "And Eb and Zeke

32

Satterwaite are contesting over who is a better shot … the others are merry. I do not care for the smell of bad whiskey, O'Malley. There is a man who works for my sister's husband. Now and again, he drinks until he is sodden with it. The smell alone makes me sick. Don't tell the other hands," Fredi added, hastily. "I'm afraid that they will laugh at me and say that I have a stomach like a maiden girl. But it is true."

"A great pity, boyo," O'Malley remarked, as Fredi pulled the blankets over himself. "For good whiskey is the water of life and the lubrication of foine conversation and elegant philosophy – but the wise men of old advised temperance and moderation in all things. I do not imbibe any more than it takes to be cheerful and at one with the world. For I too saw what comes when a man drinks to excess … an' Mister Gilbert Fabreaux, he will have no sympathy come morning."

"That's what I thought," Fredi agreed, and promptly fell asleep, only a little disturbed by the sounds of merriment and pop of gunshots coming from the other side of the Fabreaux' sprawling rancho.

Dawn had barely begun to lighten the eastern sky, when Fredi, O'Malley and the other hands were roused first by the distant ringing of the brass boat bell which hung from the eaves of the kitchen building, and then by an offensively cheerful Gil flinging open the bunkhouse door with a forceful thrust that sent rebounding against the wall with a bang like a gunshot.

"It's time, gents," Gil sang, even at this hour, beaming like a man with a fortune waiting for him. "Drop your tackle and saddle up – the cows won't get to California all by their lonesome selves, boys!"

Fredi himself felt pretty chipper, staggering out to the washhouse to dash a handful of water on his face and comb his hair. The road to California and a fortune in gold called to him. So did the allure of adventure, of seeing new country – the very elephant itself! What wonderful tales he would have for Vati, for Johann and Magda and

Carl upon his return. He fancied himself emptying out a bag of gold, their words of admiration ... how the other young men would secretly envy him for his riches and many adventures! Lost in such pleasant and anticipatory imaginings, Fredi packed his few things, rolled up his blankets and cotton-stuffed pallet and stowed them in O'Malley's wagon.

"Dutch, I want you and the Satterwaite boys and Charlie to go out to the lower pasture and bring up the herd from there," Gil said over his shoulder as he finished one last consult with his brothers. "We'll meet at the Cibolo crossing, and go on from there."

"I don't know why I gotta take orders from this wet-behind-the ears foreigner," Zeke Satterwaite grumbled under his breath, just loud enough for Fredi to hear.

Stung, Fredi opened his mouth to retort, but Gil, who had the ears of a fox, turned around and snapped, "Because I told you to, Zeke and leastways, Dutch has worked cattle before. Now, get along – we're burning daylight."

The other hands took what Fredi said to heart, all but Zeke. Fredi wondered what was behind that animosity, and concluded it must be only that he was younger, and yet Gil reposed more trust in him than in the Satterwaite boys ... which was only right. If it came down to it, the Satterwaite boys were more foreigners to Texas than he was, for they had only come to Texas a year or so ago from Georgia and had not much to do with Texas cattle since or with book-learning either, although they could ride and shoot.

"Foreigner yourself," Fredi said, sideways out of the corner of his mouth when they were out of Gil Fabreaux' hearing. "When I came here, Texas was a nation of its own, still."

"Snot-nosed abolitionist furriner!" Zeke replied. "If'n you weren't such a tattle-tale to ol' Fabreaux, I'd take you out behind the woodshed and teach you proper manners."

"Like you would know good manners if they bit you on the nose," Fredi shot back. "Any time you wish to try it, I'm ready."

Zeke simmered, his face a mask of sullen resentment. He was a hulking boy a little older than Fredi, who had just begun to show a beard, and being rather proud of this feat, declined to use a razor on the few straggling hairs. Normally his older and more sensible brother Eb kept him more or less in line.

The eighty head of Fabreaux-branded cattle had been pastured downstream from the ranch-house, where the Cibolo made a wide bend in the shape of a pouch set in banks too steep for the cattle to scramble down. The brothers had enclosed it handily with a zig-zagging rail fence across the neck of the pouch, so it was a fairly simple matter for Fredi and the hands with him to take down a stretch of rails and begin shepherding the cattle through it. They urged them on with shouts and waving hats and lariats aloft. The cattle were the same breed as those on the Becker ranch, away up on the upper Guadalupe, but slightly more accustomed to men and horses; tall and slab-sided beasts with horns that swept out and tilted forward or up.

Fredi had heard tales of how in Mexico and in old Spain there were men who made a grand show in an arena of provoking the bulls by waving a cloak at them, and dodging the horns when the animal charged. He had never actually seen such a show and found it hard to imagine how any sensible man would do such a thing, willingly. *Well, maybe if they paid him a lot of money,* Fredi thought. He wondered if the Mexicans in California did any such thing. Vati had said that California once belonged to Mexico, just as Texas had. That was another thing to look forward to seeing.

The Fabreaux cattle herd moved as a stream did, following the easiest way over the beaten track toward Bexar and the west beyond. They plodded steadily on; brindle, brown and black, white and brown spotted, gray shading to blue, a river of backs and heads, punctuated with horns, while the dust of their passing boiled up like smoke from a fast-moving grassfire. Away up ahead and almost out of sight in the rising dust, Fredi could see the pale canvas covers on the freight wagons, bobbing and bellying like a sail, this way and that as the great iron-shod wheels crossed over ruts and rises in the road.

The drovers spaced themselves along either side of the cattle-stream, watchful for any rebellion, any cow who thought to turn aside to browse at a tempting patch of green grass – and for anything that might cause them to turn aside, out of a sudden fright. Any sudden motion – a flurry of birds starting up from a nearby thicket, a stray dog barking, white sheets pegged out on a clothesline, flapping in a sudden gust of wind – could set off a maddened stampede. Fredi had once been thrown from his pony and gotten a broken wrist out of it, when a young longhorn heifer brought into the close-in pasture at the Becker place had panicked at the sight of washing-day laundry billowing in the breeze. No buckaroo would ever go wrong in underestimating the facility for the near-wild cattle of Texas to panic and stampede in all directions. An ounce of vigilant care was more than worth a pound of effort to retrieve the stampeded strays.

Three days later, the massive herd passed through the dusty streets of Bexar; a river of cattle clogging the narrow street, pooling in the old military plaza under the squat gray dome and tower of San Fernando. Fredi felt rather as if they were part of a parade, for so many people watched from doorways and upper windows, watched with interest and no small amount of awe. All the way to California, ran the whispers and cheers from bystanders; from the front of the old commander's house in the plaza, a pretty Mexican girl looked at him with an admiring smile, and blew him a kiss on her fingertips. Fredi gallantly tipped his hat to her and felt that life at that very moment had not much better to offer him.

The days slipped away, each one much like the one before, as they moved the slow-moving herd west and north, away from the oak-shadowed hills and wild-flower strewn meadows that Fredi knew best. Once they crossed that range, the rivers dwindled to streams, and then to bare trickles, guarded by stands of cottonwood trees with their leaves trembling in the slightest breeze, rather than the tall gray stands of cypresses adorned with feathery leaves. Such hills as there were became scattered eminences clothed in drab green sage, sprinkled here and there with spike-leafed yucca plants; which sent up a single stem taller than a man from the center of a cluster of gray-green leaves, each as sharp as a bayonet. The tops of the newer plants were adorned with clusters of creamy flowers, the oldest as bare as a lance set on end.

"That's why the Spanish called it the *llano Estacada*," Gil Fabreaux explained one evening to O'Malley. "The staked plain, as it looked like that from a distance."

The drovers, wranglers and teamsters had formed themselves into messes, for the evening meals, six or eight congenially-inclined, as if they were a military company on the march. Every evening when they made camp, Gil issued a slab of salt-junk or dried meat, and a measure of beans, cornmeal flour or dried tack biscuit, sugar and coffee to each mess, which they cooked over a communal fire. Gil made it his habit to dine with different messes. Tonight he sat with Fredi, O'Malley, the other two teamsters and their helpers. The sun had just slipped below the horizon in the west, leaving a pale yellow smear where it had been, and a few clouds whose colors were fading from dark red to purple in the twilight sky.

"A desert it is," O'Malley shook his head in wry despair, and Gil laughed. "You have not yet seen anything like a desert, yet, O'Malley. Just you wait."

"Aye, I suppose I must." O'Malley took off his battered top-hat and wiped the inside of it with a grubby handkerchief. They had set up evening camp at a place of Gil's choosing, and set the cattle to graze on the sparse grass in the bottomlands between two ranges of low, gravelly hills. They had to dig for water that afternoon, setting several barrels with the tops and bottoms taken out into the resulting excavations to create small wells. Now O'Malley continued, "The good lord spare me, but I never thought since I left the dear home hearth in Ballymoney that I would see a place where water is rarer than whiskey."

"I thought you came from Ballycastle in Antrim," Fredi observed, with lazy curiosity and he thought that O'Malley appeared briefly taken back. "Did I, boyo? An easy mistake on my part – just down the road a little. I went to school in Ballymoney."

Gil chuckled, "You know, O'Malley, I could have sworn that you told me once that it was Ballymena that you were from."

"Well, they're the three o' them all small places and close together," O'Malley said, sounding faintly aggrieved. "So many places that I have seen in my travels since then. They fair run together in my mind, y'see."

"Then tell us of some of them," one of the other teamsters drawled. He lounged on his elbow, a thread of smoke from his pipe rising in an aromatic cloud. "Did you ever see any o' those nobility an' crowned heads o' Europe, an' such? Or Jenny Lind singing … you must have heard of her, the Swedish nightingale?"

"Of course I do know of her," O'Malley answered, but he shook his head sadly. "I did see that nightingale of a girl with these my very own eyes, three years ago it was, when she came to New York an' I was there for reasons of my own, ye see. I saw her but no' to sing, for her concerts were in such demand that only the rich could afford a ticket. "

"What did she look like?" Fredi asked, honestly interested. There had been the most astonishing stories about Jenny Lind in the German and American newspapers alike, and some sketches of her, in which she looked very much like any other young lady.

"A pretty little bit of a girl," O'Malley replied, with the air of a man about to tell a good story. "She wore a blue mantle and a blue bonnet trimmed with light-blue ribbons and pink cabbage roses, an' she smiled just the once at the crowd. There were two gentlemen with her – I was minded of the sight of a sweet little white kitten, guarded by a pair o' gallant mastiffs. They say that at her first concert, the audience cheered for so long that she was quite taken back ... so overwhelmed that she lost her voice for some minutes, never having sung in front of so large and enthused an audience ... oh, she was received like royalty, so she was indade. More notice was taken of her than of real royalty, so I can swear."

"Have you seen real royalty, too, Aloysius?" Gil asked, with a touch of skepticism in his voice. O'Malley replied, the Irish in his voice coming out even more with indignation. "So I have, sor – did I not say that I have looked on the crowned heads of Europe? Well, the Queen of England and her great Dutch princeling, too. It was in London, so it was, and I a lad just come over from Oireland. Niver ask me what my business for that journey was, for I do not wish to lie to me friends. There I was, enjoying the spring air in Green Park, when I should see a foine open carriage an' four come bowlin' along, and three-four outriders all before and behind. There were two ladies in the carriage, one with a parasol in her hand, sitting across from the other lady an' the gentleman. There was a small crowd gathering and I heard someone cry out, 'God bless 'er Majesty!' and the one lady waved with her hand – just like this," and O'Malley demonstrated, lifting his right hand and waggling it at the wrist. "And then the carriage was passed as close to me as … as near as I am to you, boyo."

"The Queen of England herself?" Fredi asked, breathlessly entranced. "As near to you as across this fire?"

"Aye, so," O'Malley answered, with triumphant relish. "I kissed my hand to her, and I swear that she waved to me. She was as pretty as Jenny Lind … anyway, from the chin down – a neat figure, as well as can be told. But otherwise, a round little face, with round big eyes, staring like an owl or a porcelain doll. And her husband, the Prince – he was a lanky man, with side-whiskers that looked like nothing so much as a lady's muff glued on, along his jaw. If it were no' the Queen an' her man, you'd have never looked at them for a moment."

"What were you doing in London, then?" Fredi asked, most curious. It seemed sometimes as if O'Malley had been everywhere.

"This and that, boyo …for my own education," O'Malley sounded evasive. Gil chuckled. "You're full of stories, man. You talk as if you were a die-hard Fenian. You had a derringer in your pocket and were waiting for the Queen's carriage to pass in front of you and then you had to skip town just ahead of arrest for trying to assassinate the monarch."

Fredi was almost certain that Gil was making mild sport of O'Malley, so there would have been no real reason for a brief flicker of … something in O'Malley's expression. Was it apprehension, or just a lightning-flash of terror, instantly gone and replaced so rapidly with O'Malley's usual amiable humor that Fredi was not certain he had seen anything at all.

40

"I had reasons of me own, Mister Fabreaux," O'Malley replied at last and Gil laughed.

"I am certain of that, Aloysius. Besides, if you were a Fenian and meant to shoot at the Queen of England, it's nothing to me. You're in America now." Gil looked very shrewdly at O'Malley and added. "Like I would give a good goddamn about your reason to leave Ireland; whatever it might have been, it's no business of mine."

"There was a man in Fredericksburg – one of Prince Solms' trusty men, too – he had to leave Prussia for having killed a man in a duel for insulting Prince Frederick," Fredi said. "No one thought any the less of him … although my father said it was all quite silly – duels over an insult to a prince."

"Best keep the dueling personal, eh, Dutch?" Gil chuckled again. "There's sense in that. My brothers say that our father killed two men dueling and it was better for his health to leave New Orleans for Texas. He always did say that you weren't really a man until you had fought at least one duel."

"We all have our reasons," O'Malley answered, although his face in the firelight appeared oddly strained. For the first time, Fredi did wonder what had brought him to Texas besides wanderlust.

Summer came on, as they came out of the hills and moved slowly westward. The days became unbearably hot, dragging on like a season in Purgatory. Cattle and men parched alike, choking on the dust, a cloud that rose from their passing like the pillar of cloud that led the Jews out of Egypt. Fredi dreaded those days when he must take a turn at riding at the back of the herd. He and the other drovers tied their neckerchiefs high over nose and mouth, but dust still gritted between their teeth, and thickly powdered their hair and clothing. It flavored the food that they ate, their sweat made dirty rivulets down their faces and arms, and they blew dirt-colored snot from their noses. Fredi was certain that if he had taken off his trousers, they would be so thickly caked with dust and old sweat that he could have propped them in a corner, stiff as a board. The cattle bore it stoically … although they tended to wander at night, mooing querulously in constant complaint the next day when they were forced to move on.

At high mid-summer, they reached what Gil said would be the last water for many miles – a discouraged rivulet with muddy banks much churned by cattle on the trail ahead of them. It turned out that many another Texas cattle rancher looked to the rich takings in the California market and made plans accordingly, moving their herds along the established trail. The bare dun-colored desert stretched out on either side, with a scattering of low and sunbaked hills on the distant horizon.

Gil held council that afternoon, grave and forthright as ever. "I didn't think it might have to come to this," he said. "But we're still more than forty miles from Hueco – that's the next good water in this godforsaken hell-hole … and the daytime heat will start killing the weakest cows very soon. We'll rest them a while here, fix some good grub and start out after sundown."

"On the trail in the dark?" Eb Satterwaite looked skeptical, and Gil replied, "Full moon, Eb – it's near as bright as day. Nothing to worry about."

"Hueco," Fredi mused, "That's 'tanks' in Spanish – does it mean there is plenty of water there, Gil?"

"Great pools of it, Dutch," Gil answered. "Fresh and plenty, seeping out of the rocks and caves – then we'll be close to the Rio Bravo. One or two more dry spells before we strike the Gila River, and then we just follow it most of the rest of the way." He smiled at Fredi and at them all, the beard-grizzled or dirty boy-faces hanging on every word and hoping for reassurance. "Don't worry, fellows. We'll be in California by Christmas at the latest; my word on it."

They rested the afternoon at that muddy trickle, taking turns by twos to guard the cattle while the others slept in their clothes, lying on their blankets in the shade of the wagons. At sundown they roused themselves, and ate a hasty meal of bacon and cold bread or hard-tack, and beans which had been left to stew in the ashes of the midday cookfire. They finished the last of the coffee, Gil observing cheerfully that it should keep them well-awake.

"Pity we can't feed it to the cows," one of the other hands observed, to a general guffaw. "It would sure keep them moving."

"I dinna think that coffee would so affect cows as it does the human kind," O'Malley mused. "Still, I speculate such an experiment might prove interesting to gentlemen of science."

"I seen pigs get drunk from eating the mash from making apple cider," Eb Satterwaite ventured, and the conversation on that topic, to include varied personal reminiscences of the antics of farmyard animals overindulging on fermented fruit continued until the moon had risen high enough over the horizon to lend a ghostly semblance of daylight to the desert and the half-seen trail ahead. Fredi rubbed the velvety nose of his cow-pony in rueful apology, as he slipped the bridle over the pony's head.

"Sorry, Fleck," he said. "No rest for any tonight ... not until moon-set." He had become quite fond of the pony which Gil had allotted to him in addition to the one that he had brought from the Becker ranch. It was hard work, cattle-droving, and even harder on the horses. Each of the hands had two from the remuda to use, if they had not owned their own.

The wagons went first, as the moon rose – a gleaming ivory orb that looked the size of a man's fist. Charlie rode ahead of the wagons, on scout and distinguishable in the distance by the rifle that he held crossways and at the ready across his pony's withers. The very last of twilight fled, and the moonlight lay cold and serene on the rolling desert – a desert that Fredi discovered was more alive after dark than during daylight. Small things rustled, chittering and squeaking, in the sparse thickets close at hand, and once a shadow with a pair of briefly gleaming eyes fled from practically under Fleck's hooves; a desert fox, hunting mice. Now and again an owl swooped overhead, a silent shadow on feathered wings outspread. The teamsters hung lighted lanterns from the rearmost wagon-bow to guide the drovers and the cattle as they moved ahead along the trail – appearing in the distance as if they were golden fireflies, bobbing and jostling as the wagons found every rock and rut in the trail. It gratified Fredi, discovering that the trail itself was perfectly visible in the moonlight; seeming to gleam just as they did with a cobweb-shine in every story that his mother and sister had ever told of fairy paths through the dark woods.

The cattle moved at a stoical plodding pace, only the crunch of their hooves on the gravely trail, and an occasional querulous mooing breaking the night silence. The day's heat fled with the setting of the son; Fredi knew that now, after weeks and weeks of traversing the barren deserts. Funny that it could be so, but he accepted it without question. And anyway, it was better for the cattle; they would not feel the lack of water so much, walking on and on in the cool darkness. They had no water but that in their canteens and in the water barrels on the side of the freight wagons – enough for the men, but not a drop for the cattle.

Fredi wondered about Hueco. Pools of good, clean water, among caves and rocks, Gil said; a miracle in the desert. He thought on that for a good while; the best part of his mind never relaxing vigilance on the cows, but he had gotten to the point of being able to set aside a part of it to muse on matters which interested him, to wander in imagination while the thinking part tended to business. There were the stars overhead, the constellations swinging silently across the velvet-dark sky, with the Milky Way twisted like a length of gauze among them. His father had said often that every single star in the night sky was actually a sun, so far distant that they only showed as faint silver sparks to human eyes. Fredi could not imagine a distance so vast – farther away than California, or China.

Time stood still; Fredi felt as if he would always be in the middle of this nighttime trek – the cattle and the silent stars, the lanterns on the wagons far ahead. Now and again he sipped carefully from his canteen, spoke to Gil, who rode past on a regular patrol of the moving column of men, horses and cattle, or waved his hat in warning at a cow tempted out of the column. A clear night; he was grateful for that. Storms, with lightning and thunder were practically guaranteed to panic the cattle and to compound the mild miseries of a nighttime ride with being soaking wet on top of it all.

Sometimes, he felt that he had fallen asleep, lulled by tedium and the regular sway of Fleck's stride, waking with a start to wonder if he had been asleep and dreamed all of this; the night, the cattle, Gil and O'Malley, the trail to California and all of it. How strange and unsettling it was, that Johann was not a part of this – was not a part of his waking and breathing thoughts, every day as he had been since they were born. His brother, his other half, whose thoughts he had been able to sense and know since they were of an age to have thoughts. But Johann had always been different; Fredi had known this always. Everyone always said that Johann was clever, brilliant, even; certain of his father's friends who had more of brains themselves than tact and sympathy often and frankly averred that Johann had a larger portion of intellectual acuity than his twin. It saddened Fredi to know that everyone thought he competed with his brother as gladiators in the arena, but at least Vati and Carl had never treated with himself and Johann as if one or another of them were the better. They just –

were. They were two brothers, each possessing different skills when it came to the long grand joust of life. Now it occurred to Fredi that in this sphere he had the better of Johann. His brother went back to the Old Country, in obedience to custom and the wishes and direction of his fathers' friends. It was only right, because Johann knew and honored and revered all that which came from the Old Country but Fredi had the new world in his bones, just as Carl did – for all that his brother-in-law still held to the old ways of things.

The stars faded and the moon set at last; the sky at their backs paled with the coming of dawn. When it was light enough to see, Gil directed the making of a dry camp in a shallow valley. The cattle spread out to graze on what sparse greenery there was, with a noted lack of enthusiasm. They sounded plaintive, unhappy at the poor pasturage and lack of water. There was nothing to be done for it but rest during the heat of the day, try and keep them from straying too far, and start again at sundown. Fredi felt remorseful enough to pour a little of his own water into a basin for Fleck and Paint to drink.

"Don't go getting all sentimental now, Dutch," Gil rebuked him. "We don't have all that much water to spare."

"It ain't right to look at 'em suffering so," Charlie ventured, in a quiet voice. He sat on his heels nearby, having done the same thing for his own horse. "An' not do something about it, ifn' you can."

"There'll be all the water they can drink at the Hueco Tanks," Gil answered, although it was plain to Fredi that he didn't relish seeing the beasts tormented and suffering from thirst. "Two, three days more – that's all. They can hold out, as long as we don't push 'em too hard."

"Likely they'll smell the water, an' push themselves," Charlie said. "We'll need to take care then, Gil."

"Absolutely," Gil nodded, but the strain in his features remained.

Chapter 4 – Hueco Tanks

They reached Hueco by the dawn on the third day; just as Charlie predicted, all the cattle in the herd and under harness smelled water from afar. They picked up a steady pace; and their agitation was as palpable as the eternal dust that rose from their feet.

"Hold 'em steady, boys!" Gil urged them, as he rode steady patrol, up along one side of the moving column of horses and cattle and then down the other. "It's not that much farther."

"Good to know," Fredi remarked to Paint, whose ears twitched as if he understood. No doubt his pony scented water also, and if not, had sensed the disquiet among the cattle.

The Hueco appeared first as a tumble of up-thrust gray boulders erupting from the desert floor, piled one on another random jackstraw arrangements. Those harsh eminences were entirely naked of trees and bushes, save those which edged the feet of those cliff-like slopes … and the pools and lakes of water, blessedly sweet and pure, tasting faintly of clean stone and reflecting the blue sky overhead. The cattle jostled each other, barging into the closest pools, clustering around it as bees did on a drop of spilled honey, and drinking of it long and deeply. Paint waded into the nearest pool, hock deep to drink of it. Fredi could hear the water gurgling in his pony's stomach. He himself knelt on the gravel at the pool's edge, scooping water in his cupped hands, drinking just as eagerly. When sated, he dipped up a larger portion of water in his hat and poured it over himself, feeling as if he were fully awake for the first time in days.

"How much farther is it to California now, Gil?" he asked. Gil slouched in the saddle of his own horse, looking down and grinning in relieved happiness.

"We're nearly halfway," he answered, cheerful as ever. "And that's the longest stretch without water, until we get to the stretch between Yuma Crossing and the mountains. Still eager to get to California, Dutch?"

"Oh, yes," Fredi answered. Halfway; and what other marvels were there to be seen?

They stayed at Hueco for three days, letting the cattle recover strength from the desert crossing. It was high summer now, and the heat relentless – but being near the shallow desert rivers meant that they had water at nooning and at the evening camp. Such rivers were ordinarily a relative trickle down the center of a wide swath scraped out of the earth, often stagnant and muddy, so sluggish was the current. They were most often fringed with reeds and cottonwood trees.

"Haven't you noticed? Always where there are cottonwoods, there is water," Gil explained to Charlie and Fredi one afternoon. The tree in whose shade they were resting for the noon-time halt was a particularly tall specimen, with a pillar of a trunk so massive that the three of them holding hands could not reach around.

"Even if you must dig for it," Charlie answered, nodded. Next to Gil, he had the best sense of things in this track wilderness. Charley always knew what direction they were heading in, although Gil had the advantage of having been along the trail before. Now Charlie narrowed his eyes, looking off toward a distant horizon, where a line of mountains marked a jagged blue line against the sky; a line of shadowy blue only a few shades darker than the clouds which crowned them. "But I'll bet no one will be digging for water up there," he jerked his chin toward the cloud-crowned heights. "It's getting ready to storm."

"You think?" Gil squinted in the direction of the mountains. "I do believe you are right. That sounds like thunder to me. Eb, Dutch,

Aloysius!" He called over his shoulder. "We'd best get moving, boys!"

"Why?" Fredi asked, much puzzled. They had only just eaten – customarily, they would rest for another hour or so. "That storm is miles away from here – we'll never have a drop of it fall on us." O'Malley, peacefully blowing smoke circles from his pipe, set it aside and looked as doubtful as Fredi.

"This riverbed comes down from those mountains," Gil picked up his saddle. "You can look around – see all that wood and old brush stuck in the low branches? Water came and carried it up there. Saddle up, boys – let's get the cows and wagons on the far side of this before it floods again."

"Seems unnatural, beggin' your pardon, sor …" O'Malley ventured, and Gil cut him short. "Not for out here, Aloysius. Pack your traps and get those mules moving."

Privately, Fredi didn't think there was cause for alarm, but he trusted Gil's word. He was the boss-man, and anyway, since none of the many decisions Gil had made as trail-boss had come awry, Fredi was inclined take him at his word. Besides, some of the other hands were looking uneasily in the direction of the mountains and at the wide dry creek-bed as they untied their horses from sturdy branches or from a lariat run between the two freight wagons. Obviously mighty surges of water had carved it out on previous occasions. Fredi couldn't swim and had no wish to learn.

The wagons moved ponderously, the two teamsters walking at the side of their lead team; O'Malley already had his light mule-drawn wagon moving ahead, up along a place where the creek bank described a gentle slope. Overhead a few puffy clouds floated in a sky of pure blue – not a hint of rain to be seen, although the line of gray cloud piled up over the distant horizon like a sullen drunk in the corner of an otherwise happy celebration.

The trail that they followed had been well-traversed this year and in previous seasons, clearly marked by old ruts and broken sagebrush, grazing grounds now barren of any greenery, and the cold-ash remains of old cook-fires. It followed the line of the river, now close and now swinging away as the terrain allowed. In mid-afternoon, a little more than an hour since breaking up camp and moving on, Fredi became aware of an odd sound – a kind of low rumbling, almost more felt than heard. He thought at first that it was the cattle; that part of the herd ahead of him had panicked, begun to stampede. He took off his hat and waved to Gil, riding back alongside the moving herd. Without any particular urgency, Gil waved back, and waited until Fredi caught up to him.

"What's that sound, Gil?" he asked when they were close enough.

"Water – it's flooding down from that rainstorm. Ain't you glad we crossed over when we did?"

"It sounds hellish," Fredi looked down into the riverbed. "And we never had a drop of rain on us!" This was something he had never seen before. Rivers in Texas flooded when it rained, but when the water rose, it didn't come suddenly under a clear sky, or with such a dreadful noise. The rumbling sound came louder now, rumbling and grinding, as if a giant were shaking a million pebbles in an immense fist. But Fredi could see nothing out of the ordinary; the tiny meander of clear water in the river bottom appeared completely unchanged. And then, the sound came clearer, a rush of muddy water at the upstream bend, foaming, churning and falling, to the height of a horses' back. The sound of it filled his ears. It didn't even look like water; rather more like the earth itself turned liquid, carrying along in it all kinds of trash, sticks and stones, an inexorable flood, overwhelming the small trickle and sweeping under what had grown along the river bottom. In a trice, the riverbed was filled from bank to bank with a waterfall-torrent, the color of mud. And this, even as far as the eye could see, in a sere and almost bare land, as dry as the dust that fumed up from the feet of the cattle herd.

Gil nodded. "You never want to be caught in one of those sudden floods, Dutch. Never set up a camp in a dry creek-bed, or even close in to a riverbank, less'n you can see how high the water has been in the past."

Fredi looked at the muddy flood-water rushing past – the rock-grinding noise even louder. The very least that someone caught by surprise could expect was a wetting – and the worst, to be tumbled and ground to pieces until they were drowned, dismembered and dead. Yes, many indeed were the strange sights to be seen out beyond the frontier.

Fort Thorn, when they reached it almost a month's worth of travel later, presented another strange sight – an oblong of rough plank-sided dwellings, crudely roofed with thatch or crude plank shingled and every part of it whitewashed clean. The stripes and stars of the American Union fluttered from a tall pole, the only thing of bright color in the whole landscape. There were the blue coats of soldiers at drill on the parade-ground below the flagpole, and everything appeared to be very tidy, very orderly. The hills rose up into mountains west of the fort, pale violet color in the distance. After the barren deserts they had passed through, green marshes at the foot of the low bluff crowned by the fort struck them all with the promise of water and rich grazing for the cattle, especially where the rushes grew lank and tall.

"They've finished a lot more of the fort than when I came here last," Gil observed, when he ate with Fredi's messmates that evening. "It's good to see, what the war with Mexico gained us."

"Enough desert to satisfy any Arab," O'Malley observed, and slapped at a pesky mosquito. "Tell me – did we gain anything o' worth from that excursion?"

"California," Fredi answered. "And … my brother-in-law said that it also put Santa Anna's army to the trouble of staying on their side of the Nueces for good and all. He says that they came raiding into Texas many a time."

"They still do," Gil grunted sourly, taking another piece of baked bread from the long-legged iron skillet. "That scoundrel Juan Cortina helps himself to any cattle he pleases north of the Rio Grande."

"But he is only one man," Fredi began and Gil added, "With a pack of hired bravos and thieves at his back. He'll meet a Ranger company someday … somewhere where there's a good stout tree and a length of rope, and I can't promise I'll even grieve all that much." Now Gil slapped at a mosquito himself.

"So, what do the brave soldier boys do out here, then?" O'Malley asked. "Poor lads, I do not envy them in the desolation of this establishment."

"Guard against the Apache raids," Gil answered. "The 'pache are almost as good at stock-stealing as the Comanche. Once we're beyond the fort, double the night-guard."

They did, however, sell five head of cattle to the soldiers at the fort. Up close, they looked a poor body of men; most of them ailing or poorly and just well enough to totter about performing light duties. The captain in charge of the company told Gil that all of his fittest troopers were out on scout, adding the unneeded observation that of all the US Army posts in the west, this was the unhealthiest of them all. Something to do with the night air over the marsh, he thought.

The trail climbed up into the mountains flanking a fresh-water stream which Gil told them was the Rio Mimbres, a grade so steep that for several days, the teamsters double-teamed the heavy freight wagons. Toward the summit, they drew up first one wagon and then the other, hitching all the draft oxen to one wagon, taking it a few miles up the trail, then unhitching the teams and going back for the second. It was a laborious business; for almost the first time on the trail, the herd moved advanced at a brisker pace. Just as in the stretch of desert around Hueco, it was hot during the day and bone-chillingly cold at night. Tempers ran short – which was probably why Zeke Satterwaite's veiled animosity toward Fredi finally boiled over into open conflict. On a certain morning as the drovers broke camp, Zeke Satterwaite misplaced his pocket-knife.

The first that Fredi knew of it was when Zeke grabbed Fredi by the shoulder from behind, spun him around and snarled, "Where is it, you thieving little c---sucker! I know you have it, you was looking at it all the time last night, when me an' Eb was playing mumplty-peg…"

"What was I looking at?" Fredi stammered, honestly puzzled at both the accusation and the animosity behind it. All during this long journey from the Fabreaux place on Cibolo Creek back in Texas, he had never been able to figure out why Zeke Satterwaite was always ragging on him in subtle ways. Since the Fabreaux outfit was a sizable one, and he and the Satterwaite brothers weren't in the same mess of an evening, they were able to stay out of each other's way. This had mostly been a matter of chance rather than deliberation.

"My knife, you nigra-loving Dutch thief – I know you stole it."

"I don't know anything about your knife!" Fredi protested; he had observed in a casual way that Zeke had one, but not that it was any finer than Fredi's own, which was nickel-silver with a plain bone grip and come all the way from Germany.

"You liar!" Zeke Satterwaite, enraged beyond all reason, swung his fist – and it crashed on Fredi's jaw. "Take that, you thieving Dutch bastard!" Fredi was distantly aware of his mouth filling with blood, the coppery taste of it, and an insensate wave of anger. It seemed like a red mist fell over his eyes; he saw nothing beyond the jeering look on Zeke's face.

Without quite being aware that he was doing so, Fredi launched himself at Zeke, an unthinking impulse, the red mist in his eyes and a roaring in his ears, aware in a tiny corner of his mind that he was shouting rich curses in his native tongue and hitting with his own balled fists, hitting again, and again, regardless of the pain in his own knuckles as it brought out the crunch of something breaking under them. He hit until he was breathless, either from that exertion or from shouting, until at last some great and irresistible power dragged him free, away from the object of his punishing fury. He fought against that power also, but that it had him by the upper arms in an iron grip, pulling him off the sprawled body of Zeke Satterwaite.

Fredi gasped, coming back to himself and a rational mind. The red mist faded, he was aware of being immensely heated, although he stood in front of a forge-fire. To his vague astonishment, it was Charlie and O'Malley holding his arms tight-prisoned, while Eb Satterwaite knelt at his brother's side. Zeke lay prone in the dirt, barely recognizable with all the blood leaking from his nose, which looked to be broken. His lips were split; also leaking blood, his eyes swollen shut and already turning dark purple. To Fredi's confused gaze, Zeke looked as if he he had been run over several times by stampeding cattle. *What had happened – had he done this?* The other drovers, arrested in the middle of breaking camp, saddling their ponies or packing up their bedrolls … they were all standing around, staring in astonished horror. *What had happened?*

"Ah, Freddy-boyo, come back to yerself," O'Malley crooned into his one ear, while Charlie observed into the other, "Dutch, I think you hit him enough to repay the insult. Leave off, before you kill him."

"Gone like a berserker, he has," O'Malley observed with the air of a lecturer, over Fredi's head. "I've seen it before – the battle-fury, like the great champion of Ulster, Cuchculainn. They say that when the rage was on him, you'd have to throw buckets of cold water…"

"Cold water, we don't have." That was Gil's voice, impatient and exasperated. "Zeke, you stupid bastard, picking fights with the other hands is a firing offense. Count yourself lucky we're here, not back in Texas, and I might make you walk, from here on out."

Fredi struggled to regain clear sight and composure, wrenching his mind back onto the road of English. "I'm not Dutch … I was in Albeck of Bavaria born and bred. Not Holland." Fredi's sight and awareness cleared a little more; Charlie and O'Malley still held him pinioned, as Zeke Satterwaite moved and groaned.

"Well, you ain't killed him, Dutch, but it's better than he deserved for throwing the first blow," Gil pronounced.

"He said that I had stolen his knife," Fredi stammered, horrified. "His little knife … that he was playing with last night."

"His pen-knife?" Eb Satterwaite's countenance reflected an expression of mixed embarrassment and horror. "Good lord Almighty! Zeke, you damned fool! You dropped it sometime last night. It was on the ground by where your bedroll was; I found it just now." Zeke Satterwaite groaned again, struggling to rise. His brother propped him to a sitting position, daubing with his own neckerchief at the bloody mask of his face. "Swear to God, Zeke – if Dutch here hadn't gotten there first, I'd whip you like a rebellious nigra! What did you think would happen, accusing him of taking your damned knife and then taking a poke at him? You're damned lucky he didn't call you out, right then and there. Too damned big for your britches – didn't Pa and I always tell you that?" Eb looked up at Fredi, shamefaced. "Sorry 'about this, Dutch. I swear to God, I don't hold anything against you on this account. Zeke was in the wrong and you were in the right. I'll say the same to anyone."

"I didn't mean to hit him that hard..." Still shaken at what he had done, Fredi started an apology, but O'Malley observed by way of comfort, "Of a certainty you didn't, Freddy-boyo – it was the rage o' battle on you, the berserker-fit." He slapped Fredi on the shoulder in a manner meant to be comforting, adding in a louder voice, with the intention of being overheard. "Such a mild and obliging Christian lad! You'd think to look on him that he was raised on milk and water by maiden aunts ... but a tiger when his temper is up. Niver make him angry, lads – that's my best advice to you all, now."

"But I didn't..." Fredi protested and O'Malley cut him off. "Niver mind, lad; young Satterwaite has learned himself a valuable lesson, you will see. Never underestimate an opponent." O'Malley lowered his voice to a confidential murmur. "Freddy-boyo, take this as my good advice; you now have a reputation as a bonny fighter, not to be trifled with by any man misled into thinking of you as a mere harmless lad. Keep your mouth shut, that's what I say."

Charlie nodded, in silent agreement, and handed Fredi his hat, which had gone flying at the start of the encounter. Meanwhile, Eb continued upbraiding his brother, while the other hands looked on with expressions half of horror and half of dawning respect, until finally Gil barked, "We're burning daylight. Eb, put your worthless lump of a brother in Aloysius' wagon, see that he's comfortable, but his wages are docked for the time he can't work, and another week on top of that for picking fights." Gil swept them all, his lips tight in exasperation. "You all – what is this, Dr. Barnum's theater and house of curiosities? Get back to work. And Dutch," he added, in a slightly softer tone, but still loud enough to be heard by the other hands and teamsters, now making an elaborate show of tending to their hitch-up duties. "Next time you're righteously provoked, don't go all mad-dog and hurt 'em so hard they can't work."

"Yes, Gil," Fredi answered, inwardly relieved, but still baffled over what had come over him. He had not intended to hurt Zeke that badly in the fight, so badly that he had to ride in O'Malley's wagon for almost a week, his eyes all swollen nearly shut. Fredi's blows had cost him two teeth, so he could only eat cornmeal mush. Fredi's own knuckles were cut and skinned, and he wondered if he hadn't broken a bone or two in his hands as well. The memory of his insensate fury had come over him, and how he had beaten Zeke Satterwaite nearly to insensibility continued to haunt him.

"I had not meant it," he confessed to Charlie, one evening when they were on night-guard together and could speak privately as they watched over the herd and the slumbering camp. They sat on their saddles, their horses paused on a slight eminence where they could oversee most of the herd. The moon was a pale new thread, overwhelmed by brilliant starlight. "I don't know what came over me … he hit me, and I … well, I forgot everything. I think that I would have killed him if you and O'Malley hadn't pulled me off."

"That you might have," Charlie grinned, which Fredi could see clear in the dark. "Did you ever do anything like that before? You went for him like a wild-cat – that I saw plain enough. Tell you what, Dutch; it's raised your estimation in the eyes of the boys, my word on it. There ain't a man-jack of them would cross words with you now." His voice went sober and deliberate. "Not a bad thing, I'd say. Ruffians would give you a wide berth, and consider their words careful in speaking to you."

"But it's not something I thought I might ever do, Charlie. I couldn't rightly think straight. It was like something else took over, once I lost my temper."

Charlie was silent for a long time, until he said, finally, "Then it 'ppears like you must guard your temper, Dutch. Seems to me that every man has a demon riding them; Zeke – his demon is that he likes to bully those smaller and weaker than himself. Well, now he knows that you ain't smaller and weaker. Mebbe he'll ride herd on his own demon from now on. Likely not, though. What a man is at a certain age, that'll what he'll be the rest of his life. Zeke, he strikes me as one who will never get any wiser. As for Eb, I think his demon is Zeke, and trying to keep him out of trouble."

"I like that thought, Charlie." Fredi thought on it for some moments, obscurely comforted. Charlie was a good egg, with a good head on his shoulders; for all that he was only two or three years older than Fredi. Talking to him was like talking to Johann, even if Charlie couldn't read and could barely write his name. "A demon ... a particular curse to be overcome; that's something like what my father would say. He's a very wise man, Charlie. He reads books and he knows things, more than what I have ever brought myself to think about. What do you think your own demon is?"

"Ambition," Charlie grinned again. "I want land and property, with the finest cattle that ever set foot on earth, grazing on it. I want to be my own man, with no one believing himself to be my master."

"Gil's all right," Fredi felt obliged to speak up. He had never taken Gil or any of the Fabreaux brothers for any of what his father or the other greybeards from the Old Country had called the Firsts – the nobility. "He's not a master; he works with us as readily as any of the boys. Do you reckon he has a demon, Charlie?"

"Likely," Charlie answered; thoughtful in his usual way, on this starlight night, when everything and everyone else around slumbered – the cattle in their bedding down, the men in their blankets. "Every man has one, I do believe. If I had to guess, I would say that Gil's demon is that he has to prove himself to his brothers. He fears that he has no respect from them, unless he undertakes this venture and earns a good profit by it."

Fredi considered that with care for some moments and then nodded. "Yes, I do believe you are right about Gil. What about O'Malley; does he have a demon of his own?"

"Beyond strong drink?" Charlie laughed shortly, and considered a moment. "Inconstancy; like a girl who flirts with every man she meets. But O'Malley, I believe that he flirts with ideas. Grand ideas, mostly ... until he meets another one, and flirts with it."

While Charlie spoke, both his and Fredi's eyes were scanning the horizon, the margins of the restlessly sleeping cattle herd, alert for any untoward motion, or sound. A rustle of reeds by the waters' edge against the direction of the fitful breeze, a sudden gleam of starlight on a knife-blade, a swift shadow too large to be an animal ... such small occurrences must be seen and noted by those on guard. Fredi rather liked standing watch – it was quieter, even if it was almost as boring as the daily trudge. The night held no terrors for Fredi; he had been out on round-up with his brother-in-law often enough, and Carl was as canny as an Indian himself. Abruptly, Charlie continued. "Did you ever notice that O'Malley never tells quite the same story about how and why he came to leave Ireland?"

"Gil said something once about O'Malley being a Fenian and trying to assassinate the Queen of England," Fredi mused. "I think he was joking, but O'Malley looked almost frightened for a moment."

"Do you think Gil was right?" Charlie asked. "What's a Fenian?"

"An Irishman for independence of Ireland," Fredi answered, vaguely pleased to know something that Charlie didn't. "And revolution against British rule. There was a lot about it in some of the newspapers that my father reads. He takes an interest in that sort of thing. He was a revolutionist himself, when he was young. But in

Germany, and against the Firsts – that's what he and his friends call the nobility and royals back in the Old Country."

"He's full of stories," Charlie said, and Fredi nodded agreement. "O'Malley is – all of them interesting, but you never know which of them to believe are true."

"It could be that he doesn't even know himself anymore," Fredi ventured. They sat and watched from the top of the hill a little more, their horses chewing meditatively on their bits. "He says that he will stay in California, once we get there. Since there are so many Irishmen there already; he says that we should partner up and find a gold mine of our own. Are you going to stay in California and look for gold, Charlie?"

His friend shook his head; Charlie, who had thought everything out beforehand. "No," he answered. "I don't think so, Dutch."

"Why not? Do you have a girl, in Texas – one that you're sweet on? Having a girl is the only reason I'd give up a chance to strike it rich in the gold diggings."

"I don't have a particular fancy." Charlie shook his head. "And I don't intend to court serious, until I can support a wife. I took on with Gil for the wages, to get a start on my own ranch. I know all about cattle, I don't know anything about gold mines and I'm not interested enough to take the time to learn."

"I don't know that I am particular fond of cows myself," Fredi allowed. "But I am particular fond of the notion of getting rich."

"You'll never get rich working for someone else," Charlie pointed out. "That's why I have my mind set on my own ranch. If you don't strike it rich in the mines, Dutch – will you come back to Texas and settle down?"

"I reckon I want to see a bit of the world, before I do," Fredi thought about it for a moment.

"We're seeing as much of it as I want to see," Charlie agreed.

Chapter 5 – End of the Trail

The heat of summer faded, even though they were still crossing through desert country. It was still cold at night; Fredi was profoundly grateful for the warmth of the bedroll that he slept in, although as it came about, he and the other drovers more and more often took shelter at night underneath the wagons. With the cooling of the nights came rain, most always in the afternoon about the time that they had chosen to set up camp. Gil had the teamsters park the wagons a couple of yards apart, and to string the wagon covers together on ropes, running between the hickory hoops which ordinarily supported the cover, together with a length of canvas between to make a shelter against the rain, which came in a furious drenching flood for an hour or so. They could often see this rain coming in at some distance; a gray veil hanging from beneath a tower of clouds, the scent of moisture striking dry soil arriving on gusts of a suddenly-active breeze. Those daily rains made the desert around them bloom, as much as it was a discomfort to the drovers, sleeping on pallets laid on suddenly-muddy ground. Grass came up, lush and green, and the cattle drank eagerly of the fresh rainwater wherever it accumulated – in small and temporary rivulets, or even from those puddles accumulated in the low places along the trail. O'Malley shook his head in dismay and disbelief.

"I swear, 'tis unnatural. This is September, nearly November, when all should be drear and dead ahead of wintertime, yet everything is as green and blooming as spring in Antrim."

"That's the way of it in this part of the world, Aloysius," Gil chuckled at the Irishman's befuddlement. "Autumn and winter are green and blooming; summer is bare and dry. And the oak trees are green the year throughout."

"'Tis unnatural," O'Malley grumbled.

Zeke Satterwaite was able to mount up and go back to work after a week or so of jolting along in O'Malley's spring-wagon, although it took a good while longer for the bruises from Fredi's beating to fade from livid red and purple to yellow. There was a definite change in the shape of his nose and with two teeth missing, what Zeke had in the way of good looks had definitely fled.

Fredi tried approaching him once or twice to tender an apology. He did feel he owed Zeke that much, but Zeke walked away the first time that Fredi tried and the second time, he snarled, "You keep away from me, you nigra-loving foreigner." As Zeke appeared disinclined to seek out Fredi's company in any way, Fredi left the matter alone. If Zeke wanted nothing to do with Fredi, Fredi was content with having nothing to do with the Satterwaite brothers for the remainder of the journey. He said as much to Charlie, one evening.

Charlie, leaning on one elbow to light his pipe from the embers of the cookfire, answered, "Told you so, Dutch; he don't want to risk another beating, but I'd not turn my back on him entirely. He's the kind of sneak who would think long and hard about what you did to him, build up a good grudge and stick a knife in your back in a dark alley in Bexar or some other place. I've hear tell that the gold camps are pretty lawless."

"I'll keep an eye out," Fredi replied. "California's a big place. You're certain you won't come with us, once Gil sells the herd and gives us all our wages?"

"I'm certain," Charlie answered. Fredi had asked him several times. So far, Fredi and O'Malley's plans were for going to San Diego, and seeing about working their way north. If worst came to worst, O'Malley intended selling the mules and his wagon, and taking ship on a coastal steamer for San Francisco and the gold mines. What was left of the goods and supplies in the freight wagons were intended to be sold in San Diego. They were close enough now that such plans did not seem like a dream out of reach.

They had swum the herd over the Gila River at Yuma the day before. Apache country was far behind, so a night-guard was no longer such a necessity. So was the cruel desert, and the cattle fattened on the rich winter grass. Because there was a military post at Yuma, with a regular courier and supply wagons going back and forth, Fredi and some of the other hands wrote letters to be sent east to friends and kin, entrusting them with the last of their coin money to an Army wagoneer who promised to post them on when he got to Bexar.

In the middle of November, the herd reached a place called Warner's Ranch, a resting place on a heavily traveled trail, set in a shallow valley between gently rolling hills, covered in grass like plush velvet upholstery on an overstuffed chair. Cattle and sheep roamed everywhere, for the lands around were rich and the weather temperate. The end of the trail, for Gil and the Fabreaux herd; Fredi looked down from the last heights with a certain degree of regret, seeing the roofs of the rancho – a rambling and comfortable house of adobe mud-brick, with stables and barns, quarters for the many tame Indians who worked there, and for visitors like themselves.

Gil, gone out on scout ahead of the herd, came riding back smiling from ear to ear. "Almost there, boys. The folks at Warner's are going to send messages out to buyers for the herd and they're going to purchase half the herd themselves, looking to sell in the diggings in the spring. It's a going business. As near as I can see it's not the miners getting rich from finding gold, it's the storekeepers selling them the vittles and tools they need, and the tavern-keeps selling them the panther-piss they need to keep themselves merry with. And Dona Vincenta is coming to meet us; a great courtesy, since we have come from such a distance with so large a herd."

"I thought this was Warner's rancho," Fredi ventured, in some confusion.

"There was a court claim on it – went on for on for decades, over whose land grant was the legitimate one," Gil explained, scratching his jaw, as he and Fredi sat side-by-side on their horses, just at the high point in the trail which led down to Warner's. "Either Don Jose Warner or Dona Vincenta Carrillo… I have it on good authority that the lawyers got rich and fat and retired to ranchos of their own over the course of settling the matter of ownership of this valley. No difference to me; a buyer is a buyer, and Texas cattle are Texas cattle. The good lady has offered me a price almost good enough to have made it worth my while."

Dona Vincenta Carrillo turned out to be a handsome and forthright woman of certain years, beautifully dressed in a full-skirted silk dress. She and a slender boy a little younger than Fredi presently rode out from the rancho and approached the foot of the hill where Gil and Fredi waited. When she was closer, Fredi could see that she rode astride like a man, her ankles peeping shyly out between the ruffles of her petticoat and the tops of her high-buttoned shoes. Fredi had not seen such splendid horseflesh since the 4th of July horse-races among the Fredericksburg Germans, or the meeting with Sally Doyle at the Fabreaux place. He wondered idly, if these two formidable matrons would ever chance to meet – they seemed to be in the same trade and to possess the same command over horseflesh, cattle, and lesser human beings.

"The lady speaks no English," Gil said, when they were still at some distance. "Her son translates."

"I speak some Spanish," Fredi volunteered, and Gil nodded. "You have a better grip on the lingo than I do, Dutch. Come along with me to meet them halfway.

The boy spoke English beautifully, without any trace of an accent that Fredi could tell – his own accent still marked after half his life spent in Texas. "I am Señor Jose Antonio Yorba, this is my mother, Madame Vincenta Yorba Carrillo. You are most welcome to the Valley of San Jose, Señor Fabreaux …you and your friends and companions. You are invited to stay at our house … our hacienda for as long as you wish, and for no more than the pleasure of your company."

"I thank you for the hospitality," Gil tipped his hat toward Dona Vincenta, who nodded regally. "I am told that it is legendary along this part of the trail – it was a long journey for us, and to sleep in a bed under a solid roof again will be a pleasure that we have not enjoyed for many months. This is Freddy Steinmetz, one of my most trusted fellows. He speaks Spanish, as well as German. His folks were educated, so I can assure you of his gentlemanly manners … although you might doubt that, trail-worn as we all are."

"You are from Germany, not Texas?" young Jose brightened with interest and Fredi warmed to him at once. Jose reminded him very much of Johann; the names were the same in different languages.

"I am … I was," Fredi answered. Following Gil's example, he took off his own hat, somewhat abashed for having forgotten the courtesy. "Thank you, ma'am … *Gracias, Dona Vincenta, gracias por la oferta de la hospitalidad.*"

"De nada," the lady replied, seeming to dismiss any inconvenience to herself or her household, although Fredi reckoned that it must be considerable … until he actually became better acquainted with the Carillo's extensive establishment.

They rested there for two weeks, although with the sale of the cattle well in hand, nearly twenty of the drovers took their wages and departed the same day that Gil paid them – either returning to Texas and their families, or in hast toward the gold diggings – despite knowing that most of the mines would be wintered in until spring.

Charlie departed last of all. "I'm not looking forward to some of the trail," he said on the morning that he departed east. "But Mama and Papa Sheek will be looking for me, and I don't want them worried none. Good luck in the gold mines, Dutch. You too, O'Malley; don't enjoy yourself too much."

"Nothing to fear, Charlie-boyo. I am a will-o-the-wisp, a restless spirit, never lingering long in any one place."

"You've just met someone who tells taller tales than you," Charlie grinned, and then he was gone, a rapidly diminished figure on horseback, riding up the hill to the east.

To remain for more than a few days at the Rancho Valle de San Jose was a considerable temptation. It was a welcoming place, comfortable and well-appointed with many expensive luxuries imported from the east; elegant furniture in the latest fashion, many books and even several very fine clocks, which chimed the hours. The hacienda's various wings and outbuildings sprawled this way and that; a ramble of rooms, and a small garden and orchard. Fredi and O'Malley found themselves taken to the heart of a large family, as Dona Vincenta had been married twice and produced a goodly brood of children, the youngest of whom still an infant, with her husbands, although she was still as slender as a girl.

Her second husband, Don Jose-Ramon Carrillo, proved a most engaging character; although a man somewhat older than his wife, and exceedingly mild and soft-spoken in character and conversation, he could tell of the most amazing adventures he had undertaken as a soldier and rancher. He spoke English quite well; having associated with many of the American settlers and soldiers in who had drifted into California in the days before gold was found. He had lived there all his life, being born of a family which had been established in California since the days of the Spanish. Fredi quite liked Don Jose-Ramon although he was never entirely certain if the latter was teasing his listeners with accounts of his adventures – such as the time when he had fought and killed a mountain bear with no more weapons than his hunting knife and the leather apron from his saddle.

"I saw the bear at some distance," Don Jose-Ramon said, from his chair by the fireplace in the parlor, on a day when rain made venturing out of doors a wet and uninviting prospect. The Don and a handful of his guests – Fredi, Gil Fabreaux and O'Malley and a number of visitors from other ranchos – were regaling each other telling stories to pass the time on a rainy winter afternoon, when clouds pressed down on the hilltops like a heavy gray featherbed. "In the hills to the north, a good way to the north from here; he was a huge, golden monster. I was with friends. I was younger and reckless of danger. I proposed some sport; I would dismount and fight the bear…"

"Surely, they did try and discourage you from this rash attempt," O'Malley interjected. Don Jose-Ramon smiled. "Ah, but a matter of honor, my dear friend. A matter of honor and a challenge. I had sworn that I would take the bear on those terms. I took up my hunting knife and the *mochila* from my saddle and went to meet my foe."

"Aye, like a warrior of old, with a sword and shield," O'Malley nodded. Don Jose-Ramon beamed, relishing the memory in the retelling at least as much as he had enjoyed the fight itself. "I had the *mochila* around my left arm, the knife unsheathed in my right, like so … and the bear charged, roaring hideously and rising to stand up on hind legs! It bared claws and struck at me, but I parried the blow with my left arm – wrapped so in the *mochila*, so that the blows of it's hideous claws had no effect as I thrust with my knife – again and again! I stabbed upwards, feeling my knife sink deep into its flesh –

the bear bellowed, enraged! I stabbed again and again, as its blows against me weakened! I parried with my left arm – and at last the hideous creature fell at my feet, quite dead. I was unharmed, but for some small wounds from its claws on my hand and cheek – You may see now that I had some slight scars for my trouble … and a most magnificent bear skin for my dogs to sleep upon."

"A veritable Nimrod," O'Malley lauded their host; to Fredi it seems that O'Malley did so as much for Don Jose-Ramon daring in confronting a mountain bear with only a knife in hand as for his facility in making a splendid story of it. "I envy you, sir, most heartily! Not that I would ever wish to copy such a feat, but that I would want to witness such."

"You will have such a chance," Don Jose-Ramon exclaimed in an enthusiasm of hospitality and good will. "For there has been a bear seen in these hills – not the equal of this big fellow – but of a good size and hungry. In this mild climate the bears do not retire to a den to sleep throughout the winter. In the spring, such a bear is a danger to my young calves … so, if the weather turns fair tomorrow – we'll go on a bear-hunt, my friends! I will show you how we hunt for bear … better yet, if we can capture it alive – a bull and bear fight! Now that is a sport the like of which you will not have seen anywhere else in the world!"

"Not in this century," Gil Fabreaux observed, but even he was interested in such an excursion. "I have heard of such contests, but have never seen one, or met anyone who had."

"Then it will be our pleasure to provide such amusement to our guests!" Don Jose-Ramon promised, in a fit of extravagant hospitality which Fredi and the other drovers from Texas had already come to expect from their host. As O'Malley observed the next morning in admiration, "Oh, he's like one of the grand kings of Ulster – King Conchobar mac Nessa himself, with his grand house, offering hospitality to all and asking for nothing more than his guests bring news, songs and stories from far away. I would, if I were so inclined, nominate myself to be his bard, and sing the epic tales of the heroes every evening at supper."

"If we find this bear that he talks of, you'll have a good and proper ode to sing," Gil Fabreaux observed. The rain had let up overnight, leaving the bare ground scattered with puddles, and the edge of every blade of grass and leaves on trees bejeweled with crystal drops, which caught the sun and glittered, while an infrequent gust of breeze sent drops splattering to the ground underneath. Two of Don Jose-Ramon's houseguests came with the party; gentlemen of California from neighboring ranchos, with Fredi and Gil rode their cowponies, and O'Malley one of his team mules, in serene indifference to the fact that he cut a ridiculous figure, with his legs dangling on either side.

"He looks like Sancho Panza," murmured young Jose with an impish smile to Fredi, who managed to keep a puzzled expression from his own face. He didn't think any of the Carillo hands were named Sancho, and in any case O'Malley looked like no one but himself, threadbare green coat, battered top-hat and all.

The boys followed after Don Jose-Ramon and the other men, up into the hills above the rancho and its outbuildings. Now and again they encountered wandering cattle, especially in the meadows, often up to their shoulders in lush new grass, but Don Jose-Ramon's path lay in the direction of the angular barrier of the hills which shouldered up, blue and blue-green in the distance, the peaks of the tallest lightly dusted with white. Birds started up from that grass at their approach – fat and clumsy quail with white-spotted wings and a comic tuft of black on their heads. Now and again, as they rode up into the narrow, twisting canyons in the lowest of the hills they were serenaded by the welcome sound of running water.

"These waters only run after a good rain," explained Don Jose-Ramon. Soon their party climbed into the lower foothills, patched in places with gray chamisa scrub, in places as thick as the fur on a buffalo-hide robe. After some miles, Fredi cared little if they found a bear or not, but the men seemed happy enough; a day on horseback away from the hacienda with no duties to do with cattle to burden them. He relished the out of doors, the clean smell of rain-wet earth and grass, the vaguely spicy scent of bruised sagebrush and chamisa which brushed their knees and the flanks of their horses as they followed Don Jose-Ramon along increasingly narrow trails. The sunshine that fell on them was bright but not warm, and that the prospect before him was slightly but deliciously unfamiliar.

"I like that which is different," he explained earnestly to young Don Jose, who nodded in agreement.

"You have the soul of a wanderer, Fredrick," Don Jose replied. "My mother would say that you are one fated never to be happy to settle in one place, until you are an old, old man, and maybe not even then. Now I was sent to school in Boston, but I was never so happy as I was to return home and know that I would never have to leave here again… hsss! I think my stepfather has found his bear!"

They drew rein, noting that Don Jose-Ramon was pointing at the hillside below; a hillside covered deep in dark green and gray scrub bushes, with small trails made by rabbit and deer in between. On the far edge, something moved among the brush, a thing so large that Fredi thought at first looked like a buffalo; something with hulking withers covered in shaggy pale-brown fur. It did not move like a buffalo at all, though. When it lifted its nose to sniff at the air, Fredi could see quite plainly that it wasn't a buffalo – but a thick-legged, sharp-nosed bear. Even at a distance, it didn't look to be dangerously large. Don Jose-Ramon stood in his stirrups, taking his riata from his saddle-horn; he swung the fist with the riata in it over his head and shouting, spurred his horse downhill at a perfectly breakneck pace.

The others plunged after, with slightly more care; the ground under the guise of the chamisa was broken with gullies, stones and animal burrows – a perfect invitation to a broken leg for a horse and a broken head for a man. None wanted to seem a coward when Don Jose-Ramon led the way with such reckless courage, least of all Gil and Fredi. Still, he was almost upon the bear, swinging his riata in a wider and wider loop, while the others were still negotiating the hillside.

With a shout of surprise, Don Jose-Ramon, his horse and the bear all at once vanished; a sudden chasm appeared to swallow them all up – a deep gully or pit, veiled by the sage and chamisa, until man, horse and bear toppled headlong into it! A titanic struggle shook the branches at the edge, Don Jose-Ramon's voice cursing – so at least they could be certain he was relatively unharmed by the fall. But the very existence of ground so broken dictated a measure of prudence and a slightly slower pace, and it was some minutes before Fredi, Gil and Don Jose, with the others approached the edge just to see the bear emerge, scrambling for a foothold on the opposite brink. Before any could react, wielding their own rope or long-gun, the bear vanished into the brush, although it could be tracked for a short distance by the violent movement of the branches.

Fredi looked down into the gully – a little less than chest-high to a man on the near side – to see Don Jose-Ramon's horse, standing with its saddle awry, the whites of its eyes showing all the way around, and Don Jose-Ramon leaning against the bank, both he and the horse gasping for breath after some mighty exertion. Don Jose-Ramon was covered in mud, both from the fall, and from what had been clawed down from the far bank as the bear escaped.

"*Dios mio!*" Don Jose-Ramon exclaimed, with a groan. "He got away!"

"Did you fight him?" Fredi asked, while the others clamored the same question in two languages. "Is that why the bear ran away?"

Don Jose-Ramon laughed, wincing as he did – very obviously having taken some bruises in the fall, if not a broken bone or two. "*Mi hijo*, no – for that bear had no fight in him, not after the fall. All he wanted was to get away ..." Don Jose-Ramon laughed again, a self-deprecating laugh, of deepest amusement. "As for myself, I had no fight left in me, either! He climbed halfway up the bank, and hung up on the edge. So I put my shoulder under his rump ... and gave him a boost. *Ay mi! bastardo pesado!* I have strained every muscle in my back!" Groaning, he accepted helping hands from above, and scrambled gracelessly out of the gully, while Gil and Fredi followed the gully downstream, searching for a place low enough to descend into it and retrieve Don Jose-Ramon's horse.

"So much for a bull and bear fight," Fredi observed, much disappointed, and O'Malley clapped him on the shoulder and exclaimed, "But the song that the bard could make of our good host lifting a bear – now would rival any story in the old tales, boyo."

Don Jose-Ramon, much recovered in spirit, if not in body, by they time they returned to the hacienda, still insisted on a grand fandango to take the place of the proposed bull and bear fight – to honor Gil and his journey, but it was by then December and Gil was – like the others with family in Texas – desirous of returning as soon as possible. They turned down the suggestion of a contest between Gil and Fredi and their own vaqueros with as much grace as could be mustered.

Chapter 6 – Señor Frijoles

With some trepidation, Fredi and O'Malley set off toward San Diego from the Cabrillo rancho on a crisp morning the week before Christmas. Their footsteps crunched through frost on the grass; the dusting of white on the tallest mountain peaks was rather more marked than it had been before. Fredi, sitting on the wagon-seat with Nipper curled snugly at his feet, reflected with regret on selling Paint to Don Jose-Ramon. He would miss the cow-pony, he admitted to himself – but Don Jose-Ramon had paid generously, far more than Paint was worth in Texas, and had assured Fredi with every appearance of sincerity that Paint would be treasured for the fine-trained cattle-handling Texas mustang that he was; a set of silver-trimmed riding tack, a drink of beer from a porcelain basin every day, and a stall made from the finest mahogany wood would not be out of the question, Don Jose-Ramon grandly assured Fredi.

"Besides, boyo – we're off to mine gold, not drive cattle," O'Malley pointed out, by way of a final convincing. Fredi did keep his saddle, wrapped in length of canvas in the back of O'Malley's spring-wagon. The coins from the sale of Paint, plus eight months' wages from Gil made him feel as rich as if he had struck a promising gold mine already.

O'Malley's own wages were part-paid in the remnant of unused and unsold supplies now packed in the spring-wagon. Together, Fredi and O'Malley planned to sell some of them in San Diego, buy what else they needed in the way of equipment for a season in the diggings, and work their way north, hiring out as day laborers, or hauling freight, as the opportunities presented themselves. Don Jose-Ramon considered it a workable scheme and had good knowledge of San Diego – the largest and most well-established town in the locality, for his family had been long-associated with the founding of it, in the time of Spanish rule. "Take the branch of the trail which heads south from here," he advised them. "The main road leads toward Los Angeles ... pooh – a dry and dusty place, of no particular moment. But San Diego is on the sea, and long-established in this country. My grandfather was a soldier of the presidio there, and my mother inherited a grant of land for his service ... a fine place it was before..." A sudden shadow of anger and resentment passed across Don Jose-Ramon's patrician features; gone as suddenly as it appeared, leaving Fredi to doubt that he had ever noted it at all. "But our fortune is now made in beef rather than grease and hides, so allowance must be made! *Vaya con Dios*, gentlemen! My house is yours, you are welcome at any time, day or night," Don Jose-Ramon promised extravagantly, as O'Malley slapped the reins on the backs of the mules and the wagon jolted away from the sprawling façade of the Castillo hacienda.

"I wonder what he meant by that," Fredi mused, as soon as they were out of sight, along the beaten trail tending west. "About being a fine place, before ... he seemed quite angry for a moment. What do you think, O'Malley?"

"Fredi-boyo, I think our Don Jose was looking the last on things as they were when he was young, and lamenting the future as it bore down upon him and his own." O'Malley leaned back in the seat and spat out the side of the wagon as the mules leaned into their harness. "I have gathered, ye might know, that the grand establishment that his mother had was in the north and close to the gold diggings – that property overrun by squatters, by tinkers and thieves. I do not have this intelligence from him, mind you – but from inference. These men – they were lookin' after gold, ye see, with no other thought in their heads. Gold in the streams and riverbeds, free for the taking wherever ye can find it, and they came in the hundreds and thousands, breaking down the pasture fences, spoiling the wells, killing the cattle and taking their bit of digging for their own, for they had the labor of it, ye see, Freddy-boyo. They thought they were in the right through hard work. Aye, but the landowner ... that's another matter, indade; a hard thing to see your own lands overrun and everything you thought was yours wrecked and spoiled, with no recourse, or gone all black and rotted and no way to feed ..." O'Malley added, with a laugh, and a momentarily desolate expression on his countenance. "No, I've never had the pleasure of owning so much as a tiny plot o' land, meself. My father was an ordinary cottar, somewhat richer than the neighbors, although not by very much as you count such things in America. And I was a clever lad, and taken up by landlord's factor and sent to school. But I know the stories that were told. And I remember..."

"We won't do anything like that," Fredi declared impetuously, for he could indeed imagine how his father or Carl Becker would feel about destructive trespass on their acres.

"Aye, Freddy-boyo, of course we won't," O'Malley assured him, slapping the reins over the backs of his mules, so that they left the rich and mild valley at a gentle jog.

Fredi smelled the ocean, long before they saw it, just as he had approaching Indianola, so many months before. The wagon came bumping down the track, rutted with the passage of many wheels and the hooves of the draft beasts which pulled them and the view of San Diego opened out before them. The saltwater smell, borne on the light westerly breeze took away something of the smell of two bales of hides in the back of the wagon. For a small sum, O'Malley had agreed to carry the hides to a factor in San Diego from a small rancho along the road they had traveled. The rancher had thrown in a night's hospitality and a good meal, so they could hardly refuse. And the stench of the cured hides would have been even more intense and unpleasant if it were summer, anyway.

At the peak of the final range of hills, the town lay spread out below them, edged with a shining reach of water dotted with the hulls and masts of sailing ships and the odd side-wheel steamers. Beyond that was a long and low barrier island; the sea lay on the far side of it – deep blue and stippled with white wave-crests and bands of silver where the rays of the sun lay at an angle between the clouds. A tall thumb of land that stuck out from the north bore a small white tower upon it, surrounded by a cluster of white-painted buildings, like so many sugar-cubes. The little grid of streets nestled below the shoreline and the last hills was dotted with buildings; some of frame with shingled roofs and others of sundried brick, topped with pale rust-colored tiles. Small orchards and gardens adorned the outermost streets and dwellings, punctuated by tall palm trees, standing like up-ended feather-dusters.

"Where we to bring the hides?" O'Malley sneezed at the dust rising up from the road, and Fredi answered, "He said it was on Fifth Street, not a stone-throw from the shore."

"Well, we shall deliver them with all dispatch, Freddy-boyo," O'Malley beamed with happy anticipation. "And then we will pursue those amusements thought proper for a gentleman; spirituous liquors, lovely women, and music, all in a single congenial place."

"A casino?" Fredi offered, in some doubt. Back in Fredericksburg, Captain Nimitz's establishment – hotel, beer-garden, and theater – hosted weekly entertainments; concerts, theatricals and dances of the respectable kind, guaranteed not to put a blush on the cheek of the most gently-raised maiden girl. Fredi knew that he was equal to that which would have been expected of him in such a venue. But there were less-respectable, more rowdy places and that he was in two minds about visiting them. Mostly, he feared that he would be laughed-at, for being a relatively beardless boy. It galled him sometimes that he still appeared to be no older than a lad fresh from the school-room, short of height and wiry, rather than tall and muscular from an early age, like his brother-in-law. No one had ever slighted or disrespected Carl Becker; Fredi could not imagine any circumstance where anyone would have done so. Besides, Carl had gone for a soldier in two wars and served as a Ranger fighting the Comanche with Captain Jack Hays for many years. *Perhaps,* mused Fredi, *Going to the gold-fields might do something of the same for me.*

"Aye, there could well be games of chance," O'Malley replied. "Trust me, boyo – I'll not be risking our stake on a fortunate turn of the cards or buckin' the tiger … well, not over more than we may afford from it."

"Not more than five dollars," Fredi insisted, for he already had observed O'Malley playing cards at the Carillo's. "You think you are a cannier player than you are."

"That cuts me to the quick," O'Malley protested. "What's the harm in a game of chance, as a way of passing the time with other gentlemen?"

"Depends on if they are worse players than you are," Fredi retorted. He knew that he was not good enough at flipping cards to come ahead very often, although Carl – who was – had often tried to teach him and Johann. O'Malley, to be kind and in defense of their purse, ought not to be allowed anywhere near games of chance played for money. O'Malley struck his breast, with an exaggeratedly tragic expression, and Fredi laughed, because O'Malley seemed not to be offended unduly at having his prowess at cards so questioned.

"I promise, boyo – nothing more than a few pennies of my own!"

They easily located the merchant contracted to buy the rancher's hides, and helped unload them with good spirits, it now being late afternoon, with the setting sun glancing off the wavelets out beyond shore, giving the ocean a look of silver-blue crape silk.

"You'd best look for a room with Mr. Lloyd at the United States House," advised the merchant, as he spat around into the street outside his establishment, without disturbing the straw lodged in the corner of his mouth.

"Too much," Fredi whispered. "We have to save our funds for the gold mines. We can sleep in the wagon…"

"We can splurge, surely," O'Malley answered, at his most happily expansive. "Since we traveled across half the continent to be here, sleeping under the wagon or out in the open air. I have a longing for a good bed and a roof overhead, since the Lord and his angels know when we may indulge in such again. Freddy-boyo, might we take advantage of the opportunity? Here we are, arrived on the shores of the world's great ocean, after may toils and troubles. Might we indulge ourselves with a spot of that small luxury which comes a working mans' way?"

"All right," Fredi agreed, with ungracious reluctance. The mules, after all, did have to be grazed somewhere, for as long as they remained in San Diego. Perhaps the liveryman could know of some work that he and O'Malley could do to offset the expense of remaining in San Diego.

Like Bexar, the life of this town centered on the main plaza – a substantial square defined by many fine buildings and mansions in the Mexican style – of whitewashed adobe, crowned with rust-red roof tiles and adorned with long cloister-galleries on the ground floor and narrow balconies above. The newer were of brick or framed lumber, as the Americans favored, but it all blended into a harmonious whole, in the fading twilight with mellow golden lamplight shining in windows and open doorways. The air was mild, slightly tinged with the scent of saltwater and flowering citrus, which beat back the usual odors of horse dung, privies and wood-smoke. It was warm for midwinter, Fredi thought. No wonder there were flowers everywhere – and bright magenta bougainvillea vines swagged the balconies like bunting. There was a grand new establishment built of brick going up along one side of the square; lights, laughter and music spilled out into the evening air. O'Malley, resplendent in his battered top-hat and green coat, strode ahead, tipping his hat to the ladies, as animated as a butterfly skipping from flower to flower, with Nipper darting in his wake.

At one particularly well-lit establishment, with the sound of lubricated merriment pouring into the plaza, O'Malley turned to Fredi. "Ah, Fredi-boyo, 'tis music to my very soul, after so long and dusty a trail from Texas; this looks to be just the place for a convivial evening."

"I s'pose so," Fredi yielded, still dubious. They had dined at the boarding house; good substantial fare, but the lady of the house dealt out helpings with a miserly hand and he was still hungry. He followed O'Malley into the place, feeling like the tail of a particularly exuberant kite. O'Malley ordered whiskey at the bar – a half bottle for himself. Fredi asked for beer, not entirely certain if he would get it, but the barkeep produced a gray stoneware bottle from under the bar. A haze of tobacco smoke hung just under the tall ceiling. The two of them retreated to a quieter corner, where O'Malley looked around for potentially congenial companionship.

The closest table to them was occupied by a handsome, broad-shouldered man in an elegant Mexican suit of clothes. Although his hair and mustaches were sleek and black, his complexion was too ruddy to be anything but of the upper classes, or an American with a taste for fancy dressing. A pair of revolvers in fancy belt holsters argued the latter – that and the large knife thrust into the top of his elegant boots. This Adonis was idly shuffling cards and nursing a small drink, brought to him by the barkeep's assistant, a young Mexican boy who got a small coin flipped at him for his trouble.

"Muchas gracias, Señor Frijoles!" exclaimed the boy, giving the table-top a hasty wipe

"Are ye waitin' on a friend, or may we join you?" O'Malley asked, the Irish in his voice coming out at full strength, and the man pushed one of the empty chairs in O'Malley's direction with his booted toe, saying, "Suit yourself, friend."

"Polydor Aloysius O'Malley, at your service, sor!" O'Malley swept off his top-hat and dropped into the chair, waving Fredi to another. Nipper curled up very small underneath it, his bright little brown eyes eyeing Señor Frijoles with wary curiosity. "And this is my young friend, Friedrich Arthur Steinmetz. We've just come over the southern trail from Texas, with a fair herd o' fine cattle."

"Texas, eh?" O'Malley's new acquaintance exclaimed with an expression of passionate interest, which lit up his features in a most engaging way. "I came from there myself, as a matter of fact. Fauntleroy Bean, at your service, Mr. O'Malley. I stopped over a while in New Mexico Territory, myself – but there was an unfortunate reversal of fortune. Fortunately, my brothers all have had prosperous enterprises here in California."

"Alas, it does come about," O'Malley sighed in sympathy. "Unfortunate reversals; I've had to leave at speed, between sunrise and sunset of a single day. Lucky it is for you, that you had kin to give succor and refuge in your hour of need. I salute you, sir, fortunate you are indade."

"And are you not fortunate?" Fauntleroy Bean asked, in a casual manner and O'Malley replied, "Fortunate in friends, fortunate in my recent employment … yet alas, unfortunate in love and matters political, back in my fair green isle."

"A lot of that going around," Fauntleroy Bean sighed heavily. "I've had to leave in a hurry myself, now and again."

O'Malley sounded as chipper as a sparrow finding a few tasty crumbs in reply. "Yet, my dear sir, I hope to be fortunate in future. Young Friedrich and I hope to strike it rich in the gold mines, come spring."

"You could be fortunate tonight, with a turn of the cards in a friendly game," Fauntleroy Bean ventured. When O'Malley looked as if he was about to agree, Fredi said, "It's not a friendly game if there's money wagered by strangers."

"Oh, pish, Freddy-boyo – there's no fun in it without a small wager between gentlemen," O'Malley waxed expansive and Fredi scowled. This was not what they had agreed on, and it did not escape Fredi's notice that another patron of the saloon looked sharply at them, and said something to the young Mexican boy, now clearing away dirty glassware and empty bottles.

Fredi frowned in puzzlement. He could just catch the words, but they made no sense; "Fetch the Sheriff, Leo, Fauntly is about to skin another greenhorn." The Mexican boy departed abruptly.

"It's the best way to keep score," Fauntleroy Bean pointed out, as he smoothly shuffled the cards, and dealt them, talking all the while. "Play for penny stakes, then. It's all in fun then." He seemed equally gregarious as O'Malley and well-acquainted with the town. Fredi relaxed his guard somewhat, after they played a couple of rounds, with the small copper coins going back and forth on a fairly equitable basis.

Bean was at least a respectable citizen of San Diego, if a trifle flamboyant in sartorial matters and after some twenty agreeably-passed minutes, he asked, "Do you gentlemen mind if I deal in another friend, when he appears? It's more interesting a game, with more than three players … since you are new-come to San Diego, it's the best way to make new friends."

"They might not mind, but I do, Fauntly," observed a voice over their heads – a new voice, in English faintly tinged with an accent – not German, but something close. "I'm getting tired of warning you about games of chance with those newly-come to town. It's bad for business and gives the town a bad reputation."

"Aww, Augie – I was only having fun!" Fauntleroy Bean protested, reminding Fredi uncomfortably of himself, caught in the act of some boyish mischief by his sister, or Mutti – Mama, who had died on the ship coming over from Germany so many years ago. "Is there some kind of new law in San Diego that a man can't have fun? This place is turning into a Sunday school … all long faces, psalms, and lemonade."

"It's not Augie to you, Fauntly," the man called Augie replied, a dangerous edge of anger in his voice. He was a slight and refined-appearing person, with a neatly trimmed Prince Albert beard and mustaches and an indefinable air of authority. Fredi immediately pegged him as one of the 'Firsts', from back in the Old Country. That insight was confirmed when Augie snapped, "That'll be Count Haraszathy … or Sheriff Haraszathy, whichever you can stomach. Your brother the colonel isn't mayor any more. There's no one in San Diego who'll make your bad mistakes go away, now. And," Sheriff Haraszathy added, "keep both your hands on the table where I can see them, Fauntly."

"Don't threaten me, Augie." Fauntleroy Bean's pleasant face had now gone cold and threatening, a change as abrupt as it was disquieting. Fredi had only once before met a man like that, who could go from amiable to stone-murderous in the blink of an eye, and that man was well-known to be three-parts crazy and two-parts insane, even aside from being a horse thief and likely a murderer.

"It's not a threat, Fauntly," Sheriff Haraszathy's right hand dropped casually to rest on the butt of the holstered revolver at his side. "It is a promise, and you've been warned before. Put away the cards." The sheriff turned his bleak regard upon O'Malley and Fredi, sitting frozen and silent. "Gentlemen. If I may offer some advice to you both, do not play cards for money with this man."

"It was only pennies," O'Malley explained, the picture of innocent good cheer. "For myself, Sheriff – I am a considerable man of the world, and I thank you for the consideration, but it is misplaced. My good friend here, was merely extending the pleasure of his company for the evening … there was no injury done to us, none at all."

"Then I must apologize for depriving you of it," Sheriff Haraszathy inclined his head. "But he has been warned again and again. Come along quietly, Fauntly – you know the way."

"Gentlemen … alas, I must bid good evening to you." Fauntleroy Bean rose to his feet, scattering the cards. He sounded as if he were grinding his teeth. "It has been my pleasure and a personal regret that I cannot show you more of the good times and good people in San Diego."

Fredi couldn't help noticing that Sheriff Haraszathy kept his hand on the butt of his revolver, as Fauntleroy Bean swaggered through the saloon toward the door, head high and offering a greeting to those closest to him as he passed. O'Malley dolefully regarded the scattered cards and sighed.

"I was beginning to like the fellow, Fredi-boyo," he admitted, as Fauntleroy Bean and the Sheriff vanished into the fast-falling dusk outside. "He was congenial company, but I daresay the sheriff was right. They do say if you look around the table at the other players and can't see who's being set up to lose every shilling in their purse, you should get up and leave the game, for likely that it's yourself." He regarded his whiskey bottle and the half-empty glass and Fredi his beer, likewise half-consumed.

"I think that I shall walk around the *main-platz* for a bit," Fredi said. "And enjoy the sound of music and human voices. And the presence of ladies. There was not so much of any, until we came to the Carrillo ranch."

"You do that, boyo ..." O'Malley was interrupted by the sound of pistol-shots from outside, a splattering of them, and someone shouting, "He's made a break for it! Get him! Arrest that man!"

This brought a sudden brief silence in the saloon. At the next table, the man whom Fredi had overheard, sending for the sheriff, slapped some notes on the table and remarked to his companions,

"I'll put up five dollars saying that Bean escapes from the jail if Sheriff catches him – any takers?"

"Raise you two," replied one. "If you set a limit on the time. It took him how many days to escape last time?"

"Dug his way out with a spoon, so I heard," another answered. "No, I'll not bet. Likely he'll just quit town altogether."

"Likely just bribed the jail-keep," the third man grunted. Fredi downed the last of his beer and looked across the table.

"Sounds like Bean wasn't as respectable a citizen as all that," he observed, and O'Malley answered. "It's a thing that happens to the best of us, Fredi-boyo. Me, I'll stay here for a while. A congenial place this is to me; light and laughter and song. Don't wait up for me."

"Don't forget, Mr. Lloyd says he'll bar the outside door at midnight," Fredi reminded his partner, before strolling out into the square, his hands deep in trouser pockets. He had gotten to be quite fond of O'Malley, rather as an older brother, or a cousin, perhaps. He knew also that O'Malley looked on him as a brother – like the brother named Freddy back in Ireland. Fredi wondered idly what the younger

O'Malley brother was like; why O'Malley never said very much about him – or indeed, any of the family. Looking back on the trail drive with the Fabreaux cattle, Fredi remembered that all of the men and boys in their mess talked about their families, recalled them fondly, told stories about sisters and brothers, of pranks and merriment, hard work and good meals.

Only O'Malley was silent about that part of his life, as if he had not been properly born into a family, but rather sprang whole and entirely grown, clad in a shabby green coat and battered top-hat, from a floating shell on the sea, or from the forehead of one of his ancient Hibernian heroes. Fredi briefly wondered why this would be so – and then he recalled Carl's admonition about asking too many questions of strangers and acquaintances. *A man will tell you just what he thinks you need to know,* Carl said, that one time that matter had come up. In the German towns, everyone knew where everyone else had come from, down to the village and the number of acres in the fields, why they had come to Texas, what ship they had sailed on, and who their parents and cousins were. *Among Americans,* said Carl – *it was different. Wanting to know more than what a man told you was a breach of good manners.* Sometimes, a man had good reason not to be forthcoming – and that was no ones' business at all.

Fredi strolled around the open plaza several times, to his great enjoyment. There was an impromptu cock-fight, down one side avenue, several couples dancing to the inexpert chords of an off-key violin, a mouth-organ and a small drum beaten by a drunken Yankee sailor who by the evidence of his energies, had heard of the existence of tuneful rhythm but never encountered it in practice. But the music of the orchestra was enthusiastic, and the dancers didn't seem to care. There was a one-legged sailor with a trained monkey on another corner; the monkey did tricks and begged. There was a cluster of other men, intent on some kind of game, being played on a level patch of ground, in the light of a lantern hanging from the second-floor balcony. Fredi drew close to the edge of the ground; a thimble-rigger, with a set of three half-walnut shells which he kept in motion with the speed of a gambling-man shuffling cards.

"Place a bet on which shell the pea is under? You look like you have a sharp eye, young fellow. Now – keep your eye upon the shell. Is it this one, this, or this?" The thimble-rigger looked up at Fredi.

"It's not under any shell, but between your fingers," Fredi answered and one of the onlookers scowled, hissing like a snake, "Best move on then, if you aren't going to bet."

Fredi shook his head and sauntered on. Back in Texas, Captain Nimitz had often demonstrated how that game was played. He was very good at sleight of hand, was Charley Nimitz.

On his second circuit of the plaza, he looked into the saloon where he had left O'Malley. It looked as if O'Malley had found congenial company in the form of some other Irish folk, for Nipper was dancing on his hind legs to a penny-whistle tune, while his audience cheered and clapped. The level in O'Malley's bottle had not fallen appreciably, but then O'Malley had never struck Fredi as being a confirmed and unrelenting drunkard when the occasion presented itself. For himself, he felt pleasantly tired from the day's journey, and his head buzzed slightly from the beer and the clamor of voices and music in the plaza.

Duty and habit directed his steps toward the livery stable where they had quartered the mules and parked the wagon – one last check on the stock; the habit of the trail drive could not be gainsaid. He found the stable door was locked; well, then, the mules were safe inside. They had drawn up the wagon to the back of the stable; a deep well of darkness after the lights of the square. There was a light in the window of an upper room in the house which backed on the stable and corral, but the single pale amber square merely accentuated the darkness rather than relieving it. Fredi's eyes adjusted to the darkness; the clamor of evening life in San Diego sounded here as softened by distance as the sound of surf; a gentle murmur, rather soothing in its consistency.

A soft sound from the wagon – a scraping sound, as if a booted-foot against the wagon-bed, or the boxes of goods – drew his sudden attention. This was not good; a good quarter of the value of his and O'Malley's mining stake was in that wagon. Fredi's curiosity and indignation rose as if in tandem. What was going on here? He heard the scraping sound again, a muffled curse in Spanish, barely a breath above the sounds of the night. Another man might have ignored it, but Fredi had spent too many months on the trail; in the wilderness, every sound meant something. There was a tin of loco-foco matches in the small tool-box attached to the side of the wagon. Fredi stole as quietly as a thief himself, opened the tool-box and felt for the smooth-sided tin. There; stealthily he opened it, drew out matches by feel, and climbed up to the wagon-seat. He struck one, and peered into the wagon interior.

In the brief yellow flare of light, Fredi saw the pistol barrel, pointed at him, as wide and black as a cannon mouth and the pale hand of the man who held it. A familiar face, and silver embroidery glinting on his fancy jacket; Fauntleroy, or Señor Frijoles, the fugitive from justice.

"You!" Fredi stammered, too angry and startled to be afraid of the pistol. "What are you doing!" just as Fauntleroy held a finger to his lips and whispered, "Shusssh! I need your help, Dutch! You've got to help me get out of town!"

The match flickered out, leaving them both in darkness. Fauntleroy grabbed Fredi's shoulder with the hand that didn't have a pistol in it, and hauled him bodily over the seat and into the wagon, where there was no chance of anyone seeing either of them.

"I do not!" Fredi retorted, indignant. "You're ... the sheriff arrested you! I will go and tell him ..."

"You won't, Dutch," Fauntleroy Bean answered, insultingly self-assured even in a hoarse whisper. "Because if you breathe a word to Augie, I'll tell him that you and your Fenian friend are in on it – I'd say that I paid you in gold to smuggle me out of town. Hell, I'll tell him it was your notion!"

"Why would he believe you?" Fredi demanded, aghast and astounded at Bean's bald-faced effrontery. Being arrested and jailed was about the worst humiliation he could imagine; *What if Vati ever heard about it? What if Johann did?* "It was you that the sheriff arrested – why would he take your word for anything?"

"Because Augie knows me," Fauntleroy Bean sounded smug. "And my brother – he's a general in the militia – was mayor here, until a while ago. And Augie doesn't know you, Dutch, or your partner, either. You'd be locked up for months ... too late to go prospecting. This wagon of yours? Confiscated in lieu of a fine, or because it was used to commit a crime."

"I don't believe you!" Fredi insisted, although with a sinking feeling in his stomach. Sheriff Count Haraszathy didn't know either of them and he <u>did</u> know Fauntleroy Bean. *Who would the law sooner believe; a gambler with a brother in high places, or a couple of strangers?* Fredi knew absolutely that he didn't want to gamble possession of the mules, the wagon, and everything in them on the answer to that question.

"Aww, Dutch, I'm cut to the heart," Now Fauntleroy sounded wheedling. "Look, I will pay you. I promise – I mean that. Or my brother will. Take me north to San Gabriel. My brother Josh has a saloon there. Then we're all square. Just get me away from San Diego. I'm about sick of the place anyway; they don't cotton to men having real fun here anymore. Don't you trust me, Dutch?"

"About as far as I could throw one of the mules," Fredi answered. Fauntleroy Bean laughed, in wry acknowledgment and conceded "You are likely right in that. Tell you what; I'll pay you to get me out of town and Josh, he can put you in the way of hauling supplies to his place through the winter. He's a big man in these parts. He'll do right by you for me. What about it?"

"I'll talk to my partner," Fredi conceded, still dubious about any agreement with Fauntleroy Bean. If there was a man less worthy of trust in these parts, Fredi hoped sincerely never to meet him.

"Good lad, Dutch." Fredi could hear Fauntleroy Bean moving in the dark, the rustle of fabric – likely O'Malley's warm many-caped coachman's overcoat. "Say … I wouldn't have told on you to Augie. I was just saying that. If he does catch me tonight, well …I won't say anything. I promise. I'll just hole up here for tonight, and you and your partner drive away tomorrow morning. Josh'll make it worth your while. I'll swear any oath you like on it."

"Of course you will," Fredi mumbled, half-under his breath, as he clambered out of the wagon; the wagon-yard lit by starlight, and a moon somewhat veiled by fog which diffused but did not block any of her light. After the inside of the wagon, the night looked as bright as daylight. He wondered what O'Malley would say.

Chapter 7 – The Headquarters Saloon

Fredi sauntered away from the wagon-yard, hands jammed deep in the pockets of his round jacket, his bearing and general air being elaborately casual. He kept to the shadowed side of the street, making his way back to the boarding house, hoping with every step that he had attracted no interest, especially from the Sheriff. He also hoped Sheriff Haraszathy had no abiding interest in turning San Diego upside down, looking for Fauntleroy Bean. It didn't seem as if there was. *What would O'Malley say?* Well, Fredi reasoned to himself, they had a promise of payment, for assisting Fauntleroy out of town, and that would be worth something.

At the boarding house, lights glowed from the parlor downstairs. Fredi stole past the doorway on tiptoe and climbed the stairs to the boarder's room, hoping that O'Malley had returned, and they could make some pretense of speaking privately. To his relief, O'Malley had returned. He lay fully-clothed on top of the blankets, snoring loudly. There was a candle in a metal holder wobbling perilously in a pool of softened wax on the crude wooden wash-stand, the single point of light in the room. They were alone in the room, but for Nipper, curled in his usual neat ball at the foot of the bedstead. Fredi shook his partner's shoulder, to no avail. The odor of whiskey and tobacco smoke was strong on O'Malley's clothing and on his breath.

"Wake up, O'Malley," Fredi begged in a whisper. "Wake up … we'll have to leave first thing tomorrow. We've got paid work, if we go to San Gabriel, first thing… wake up!" He shook O'Malley even more. The other boarders would be coming upstairs any minute.

O'Malley stirred, but only came partially awake. "Freddy lad – let me sleep … I must visit Orla in the morning before I go to Derry." And then to Fredi's utter horror, O'Malley began to weep, great shuddering sobs. "Ah, but she is dead, sweet lovely Orla … why did ye do it, Orla? Father Patrick said it was for shame…Dead, all of them, dead and buried …" His voice and the weeping diminished into incoherent mumbling, and then into sleep again, and Fredi sat back on his heels, taken back. O'Malley told many stories along the trail drive, and at the Castillo home-place, but never anything about a woman named Orla, or about leaving one or many dead and buried.

Well, perhaps he could get some sense into – or out of O'Malley in the morning, Fredi concluded. He blew out the candle, undressed as far as his shirt and crawled into bed.

In the morning, O'Malley was little the worse for the evening, only squinting as if the fog-shrouded sunrise made his head hurt. As soon as they were finished breakfast, a meal for which O'Malley appeared to have little appetite, Fredi hustled him away toward the livery stable, Nipper trotting purposefully after.

"We have to leave this morning," he said, as soon as they were out of any hearing.

"We do, boyo?" O'Malley squinted blearily at him. "I tell you, I was no' drunk an' disorderly last night. I did no' get into a fight, either … Nipper and me, we had a good time, didn't we, Nip?" He snapped his fingers at Nipper, who now capered alongside them, ears and tail up. If dogs could grin, Nipper was grinning.

"Remember Señor Bean – Fauntleroy Bean, who played cards with us until the sheriff came?"

"Aye – that I do recall… in a haze, but I do recall it. He was no' supposed to be playing cards, an' yet he was. The sheriff took him away, didn't he?"

"Yes," Fredi decided that short answers were best. "But he escaped from the sheriff. He's going to have his brother pay us for getting him out of town. I found him hiding in our wagon last night."

"Oh, did ye now? Is it certain that he will still be there, this foine morning?

"He said he would be," Fredi answered, his heart lightening. If the elusive and faintly criminal Señor Bean was not in the wagon, then they were free to seek out other employers. "It's not like we signed a contract or anything…" And Fredi decided that O'Malley might as well know the worst of it. "Likely it'll be his brother that pays us, rather than him."

"Oh, Freddy-boyo!" O'Malley looked as if his head pained him even worse. "And if his brother is no' the least fond of him? What then?"

"Why shouldn't he pay to get his brother out of trouble?" Fredi demanded, honestly puzzled. "My brother would give the last penny in his pocket for me, if I asked it. Wouldn't yours?

"No, he wouldn't." O'Malley riposted. "Because he had neither pocket nor penny, being a poor Irish crofter lad, and second because he is dead these six years an' more."

"Oh," Fredi considered this startling intelligence. "I'm sorry to hear, O'Malley – indeed I am. On the ship, coming over, was it? My mother and my sister Liesel's little baby …"

"No," O'Malley's voice was curt and sharp, as it almost never was. "Not on ship. Of the Hunger, in Ireland it was. It's something I'd rather not be reminded of, Fredi-boyo, if ye do not mind."

"I won't speak of it again," Fredi promised. He translated the 'Hunger' that O'Malley spoke of into German. Famine, that's what he meant. Vati had talked of it now and again, for he and his friends sent letters back and forth. The potato crop had failed in many places in the Old Country, of a particularly destructive blight. If there were no other crop to feed the farm folk with, they would and did starve. Fredi shivered; he had been so long in a bountiful if sometimes harsh country, that the prospect of having nothing to eat at all was more like a frightening story that the older folk would tell.

The livery stable was open at this hour of the morning, a bustle of men, horses, wagons and mules. Their wagon sat by itself in the wagon-park behind the stable, canvas cover drawn tight over the contents.

"If our guest is here," O'Malley said at last. "We shall make ready to hitch the mules. The road to the north is well-marked. The King's Highway, they call it. I don't know why, as there has never been a king here. I suppose it was established by the authority of the King of Spain, all this time gone."

Fredi scrambled up to the wagon-seat and peered inside; there was a great lump of O'Malley's coachman's overcoat, with Fauntleroy Bean's elegant boots sticking out from one end and faint snoring sounds coming from the other.

"He's here, all right." Fredi breathed, just as the sleeping form underneath O'Malley's coat twitched and sat upright, knuckling sleep from bleary eyes. "Hey, fellows – what kept you this long? Can we get a'moving now?"

"Tell him what you wanted from us," Fredi demanded. "About your brother and the saloon…"

"The Headquarters in San Gabriel, it's called – right close to the old Spanish mission. Josh, he's a colonel in the militia, so he named it that." Fauntleroy Bean yawned, a particularly jaw-cracking yawn. "I don't have any money save what's on me, but Josh is good for it. He an' Sam promised Mama they would always look after me."

"We do no' need any excuse to linger, then," O'Malley snapped his fingers at Nipper, who leaped up to the wagon-seat, as nimble as if he had trained for a circus show. "You see to the mules, Fredi-boyo, I'll pay the liveryman. And how do we find this Headquarters Saloon place, then?"

"Only saloon in town," Fauntleroy Bean answered, the good cheer of the previous night restored as if by a miracle.

They departed San Diego with some regret, for it had seemed a pleasant and welcoming place to both O'Malley and Fredi. The old King's Highway led north, near to the coast at first where the gentle salt-smelling breezes fanned them. Gradually the highway veered inland, crossing over a number of tidal salt-marshes, where the reeds grew higher than a man, and rustled in the moving air. Fresh green grasses cushioned the inland hillsides, hillsides which looked as soft as a pillow at a distance. They were dotted with oak trees; gnarled trees which sported small dark green leaves, curled at the edges.

"Another blessed land, never touched by the blighting hand of winter," O'Malley remarked.

"It's foggy most days," Fauntleroy Bean pointed out, from the back of the wagon, lounging like a lord on the stacked bags of flour and beans, cushioned by O'Malley's overcoat and Fredi's bedroll. O'Malley had suggested that he not show himself until they were a fair distance from where anyone from San Diego might recognize him. "And in the winter sometimes, it rains. And rains. For six months a year, you can barely see your hand in front of your face in the mornings. And the winds blow down from the mountains late in summer – it's like God opened the oven-door of Hell."

"It cannot be hotter than Texas in the summertime," Fredi pointed out, and Fauntleroy laughed. "Then you'll be used to it."

It took a little more than a week to make a leisurely journey along the old highway; a well-traveled and mostly level road, which uncoiled in wide and lazy bends, only gradually climbing toward the mountains rendered blue in the distance, crowned with white on their very peaks and sometimes shrouded with clouds. They passed through many small towns, the oldest of which had been established by the Spanish, usually coalescing around a mission, like nacre in an oyster-shell. O'Malley marveled at this, and went to every one as they passed, to say his prayers and dedicate a candle.

"'Tis a wonder an' a delight, Fredi-boyo – to be in a country where the True Church is not slighted."

"Was it not so in Ireland?" Fredi asked, much curious.

"'Tis better than it once was," O'Malley replied. Sometimes Fauntleroy Bean accompanied him, although not for purposes of devotion, but to rather flirt with any young women who happened to be about, which mildly annoyed O'Malley. The churches and cloisters were usually very fine but Fredi noted that much of the orchards, fields, and vineyards which once had surrounded the missions had the look of neglect; vines reverting to their wild and tangled nature, and untended trees dropping wizened olives and citrus fruit onto the ground underneath their branches, the scent of rotting oranges and lemons particularly sharp and distinctive.

The mission at San Gabriel was one of the largest mission churches they had passed yet, adorned with a campanile wall, each arched void in it filled with a bell. The building was well-kept, whitewashed clean, and the cloister buildings also kept in good steading. It looked as if there were a christening being performed, with the priest in his vestments blessing the parents at the door. As the mules clomped past, Fauntleroy Bean tipped his hat and blew a kiss toward a bevy of handsome young women in bright Mexican silk dresses, their lace veils hanging from elaborate bone and ivory combs. The ladies giggled, and a young gallant with them scowled in a most threatening way.

O'Malley scowled also. "Ha' ye no decency, Faunt'ly? They're going to Confession!"

"That's where you meet the sweetest and juiciest of them," Fauntleroy Bean pointed out, utterly unaffected. "Lovely little gardens wherein to put the old Nebuchadnezzar out for a graze. I see it my duty, giving them something exciting to confess to. And it gives the old padre a thrill as well."

O'Malley – to Fredi's mystified astonishment actually looked rather red, especially around his ears. *Nebuchadnezzar, out for a graze? What did that mean?*

"You're a heathen, Faunt'ly, and a blackguard of the worst sort. I shouldn't be surprised to hear that you were killed by a jealous husband or suitor, some day!"

"As long as it happens when I am an old, old man!" Fauntleroy answered with a jaunty air. "Ah, there is the Headquarters Saloon; Brother Josh's home away from home. Present your bill, boys, for Josh will serve up the fatted calf, for certain!"

The Headquarters Saloon proved to be a vast timber-beam and adobe ramble, two stories tall, and with a deep gallery or verandah across the front, all of it roofed with pale rust-colored tiles, bowing a bit as the roof-beams which supported them sagged under the weight. It looked very much as if it had been built at the same time, in a similar design and contiguous to the rambling mission cloister, though it did not bear the same outward appearance of good repairs as did the mission buildings. Fauntleroy Bean leaped down as soon as O'Malley brought the mules to a halt, and strode across the gallery toward the open double-doors, swaggering as if he owned the place and not his brother. O'Malley tied up the mules, and then he, Fredi and Nipper followed on his heels.

Since it was only early afternoon there were only a few committed drinkers in the place, three of them leaning up against a particularly ornate bar, while a tall dark-haired man who looked like an older and more run-to-seed version of Fauntleroy Bean stood behind it, idly polishing glassware with a slightly grubby cloth.

"Hey, Josh! I'm here! Aren't you glad to see me?"

"I would be, if I knew why you suddenly took it into your head to leave San Diego," growled the man addressed as Josh, while the three loafers exchanged furtive grins and settled back to observe an unexpected diversion. "H'lo, Faunt'ly. I take it that this sudden excess of family feeling is due to some light o'love with a jealous man?"

"I thought you'd be happier," Fauntleroy grumbled. "No, it was Augie. Now that he's sheriff, he has purely taken against me, for no reason at all that I can see. It's got to the point where I can't have any fun, without that sour-pickle-faced kill-joy hangin' over me and putting a stop to it. I couldn't stand it no more, so's I had these boys bring me in their wagon to San Gabriel. I promised that you'd pay them for it."

"I figured as much," Josh Bean answered with a heavy sigh, and an unexpectedly shrewd and rather sympathetic glance at O'Malley. "How much did he promise you, boys? Not over twenty dollars American or gold in equivalent, I hope."

"That would be considerate of you, Colonel sor." O'Malley answered, in some disappointment. Both he and Fredi had expected more, and Josh Bean sighed again. He opened a drawer in his side of the bar, and fished out a handful of coins, counting them out on the bar, before shoving certain of them across to board to O'Malley.

"There you go, boys. I hope he didn't put you to any real trouble. Kin – you know? It's an obligation, none the less."

"Well, I think the world of you, too, Josh," Fauntleroy Bean scowled and his brother snapped, "Faunt'ly, I've hauled your ass out of the fire for about the last goddamned time! Is it too much to expect you to act like a grown man?"

"I guess it must be, Josh," Fauntleroy Bean answered, his handsome features a mask of pain at unjust betrayal. "But Momma an' Poppy, they asked you and Sam to look after me, and you both promised you would."

"I did and I've had a good few years of regretting it." Josh Bean eyed his younger sibling with a severe expression. "And don't think you're going to laze the day away courting pretty señoritas…"

"He does have a good sense of his brother's inclinations," O'Malley murmured an aside to Fredi, who kept his own expression noncommittal. They had both gotten to know the exasperating Fauntleroy very well during the journey.

"And the evenings playing cards," Josh Bean continued. "If you're living under my roof, you're working under it as well." He balled up the towel and tossed it across the bar to Fauntleroy, who – although surprised – caught it in a swift reflex. "Put your things in the first room at the top of the stairs, take off that fancy coat, and roll up your sleeves. There's three basins of dirty glasses in the back."

"Aww, Josh…" Fauntleroy protested, but he went up the stairs like a truant schoolboy.

"Beggin' your pardon, Colonel sor," O'Malley ventured with delicate courtesy, the Irish in his voice at full strength. "But your brother may have forgotten to mention, we are also looking for work ourselves, for a month or so, until the season opens in the gold mines. Freddy and I have a wagon, we'd be able to do a little freighting or even mucking out stables, if that is all there is."

"You don't say," Josh Bean scratched his jaw. "Fact is, I might have a job for you, in a week or so. You know anything about hauling a piano? I ordered one from the east last year and the damn thing finally arrived in Los Angeles a month ago, but the regular freight-man says there's no room for it in his wagons that he can see, until later in the year. I think he's trying to hold me up, making me pay the extra on it, over and above what I'm paying him for regular freight. I'll make it plan – I want my damn piano, and soon."

"We can accommodate you, sor, on account of our friendship with your brother." O'Malley allowed, "He spoke well of you, as a generous and public spirited man, an officer in the militia, too. I would ask you that it be worth our while, since the piano is a delicate and valuable thing."

Josh Bean's manner thawed a degree or two. "I'd make it so," he allowed, bringing a bottle from under the bar and pouring out three small measures into the newly-polished classes. The three loafers looked on hungrily. "Irisher, are you?" he asked. O'Malley beamed.

"I am, indeed. Polydore Aloysius O'Malley, at your service, but my young friend and business partner here is merely a Dutchman, although there is nothing wrong with that."

"Freddy Steinmetz," Fredi nodded, and took the third tot before O'Malley or one of the hovering loafers could confiscate it. He wasn't certain that he really liked the taste of it, warm and slightly oily-tasting, but the warmth spread from his tongue, to his throat and at last to his stomach. He decided that he rather liked Josh Bean, seeing that he was a trustier man than his brother. And whiskey was what men drank when doing business.

"When do you want your piano?" Fredi asked, obscurely proud that his voice sounded deep and manly – or at any rate, not like a boy's treble.

"I shall leave that to your discretion," Josh Bean replied. "But sooner rather than later."

"It will be our honor," O'Malley downed his own tot in one swallow. "T' convey such a valued instrument to this … outpost of culture an' civilization."

"Damned right about that," Josh Bean sank his own drink, and the three loafers visibly wilted. "Los Angeles is a damned contrary place – if it isn't as dry as a bone, then it's pissing down rain until half the town floats out to the sea. And if there isn't some poor Mex bastard being hanged from the public gallows, then it's been a damned dull week. You go there, fetch my piano and bring it back here. That'll be worth fifty dollars to me in cash or gold, whichever serves."

He stared into the middle distance moodily, just as Fauntleroy came downstairs, coatless and with his shirt-sleeves turned up.

"Hey, Josh – I'm ready to work."

"That'll be the first occasion ever!" Josh growled.

With a show of bad grace masking considerable generosity, Josh Bean suggested that O'Malley and Fredi bunk down in one of the back rooms at the Headquarters. He was also generous in allowing them put the mules in the stable around back, where a single saddle horse looked moodily into a trough filled with oats and old grass hay. Fredi wondered at first why Fauntleroy's brother put on such a grudging pretense, and said so to O'Malley. O'Malley, with a cask of flour on his shoulder, squinted thoughtfully.

"I think he dislikes the thought of folk seeking to take advantage of his nature, in the same shameless way that Faunt'ly does. For all he knows of us, we might be o' that same ilk. 'Tis why I am giving him this flour, ye know. We are not poor tinkers, boyo."

To Fredi's vague surprise, Fauntleroy Bean did take to the work that his brother set him at; mostly tending bar on the busiest evenings. Since it was the only public saloon in town, even its slackest times were busy and the evening hours sometimes approached a near riot; a situation usually quelled by Josh Bean twitching back his unbuttoned frock coat to show the enormous dragoon revolver holstered at his waist as he demanded courtesy and order in a parade-ground bellow. It was an effortless display of authority. Fredi could not remember having seen it bettered, even by Gil Fabreaux on the trail from Texas. Still, he was glad to help hitch up the mules again, and go to Los Angeles to collect the new piano.

"'T'will add a refined element to the Headquarters, boyo; music hath charms, y'see."

"Do you think Colonel Bean will know of anyone to play a piano?" Fredi asked. There was a single piano in Fredericksburg – in the Nimitz Hotel Casino, where there was a stage for theatricals, and sometimes Captain Nimitz allowed the ladies to come in and have musical evenings.

"For a certainty," O'Malley replied. "I do ... in me youth, I was considered a musical prodigy. A minor one, not in the same league as Mozart, o'course. It has been some years since I sat down before the keyboard." The wagon jostled over a rut in the trail, and O'Malley fell silent, lost in consideration or memories, Fredi thought. He looked at the muddy track unspooling around the base of a gentle hill, the grass growing green and lush on either side of it; rich green velvet on an upholstered chair. The mountains beyond the hills were veiled in white snow, pure and clear against the deep blue sky.

"Why did you give it up?" he asked.

"What, boyo?" O'Malley half-turned. "Playing piano? Oh, boyo – one of those things. The patron who saw to my education couldn't continue sponsoring me in society. Truth to tell, it was becoming less of a joy to me, more of a labor and a means of supporting my crippled father ... and then I was distracted. It was a long time ago; I hardly think of it now."

"Still, you could make more money for playing piano than we can for sweeping stables or teamstering," Fredi pointed out. This knowledge added a whole new aspect to their potential employment prospects. He wondered why O'Malley had never mentioned it. Come to think on it, there was a <u>lot</u> about O'Malley left unmentioned.

It was a journey of two and a half days to reach Los Angeles, which reminded Fredi rather of Bexar when they reached it; a plaza with church, and many ranges of adobe buildings in the Mexican style lining the sides, and the roads which wandered on every direction into the meadows, marshes and oak tree stands on either side. There was a river, too; a sluggish and muddy one; nothing like the fast-flowing clear stream that wound through Bexar in a rush-fringed crystal ribbon. As Josh Bean had predicted, there had been a hanging in the last day or so; an associate of the notorious bandit Joaquin Murietta, or so they were breathlessly assured by the gentleman at the freight office.

"I would wonder, myself," O'Malley mused quietly, "if it were truly one of Murietta's henchmen. If so – which Murietta? They say there are several, each one fiercer and more daring than the other."

"Likely, every Mexican bandit in California is called Murietta," Fredi answered, as they followed the freight agent to the back room of his place of business. Fredi looked around; crates and barrels predominated, along with piles of excelsior. The largest crate held the piano; marked with hastily painted letters directing the contents to Mr. J. Bean, at the Headquarters Saloon in San Bernardino, Upper California. Just as they hastened to confirm that the crate did indeed contain a piano, a spattering of gunshots came from close by. To Fredi, it sounded rather like a fistful of pebbles thrown with force into a tin wash-pan, but their guide as well as O'Malley suddenly ducked behind the shelter of the crate.

"Another duel in the streets," commented the freight agent, when there was nothing more following on the initial exchange. "Second one of the morning."

"Does this happen often?" Fredi was shocked enough to ask. Even if it was a common enough thing in Texas, duelists usually had the courtesy to take it out of sight and range of innocent bystanders. The freight agent laughed, in hollow amusement. "They say that this place is even more dangerous than the gold camps, young fella."

"A good enough reason to start back, once we get this lovely music-box loaded on the wagon, boyo." O'Malley nodded. "Is there a way, sor – that you can open the crate and assure us that Colonel Bean's piano is indeed within and undamaged? I mean no disrespect to your good self, or to cast aspersions on your management of this foine establishment – but by the look of it, this instrument has passed through many hands on its journey. We will no' be paid if it turns out to contain nothing but a tombstone weight, or has been smashed beyond repair."

The agent scratched his jaw, and nodded. "Seems right enough – I'll fetch a crow."

Within a few minutes and deft work with a prying-bar, he had one end of the crate pulled free, with a screech of protesting nails. A few flakes of tight-packed excelsior fell away, as O'Malley gently pulled them aside, and then a corner of the canvas underneath. The canvas swaddling revealed a bit of polished wood, and an elaborate bit of carving along the corner; right enough, an upright parlor piano. O'Malley tucked the canvas back, as if he did so with a blanket around a sleeping child, patted the flattened wad of excelsior around it, and gestured to the agent, standing by with a hammer.

"Thank you, sor. She's a lovely bit of music-making and worth ivery penny of what the Colonel paid for her. Help us get it onto the wagon, and we'll be on our way."

"Glad to have it off my hands," the freight agent answered, although he did not look all that happy, Fredi thought. Likely he had been planning to bill Colonel Bean for storage. The agent whistled to a pair of raggedy laborers, who looked a little like Mexicans, but more like Indians, like the Yumas that Fredi had seen back at the end of the trail from Texas.

Ragged and not entirely sober the laborers might have been, but they eased the crate with the piano into the back of the wagon.

O'Malley and Fredi lingered long enough to savor a meal at a chop-house on the plaza before retracing their tracks southward and in the direction of the mountains which rose up like a high wall topped with shards of white glass. Fredi fancied that every time the wagon wheels rolled through a particularly deep rut that he heard a faint musical protest from the crated piano. When he said as much to O'Malley, the latter nodded and pursed his lips.

"Aye, the sweet thing will need careful tuning – the great Chopin himself could not get a true note from it, not after the long journey and much rough handling. I'll set to work to see what I can do, once we have it installed in the Headquarters."

"If you do the work of a piano-tuner, make certain that you are paid for it," Fredi advised. There were times when he wondered if O'Malley ought to be out and about without a keeper. This was one of them.

Chapter 8 – Where'er You Walk

On their return to San Bernardino, any number of willing volunteers assisted with moving the precious crate from wagon-tail to saloon, with Colonel Bean and O'Malley hovering, watchful and protective.

"Gently, go gently with it now," Colonel Beam commanded. "I paid top dollar for it, all the way from New York."

"Sure now, don't open the crate as if you are cracking a nutshell," O'Malley crooned. He had a long iron crow in hand, and as soon as the crate was positioned next to where Colonel Bean had indicated where the piano should go, O'Malley deftly inserted the point of it into the right places, directing the various interested hangers-on to pull away the planks which made up the crate top and sides as he loosened them. In a few moments the piano stood revealed in all of its varnished and ivory-keyed glory, the protective layers of excelsior and canvas stripped away.

"Careful, boys, careful!" O'Malley urged four men – including Fredi – as they bent their backs and lifted the piano up from its discarded chrysalis of wood, excelsior and canvas and shifted it just a little way, to place it against the rough-plastered wall of the Headquarters. Buried deep in the mound of excelsior tucked into the recess underneath the keyboard was a smaller and barrel-sized bundle which proved, once removed from that smaller wrapping, to be a small stool with what looked to be one seat mounted over another on a large threaded screw. It was of the same wood and styling. or close to it, as the piano. O'Malley divested it of the last of that packing material and set it before the keyboard with an expression once ecstatic and nostalgic.

"'Tis made to compensate for the height of the performer," he said. "A clever device! This one from the Parker Company of

Connecticut ... but nay, boys – I will not play a note, until I have seen to the proper tuning of this lovely and long-journeyed lady. Shoo, then. Take all this clutter away with ye."

"Yes, do as he says," Colonel Bean encouraged them, and then turned his regard on O'Malley, who was caressing the ivory keys, with small pressure upon them to bring forth a note or two – then lifting the hinged lid to peer within, shaking his head as he did so. "You tell me that you can tune and play it? Well, that's a fortunate occurrence ..."

"For which he will expect to be paid, accordingly," Fredi spoke up. Both the older men looked on him with expressions of mixed dismay and calculation. No matter; Fredi looked straight at the Colonel and said, "For fetching this from Los Angeles, we were paid well. Fitting it to be played and playing upon it is more skilled work. If there is another such in San Bernardino..."

"Freddy, boyo," O'Malley sounded distressed, and the Colonel looked positively thunderous, but Fredi continued, undismayed. "Then send for them, if they can offer a better rate. $25 dollars for properly tuning the piano, and $5 an evening for playing it. That's our offer, for the rest of the winter, until we head north to the gold-fields. What's yours?"

Colonel Bean appeared to chew on his mustaches for a long moment, while Fredi held his own firm countenance and O'Malley looked from one to the other with increasing dismay. Finally, the Colonel replied, in tones which seemed as if they had been squeezed reluctantly from him, "Yes on the piano tuning, although I doubt anyone in this dusty hell-hole could tell the difference. For an evening, $3 – but he can keep all the tips."

"Done and agreed," Fredi said, before O'Malley could demur. He was breathless with this achievement; quite better than he had hoped for, all things considered. "For as long as we stay in San Bernardino –

until the snows melt in the Sierras in the spring and we head north to the gold-fields. Shake on it, sir?"

"Agreed and done," Colonel Bean shook hands with the both of them, and it seemed to Fredi that Josiah Bean regarded him with newly-fresh respect. "You drive a hard bargain, boy."

"I'm not a greenhorn, fresh off the boat," Fredi replied. "Though I might sound when I speak English as if I am – a foreigner, newly come."

"Aye well, perhaps a little," Colonel Bean admitted. Fredi only smiled, thinking of how this would fatten their stake.

It took O'Malley some days to properly tune the new piano; it seemed to be tedious work, involving incessant fiddling with a peculiar little tool, tightening or loosening the steel pegs that secured the metal wires inside, while O'Malley whistled tunelessly to himself. He seemed happy enough at the task. Fredi became quite bored of watching him after a day or so; no, tuning a piano was not a skill that he could ever acquire, not when he couldn't hear any significant difference at all between notes. And it turned out that Fauntleroy Bean had been giving scant time to his duties as a bottle washer.

"He's running after some pretty Mex girl again, I swear." His brother growled, upon discovering two full baskets of unwashed tumblers, tin cups and beer-mugs. "Damn him, I wish he wasn't so well-grown, I'd tan his ass with a willow-switch until he couldn't sit down for a week."

Fredi, seeing his duty plain, rolled up his shirt-sleeves and volunteered to work his way through the detritus of the previous night's drinking, not omitting to set a price on his labors over the dish-tub. Late in the afternoon, while throwing the last pan of dirty water out into the stable-yard, he spotted Fauntleroy strolling in from the direction of the San Gabriel church, swaggering like a tom-cat.

Fauntleroy had not seen Fredi, who waited until Fauntleroy had tiptoed into the back room – rather obviously hoping not to be seen.

"The Colonel's mighty angry with you," Fredi said, from beyond the doorway into the saloon. Fauntleroy jumped. "Sweet Jesus, I didn't see you, Freddy. Aww, Josh is always angry with me. It's in his nature, I guess. What's he mad about this time?"

"About the usual; sparking pretty women and not doing your job here." Fredi added, since he was curious, "Are you courting a girl, Fauntly? Is she pretty?"

"The prettiest," Fauntleroy's handsome countenance wore an expression of smug assurance. "She's aflame with love for me … can't keep her hands away. It's like wrestling with an octopus. And the things she can do with her … lips. You'd be on fire, Freddy. Dona Inés is kin to the Ortegas – big landowning family in these parts. She's supposed to marry some distant cousin of theirs, but what do you know? She might just marry me instead."

"The Colonel won't like that," Fredi could feel his heart sinking. Fauntleroy Bean could not go two weeks without getting into trouble; gambling trouble, woman trouble or fighting trouble. No wonder the Colonel looked so much older than his brother; being responsible for Fauntleroy Bean would tend to age a man considerable. "It'll make trouble for him."

"Ol' Josh can take care of himself," Fauntleroy assured him, as the sound of gentle piano notes floated into the back room.

"He's finished tuning the piano," Fredi exclaimed with much delight, immediately losing interest in Fauntleroy's current light of love and in twitting Fauntleroy about it. Also, he was nearly done with the work of washing-up from the night before.

In the near-empty saloon, O'Malley sat before the piano, his eyes half-closed as his hands wandered purposefully over the keyboard. The music was slow and stately, with a touch of melancholy, enough to bring tears to the eyes of the sentimental; loss and longing and regret all mixed together. Fredi stole closer. The tune was halfway familiar. Perhaps he had heard it at one of the Sunday recitals back in Fredericksburg, when Captain Nimitz opened up the casino-ballroom in his hotel for a concert or some such.

"From an opera by Handel, boyo – one of your countrymen," O'Malley explained, as if in answer to Fredi's unvoiced question, his eyes half-closed as he played; no music on the stand before him, he was playing from memory. Fredi was immediately awed by the magic of it – such a complicated piece, with so many notes! "A concert-master to kings and princes, and a favorite of the Earl of Cork, no less."

"No – he was from Halle in Prussia," Fredi objected. "We were from near Ulm in Bavaria…"

"No matter …" O'Malley played on, singing half-under his breath to the notes that he played. *"… Where'er you walk, cool gales shall fan the glade … Trees where you sit shall crowd into a shade … Trees where you sit shall crowd into shade! Where'er you tread, the blushing flowers shall rise … And all things flourish …"*

"Sounds like a funeral," Fauntleroy said, disparagingly. "Christ Almighty, don't play anything like that for the house tonight, O'Malley. Play something cheerful; get the boys into a drinking mood."

O'Malley clashed his hands onto the keys in one discordant rush – the melancholy mood instantly shattered into a thousand jagged pieces. "How about this, Fauntly, for a good drinking mood?"

He launched into another tune, in brisk waltz-time, which sounded partly familiar to Fredi; he rather thought it was one that the older Fabreaux brothers were wont to whistle when the mood took them – a rather lewd and suggestive ditty when it came right down to it.

"Will you come to the bow'r I have shaded for you? I have decked it with roses, all spangled with dew…"

"Just the ticket, O'Malley," Fauntleroy said, with a broad and appreciative grin, just as Colonel Bean came out of his office and passed close by his brother. "Oh, it's you, finally," he said, and sniffed. "I know where you have been all afternoon. You have the stink of a woman all over you."

"Jealous, Josh?" Fauntleroy's grin widened. His brother snapped, "I swear, Fauntly, if you have loosed your Nebuchadnezzar to romp with the wife or daughter of a jealous man and it brings down ill-fortune on the Headquarters, I will cast you off entirely. I mean it, Use some discretion, for the love of your life! Try a whore now and again; at least, such will go away once paid!"

"But's so much more fun, this way," Fauntleroy Bean replied, unrepentant.

"Get ready to open the bar," Colonel Bean snapped, and Fauntleroy looked as if he were about to make a reply, but thought better of it.

O'Malley was still playing, to the world oblivious of all save music, but as Fredi hovered uncertainly, O'Malley murmured, "Boyo, has the good Colonel paid us yet for our work?"

"He will, as soon as I remind him that the piano is now playable … why?"

"I sense choppy waters ahead, Fredi-boyo." O'Malley looked at the ivory keys, responsive to his hands. "We may have to leave in a hurry."

There was no particular incident occurring in the following days which suggested that O'Malley had reason for concern. After a day or two, Fredi's naturally optimistic nature reasserted itself, and he left off worrying. O'Malley at the piano proved popular almost at once;

the Headquarters Saloon was packed every evening, with drinkers and onlookers spilling out into the veranda and the street, listening to O'Malley play. Fredi, greatly daring, negotiated that the Irishman would play for at least three hours every evening, but a break of ten minutes or so every hour. O'Malley complained now and again of how his hands ached from the unaccustomed exercise, and that all that the drinkers in the saloon wanted to hear were rather silly popular songs, generally the lewder the better.

"It's a betrayal of my training," he complained, one evening, "to perform like a lowly barrel-organ grinder, with only a single tune and a monkey dancing around begging for coins…"

"It fattens our purse considerable," Fredi answered, not without sympathy. He had concocted a hot mustard plaster for O'Malley to rest his sore hands on, after the evening's work. "And it's not as hard as loading wagons, or digging wells would be."

"Aye, boyo. I should not complain," O'Malley acknowledged, although Fredi thought the Irishman appeared worn, the shadows dark under his eyes and new lines graven in his countenance. "Gold-mining … now that will indeed be hard work, but it is for ourselves, and not at the bidding or purse of another. An' speaking of that – where was Mr. Fauntleroy this very evening? I thought he was to tend bar. The Colonel was not a happy man this evening, boyo."

Fredi sighed. "He's got a woman. He told me so the other day, when you were finishing with the piano. A Dona Inés de something or other Ortega. I guess that he went to see her."

O'Malley chuckled, a dark and cynical sound to it. "I hope she is worth the trouble, boyo. Is she at least a comely woman?"

"If she is the one that I saw him kissing in the corner of the cloister where they thought no one could see them, then she is. Very pretty. She is tall like my sister Magda, with long black hair. She was wearing a yellow shawl embroidered with red flowers. You may have seen her at Mass."

"Oh, that one!" O'Malley chuckled again. "A bold filly with spirit and promise, but old to be unmarried. I have noted her, now and again, though we have never spoken. I would not dare, myself ... there are certain fine women given to season their everyday meat with a sprinkling of madness. I fear that she is one of them and perforce dangerous to the life and soul of a mere ordinary man."

"She is supposed to be engaged to marry a cousin, or something," Fredi answered, at which O'Malley's countenance lost all hint of the merry good-humor that had been upon it, as the hot poultice eased the ache of his hands, after a long stretch at the piano.

"This will not end well, Freddy-boyo" he replied, suddenly and deeply serious, such as Fredi had never seen him. "I would say that we should leave for the north, even before the snows melt in the high Sierras. Fauntly Bean runs a dangerous course, and that is his choice in doing so, but this may all turn unfortunate and I would rather be on the long road north when it does."

Fredi shook his head, answering, "But while you are earning so much at the piano, and me in doing that which needs to be done. For all that the Colonel complains, he is a generous employer. We should stay as long as we may."

"And our porridge-bowls upturned as long as it is raining oats?" O'Malley appeared even more depressed. "Yes, of course; but the time of our departure must be carefully calculated. "'Tis a dangerous game, Fredi-boyo. I know this from bitter experience."

"Another two weeks, O'Malley," Fredi answered, thinking over what would be added to their stake. Yes, that would add at least a third again to what they already had. O'Malley said nothing more regarding a departure, but now and again, Fredi noticed that in the slack hours of the day, he was mending the many-caped overcoat he had worn over the long trail from Texas, while Nipper sat at the Irishman's feet, with his muzzle dropped on his paws, his eyes open watchfully.

For a disaster, Fredi later reflected – the result of Fauntleroy's flirtation with the Ortega woman – it certainly blew in with very little warning. Five days after his conversation with O'Malley, Fauntleroy Bean went from the back door of the Headquarters on a Sunday morning without saying a word to anyone save Fredi, who was carrying in a bucket of water for washing-up. The bells in the San Gabriel mission church rang for the early Mass. Fauntleroy wore his best and flashiest set of clothes; the Mexican coat trimmed with silver and a flamboyant silk sash, and nothing like plain work trousers and shirt to do chores in.

"There's the washing-up to do," Fredi reminded him. Saturday nights brought an especially large crowd to the Headquarters, including many local ranchers and their families desirous of attending Mass the following morning, and sometimes there might be trouble in the saloon between the Anglos and the Mexicans. Of the latter, a few were whispered to be dangerous men, allies of the notorious bandit Murietta, and banned from the Headquarters as outlaws and villains. The Colonel kept an especially watchful eye on the Saturday night crowd, for his detestation of Murietta and his crowd was a byword in the dusty streets of San Bernardino. O'Malley had been kept at the piano for hours – even now, he still slept.

"Sorry, Fred. Gotta see a man," Fauntleroy replied over his shoulder, his handsome countenance uncommonly grim. Fredi scowled. Fauntleroy was off to his woman again, although why he had both of his heavy Colt dragoon revolvers in holsters strapped around his waist was a mystery. Probably going to show off for his woman, although why he needed revolvers for that was a mystery.

Fredi looked at the washing to be done – good thing he had negotiated wages for doing such chores with the Colonel, who had about given up on the thought of his scapegrace brother ever doing anything more useful than tending bar for a couple of hours. Not for the first time, he wished that the Bean household contained a woman. Wasn't washing and cooking and laundry women's work anyway? It had always been thus, as far as he was concerned, but it seemed that women were few and far between in California, especially of the respectable sort, or so he had been told.

He set to work with a will, hearing the Colonel's distant voice, coming from his little cubby of an office off the main bar. Fredi had diminished the piles of smeared and sticky containers by a considerable degree by mid-morning, carrying trays of clean-polished glass, beer-mugs and cups back into the bar; like arranged neatly with like and regarded his handiwork with a degree of satisfaction. It wasn't gold-mining, or cattle-droving, but it would do. The fact that it would all have to be done over again the following morning … well, he would think about that on Monday morning. He wondered if he should go to the Colonel and remind him that his and O'Malley's wages were due but there was someone in the office, and it sounded as if the Colonel were arguing with someone in Spanish.

On his return to the back room for another tray, he was astounded to discover that Fauntleroy's woman standing here, Dona Inés, breathing as if she had just run a footrace. The hems of her skirt and petticoats were dabbled with dust, and her hair hung witchlike and disarrayed around her face under that flamboyant yellow and red silk shawl.

"Quickly!" She cried in Spanish, gasping for breath. "You must come with me, now! They are going to kill him!"

"Who?" Dona Inés' panic temporarily bereft Fredi of his composure and his command of working Spanish. "Where? Let me get the Colonel!"

"There is no time!" Dona Inés clutched at his arm, her fingers like steel bands on his arm. "Now, before it is too late!"

"Colonel Bean!" Fredi called, hearing angry voices from the Colonel's office, as Dona Inés pulled him after her, out the door; whatever danger it was that she feared, it gave her terrifying strength. The wide street beyond the stable was empty; no one around, for it was the hour of Mass. The good and devout were in church, those who were neither must be sleeping off their revels of the night before. Fredi looked around, half-desperate for assistance, half-embarrassed at being pulled along by a woman.

No, and the Colonel hadn't heard him and Dona Inés was almost running, so compelling and urgent her fears. Now they had left the huddle of San Bernardino behind them, the tall campanile wall of bell-niches and the mission church itself towering over the lower roofs of rusty-red tile or sun-faded wood shakes. The small creek which supplied the mission orchards and decayed vineyards burbled to itself. Heedless of her skirts, Dona Inés splashed through the ankle-deep water. There was a trodden path she followed, muddy with recent rain, and the new green stems of this year's grass crushed to the ground. Someone had been along here, several someones, including at least one horse.

"What was going on?" Fredi gasped, having recovered enough of the Spanish learned from Carl's Mexican stockman, in the years that Porfirio had spent at the ranch. "Who is going to kill ... who! Tell me!"

"Don *Leroi* Bean," Dona Inés answered. "In a duel – between him and certain friends of my affianced! I did not think they were serious

… but at Confession this morning … a friend whispered to me! They will kill him if he wins the duel!"

Fredi whispered to himself, "They'll have to get up early in the morning and move fast to do that!" This was the trouble that O'Malley feared. He wished that Dona Inés had not rushed him from the Headquarters. He had no weapon on him other than the hunting knife at his belt, a thing so much a part of his usual attire that he donned it as readily as his shirt.

"Dona – Lady … what do you want me to do? I would rather go back for the Colonel, for my own revolver…" he begged.

"No! It will be too late!" she insisted. The path had already taken them toward the low hills which overlooked down, hills thatched with scrub and oak trees, beyond the once-cultivated grounds of the mission – an isolated place, but not more than a quarter of a mile from San Bernardino. Yes, that would be the perfect dueling-ground; an oval stretch of meadow in the lee of a hill – the first of those which rose in higher and higher ranks until they became mountains, veiled by mist and distance.

A single gnarled oak tree towered over the dueling-ground, and Dona Inés cried out. "Mother of God, they have murdered him!"

A man's body hung from a slim leather-braided lariat strung over a lower branch of the oak tree; hanging close to the ground, his head at an unnatural angle. Fredi recognized the clothing before the face – engorged and red, gagged with a bright handkerchief. Dona Inés let go of Fredi's arm and ran, weeping and stumbling over the rough ground, incoherent with grief. Fauntleroy's eyes were open, almost bulging from their sockets; strange and strangled groans came from his mouth, muffled with the handkerchief. No, he was not dead, but close to it.

Fredi's knife seemed to leap to his hand. The friends of Dona Inés's affianced must have been in a hurry; having strung up

Fauntleroy and left him to strangle slowly. They did not see that the lariat had stretched and the tree-limb bowed from his weight and that Fauntleroy's toes brushed the ground.

No time to search for the lariat-end. Fredi grasped at the lariat with one hand, as far as he could reach, pulling it down with all of his own weight, as he slashed at the tough leather braid with his knife in the other.

"Stand fast!" he shouted in Fauntleroy's ear, in German and then in English. "Don't faint like a girl, damn you!" Fauntleroy groaned in response. The lariat had drawn blood, from under his chin, rubbed raw in the struggle, drawn a cicatrice of raised and reddened flesh about his neck. Dona Inés may have been far gone in hysteria, but she tore at the knots binding his hands; strong silk strips torn from his fancy sash, Fredi noted with a quiet corner of his mind. The tough strands of leather parted; Fauntleroy crumpled at the knees and lay gasping on the ground.

Fredi pulled the noose from his neck, and the gag from his mouth; Fauntleroy's eyes had rolled up in their sockets so only the white of them showed – dotted with tiny flecks of blood – and his chest heaved like a winded horse, drawing in great tearing gulps of the air. Dona Inés wept over him, holding his head in her lap, her tears falling onto his face, murmuring passionate endearments.

At last Fauntleroy's eyes opened; his breathing slowed to something more normal. "I have to say I love a woman who knows the perfect time to make a display of her charms and devotion," he gasped; his voice sounded hoarse, as if his throat had been stretched as much as the lariat.

"You're an ass," Fredi said, at least as much from anger as relief. "Did you not think of taking a second? Or telling the Colonel?"

"No need," Fauntleroy lay his head back in Dona Inés' lap. "Pistols for two, breakfast for one, Freddy. You should know. I thought they were honorable men…"

"Like you would know the kind," Fredi was still angry – overwhelmingly with Fauntleroy for giving him such a fright and then to be so insouciant about it. "What happened that you were caught so by surprise? Did you kill your man, at least?"

"I did," Fauntleroy made as if to languish in the lap of Dona Inés, like the dying King Arthur in the vessel taking him to Avalon. "Or at least – he didn't look to fitten' when last I saw him. As we finished our business, his friends sprang out of the bushes. They caught me by surprise, taking both my pistols. They strung me up and then rode away with him. In search of a doctor or a priest, I didn't care which. Glad I am so have seen the both of you…" he assumed the most pathetic expression, and looked up into Dona Inés' eyes. "*Querida* … my darlin' girl, I could not have lasted much longer … and it was all done for love of you."

Fredi thought he might gag from the false sentimentality. Could anything be more like the overwrought novels and stage-plays that some in Fredericksburg, especially among the fair sex, adored? He thought – upon no more demonstration of it that she had the wit to go for help on hearing a mere rumor – that Dona Inés was a sensible woman, even if she was carrying on now in the most operatic fashion.

"We need to get you to the doctor," Fredi suggested. "Or at least, back to the Headquarters. Shouldn't we send for the sheriff? They tried to murder you, after all."

"Not certain I want to do that," Fauntleroy coughed, his face contorted with the pain that the effort cost him. "I'd have to say why. And it would embarrass a lady. Besides … even if it happens all the time, with a dead man dueling's still an offense the sheriff is bound to take note of, even if only a Mex. I don't want to tell Josh. He'll be mad at me for weeks."

"As if that has ever been a concern of yours," Fredi replied, exasperated. "Get up, if you can." He and Dona Inés assisted him to stand, which he did, groaning all the while and rubbing his neck.

"God, that hurts," Fauntleroy complained. "I can't turn my head this way at all."

"Don't worry about your head, just put one foot in front of the other," Fredi encouraged him. With Dona Inés at Fauntleroy's other side, they walked him back down the path they had come. Fredi paused only to collect Fauntleroy's gun-belt with the dragoons still in it, which someone had thrown into a bush where a loop of leather had caught on a branch. Fauntleroy groaned and complained the whole way. When they came within sight of town, Dona Inés suddenly flung both of her arms around Fauntleroy and kissed him.

Fredi had gotten back into the habit of Spanish, and so understood very well when she exclaimed, "I must go, my dear Leroy ... we must never see each other again! They will kill you for certain, and I cannot bear that thought! Go with God, and know that I shall always remember our times together!"

"It's for the best, I understand," Fauntleroy consoled her, with cheerful agreeability, returning the embrace and the kisses with enthusiasm. Still, when Dona Inés tore herself away, and ran ahead of them, hastily twisting her hair into a proper bun and folding her shawl over her head as she did so, he appeared even more cheerful. "An' Josh said that at least whores go away," he mused.

Fredi shook his head; "You are the worst kind of scoundrel, Fauntly; disporting with a respectable lady, about to be wed..."

"Well, I never heard her say no," Fauntleroy answered, smug. "Her intended is rich – which is what she wanted, but she wanted to sport with a scoundrel first." He leered, adding, "Well, she has some warm memories now, I reckon. Close your mouth, Freddy, before you catch a fly or two."

Fredi obeyed, for once at a loss for words; for a rakehell back in the Hill Country, there was always Mr. Zink the surveyor, who seduced other men's wives and fought duels indiscriminately, but at least Mr. Zink showed some discretion about his activities. Fauntleroy Bean was utterly and completely unashamed of them.

They returned to the back of the saloon in silence; Fredi not having thought of anything else to say, and Fauntleroy recovered to the point of being able to walk without assistance. The Headquarters was unaccountably silent, even for a Sunday, as they came in from the stable-yard.

"If you don't want to tell the Colonel about this," Fredi advised, "then you'd better wash up and put on your regular clothes. You look like you've been ridden hard and put up wet."

"You won't say a word?" That was as close as Fauntleroy would ever come to begging, and Fredi shook his head. "I won't say anything – but if he asks, I won't lie."

"No reason for him to ask," Fauntleroy had recovered some of his usual jaunty manner, but in the next moment, O'Malley appeared in the doorway to the saloon.

"They are wondering where you were. The Colonel's been shot, and they don't think he will live."

Chapter 9 – El Camino Real

"They say it was one of Murrieta's old gang," O'Malley explained, with a somber face. "The Colonel had wrathful words with a Mexican last night, threw him out of the place. This morning, they had words again when the man came to complain. The man went away, but waited and shot him down like a dog in the street. He escaped, although those who saw it raised the hue and cry. They were looking all over for the pair of ye; where have ye been, all this time?"

"I had an errand, and asked Freddy to come with me," Fauntleroy answered, on the instant, as if he did not even pause to consider a lie. "Where is my brother now?"

"In his own room, sor," O'Malley looked so very grave and sympathetic. "I fear that it will not be long now for your brother. But he is not suffering."

"That's good," Fauntleroy answered. He seemed dazed, uncomprehending; likely for the second time in a single day. Fredi wondered who would run the Headquarters. Fauntleroy enjoyed looking like a big man, behind the bar, but had no relish for the work involved. That had been obvious within days, even to Fredi. "I suppose that we shall open tonight just for friends of Josh's. No piano – we'll keep it quiet from respect."

"It's all happened so sudden-like," Fredi said, later that afternoon to O'Malley. They sat on a bench in the veranda of the Headquarters, with Nipper at their feet. The late afternoon sunshine blazed on the plastered walls of the mud-brick, a welcome counter to the cool breeze wandering from the east, seemingly chilled by the snow lingering on the tallest mountain peaks. "No warning. And in the space of an hour, everything is turned upside down."

"It's like that, Fredi-boyo," O'Malley meditated on the smoke from his pipe, rising into the air. Fredi had already told him of the mornings' escapade with the duel, Dona Inés and the almost-hanging. "Sometimes ye can see the bad fortune coming – see it for miles – and then sometimes not. I think should leave here soon, as we had planned. The doctor does not think that the Colonel will last the night. Young Fauntly attracts misfortune to him, and I do relish the thought of standing next to him when the next parcel of it arrives."

"For loyalty to the Colonel, should we not stay a while?" Fredi asked, for the Colonel had been quite decent to them both, if sometimes blunt-speaking.

O'Malley shook his head. "'Til he has been put into the ground and the words read by the priest; not a moment longer, boyo. We take the pay that is owed and we go north."

Colonel Josh Bean died very quietly, just before dawn the next morning. Fauntleroy, very pale, and with his shirt collar buttoned high and cravat tied likewise to hide the marks on his neck told a small handful of friends the next morning.

"I suppose since I am his brother and he owned the Headquarters free and clear in his name, that it is mine now, to order and run as I see fit," he added, in closing. The various friends looked sideways at each other. Their opinions of Fauntleroy Bean likely were similar to O'Malley and Fredi's but it was the only saloon in San Bernardino.

"I daresay ye will close the Headquarters until the burying," O'Malley suggested in a gentle voice. "'T would be suitable."

But Fauntleroy shook his head. "My brother had many friends and much respect among the citizens of this place. If they come to pay their respects, I may as well open the bar."

There was an uneasy silence, in which Fredi cleared his throat. "We are owed our wages for this last week, Fauntly, for working in the back, and O'Malley with the piano."

"How can you bring up money, at a time like this?" Fauntleroy had every appearance of being in grief and wounded to the quick. "I'll … look at my brothers' account books, and see what I can do for you boys."

"I'd be grateful, Fauntly." Fredi was reassured on that score but only for a day. Fauntleroy emerged from the office at mid-morning with an opened account book in his hand, just as Fredi went past with a tray of clean glasses and tankards, saying, "I've been going over Josh's accounts, Dutch, and here's no money to pay you boys, what with the costs of burying Josh, and the loss of business on account of closing to the general public over the last five days …"

Fredi regarded Fauntleroy with stone-faced disgust. The Headquarters Saloon, never mind who was in charge, owed O'Malley for a week of pounding the piano keys, and himself for the same week, running errands, sweeping the floor and washing tankards and cups. This was no better than being treated as a Negro slave. Fauntleroy owed his freedom and his life twice over to O'Malley and Fredi. This was galling, since there was damn little they could do about it now, dependent upon Fauntleroy's willow-the-wisp good will. At that moment, Fredi realized that he had enough of this kind of smiling-faced treachery. He and O'Malley were cheated of their wages, and that was an end to it.

He dropped the tray onto the tile floor, hearing the tray hit with a clatter and the glassware with a satisfactory smash. "We're gone north to the gold mines, then. Look to some other poor fool to clean that up for you or do it yourself." He turned on his heel, and walked away, leaving Fauntleroy no doubt staring at the mess in dismay. For himself, Fredi no longer cared; he went to the tiny room in the back of the place where he and O'Malley had been quartered. O'Malley was there, sitting by the small window where the light was best, mending the hem of his overcoat with needle and thread. Fredi rolled up the pallet and blankets that he had slept on and under since leaving Texas.

"We're going, O'Malley," he said, over his shoulder. "Fauntly says that he cannot pay us our due so I have quit, and told him we are for the gold mines."

"Indade," O'Malley observed – sounding not all that distressed about it, or even very much surprised. "The open road calls to us, then. And we have many hours of daylight left to us if we leave at once." He made a knot in the thread and snapped it short, shaking out the overcoat as if to admire his own handiwork. "A pity about the piano, though. 'Tis a bonny and tuneful thing, abandoned in this place!"

"We'll find work for you playing another," Fredi said through his teeth, as he bundled the last of his meager possessions into a carpetbag and shrugged his own jacket over his shoulders. "Gather your own trash and traps, O'Malley; we're done with this place, this very minute."

"Before Fauntly gathers his wits and cozens us to remain, pleading with sweet words and promises?" O'Malley nodded agreement. He whistled to Nipper, who came awake in an instant, and bounded from where he had been curled up in a tight brindle ball at the foot of O'Malley's pallet, resting his paws on O'Malley's knees.

"'Tis on the road we are, little fellow!" O'Malley said to his dog. Nipper seemed agreeable enough, and much more philosophical about it than Fredi felt. They gathered their small baggage and went out to harness the mules. Nipper bounding ahead of them all the way, looking over his flank at them, and hopping up to assume his usual seat in the wagon as O'Malley whistled to the mules in the small corral at the back of the Headquarters. The corral and the stable-yard were deep in trampled mud after a week of on-and-off rain, the droppings of many animals, and pans of dirty dishwater thrown out from the back steps of the Headquarters. O'Malley tossed his many-caped overcoat into the wagon-bed. Nipper burrowed into it at once, for the morning again was chill and the day promised more rain, if the gray clouds gathered like a cloak about the peaks of the mountains were any indication.

They set to the business of harnessing the mules, two and two, to the wagon, a task at which they and the mules were so accustomed that it was accomplished in relative silence and a few minutes by time. When they were nearly done, Fauntleroy Bean appeared in the kitchen doorway, his cravat already undone and shirt collar unbuttoned, revealing the livid marks about his neck still remaining from his near-hanging. O'Malley was already in the wagon, the reins in his hands.

"Fellows … Fred, Aloysius, you should reconsider," he began, his countenance set in an earnest and tragic expression. "It's just that there isn't any money for wages at present, after the expenses are considered. My word on it. The Headquarters is in a bad way, with my brother dead – and a worse, if you are gone…"

"Not our concern," Fredi snapped, still furious almost to the point of reverting into his first language. He felt again that unreasoning red mist of anger about to descend on him, that mindless and heedless fury that had led him into pounding Zeke Satterwaite into a bloody pulp. If Fauntleroy Bean laid a hand on him, Fredi knew without a doubt – that particular battle-fury, as O'Malley had called it – would descend again. He was that angry over the lost wages, over the way that Fauntleroy seemed determined to treat them both as carelessly as he did his various lovers. "Your word … it is a worthless thing. Not like your brother. He was honest and fair to us. We are on our way. You cannot cozen us into remaining." He turned away from Fauntleroy, who started forward, looking as if he was about to stay them with a hand outreached, even as Fredi mounted up onto the wagon-seat.

"Freddy … Aloysius," Fauntleroy pleaded, as if he was an honest man unfairly reproved, which infuriated Fredi even more. He kicked out, his contempt unrivaled, and his toe caught Fauntleroy Bean fair in the chest with sufficient force to topple the man backward with a satisfactory splash, down into the pool of muddy dishwater and accumulated cow, mule, and horse-pats at the bottom of the step into the kitchen.

"Well-done, Freddy-boyo," O'Malley observed with satisfaction, slapping the reins over the backs of the mules. Fauntleroy, stunned for once into speechlessness, levered himself with one elbow into a sitting position, mouth open with shock as the wagon rolled out of the yard and into the street.

"We tell everyone we meet what you have done," Fredi shouted, over his shoulder as they rounded the corner, not caring that he was shouting in an incoherent mixture of German and English. "That you are a cheat, a liar and a fornicator … see how many customers come to the Headquarters now, eh!"

O'Malley chirruped to the mules, and grinned at Fredi. "Well, boyo, so now ye see? There's many of his like in the world, I'm afraid, and Fauntleroy Bean is far and away not the worst of them."

"I'll take very good care not to take wages from any such!" Fredi's anger still burned hot, and O'Malley looked at the road unrolling ahead of them, the dusty road which led north, toward Los Angeles.

"'Tis a luxury, having such a choice, boyo." The Irishman sounded as if he were admonishing. "But aye, I am thinking that no' so many will work for a promise of wages now. In good time, Fauntleroy Bean will have the reputation which he deserves. We still have a foine stake for setting up a claim. It's only a week or so that he cheated us of; no so much, considered against what we have already. As for us now … the snows still lock the high mountains in winter for another few months. 'Tis too early to commence our journey to the diggings; what say you to San Francisco, and searching for work there? The biggest city in the land likely will offer us any number of opportunities."

"Even for playing the piano?" Fredi, good-humor restored by the thought of as large a city as any that he had ever seen in this country – bigger than Galveston even – was not above teasing his business partner a little. O'Malley laughed. The freshening breeze tugged at their caps, and at the overlapping capes of O'Malley's overcoat.

"Aye, boyo, and it pays well! When the diggings open, we can load up the wagon and haul supplies into whatever mine-camp seems to be most promising. They say that rich strikes are happening every week, from Mont-Ophir in the south to Rich Bar in the north!"

"And why shouldn't we be among those striking it rich?" Fredi ruminated over all the stories he had heard; pebbles of pure gold, the size of a man's thumbnail, scattered among the gravel at the river's edge. That was a picture more alluring than laboring away, hauling freight and driving cattle or washing glasses and bottles in a saloon. He could hardly wait. Once again he relished imagining his return to Texas, richer than one of the Firsts, and repaying his brother-in-law every penny of the money lost to robbery on the road to Indianola.

That seemed now to have happened a long time ago, although in truth it was barely eight months. Fredi thought smugly that he had become very wise in that time; he and O'Malley's stake was secreted in several places; a small portion carried on his own person and on O'Malley's, but the largest part in a small sack concealed in a cask of cornmeal in the back of the wagon. No one would think to look for money in the meal cask, O'Malley had said, quite early on, and Fredi agreed.

Chapter 10 – O'Malley's Grand Party

They had gotten to a point halfway between San Bernardino and Los Angeles when disaster struck. It was a particularly deserted stretch of road, not a lonely house or a tiny settlement in sight. The sun, sliding down the western sky was still gilding the hilltops, and tinting the snow on the distant mountaintops in hues of rose and gold, but the valley bottoms were already abandoned to shadow.

Fredi had already suggested that they make a wilderness camp of it for the night, picket the mules to graze, and sleep under the wagon, but O'Malley hankered to spend the night under a roof, and held out for traveling another mile or so, in hopes of encountering a dwelling-place, a town … anything. Shadows filled the valley, deep and darkening, even as O'Malley looked wistfully ahead for a lantern-lit window. Just as Fredi was about to say that there was no such thing in sight, and they should make camp while they still had light enough to unharness the mules and ensure that they were not bedding down on top of an ant-hill or a nest of rattlesnakes, a male voice called to them in Spanish, from the deeper shadow beside a tall thicket of chamisa.

"*Hola*, my friends … it's late to be on the road – may I ask where you are going?"

"To Los Angeles," Fredi answered, having no suspicion in the least until the metallic click of a pistol cocking alerted him – too late. Even as O'Malley made as if to send the mules hurtling forward, another man-shaped shadow emerged, deftly catching the lead mule's headstall. Fredi leaned down, reaching for the shotgun which O'Malley kept within reach, under the wagon-seat. The man with the pistol stepped out of the shadows, the last of the twilight etching a pale line down the barrel. That pistol pointed straight at Fredi's stomach, from hardly an arm-length away, and there was another pistol aimed at O'Malley; at least three men that Fredi could see, and at least two more that he could not, but sensed their presence anyway.

"Not tonight, I think," said the first man, suave and confident. Now Fredi could see that he had a dark kerchief over his face, and his heart sank. This did not look good. There had been many a tale of Murietta and his bandit gang told in the Headquarters Saloon. Not everyone in San Bernardino was wholly convinced that Murietta and his chief henchman, Three-Finger Jack Garcia, had been killed by Captain Love's Ranger company a year or two before, although many claimed to have recognized the bandits' pickled head when it was shown around the gold camps afterwards. "Alas, we are poor men and you are rich – and is it not said that those who have must share with the poor and hungry?"

"And we are very hungry," commented the man holding the mule's headstall. The wagon rocked slightly on its springs, as if someone were climbing over the tailgate. Nipper growled from his nest at their feet in O'Malley's folded overcoat. O'Malley twisted around to look back into the wagon-bed, bidding Nipper to be still. Fredi could hear O'Malley whispering to himself, very low in English which sounded like prayers.

"We're being held up by road-agents," Fredi said, keeping his voice level with an effort. Everything they owned between them was in the wagon; the cargo it carried, the mules which pulled it, and most especially their stake in coins and notes, secreted in the cornmeal. "We are not rich," he protested. "But honest and hard-working men! We are heading for the gold mines, not away from them. Why should you steal what we have from us?"

"You have more than we," the bandit leader replied, in an irritatingly reasonable manner. "And we have nothing, so you are rich indeed, by comparison. Come down from the wagon, my friends – slowly and keep your hands clear where we may see them."

"He's telling us to get down," Fredi translated for O'Malley. "And to be slow and careful – there are at least three guns trained on us."

"I'll not die like a dog in the road," O'Malley said through his teeth. "Give them what they ask for, boyo. Do just as they say. Nip – to me. Tell them I'm wrapping Nipper in my coat. He's just a poor little doggie, but he is loyal above all."

"Your valuables, my friends," ordered the bandit leader, once they had obeyed. "Go on. Keep nothing back, not a single *centavo*, for Jesu Cristo rewards in heaven those who are generous to the poor."

Fredi and O'Malley stood with their backs to the wagon-wheel, Fredi with his hands raised and O'Malley holding Nipper, tightly wrapped in his overcoat under his arm. Inside the wagon they could hear one of the bandits ransacking what it held, while Nipper whined in distress. O'Malley held the dog fast, swathed in the overcoat's folds. With one hand the bandit leader held out a coarse sack which might once have held sugar or salt – brandishing in the other an old-fashioned dragoon pistol. It only held a single shot, but at that range, a man couldn't miss. Close as they were, Fredi could see the hilts of three or four more, tucked into the leader's belt and the front of his short Mexican jacket. Another bandit, similarly masked and armed, stood by and holding a small pierced-tin lantern aloft, so that there was light enough to see by it, as darkness closed down over the valley like a pot-lid. *Who knew how many other guns were trained on them, held steadily by how many bandits?* He thought that he could hear horses close by, whickering to each other, their bridle-bits jingling. There was no advantage to himself and O'Malley in this, Fredi acknowledged bleakly. Not even Carl Becker could have overcome this many … and in any case, his wood-wise brother-in-law likely would not have fallen into an ambush like this in the first place.

With an insouciance remarkable to Fredi, O'Malley surrendered his pocket-watch; a cheap and battered thing of tin, and twisted off the tiny jet signet ring from his finger. With a sigh, he added his purse, containing his small share of their stake, which he carried for such small expenses as they had, in order that the avaricious might not observe the larger store of money. Fredi, the bag and the dragoon pistol put before him, added his own small share, and the patent Colt revolver which he had bought from Gil Fabreaux's brother, all these months ago. The two bandits regarded them in reproach in the speckled lantern-light, obviously disappointed over the meager takings.

Stung, Fredi protested, "I told you that we were plain working men! Who other than such would be on the road at this time and season?"

At his side, O'Malley groaned faintly. "Boyo, have a care. We give them what they want, that we may go in peace..." he crossed himself in the way of Catholics in the old church with his free hand, murmuring, "...pray for us now and in the hour of our death..."

Seeing an advantage or sorts – *did this bandit understand English after all?* – Fredi said, "He is one of your old church, as devout as a man can be said to be in this wilderness. We have given to you what we can."

"Not all!" the bandit leader sounded as if he leered triumphantly under the kerchief over his face, as one of his gang came over the wagon-seat, with a dusty sack in his hand. Fredi's heart sank, all the way into his boots. *Their stake!* All the money they had in the world, their wages from six hard months on the cattle trail, and what they had earned since! The sale of Paint lay in that bag, that and the price of his and O'Malley's long hours of work, pounding piano keys and laboring over the wash-pan in Colonel Bean's saloon.

The man with the cornmeal dusty bag emptied it into the larger one, the coins and notes jingling and rustling as they fell. Fredi and

O'Malley watched, helpless and impotent. To add insult to injury on top of robbery, the bandit chief looked at them both in reproach.

"My friends, you are certainly very poor rich men, if this is all you have! Little notes, small coins of less value…"

"We were cheated of our wages," Fredi replied, indignant, as that particular injustice still stung. "We worked for Colonel Bean, at the saloon in San Bernardino; all these weeks and his brother did not pay us, saying there was nothing from the profits!"

"*Los Frijoles?*" the other bandit murmured; not sympathetic, but appearing to flirt with the notion. O'Malley's gaze went back and forth between Fredi and the two outlaws, but the Irishman sensibly appeared to think better of speaking. Fredi wondered briefly again, if the bandit understood English. Bundled in the overcoat, Nipper whined again, still distressed, but not as much as he hand been when the bandit first began searching the wagon.

"Yes – the Beans. We worked without pause or rest for … many weeks. And at the end of it, Señor Leroy refused us our wages."

"And what did you do … for *los Frijoles*?" the bandit leader asked again, seeming interested.

"I washed in the kitchen," Fredi answered. "And we hauled a piano from Los Angeles. Señor O'Malley played upon it nightly for many hours, which brought many customers into *los Frijoles'* establishment and enriched them mightily. We were promised a generous wage of five dollars for each night that he played but that bastard Señor Leroy cheated us in the end. So we left."

"*Aye-yi-yi,*" the bandit leader whistled in sympathy, as an interested murmur of Spanish rippled among the others of his gang. "You were cheated … such is not an unknown occurrence, but usually not inflicted upon those of their own kind. But I am a gentleman and a merciful one – unlike those gringos …" He reached into the large bag which held everything that his men had looted from O'Malley and

Fredi, and scattered a random handful of coins at their feet. "Thus, I return to you a portion. Alas, we are poor men ourselves, and cheated of our rights on every hand, or else I would return even more. We will leave you with your wagon and the mules. Count yourself fortunate, my friends, that we have no use for them. But we do languish for music and amusement ..."

"Oh?" Fredi regarded the bandit chief with wary courtesy. "We don't have a piano – or anything but a penny-whistle. What would you have us do?"

"If your Señor O'Malley would come with us, for a few hours," the bandit leader replied. "There is a rancho ... some little distance from here, where there is a piano, but no one there alive to play it."

"They want you to come with them, to play the piano," Fredi relayed to O'Malley, who nodded briskly, and seemed to fear no peril. Fredi wondered exactly how often O'Malley had been in tight, dangerous situations; he certainly seemed cool enough.

He handed the bundled overcoat with Nipper in it over to Fredi, saying, "Keep the little doggie safe with you, for he may try to run after me and become lost."

He looked as if he were about to say more, but thought better of it.

"Fetch him a mule," the bandit leader jerked a thumb at the nearest of his men. In a few moments they had unharnessed the four mules, scattering three of them into the darkness with shouts. O'Malley mounted the fourth, while Nipper whined in Fredi's grip.

"Mind the wagon," O'Malley said only. "The mules won't go far – but take care of Nipper," he added over his shoulder, as the bandits let him away.

Gone out of sight in an instant, out of hearing in another, muffled hoof-beats falling soft on the dust of the road and Fredi was alone, save for Nipper. At least the dog was not struggling to get free any more, but burrowed deeper into O'Malley's coat. Fredi put him back into the wagon. Getting down on his hands and knees, he searched by touch in the darkness near to the wagon-wheel for the coins scattered at their feet by the bandit leader.

He regretted the loss of his revolver but at least the bandits missed the shotgun under the wagon-seat. Fredi sat back on his heels, struck by a little niggling thought, a sense of something not quite right. He could have sworn that there had been more in the bag containing their stake. The bandit leader had been disappointed with what was found in the wagon. Surely there had been gold coins in their stake. Yes, he was certain of that; he had the price for Paint in gold eagles, and O'Malley was paid the same for his piano-playing. He reviewed the moment when the dusty bag was emptied into the larger; had he seen anything like the bright glint of gold? When the bandit leader threw down a fistful of money at random, surely there would have been at least one gold half or quarter-eagle among them...

But there was not – only copper pennies, with a few silver three-cent pieces and half-dimes. Fredi retrieved a tin lantern from the wagon, lit the candle within and searched the ground on hands and knees for any coins he might have missed. Nothing ... and he wondered just what O'Malley had been about to say to him, before the bandits vanished into the night with him.

Not daring to venture far from the wagon in search of the mules for fear of becoming lost in the dark, Fredi eventually settled on his bedroll underneath it, holding Nipper still firmly bundled in O'Malley's heavy coachman's overcoat. Much to his surprise, he fell almost at once into a very sound sleep, and remained in that condition until wakened just before sunrise by the lightening sky, the cooing of doves in nearby bushes, and the pattering of fat little quail searching for bugs in the leaf-mast under them. The night had been chill enough and Nipper had not been tempted until then to unravel himself from the toils of O'Malley's coat. He shook them off, trotted over to the nearest bush and cocked a leg to piss against it. Groaning, Fredi followed suit, and wondered now what he was to do, penniless and alone save for a small black terrier dog, without mules to pull the wagon. The wagon itself now represented the larger part of his and O'Malley's fortune, and he was loath to abandon it.

Might as well go and search for the mules, first. Perhaps he would strike it lucky. It would be about time, for there was nothing but bad luck in the last few days. He had no appetite for breakfast, for worrying about O'Malley and the mules. He rolled up his bedroll and blankets, pitched them into the wagon, shrugged the overcoat over his shoulders against the chill and whistled to Nipper.

"Let's go find those mules, hey, Nip? There's a good dog. I know of sheep-herding dogs," he mused aloud. "Why can't you be a mule-herding dog?"

He examined the hoof-prints of shod beasts, trodden into the road, and into the grass to either side, but the prints of the mules were indistinguishable from those of the horses ridden by the bandits to his relatively unskilled eye, and all in a muddle anyway, on either side of and ahead of the wagon, sitting forlorn by the side of the road. He wasn't anything like the tracker that Carl was, although he was good enough at straying cows.

Fredi took his lariat from the wagon, and strode off in the direction most heavily marked by disturbance of the mud, crushed grass and small broken branches, in hopes that fortune would favor him and that three mules had not wandered very far from water. From the darker line of green at some distance, it appeared likely that they had gone in that general direction. Fredi gloomily wished that he had kept shrewd Paint, sold at Warner's for a price in gold now gone to a bandit's purse. It would be a damned long walk to the water, and a hard chase on foot if the mules weren't cooperative. Before he had ventured very far, he heard O'Malley's distant voice, raised in song.

Nipper, trotting at Fredi's side one moment, made like a small black lightning-bolt in the next, soon lost in the low brush.

"You took your time about it," Fredi gasped, when he emerged onto the track again, to see Nipper capering happily alongside the mule that O'Malley rode bare-back. Now and again the small dog leaped up, clear of the ground. "They must have showed you a grand time."

"Oh, Freddy-boyo, they did indeed," O'Malley groaned, even though his countenance seemed unreasonably cheerful considering that the bandits had deprived them of nearly all their stake. "Although 'tis a matter of me, showing them a good time … the poor lads wanted to see someone playing a piano properly, y'see. I thought of it as a command performance, boyo. They heard all about the piano at the Headquarters Saloon an' the wonders of m' performances there – but bein' in the outlaw trade, they could no' partake of them in person."

"Where did they take you to?" Fredi demanded, but O'Malley only shook his head.

"It was dark, an' they tied a blindfold around me eyes, and again this morning when they led me away. It was a room in a house like Dona Vincenta's, of that I am certain although it was only the one room that I saw, sore neglected, an' all covered with dust. The piano was in abominable tune an' a torment to my own ears … but it pleased the audience well."

"Glad that it pleased someone," Fredi observed sourly, resenting O'Malley's good cheer on this disastrous morning. "They stole our stake from us, O'Malley, and unless we can recover the other three mules, no chance of earning another one before spring."

"Our stake? Pish-tush, boyo. All they took from us last night was some small coin, your revolver and my timepiece," O'Malley's countenance reflected such smug satisfaction that Fredi almost wanted to hit him, hit him again and again. "I took the precaution – well-justified you must admit now – of sewing the most of it, including the gold coins, into the hems of my coat, that very coat you are wearing now, leaving the lesser coin and notes as a decoy. You and Nipper between you, it was guarded well. I could not say anything to you last night. It was in my mind that Murrieta – I am certain that was him, being not dead but as alive as you or I – understood English better than he let on. Two may keep a secret if one of them is dead, you apprehend, Freddy-boyo; or one of them being a poor little doggie with no human speech at all."

Astonished and overjoyed at this news, Fredi felt along the first hem of O'Malley's heavy and many-caped woolen overcoat; yes, along that hem there were many small hard disks, buried in the doubled fabric. Only if you had thought to press the edge of that cape would one have detected their presence, and Fredi would have assumed them to be leaden dressmaker weights, inserted to make the ancient garment drape favorably.

"You could have told me," he accused, and O'Malley sighed, a great and gusty sigh.

"Ah, boyo, there was not the time, and you are no actor, experienced in the intrigues among the wicked and lawless. It is indade a sadly wicked world that we live in, and the result of a bad performance is not a matter of rotten vegetables thrown upon the stage in disapproval – but a bullet aimed true at heart or head."

"Let's go find those silly mules," Fredi suggested, his heart already lightened considerably by the intelligence that O'Malley did retain a degree of low cunning about him. He set aside, with an effort, his previous conviction that O'Malley might have to be looked after as did Vati, who was dreamy and bookish, and lived life on such a high intellectual plane that realities such as Mexican bandits never impinged upon it.

Chapter 11 – The Golden City on the Bay

Some three weeks later, as spring began to veil the tumbled hills in new green – although the lonely stands of oaks retained their same dull olive-green color – they reached the city. Fredi, at the reins of the trusty mules saw San Francisco at a long length, from a bit of the road which led along high ground, as the sun, lowering in the west turned the sea and the bay which lay between stands of oak and sand dunes to an ocean of quicksilver. They had added a little more to their stake, in transporting some small cargo between the settlements dotting the length of the old royal highway. The highway itself meandered like a drunken snake, along gentle valleys threaded by seasonal watercourses – a small and rock-studded stream at the best of times, and roaring cataracts of muddy water at the worst. Stands of oaks and aromatic chamisa scrub-brush patched the hillsides. They had not been bothered by bandits again – nor had they risked traveling by night, but searched for shelter towards the end of every day. The old Spanish friars had thought to establish a mission settlement of sorts at more or less a day's journey along the old highway; very sensibly, Fredi thought, although many of the missions had, like that in San Bernardino, sadly declined or ruined outright by neglect and the desertion of their Indian converts. It looked a rich land, Fredi thought – not as lushly green and cultivated as the countryside that he recalled as a child, but as least as temperate and bountiful as Texas.

But San Francisco was different even at a distance. No brief ramble of tumbled-down adobe walls amidst neglected plantations of orange and olive trees; this was a city which had sprung into existence within the space of half a dozen years; street after street of substantial, four-square storefronts, raveling out into suburbs of canvas shanty walls climbing the slopes of hills above the waterfront, the steepest hill in the shape of a loaf of bread and crowned with a timber-framed semaphore-signaling tower. As evening fell and the skies darkened, those tents and canvas-roofed tenements on the edges of town and on the highest hills seemed to glow from within with a rich amber gleam. This was a bigger city than San Diego, definitely bigger than Los Angeles or San Bernardino; the storied gateway to the gold mines, the Golconda of the new world. It even looked bigger than the biggest city in the Old World; Bremen-on-the-sea, where Fredi and his family had taken ship for Texas.

"'Tis a city of lanterns," O'Malley breathed, sitting on the wagon-seat, with little Nipper tight-curled at their feet. "A fairy-land, so it is – and built on seven high hills; just so was ancient Rome, Freddy-boyo."

"We find work, first," Fredi said. "And a place for the mules. And when spring breaks for good and all, we are off to the mines."

"Freddy-boyo, did anyone iver tell you that you are the hardest of taskmasters? Ye stand over me with a whip…"

"Well, someone has to," Fredi replied. "And if it weren't for me, I swear that you and I would still be working at the Headquarters in San Bernardino – and not getting paid by Fauntly Bean."

They eventually settled on a small livery stable on the sandy outskirts of town, to park the wagon and pasture the mules; if worst came to it, they could sleep in the wagon, if they wanted to venture the long walk from the city. The stable-owner – a burly man with an incongruously shaven head and a dark fringe of whiskers along his chin quoted a sum which made O'Malley blanch and then redden.

"We'll consider your proposal with all care," O'Malley nodded, and slapped the reins against the mule's rumps. "After we make a careful assay of our other options, d'ye see."

The livery owner spat into the dust at his feet and replied, "I would no' cheat a fellow countryman; the Saints would strike me down, indade."

"We'll return by evening," O'Malley was not mollified, "If we have no' found a better situation."

"I'll be seeing you upon that appointed hour," the livery owner grinned, "For there is none better within the city."

"He sounds very certain of that," Fredi confessed in a low voice, as they followed the road, winding through sand dunes patched through with stands of waving grass and the occasional scrub tree. The scent of wood-smoke and salt-water teased at them. With a tender consideration for their stake, Fredi began worrying that living in the city itself might cost more than they might earn. "But we need work – and we'll need the wagon and the mules. Any work for me, O'Malley – and for you, playing a saloon piano."

"Aye," O'Malley agreed with a sigh.

In the end, they did have to leave the mules and wagon with the livery stable on the outskirts, although O'Malley did find work – playing the piano in the glorious Bella Union saloon and music hall on Montgomery Street, but only for three nights a week. Perhaps there would be work in hauling cargo for short distances from the docks to various locations. That, the livery owner allowed, would be dependent on the good-will of the newly elected controller of customs, and any number of judicious bribes. Hearing this, Fredi was outraged to the bottom of his honest soul.

"I see the right of it," O'Malley said in a low voice. "'Tis rank corruption, Freddy-boyo, indeed. No need to glower at me, lad; it's the way of the world when dishonest men take command of it."

"Well, I don't see how honest men can let things get into such a state of affairs," Fredi simmered with indignation. O'Malley sighed, opened his mouth as if to say something and then reconsidered. Finally, he said, "Aye, Freddy-boyo, sometimes it is because honest men have their own lives and loved ones to consider; such consideration consuming the most of their hours and energies. And sometimes – often it is – that the honest men are outnumbered, outfoxed, and outflanked by the wicked. Because the wicked are most often willing to do what it takes for their own cause to prosper … and honest men are too scrupulous, and often too trusting. 'Tis a quandary, indade. But we will not remain here long enough to see it matter to us, indade."

"I was counting on making enough to break even through freighting," Fredi was obstinate. "And I don't see how it is that the wicked can – or ought to prosper, without fear for their own necks."

"The way of the world, lad, the way of the world," O'Malley assured him, with a lugubrious expression on his face.

With a regret and a hope that the winter in San Francisco would not take too much form their accumulated stake, Fredi consented to dip into it sufficiently to pay for several weeks' lodgings at a cheap boarding house on the lower slopes of Russian Hill, where many of the decidedly foreign element in San Francisco had set up housekeeping. In the end, Fredi did find work, although not what he would have expected. Methodically, be went up and down the busiest streets in the part of the city most thickly lined with substantial buildings, going to every business and asking politely if there were any work to be had. This resulted in several days of delivering messages to other businesses, running errands, some hours of helping unpack a wagon of freight just arrived from the East, of scrubbing floors, and a half-day spent washing glassware and plates at a busy saloon when their regular dishwasher appeared too drunk for his duties. He did not mind not being hired on a more permanent basis once the regular dishwasher recovered; after the Headquarters Saloon in San Bernardino, there was no work that he detested more than washing dishes.

On the following day, he continued his quest for regular employment. This quest terminated in mid-afternoon at an enterprise on Montgomery Street. The sign over the front door of the place vouchsafed only that it was the premises of a certain C.O. Gerberding & Co. A tall, albeit slightly stoop-shouldered man with a particularly aggressive set of curly black whiskers, mustache and sideburns looked up from the work on his desk, at the tinkle of a bell over the door as Fredi opened it. A curious, almost metallic odor tickled his nostrils.

"Yes?" the man demanded, with some impatience. "Can't you see I'm busy? What do you want?"

"Work, sir," Fredi replied, jolted into absolute honesty. "If you are so very busy, you might need another hand."

The black-bearded man laughed, a short bark of laughter. "Very true, lad. Do you know how to set type and run a printing press?"

"No, sir, but I am willing to learn," Fredi replied and the man laughed again. In the back of the room, two men and several boys labored around a strange metal mechanical contraption that stood taller than a man – they were methodically laying sheets of paper on a flat sliding table-top part, spinning a crank to slide the table-portion underneath the tall bit – which looked to Fredi like an enormous metal cheese-press. One man pulled a heavy lever all the way from one side to the other, held it for a count of five and then pulled it back. Out slid the table-top ... and one boy was industriously rolling a device that looked like a rolling pin with two handles attached across another surface smeared with black, tarry stuff. The smell must come from that, Fredi decided. The other boy was taking the sheets of newsprint and carefully draping them over lengths of clothesline strung from peg to peg at the back of the room. The sheets of paper rustled slightly in the draft, like the leaves on a cottonwood tree. The third boy was engaged in folding the dried sheets once, twice, and then rolling them into a compact shape. He had a canvas bag nearly full of them

"I haven't time to teach you," the man replied, "And it's wasted effort, especially if you're haring off to the mines as soon as the snow melts in spring. But as it happens, I do have a need for another likely lad; delivering the latest issue of the *Evening Bulletin* to subscribers every afternoon and selling copies on the street. Interested?"

"I might be," Fredi admitted, cautiously. "How much do you pay?"

"Depends on how many you sell," the black-bearded man corked his inkbottle and set aside his pen. "Three dollars a day for delivering to subscribers – then a half-penny for each copy of the *Bulletin* you sell on the street for a penny. I guarantee you'll make enough to make a living and then some. The *Bulletin* is the most-read newspaper in San Francisco and increasing circulation every day."

"Sounds fair enough," Fredi agreed. This was new to him. A penny newspaper, on the muddy streets of San Francisco. Well, anything once and it was a prospect that didn't involve a wash-pan of greasy water.

"We'll shake hands on it then," Fredi's new employer rose from his desk, unfolding like a jointed carpenter's rule in stages. "James King of William. You sound like a foreigner, lad. Where are you from?"

"Fredi Steinmetz," Fredi tried not to wince under the powerful, slightly ink-stained grip. "From Texas ... but we came from Germany some years ago. I thought to come to California for gold, but indeed – is not everyone in America save a few – come from somewhere else?"

"Very true, young Fred, very true." James King smiled. Fredi liked him at once – blunt, honest and fearless, like Gil Fabreaux, like Carl his brother-in-law, although a good bit more rash when it came to trading insults in print. But this was something Fredi would only discover in the following weeks. "And in California – especially so, and many of them not from as wholesome a place as Texas ... although there are some of your fellows," and a slight frown creased James King's ferociously beetled brows, "Who do not give honor to your chosen state, such as ... well some that I mention in my editorial essays. But never mind; yes, I can make honest use of your services." He turned his head and called over his shoulder. "Edwin! Here's another lad to deliver the Bulletin. Can you take him around to the subscribers on Rincon Hill as soon as you are ready? Then take him to back to Montgomery street and show him how to sell the papers. He's hired as of this evening."

"Certainly, Mr. King," the boy replied, setting aside his task and coming to stand by Mr. King's desk, where he and Fredi looked each other over in a silent moment. Fredi saw a lad of about thirteen, he thought – a pale-faced boy with a peaked owl-face, splotched with pale freckles, slender but just beginning sprout up to his adult height. The boy's eyes were rounded and hazel-brownish colored, which increased the resemblance to an owl. Raggedly-cut dark hair, again, appearing rather like feathers added to the owl-resemblance. He looked Fredi over; yes, there was some trepidation there, resolutely hidden as Edwin stuck out his hand.

"Edwin Blaine," he said. "Do you know San Francisco at all ...?"

"Fredi Steinmetz," Fredi replied. "And not well at all, Me and my partner O'Malley just got here, a week ago." No, there was nothing to fear from Edwin Blaine. He rather hoped that Edwin had a fond and careful mother; the boy appeared in desperate need of the care of such. His clothing looked too large for him, and whoever had cut his hair was no expert.

"I'll leave you to show Freddy the ropes, Ed," Mr. King had already absented himself from the exchange, his attention on the papers before him, the topmost of which was already three-quarters covered with fine spidery handwriting.

"You talk like a foreigner," Edwin observed. "But I guess there are many foreigners come to look for gold – where do you come from, Freddy? Come help me fold the last of today's issue, and then I'll take them around. Do you have a good memory? Otherwise, you had best make a note. Some of the subscribers are quite polite and generous. Ma'am Pleasant is especially nice. She keeps a fancy boarding house on Rincon Hill, where all the swells live, and often gives me a bite to eat."

"That sounds prime," Fredi agreed – and indeed it did. Walking around delivering newspapers, and then selling them to passersby – definitely better than laboring over a washtub.

He related his story in bits and pieces to the younger boy as they set out; about the tiny village of Albeck in Bavaria, with a green copper onion-dome on the little church tower, how he and his family came over on a sailing ship, storm-tossed on the Atlantic. Fredi even told how he and Johann, playing with a makeshift raft at the edge of the San Antonio River, had nearly drowned their niece Anna, when the raft floated out of reach. "It was a great fright; but just then, Colonel Hays – have you ever heard of him? He is a great hero in Texas, the best Indian fighter there is … anyway, his sergeant could swim and he dove into the water. That was my brother-in-law Carl, only he wasn't my brother-in-law yet. He rescued Anna, and my sister mended his shirt for him." Edwin listened, with grave attention, which Fredi found to be quite flattering, as the sun began to set in a brilliant gold and orange smear behind the range of hills that defined the city – a city that in some places looked to begin sliding wholesale into the bay.

Fredi's account suffered many interruptions, though; each carried a heavy canvas haversack stuffed full of folded copies of the *Bulletin*.

At an hour when Fredi would have expected folk back home in Fredericksburg to be closing their places of business for the evening, and trudging home to a good supper – San Francisco was even livelier than the old quarter around the Main Plaza in Bexar; drinking, socializing with friends, gambling on a turn of the cards or the old shell game. They sold a dozen papers out of their bags before they had gotten a block. It gratified Fredi that so many men seemed eager to read the *Bulletin* and he congratulated himself on his luck at finding employment with such a popular newspaper.

"It's as if no one has a need to sleep," he remarked to Edwin, as they trudged along the lower slopes of Telegraph Hill. As light faded from the sky, lights bloomed behind glass windows and canvas walls of the cheaper sorts of residence.

"If it isn't gold they are dreaming of, it is how to cheat and skin the greenhorns," Edwin said.

"You sound very sour and cynical, for one so young," Fredi remarked, in some surprise. Edwin snorted. "Remain here for very long, you'd be sour and cynical yourself," he answered. "I've been here … well, not very long at all, but if there is a place more sunk in vice and corruption than San Francisco then I pray I never have to spend a minute in it."

"If it made me rich, I could bear it," Fredi replied. "Me, I came to California to find myself a fortune in gold. Everyone says it's thick on the ground in the foothills."

Edwin began to laugh. "Oh, no it's not and you're a greenhorn yourself for believing all those tales they tell."

"So!" Fredi retorted, indignant over being laughed at by a younger boy. "And how would you know? How long have you been in California?"

The younger boy didn't sound as if he felt any sting in Fredi's words. "I've spent nine seasons in the diggings, long enough to know that gold isn't scattered all over the ground, like flowers in a meadow, that all you have to do is gather them. You have to look sharpish for it, dig, and pan for hours and days to find enough to buy a loaf of bread." He shrugged his narrow shoulders. "If you are lucky – then you find enough in a day for two loaves of bread. If you are really lucky, then enough for a good supper at Ma'am Pleasant's boarding house. She's the best cook in San Francisco – and her place caters only to the best sort. That's why she has two-three copies of all the newspapers for her gentlemen, and some of them, like Mr. Bell have a subscription of their own. None but the best for Ma'am Pleasant. This is her place. We go around to the back," Edwin added, as they came to a tall clapboard house on the corner; three stories tall with a mansard roof crowned with a row of fancy ironwork. Intrigued, Fredi followed the younger boy around the corner, where another, plainer gait led into the small enclosure at the back of the tall house. The chill wind whipped around the corners – but the sky was relatively unclouded, so far. Edwin rapped his knuckles on the door, which opened almost at once.

"The *Evening Bulletin*, Ma'am Pleasant," Edwin said to the young woman who opened the door.

"You are early, this evening," the young woman said, and Fredi regarded her with great interest; an oval and ivory countenance in which dark eyes were so deeply set that they had a hooded look to them. Her dark hair was smoothed back under a snow-white house-bonnet of the kind that only older women wore these days. Her dress was of fine cloth and buttoned primly up to a fine lace collar around her throat but there was still something about her … something wanton, yet dangerous. Fredi could not think of what it reminded him of, and then he recalled Sally Doyle, and how O'Malley had described her as a perilous woman, a woman as far above other women as angels were to be above men.

"I'm showing Freddy around to the subscribers," Edwin explained. "He's just starting out – but I expect he'll be off to the diggings by spring."

"Indeed," Ma'am Pleasant ventured, and turned the full weight of her regard onto Fredi. "So, you will be off to find yourself a fortune, then?"

"I hope so, Ma'am," Fredi ventured a stiff but proper bow, and put four two rolled copies of the *Evening Bulletin* in her hands. "I am properly Friedrich Arthur Steinmetz, at your service. And I hope to make my fortune in the diggings, although it is my temporary good fortune and pleasure to bring you the newspaper of Mr. James King every evening."

"I anticipate your service, for the time that you will be offering it," Ma'am Pleasant smiled, and her voice changed in some manner imperceptible to Fredi; from that crisp manner which he associated with Yankees like the Homestead brothers to something more like a honey-saturated drawl which he associated more with that handful of Southerners of his association who came from New Orleans. "An' with you being so early, I regret there is nothing I can offer you boys for a supper than sandwiches of bread and bacon."

"Grateful we are, Ma'am," Edwin said, although with a slight expression of disappointment.

Ma'am Pleasant added, "And a piece of citron-cake and an apple apiece, for you to take with you." She turned her regard upon Fredi. "But if you are still hungry when you are done with delivering the Bulletin, come to the back door later and I'll see what I have left after serving supper to the gennelemen ..." Her voice dropped to a throaty purr, which unaccountably raised the hair on the back of Fredi's neck, but in a faintly pleasurable way. No – Ma'am Pleasant might be at least ten or fifteen years his senior, but she was as fine-looking a woman as any that he had looked on since leaving San Antonio, and that Mexican girl in Military Plaza blew him a kiss on her fingertips.

Not that he had actually looked on many fine women at all. Not even Fauntly Bean's light o'love had roused any feelings in him, other than a feeling of mild annoyance that Fauntly should be trifling with the dangerous affections of a woman as good as already married.

He and Edwin took each a sandwich, an apple, and a slab of sweet-smelling cake, still warm from the oven and wrapped in clean cloth napkins and went on with their errand, munching hungrily and scattering crumbs all the way along Second Street.

When his appetite was sated, and they reached the lower slopes of another low hill, Fredi ventured, "Ma'am Pleasant – is she a widow, or what? Such a one would be very rare in San Francisco; I am thinking, what with the dearth of respectable women. Young and fair in appearance and an excellent cook, too. I cannot imagine why a paragon would not be married."

"Widow, I do believe. Twice over, I think." Edwin trudged ahead. "Mr. Bell is her special admirer. She … she has a lot of friends, especially among the nigras in San Francisco. I've heard it said that she's really a high yellow woman from New Orleans."

"Well, she looks white to me," Fredi mused. "Like some of those Californio Spanish I seen, coming over the Southern trail from Texas. So who else is delivered a paper?"

"Mr. Sherman, at Harrison and Fremont, in the green-painted house. He's a big man with the Lucas and Turner Bank. All the notable men have houses on Rincon Hill. You do one side of the street, while I do the other side. The governor asked Mr. Sherman special to command the militia company in San Francisco, on account of him having been a soldier, once." Edwin looked slantwise at his companion for a moment, before he continued. "There's trouble brewing – even the peaceable-tempered men say so. There was a heap of dirty dealing in the last election. Some of them got elected are as crooked as snakes, and it's pretty certain that the balloting was rigged. And Charley Cora shooting Will Richardson dead in the streets – the US Marshall, can you imagine? And seeming to get off by having his fancy woman bribe the jury … o'course, the gossip has it that it was the marshall's wife and Cora's woman taking a dislike to each other when they had a party on the same night, and all the gentlemen preferred party in a fancy parlor-house to tea and gingerbread at Mrs. Richardson's. That set the cat among the pigeons! Or so Mr. King says. Did you know that in eight square blocks around Broadway there are at least a hundred bawdy houses and twice that many gambling hells? The respectable element, they don't like it much – that Cora and his pals like Crooked Davy Broderick can run roughshod, shooting down an unarmed man in the street in broad daylight, while city offices are bought and sold wholesale. That's Mr. King's opinion, o'course. He says that Broderick and his pals look at the city as an oyster to be shucked for their own benefit. Me …" an errant light from the broad glass window giving into one of those nearby hells shown briefly on his narrow, owl-like features. "I'm all for leaving for the diggings as soon as spring comes. I like Mr. King, well enough but Broderick and his pals play a dirty game and they play for keeps."

"Is it dangerous, then, taking around the *Bulletin* – if Mr. King has made an enemy like that?" Fredi asked, with a slight crawling feel at the back of his neck, and Edwin shook his head.

"Naw … we only bring the papers. We don't write what's in them. But if you see a couple of Irish plug-uglies coming down the street, looking as if they are coming for you, then I would run, run as fast as you can."

Fredi made a quiet resolve at that moment, to replace the old Colt dragoon pistol that had been stolen from him by Murietta's gang. It sounded from Edwin's words that it might be more dangerous in the streets in San Francisco than in the rutted and bandit-haunted trails around San Bernardino.

"You might want to come with us in the spring, then," Fredi suggested on an impulse. "Nine years in the diggings – you must have been at it before you were even out of small-clothes. O'Malley and I are greenhorns, at gold-mining, anyway. You'd be a right handy friend."

"I might, at that," Edwin allowed, as if he was considering it seriously, with a slantwise and considering look at Fredi.

The two boys tramped up and down the street blocks of the city; hill and shore, though the substantial district of town, where buildings and warehouses of brick, stone and sawn lumber adorned muddy streets lined with brick and plank sidewalks. Light shown from windows, upstairs and down, and the night was raucous with rowdy men and women of scandalous repute at their revels ... or that portion of which was on display in the streets was not entirely scandalous, but Fredi worked very hard at keeping an incredulous expression from his face. He was half-appalled, yet tantalized by the chaotic, haphazard life of a large city, the like of which he had never experienced before. The seamy, vice-ridden waterfront district, the haphazard tents and shanties climbing up the sandy slopes of Russian Hill, muddy streets, magnificent gambling halls and theaters, jousting uncomfortably with the respectability of churches and luxurious mansions, all hung over with the smoldering threat of violence ... and fire. Sober Yankee businessmen, elbow to elbow with edgy chivalric gentlemen from the South, Chileans and Chinamen, Kanakas from the Islands of Hawaii, sailors from every nation, swaggering thugs, straight off the latest ship from the Australian prison colonies – and madmen in plenty, most of them mad for gold.

Nothing in Fredi's previous life had ever prepared him for this, not the cattle trail from Texas, or the staid and orderly streets of Fredericksburg, back in Gillespie County. No, he was no innocent country bumpkin; not he, who had come overland from San Antonio with a cattle herd, and worked in the Headquarters Saloon, but still … Should he choose to write of this to his father and sisters in Texas, and Johann, devoted to his medical studies? If he were even to hint at the depravities before his eyes, would they even believe a tenth of it?

"My brother is in Germany," he ventured to Edwin, as they stood side by side in the plaza, at mid-evening when they had delivered to the last of the regular subscribers, selling the remaining copies of the *Bulletin* for a penny each. "A student of medicine in Heidelberg. When I write to him next, I do not think that he will believe a word of what I tell him about this place."

"No, I expect not," Edwin agreed, a wistful expression on his owl-like features. "I've heard …" but at that moment, a number of not-quite sober men importuned them for copies of the *Bulletin*. When conversation resumed, Edwin said, "My mother had a friend in St. Louis when she was a girl. Ma's friend married a Choteau, but her father was rich and her mother used to send to France for her own clothes and dresses for her daughters. Every year, trunks of new dresses in the latest style. Ma wasn't half envious! All the way from France! Ma told us such tales she heard from her friend. All the music and the gaiety – nothing like here." Edwin added, sadly, as a pair of scandalously-dressed women drifted past them, attended by gales of laughter and a rustle of silk … and also a pungent whiff of rosewater. "I dream about going to France myself, someday. It sounds a wonderful place, as Ma's friend told it."

"I don't know if I ever want to go back to the Old Country," Fredi said, stoutly. "It was a hard enough journey when we came from Germany. Texas is good enough for me, once I have made my fortune here. Now, my partner, O'Malley, he has traveled through the great cities on the continent. He even played the piano for royalty. Now he's playing piano at the Bella Union. I expect that I shall have to see him to our lodging when he is finished, lest he be tempted to bet on the cards. Where do you live Edwin?"

"I sleep in the back room at Mr. King's." Edwin replied, suddenly curt. "Most times, Ma'am Pleasant gives me a good supper, on account of she wants to hear any gossip I might have come in the way of through working at the *Bulletin*. Which is only fair, I think," Edwin added after seeing that Fredi did not altogether approve of this kind of duplicity. "For Ma'am Pleasant tells me things I believe she wants me to tell Mr. King. So, I get a square meal and a little extra from Mr. King when something she has told me is useful to him. Sometimes Ma'am gives me a little extra, too. She likes knowing things. Rumors, gossip... she was the first to find out that ol' Slimy Casey was a convict in New York." Edwin added, in a lower voice. "She has many friends in the east ... important friends. I believe that she is sympathetic to the Abolitionists, as she is no friend to slave-owners."

"Truly?" Fredi marveled. "That would be another reason for me to think highly of her. My father is most fiercely against keeping Africans or anyone else in bondage and so are his friends."

Edwin regarded him, owl-eyes rounded in shock. "Are you ... are you an Abolitionist, Freddy?"

"I might be," Fredi hadn't really thought very much about the matter. "I wouldn't go around helping slaves escape their masters, but for darned certain I wouldn't offer help to a slave-catcher looking for one. I certainly wouldn't weep if all the slaves in the South were freed, or if California becomes a free state. I have enough of a chore looking after O'Malley and the mules; why would I burden myself with looking after a slave as well?"

"Some folk are touchy about all that," Edwin replied, "Even here. Especially here." In the golden lamplight falling through another window, his peaky little face appeared most grave, serious. "It's a dangerous season here, Fredi, even more dangerous than the diggings, less'n the Committee of Vigilance bestirs themselves again. If they do, it won't be a country picnic neither."

"It can't be any more perilous than the trail from California," Fredi retorted. "With Indians and sudden storms and bandits and all. Anyway, we're for the diggings in spring. If O'Malley agrees, then you should come with us."

"It's something I would consider," Edwin agreed, after a moment of contemplation. "I sure as tarnation don't want to stay here past spring."

Chapter 12 – Enchantment and Intrigues

The winter and early spring of that strange year in San Francisco presented a strange workday for Fredi; a day that only began in mid-afternoon, and extended into the late evening hours. He often slept into the mid-morning, as did O'Malley, whose day ended even later, after hours of playing piano in the Bella Union. O'Malley and Edwin conceived a curious friendship, from the moment that Fredi had introduced them, that first night that Fredi had delivered the *Bulletin* for Mr. King. Edwin was full of wistful admiration and a longing to know of all those places in the Old Country where O'Malley had played before the crowned heads and nobility of Europe. O'Malley, in turn, and like Fredi – wanted to know all of what Edwin knew of gold mining, which over the progression of many suppers and evenings of delivering and selling the latest *Bulletin* for a penny, turned out to be quite a lot. Edwin claimed to have spent every summer of the last nine years in the Northern diggings. What he had said regarding those experiences tallied very closely with what Fredi had gathered in conversation with other miners and hopeful Argonauts.

To while away the time before the daily *Bulletin* issue was ready for distribution, Fredi first found amusement by going down to the waterfront to dock and offload cargo from their holds. He relished the wonderful sight of walking along the waterfront, under the looming jib-booms of the sailing ships drawn up close, admiring the infinite variety of their carved and painted figure-heads. The innkeeper Captain Nimitz, back in Fredericksburg was a sailor in his youth and told many tales of long voyages in such ships, of storms and adventures in strange ports around the world. Fredi wondered what Captain Nimitz would think of the marvelous vista of San Francisco's waterfront. He knew enough from Edwin, and from the murmured warnings from O'Malley that he should avoid those establishments on Pacific Street run by one of O'Malley's countrymen, a hot-tempered ruffian with a bright red beard named Kelly as well as a number of other saloons with an even worse reputation. Relieved at being employed by the *Daily Evening Bulletin* and making sufficient at it that he and O'Malley night even depart San Francisco with a small addition, rather than a subtraction to their grubstake, Fredi at first disregarded Edwin's caution and O'Malley's warnings. There was always something happening; a constant bustle in the streets, music from the gambling halls spilling into the streets at any time of day or night, the arrival of sailing ships and steamers from across the water, the constant movement of the telegraph signaling arms, the tower of which crowned the tallest hill. Fredi, having lived always as a landsman, found it all exotic and deeply fascinating, spiced with that slight edge of danger that sent a frisson down his back, to the dismay of O'Malley and Edwin Blaine alike.

On one morning, when the noise from other boarders kept him from the state of deep sleep in which deep weariness usually consigned him, Fredi was moved to dress and walk out early to the waterfront. That place was still lightly shrouded in the pearly fog of early morning, and almost silent save for the dripping of condensation from eaves, shutters and porches onto the muddy ground below. The fog had the curious capacity of muffling sounds close by, but magnifying those at a distance. The voices of sailors on ships farther out in the bay, the splash of oars as someone rowed a boat towards shore, a termagant whore in the next alley, shrieking her displeasure at her pimp or unsatisfactory customer. The jib-booms looming over his head, as he walked along the wharf appeared like ghostlike, faintly seen, swaying with the motion of the tide. Fredi strolled along, hands in pockets, now hearing the rowboat ever more clearly.

The fog began to lift from the water, dissolving into a mist which barely veiled the shore opposite, and a dotting of hilly islands in the bay The town across the bay was called Oakland Township; a shy country companion to the muddy and chaotic bustle of San Francisco, where the hills behind the shoreline piled up in grey and lavender-tinged folds, paler in the distance. The single rowboat approaching the wharf was a small one with a single dark-coated man at the oars. Fredi watched with idle interest. The man didn't look anything like a sailor, and there were no anchored ships in the area from which the small boat came. It looked more as if it came over from Oakland Township, just across the narrow straits, and as it came closer, Fredi wondered why the man pulling at the oars looked familiar; a short, slight fellow of middle years with a neatly clipped short beard, yet as spry as a youth. He knew that man from someplace; not from the overland journey, or selling newspapers in the streets of San Francisco, but from back in Texas. He watched as the oarsman circled around to a small landing, shipped oars and tied up, just a few short yards away. When he stepped ashore, straightening the front of his coat, Fredi remembered.

"Captain Hays!" he shouted. The man's head turned towards Fredi, and regarded him with mild curiosity. "Are we acquainted, sir?" he asked, with mild curiosity. "I do not recollect ever having been introduced, and you are too young to have been one of my follows in a ranging company or in the war with Mexico."

"There is that," Fredi replied. "No, I wasn't ever, but my sister's husband was. You must remember him; Carl Becker. Sergeant Carl Becker."

Captain Hays' face lit at once with recognition and a delighted roar of laughter. "You, then! I remember you and your twin very well! Two bad little German boys, pottering around on the riverbank – damn-near drowning your little playmate, too. Well, I'll be damned!

Must have been ten years ago! So, you've come to California! I couldn't convince Carl of that, more's the pity. Are you rich yet?"

"We haven't gotten to the mines," Fredi confessed. "Are you?"

Captain Hays shook his head, still amused. "I'm doing well enough. Back to surveying, which was always my first profession. I'll say this for California; at least I can do it without risking my life in having to fight off the Comanche all the while. What are you doing in San Francisco?"

"Selling newspapers," Fredi replied, torn between pride at being recognized and recalled by the great hero, Colonel Jack Hays, and embarrassment at the reason. He and Johann had been very careless. That their pottering around on the riverbank hadn't cost the life of their even younger niece, Anna, was only due to the fortuitous arrival of Captain Hays and a small party of his men and that Carl Becker could swim well. Vati, Magda, Liesel and Liesel's husband Hansi had all been rightfully furious with Fredi and Johann. *"The Evening Bulletin.* My pard and I are building up our stake. We'll be off to the diggings as soon as spring comes."

"Well, then," Jack Hays clapped Fredi on the shoulder, "I wish you the best of luck in the mines, young fellow. Convey my best wishes to Carl, when next you write home. He has a fine family now, doesn't he?"

"He does, indeed," Fredi replied, feeling a slight tightness in his throat, thinking of Carl and Magda. *Damn, he simply must strike it rich – to pay them back the money for the cattle, money which they must need desperately.* "Two boys and a little daughter."

"A fortunate man," Jack Hays said, and regarded Fredi with a piercing look. He hesitated as if he were considering his words most carefully. "Should you have the opportunity, you and this pard of yours ought to consider leaving San Francisco for the diggings as soon as you can. It's a dangerous place; there have been more open murders in this place over the last year than in every other town or settlement in the territory combined. There is considerable unhappiness with the public administration of this place – the sense among those who pay notice to such matters is that there will soon be open war in the streets."

"We will consider doing so, as soon as winter breaks," Fredi replied. Selling the *Bulletin* on the streets, and hearing from Edwin over how Mr. King was locked in a bitter feud with Mr. James Casey of the *Sunday Times*; he and O'Malley had talked about this several times. At this, Jack Hays looked relieved.

Clapping Fredi on the shoulder once again, he said, "Smart lad. As soon as you can, then," and took his leave. Fredi wandered a little way farther along the wharf, considering those words. Carl always said that Jack Hays was the best and canniest soldier there was, never mind that he never wore a fancy uniform. If Jack Hays foresaw trouble, that was a matter to take careful heed. Fredi considered, took an account of his earnings, and that very morning went to a general mercantile and purchased another dragoon revolver; an old one, but still a stout bit of shooting iron. It had an engraving on the barrel, of a running fight between Jack Hays' ranging company and Yellow Wolf's Comanche warriors, which the shopkeeper was pleased to tell Fredi about. Fredi considered it an excellent omen.

Edwin Blaine, Fredi discovered, entertained an even deeper dislike of the waterfront than did O'Malley, who finally broached the subject openly as the three of them ate a meagre supper at a cheap chop-house near the Bella Union, the very afternoon of the day of Fredi's chance meeting with Jack Hays. He had thought the other two would be impressed with the story of that meeting, and moreover that Jack Hays particularly recollected Fredi.

"They are the many of such places a front for crimps and thieves," O'Malley warned Fredi, little impressed with the tale, while Edwin nodded agreement with his mouth full. "There is a reason they call that district the Barbary Coast. 'Tis the natural residence of pirates, slave-takers and godless men. In any of the low taverns, accept no drink from any man or woman, no, not even if the bottle looks sealed and fresh from the distillery, the man having an honest bluff appearance, the woman a tender one; no, not a bite to eat, or even a smoke from a good cigar..."

"I don't smoke cigars," Fredi protested. "And I have nothing to eat or drink from their hands! I am not a fool, O'Malley."

O'Malley looked at him severely, and then sighed. "And lucky for you, for it is a filthy habit, indade and count yourself fortunate. But for my peace of mind, I beg you to avoid the waterfront, Fredi-boyo. A sailor's life is a hard life, so they say, ruled by brutal shipmasters. So many sailors desert upon reaching a fortunate shore, y'see. It is one more hazard of this place. Ye are young, a promising lad and not a sailor by profession – yet are the ship captains so desperate to crew their vessels. Ye may be safe enough in broad daylight of a morning, and on the public streets, but still. There are more crimps plying their trade in the waterfront district then honest men, indade. I would advise ye not to gamble your freedom for six months or a year by walking alone through the Barbary Coast, even in a bright morning."

"I suppose I could walk to the top of the telegraph hill, instead," Fredi agreed with some reluctance, for he found the sight of ships endlessly entrancing; standing out in the bay, or tied up to the dock, the busy steam-ships threshing the waters to a froth with their great turning wheels, as well as the bales of goods unloaded from them – everything from pineapples to lumber. The possibility being snatched by a crimp was a definite peril to his and O'Malley's plans to strike it rich in the diggings. Even Edwin agreed that the streets of the waterfront district were somewhat more dangerous than the rest of San Francisco, which was, according to Jack Hays, more dangerous than the most violent camp in the whole diggings.

"When I leave San Francisco," Edwin confided. "It won't be by a misery of a sailing ship, that's for certain. What if the ship sinks? You're drowned and food for the fish."

"But you say that you want to see the great cities of the world," O'Malley pointed out. "How will you get from here to there, without crossing an ocean?"

"On a steamship," Edwin replied, and O'Malley nodded, agreeably. "On a foine vessel like one of the Collins Line, sure enough. Now, Eddie-boyo – tell us more about the finding of gold. What must be done to locate that precious ore ..."

"Panning is easy, but slow," Edwin answered, that owl-like, sharp-chinned face intense. "It works best when the color is plentiful, along a rich bar at the inside bend of a creek or a river, or at the bottom of a stretch of rapids, where the water slows all of a sudden. Find a good run of color by panning; then set up a cradle, or the Long Tom. Some say that dark gravel or sand is a good sign of color. They say to look for granite outcrops. Sometimes good color would turn up in the crevices between slabs of granite. But most often in a gravelly valley. Some say in that was a river during the Noachian flood, but dried up long since."

"Why d'ye suppose all that gold came from at the first?" O'Malley mused.

Edwin answered readily, "I heard tell that somewhere up in the highest mountains, there is a great cliff of coal-black granite threaded through the gold. It's the Mother Lode, you see. Rivers run down through the mountains from a lake at the foot of that cliff; they carry all the little nuggets and grains of gold down through the hills."

"And has anyone ever found this grand mother lode and cliff of gold?" O'Malley asked, with somewhat skeptical interest.

Edwin sighed. "No, and not for want of looking, either," he answered. "I reckon if it was there to find, what with everyone crawling up every little valley and gulch looking for gold… if it was there, it would have been found."

"You told me once that you had been nine seasons in the diggings." Frederick asked, idly. "Did you come here with family or are you an orphan apprentice?"

Edwin's thin shoulders straightened, proudly. "I came with family, over the trail from Missouri, in '48, before word got out about gold. My Pa was friends early on with Mr. Murphy in San Jose and a partner with … a Mr. Padgett, who also came over from Missouri."

"And then, what?" Fredi was intrigued; he and his family had come over from Germany when he and his twin were seven years old. It was a long and torturous journey, but with the promises of the Verein at the end of it all, and everything seemed to have worked out all right, save for Mama and his sister Liesel's little baby dying of ship-fever during the voyage. Fredi didn't rightly like to think any more of how those canvas-wrapped and weighted bodies – the small one, and the tiny one – vanished into the green ocean, while Pastor Altemuller read the words for proper burial from the deck of the *Apollo*.

"Pa was friends with some of that crew that found gold in digging out a mill-race for a saw-mill for Captain Sutter," Edwin answered. "And as soon as word got out, he said that we should go to the gold-fields and make a fortune. It didn't work out as he expected. They all … caught the cholera and died."

"Leaving you an orphan?" O'Malley ventured, his Irish accents heavy with sympathy. Fredi intended to ruffle the boys' roughly-barbered dark hair by way of sympathy. Edwin flinched aside from the touch, but Fredi wrote it off to remembered grief. In those dark days after Mama died, he and Johann could only accept sympathy from the family, not officious strangers, and very little of that. He took no offense. He had Vati, his sisters, and their husbands. Far away in Gillespie County, of course, but Edwin had no one at all.

"And then I went to Pa's partner, Mr. Padgett," Edwin's peaked face went even paler. "but he and the others were killed in the diggings by a claim-jumper last fall."

Fredi ventured, "Then now have you no kinfolk at all – of uncles and aunts, not a one?"

"Back in the States," Edwin set aside his fork, and regarded the tin plate with an expression of misery. "In St. Louis. Pa's sister Sadie – she married a man named Henry Parmalee and Ma had kin there, as well. I'm intending to go back there, as soon as I have enough of a stake. I've had enough of Californy."

"You could take service as a sailor and work your way home from San Francisco," O'Malley suggested, and Edwin shook his head in vigorous dismissal, saying, "No. Put myself on a ship, knowing what I know of the likes of ol' Shanghai Pierce and his pals to trust my life to any of them? I'd most prefer to take my chance with Indians an' Mormons, but I need a stake before I go anywhere. I owe it to Pa an' Ma."

"Understood, boyo – understood," O'Malley replied. "Faith, an' a nice fat purse o' gold would do much for any poor man but I do not expect that we will be poor for long, not with gold for the taking, like pebbles in the road…"

Edwin was already shaking his head. "It's not as easy as all that, Mr. O'Malley," he said, as serious as a judge. "It's work, as hard as any you can do, up to your knees in cold water, shoveling dirt into the cradle, looking for a bit o' color…"

"But with the advantage of being work for yourself, instead of another." O'Malley replied, cheery as a cricket. Fredi and Edwin exchanged wry grins. O'Malley lived on optimism. A bell in the nearby steeple of the Unitarian church chimed the hours, and Edwin gobbled his last few bites. "Three o'clock; tonight's *Bulletin* will be coming off the press. We'd better go now, Freddy – Mr. King will be looking for us."

On that evening, Fredi and Edwin quartered the streets of Rincon Hill; Mr. King's subscriber list seemed to lengthen by every issue, necessitating Fredi and Edwin to work separately, with their bag of rolled newsprint dragging ever more heavily at the start. It turned out that Fredi delivered to Ma'am Pleasant's; usually that fell to Edwin, and Fredi only minded because it meant that he just had an infrequent chance to admire Ma'am Pleasant's fine features and even finer figure, and wonder yet again why she might sound so crisp and Yankee-correct one moment, and the next speaking in a honey-sweet soft drawl.

She even smelled nice; a faint elusive scent of verbena, and clean starched cloth. She smelled like a woman who lived a respectable life; not like the other kind, those women who frequented the saloons and gambling hells; who, if they did not drench themselves with overpowering quantities of perfume, smelt of sweat and tobacco smoke and the unclean flesh of men who had bedded them. Fredi did not consider himself to be overly particular when it came to feminine companionship, but he drew the line at women who smelled bad.

And she most always provided a bit of bread and cheese, and a piece of cake or pie for each of them, oftentimes, no matter if it was Fredi or Edwin who came around to the back door with the newspapers for her establishment. This evening, when Fredi rapped his knuckles on the back door, it was Ma'am Pleasant herself who opened it after a moment, saying in her honey-soft voice, "You're late this evening. The gennelmun, they be asking after the *Bulletin*."

"Sorry, Ma'am – there are a heap of new subscribers, an' Edwin an' I got started late and stayed behind. I hope Mr. Bell isn't inconvenienced…"

"No," and Ma'am Pleasant smiled. "Don't you fret about that none. He's away to Sacramento on business all this week."

"Mining business?" Fredi was intrigued. As far as he knew, Mr. Bell was a banking man, but with interests in all kinds of investments, not strictly gold mines. Perhaps there might be some tidbit of news worthy of Mr. King's interest for the *Bulletin*.

"No," Ma'am Pleasant chuckled, taking the proffered newspapers from his hands. "He is a clever man and a rich one. Such do not need to mine for gold; they mine the miners. I purely forgot to put together something this minute for you an' young Edwin. Come back when you are done with work tonight, an' I'll have set aside something sweet and special, just for you."

"I will, Ma'am, and thank you." Fredi replied, unaccountably pleased by this consideration, and by the secret fondness for him which he thought he saw in her regard. She smiled again, and in a most peculiar gesture, brought her fingertips to her lips, and then kissing them, lightly brushed his cheek; a butterfly-soft gesture. "You take care, Freddy. I'll leave the back door unbolted. You let yourself straight in, you hear?"

"I will," Fredi promised again, and went on with deliveries. After completing the rounds, he and Edwin stood as was their habit at a succession of street corner locations, selling copies of the *Bulletin* until their bags were emptied entirely. Fredi was in haste to return to Ma'am Pleasant's house, although he was careful to say nothing to Edwin. He suspected – rightly, as it turned out – that her invitation was for Fredi and Fredi alone.

Edwin went off, yawning, in the direction of the *Bulletin's* office on Montgomery Street, shoulders huddled under his round jacket against the cold, and Fredi, likewise feeling the chill from the cold wind that seemed to turn every exposed bit of flesh to leaden numbness, turned his footsteps toward Ma'am Pleasant's place, wondering what it was that she had set aside for him. He was hungry; hungry for a meal, and in any case, shelter from the cold.

As promised, the door around the back of her place was not barred, although the kitchen itself was dimly-lit. A single lantern, hanging from the center of the room, over a generous work-table, cast light on a single plate, covered with another, a basket of fresh biscuits, covered with a clean white napkin and a smaller plate, with a slice of buttermilk pie on it. But it was warm, redolent with the odor of good cooking; Fredi had not been in such a comfortable, home-like kitchen since the last time he had eaten a meal at the Becker ranch home-place.

"Ma'am Pleasant?" he called, from the doorway, as he closed it behind him. "Friedrich Steinmetz, I ..."

"You're very late," she called from further within the house. There was a distant murmur of male conversation, in another room and from behind closed doors. In a moment, Ma'am Pleasant appeared in the doorway, near invisible in her dark dress. She must have been done with cooking, for her apron was hanging from a hook by the inner door. "Go ahead, set yourself down at the table – but go ahead and bar the door. And you can take off your coat and hat – was it a barn that you were born in, *cher*?"

Grateful for the warmth and for the prospect of hot food, Fredi shed his jacket and hat, which Ma'am Pleasant took away, her skirts and petticoats rustling. He sank into the single wooden kitchen chair, thinking wistfully that was one of the things which he missed the most in this world of mostly men; the gentle susurration of a woman's petticoats and dress, stirring around her ankles as she moved. If there were a heaven on this earth, Fredi decided, it would be a well-appointed kitchen ruled by a woman who looked like an angel and cooked like a goddess, dispensing her bounty on poor, starving, cold mankind.

The top plate covered a ragout of beef and winter vegetables, sauced with a flavorful gravy, and the napkin sheltered some hot biscuits, already split and spread with butter, sweet cream butter which had already melted into them. Fredi ate ravenously, only half-wondering where Ma'am Pleasant had gone, for she left him alone in the kitchen. She had not returned, by the time he finished, wiping up the last savory scraps with a biscuit. Well, he decided, if Ma'am Pleasant fed Edwin like this, in return for some small scraps of information gleaned from goings-on at the Bulletin, he would gladly be her spy there as well. He applied himself to the slice of pie.

"Do you like it, *cher*?" Ma'am Pleasant's voice floated in, from the next room, and Fredi, raising his voice only a little, replied, "I do, Ma'am. I have not eaten so good since ... not in a year or so. My most sincere thanks for a fine supper ..."

In reply, Ma'am Pleasant giggled; an oddly girlish conceit in so formidable a woman. "Oh, *cher* Freddy, you need not be so formal as that. My name is Mary Ellen. It would please me, if you would call me by my real name."

"Yes, ma'am," Fredi said, and only with an effort recollected the meaning of what she had asked, so taken was he by the fact that she had gone so far in speech toward the sweet New Orleans purr. "Ma'am ... Mary Ellen. It does not seem fitting and polite to me."

As he finished the buttermilk pie, he shoved back the chair and stood up, wondering where Ma'am Pleasant could have possibly taken his coat and hat. For it was cold outside, bone-chilling-cold, and the cheap boarding-house where he and O'Malley stayed was a good walk distant.

She appeared in the doorway at that moment, a pale face above a pale draping of garment, her dark hair flowing in a river around her shoulders, free from the confines of pins and house-cap. "No, *cher* Freddy, darling p'tit Freddy; this would be fitting and polite, for one chosen to spend the night in my bed with me. Say it – my name, *cher* – my proper name."

"M…Mary Ellen," Fredi stammered, for Ma'am – for Mary Ellen Pleasant was clad in her wrapping gown, with nothing at all underneath it; not even her corset. The parting in the gown came apart, as she walked towards him. She was entirely naked underneath, pale and smooth as an egg; perfect, with breasts above and that enticing cleft below. She took his hand, and he did not resist, He brought his hand to her breasts, resting it on the flesh of her left breast, and purred, "There … this is what you desire, my darling p'tit Freddy, what most men dream of. Do you dream of me, *cher*? Answer true, for I am a voodooienne, and I will know if you lie…"

"I have … well not at night," Fredi confessed, wondering if she had put some kind of laudanum potion in the meal he had just eaten, for he felt as woozy and light in the head as if he had drunk too much of a powerful liquor. He also had no notion of what a voodooienne might be; possibly some kind of pagan priestess. "I have thought about you in the daytime … and I wondered what it would be like, since I have never bedded with a woman, ever before."

Her other arm snaked around the back of his neck, and she pulled him closer to her, whispering, "Then wonder no more, *cher*. Wonder no more."

Fredi spent most of the night in Ma'am Pleasant's bed, only departing an hour or two before dawn, feeling as if he had fallen into a spell, an enchantment cast over him. When he put on his clothes and boots again, fumbling for them in the dimness of her bedroom, and sitting on the side of the bed to pull them on, Ma'am Pleasant stirred, and whispered, "Freddy, p'tit – come back tonight at the same hour. You 'ave much still to learn …"

"Yes, Ma'—Mary Ellen," Fredi whispered. On an impulse, he leaned down, and dropped a brief kiss on her cheek. He heard the rustle of her laughter, and she added, "Maybe not so much, *cher.*"

He let himself out, and walked down the hill in something of a daze, wondering if he had truly dreamed the interlude with Mary Ellen Pleasant – that she had taken him to her bed, and they had done … things. Pleasurable things, which he had heard something about, but until this very night … No wonder Fauntly Bean was so often accused of letting his Nebuchadnezzar out for a romp. The sky was barely pale in the east, when he let himself into the room that he and O'Malley shared at the boarding house. O'Malley slept soundly, but Nipper stirred, lifted his head from where he slept at the foot of O'Malley's pallet, and regarded Fredi briefly, his sharp little eyes gleaming in the faint light sifting between the cracks in the wooden shutter that covered the window. Reassured that it was a familiar person, Nipper dropped his head back onto his paws. Setting his boots aside, Fredi slipped underneath the coarse blankets without taking off his coat. It was cold in the boarding house at night, not hear as warm as Ma'am Pleasant's finer establishment, but he fell asleep almost as soon as he settled on the pallet with a faint scrunching sound from the straw that it was stuffed with, and wondered if O'Malley would make any comment at his absence.

O'Malley didn't, and if Edwin looked askance at when he and Fredi sold the last of their copies of the Bulletin that evening, and Fredi let it drop that Ma'am Pleasant had promised him supper again, the boy kept whatever thoughts he had to himself. That night, the next, and the next after that, all passed as if in a dream, much like the first. Each morning, just before dawn, Fredi stole quietly from Ma'am – Mary Ellen's bed and returned to his own chilly quarters at the boarding house.

Only on the last morning, as he pulled on his boots, Mary Ellen slid from under the bedclothes. She stood, veiled only in the torrent of dark hair, and shadows in the room, saying quietly, "*Cher* Freddy, you should not return here tonight, for Thomas Bell returns from Sacramento today."

"He is your regular lover, then?" Fredi assumed this, but was stung by the abrupt dismissal.

"More than that. We are in business together, as well as partnering in the pleasures of the bed." Mary Ellen touched his face, a gentle caress – and kissed him softly, once on each cheek, and then on his lips. "Love has little to do with it. *Ma p'tit*, consider this last week a gift – my gift to you and to the women who will bed with you, the gift of pleasures between the sheets."

"I see," Fredi was still disappointed. "Then it's just as well that we shall start for the diggings in a week or so, now that spring has come."

Mary Ellen shook her head, and made a 'tsk' sound. "Do not be downcast, *cher*. Our time was always intended to be fleeting. I will not say goodbye, but only farewell until we meet again."

"Then I will say goodbye, for I don't believe that we shall," Fredi whispered, still heartsore, yet knowing that he really had no reason. They were ill-matched in every respect, and besides – she had her Mr. Bell.

And that evening, when he turned his footsteps towards the boarding house, instead of the street leading to Rincon Hill, it was to find O'Malley there, industriously picking out one of the cape hems of his old coachman's overcoat. He looked sharply up at Fredi, as if he might say something, but reconsidered.

After a moment, he said it anyway. "So, you have no urgent engagement tonight, boyo. That is good, for I believe we should leave soon for the mines. It is already the end of April – sure, and the snows should be melting in the foothills by now. I have already tendered my resignation, so that we may prepare for the journey."

"I will tell Mr. King of this," Fredi replied. Yes, at this moment, there was little to interest him, and just that very day, Mr. Casey, the editor of the *Bulletin's* rival newspaper had come into the Bulletin's office and berated Mr. King in a most abusive way; something to do with a story Mr. King had published about Mr. Casey being a convicted felon, back East. Fredi had paid little attention, as he and Edwin were gathering up the last copies for delivery.

"I am also considering young Edwin as one of our party," O'Malley continued, as Fredi pulled off his boots. "He says that he has talked to you with regard to joining us. I promised that I would talk it over with you. He is most resolute on setting out to the northern diggings, on the Yuba, saying that he knows of some promising locations along the middle fork."

"He knows more about mining gold than the two of us put together," Fredi didn't feel much like discussing it. Without the allure of Ma'am Pleasant night-time wiles, the feeling of threat in the city was undiluted; a storm about to break. As much as he liked Mr. King, the man's gadfly nature would make of him a lightening-rod when the storm did break, and Fredi wanted no part of that. "I think he would be a worthy partner, O'Malley."

"Good." Again, Fredi thought that O'Malley might speak of Ma'am Pleasant, but he didn't. Instead, he added, "Well, then – we'll tell him in the morning, shall we?"

Chapter 13 – To the Mines

The wagon packed high with supplies, a canvas tent and bedrolls, as well as a contraption that Edwin said was a 'cradle' O'Malley and Fredi finally departed from San Francisco on a foggy morning early in May. They took deck passage on a relatively comfortless and therefore cheap freight steamboat bound to Sacramento and beyond as far as Yuba City for the wagon, mules, and themselves. With some difficulty they urged the mules over a wide gangplank laid between wharf and the blunt prow of the boat, drawing the wagon after, and found an open space between the neat piles of fuel cordwood and bales of goods bound for the mines, which were stacked on the main deck. Edwin with Nipper in his arms, clung to a high perch on top of the cargo, as the side-wheel steamer threshed out into the bay, heading north toward Vallejo and the old territorial capital at Benicia, and from there into the tangled delta of the American River.

It was estimated they would be a week or so at this; a considerable savings in time over driving the wagon all the way. The patchwork heights of San Francisco and the forests of ships' masts in harbor vanished very soon in a billow of fog. Within a short distance, every surface was wetted with condensation, collecting in beads of moisture. The slight vibration of the mighty steam engine below deck shook rivulets of water from every slanting surface. It felt to Fredi like the beating of a mighty heart. O'Malley, the boys and dog huddled in blankets under the dripping wagon cover, and the mules stood miserable with their noses together.

"This is the first time I have ever been on a steam ship," Fredi's excitement at this new experience overcame the misery of passage across the open bay.

"I'm glad to be away from there, Fredi-boyo," O'Malley confessed. "Between murdering swine like that devil Cora, not to mention the fires and the constant pestilential weather ... I dinna care to stay a moment longer. There's a feeling in the city like a storm about to break – a dangerous mood, when honest, well-intentioned men are becoming fed to the back-teeth with corruption and vice. There's murder in the air, an' I want none of it."

"You too, O'Malley? Mr. King was always carrying a revolver since there were so many threats against him for what he printed in the *Bulletin*," Fredi nodded in agreement.

"It's not like there is any more law in the diggings," Edwin now said, morosely. "There are brigands and bandits and claim-jumpers a' plenty."

"For certain there are," O'Malley said, agreeably. "But they are few and go against the company of righteous men, an' they have not suborned the law to feather well their own nests. So, tell us, now – there are rich diggings in the hills between ... which river is it?"

"Between the middle and north forks of the Yuba River," Edwin nodded, rubbing the end of his nose with the back of his sleeve. "They called it Coarse Gold Hill, sometimes Pine Tree Diggings. It's far enough up into the mountains beyond Camptonville, to where the snow closes down the diggings in late fall."

"And you know of rich diggings because ..." O'Malley hinted broadly and Edwin replied, "I went with my ... with the Padgetts to those diggings, over three summers to their claim, after the cholera took my own family. Pa was a partner in the diggings with Mr. Padgett. Their claim on the Yuba has been left for months ..." and Edwin's pale, peaked face was adult in its adamantine determination. "But I know where the best and most promising part of the diggings lie and if we are the first to reclaim and stake our own claim ... this will be worth the journey. I promise you fellows." Edwin blushed, boy-like, and embraced Nipper even closer, as if for security, and Nipper, who above all else hated cold and wet with an uncharacteristic passion for a dog, licked the lad's cheek, and burrowed deeper into the shelter of the blanket wrapped around them both. Edwin continued, "You are both stout fellows and have been good friends to me, so a third each of the gold in this claim; that would be fair, would it not? And we are good friends, aren't we? Three in fortune and friendship, like the royal musketeers in that French novel of M. Dumas ... All for one and one for all?"

"We are indade, boyo," O'Malley answered, comfortably, "Although Fredi-lad and I have been true companions these many months, to admit another to our fellowship, especially a trusty fellow with knowledge of the mines, is a most providential occurrence. You have a skill, complimentary to mine and Fredi's. So you see, we shall get on very well, I believe. Even more when we get out from this pestilential fog. My oath upon it, lads – there is nothing to equal this fog and misery, not even in old Eire."

Over the days of their journey, as the river steamboat chugged across the wide reaches of the bay, and threaded through the tangle of waterways which comprised the delta, the fogs thinned to a brief mist at sunrise, tangled in the stands of tall tule reeds. The air seemed drier; often in the afternoons, Fredi thought that he could see a line of blue mountains looming on the distant horizon. The river ran broad and fair, the meadows on either hand appearing more as if a purpose-designed park. Horses, cattle, and deer browsed along the banks, seemingly without fear or apprehension.

"'Tis like a noble garden planned by the great Capability, around one of the great estates of Ireland," O'Malley was wont to comment. Water-birds stalked through the shallows, snow-white egrets who stood on long, stick-thin legs, pointing their beaks at the sky. Every aspect pleased the eye; Fredi wished that he had some skill at painting and drawing, like poor sickly Mr. Petri, a neighbor back in Gillespie

County; it would surely have helped to pass the time, as the lazy days of the river journey began to tell on him. This was the most time that Fredi had been inactive since departing the generous hospitality of the Carrillo rancho at the end of Gil Fabreaux' cattle drive.

All that he and Edwin must do of a day for chores was to supply green fodder and water for the mules. The steamboat master obligingly drew near a river bank where the grass grew lush and thick, setting a plank from deck to shore, where the two boys might scramble ashore once a day and scythe armloads of fresh grass. O'Malley smoked a leisurely pipe in the afternoons, with Nipper curled at his side. Edwin talked about gold, how to search for it, and what to look for in seeking – or 'color' as he called it. He brought out one of the shallow wash-pans, to demonstrate how to take a scoop of sand or earth, and gently wash water over it, until all the grains of dirt or gravel were gone, leaving only gold, if it were done correctly.

"A lot of work," Edwin warned them, yet again.

O'Malley and Fredi exchanged glances. "Aye, well – that is nothing new," O'Malley smiled in a genial manner and put aside his pipe.

Edwin added, "And a lot of luck, too. Standing in ice-cold water up to your knees all the day, from can't see to can't see, bending over a pan, or shoveling dirt into the cradle. I'll say this one thing, though – selling penny newspapers in the street is a holiday in comparison. But you'll find out, soon enough."

They knew that they were approaching Sacramento, some miles before seeing the ramble of houses at tall trees at the edge of the water on the morning of the third day; the haze of wood-smoke in the air, a pale dust-colored smudge in the blue sky above endless green meadows and tule-marshes, which marked the town as readily as any signpost.

"We'll be here for a night," the boat's pilot and master told them, as he edged the laden steamboat to a place on the waterfront, "Before we go on to Yuba City. I got cargo to off-load and take on more wood for the boilers. Spend the night on board, or spend it ashore, don't matter none to me. Just be back before we cast off, or else you'll have to swim upstream."

"We'll stretch our legs, an' see if we can afford a hot meal," O'Malley doffed his battered top-hat to the pilot and master, "And be back aboard, before three shakes of a lamb's tail, you may depend on it ... Although," he added in a lower voice to the boys and the ever-alert Nipper. "I will be glad to stretch my legs and partake of a hot meal."

They had been dining on hard-tack, cheese, hard-boiled eggs, dried fruit and pickles, since departing from San Francisco; comestibles taken from their store in the wagon. Fredi was heartily tired of it after three days, spoiled as he was from meals at Ma'am Pleasant's kitchen, and he knew that Edwin must be as well.

"I could set my teeth well into a supper of boiled or roasted beef," Fredi replied. "Let us walk around the town, and find ourselves one last excellent meal as well as whatever entertainment this place provides of a day. But O'Malley, we ought not to be too long about it," Fredi added, with a meaningful glance, "Or be lured into a gambling hell. Remember how we were cozened into an unwilling alliance with Fauntly Bean? That should not happen again, now that we are on the threshold of the mines."

"Boyo," O'Malley protested, with an expression of hurt upon his countenance. "I promise, on my word that I will be discrete and as careful as a mother with maiden daughters ..."

"We have a partnership and property with which to take a mind of," Fredi was adamant. "You have your skills, and I have mine – and one of mine is to never be lured into games of chance with strangers and bet more than I can afford."

"Aye, but you didn't avoid the bed of an enticing woman such as Mrs. Pleasant, could you, boyo?" O'Malley retorted and Fredi flushed beet-red.

The steamboat's crew threw out ropes, from fore and aft – ropes caught and made fast by men on shore throwing a single cast about a pair of bollards. The great wheels slowed in turning, drifting forward and a little sideways, until arrested in that small movement by the ropes. The mooring-ropes snapped taut, and the boat rocked gently for a moment, until the prow rope was loosed from the stout mooring bollards set into the wharf-side at regular intervals.

"Haul away!" cried one of the men on the dock, and his fellows bent their backs, hauling at one rope and then another, until the steamboat nestled alongside the wharf, bobbing gently in the current. A single gangplank crashed down, with a noise like muffled cannon-shot.

"The gateway to Golconda, lads," O'Malley remarked, as they set foot on shore, and each looked around. Fredi felt as if the solid wharf under his feet still bobbed and swayed, as the boat had done. Sacramento, built on relatively flat land, did not present nearly the overwhelming prospect to a new arrival that San Francisco did. The buildings lining the other side of the docks were simple of plaster over brick, of sawn lumber with some small ornamentation, mostly of two stories tall, widely set apart and interspersed with tall trees, with an occasional church-steeple, flag pole, shot-tower, or tall chimney looming in the distance above the lower rooftops.

It all looked a pleasant and well-appointed city, although there was an unexpected bustle at the dockside; prosperous shop-keepers and workmen in calico shirt-sleeves moving purposefully toward the center of the city. There seemed to be a good-sized crowd. Drawn by curiosity, O'Malley and the two boys followed, since everyone seemed to be going that way, anyway.

"What is the excitement, then?" O'Malley courteously doffed his battered top-hat in the direction of an especially ragged miner, bearded like a bear and as large as one, his trousers and round jacket well-daubed with mud, testifying both to his profession and the haste with which he had come to Sacramento. "It is that we are only passing through this lovely city, and wish not to appear giving offense, d'ye see?"

"A hanging," the miner answered, gruff, yet with a gentlemanly courtesy which belied his rough appearance. "A claim-jumping, robbing, murdering scum – tried fair and square two days ago, for murders done last fall at the Pine Tree Diggings on the Yuba."

O'Malley placed his hat and hand on his breast, an appropriate expression of sorrow on his face. "'Tis sorrowful I am indade to hear of murders, but satisfied to hear that justice is being carried out …"

"Who is being hanged?" That was Edwin, his peaked face tense with agitation at O'Malley's side. "Pine Tree on the Yuba? Tell me, who did he murder?"

"Say, boy, did you not read the newspapers?" The miner scratched his bristly cheek and regarded Edwin with mystification.

"No, I only delivered them," Edwin retorted. "I did not read every article."

"He went by the name of Henry Wade. He and his pards murdered Joss Padgett and his whole family last fall, just as the diggings were closing down for the winter. Then he had a falling out with his gang – one they found in a sluice with Wade's knife in his back, and the other he shot in a duel in the streets of Camptonville – that one died, but not before he confessed it all on his deathbed. That murdering scum – there wasn't but five respectable women in the whole of the Yuba River diggings and that bastard," the miner spat feelingly into the mud at their feet, "Had to go and kill one of 'em. They never found the girl's body. Only the Almighty knows what he did to that poor child, after what they did to Mrs. Padgett."

Edwin turned as pale as death; even his lips were gray. "How ... how did they catch Wade?"

The miner spat again. "The rotten son of a whore had Padgett's watch and gold fob. He tried to sell it to a man here in Sacramento who recognized it and knew Wade for the murdering scum that he is. Boy, you sound like you got a personal interest in this hanging."

"I do," Edwin nodded, still gray-lipped. "Mr. Padgett was a partner to my father in the diggings and took me in when I became an orphan."

"Then you came fortuitous," the miner growled, looking even more like a bear. "But you better hurry, if you want to see justice being done. The hanging's set for nine o'clock. They been a' building the gallows ever since the jury pronounced. They know there's be a big crowd, coming to see Henry Wade hanged high."

"I don't want to miss it," Edwin nodded again, still pale but with a steely tone to his voice that Fredi found quite unsettling. So, obviously, did O'Malley, who looked between them both, before replacing his hat on his head.

"Boyo, while sure I am in the favor of justice administered rightly upon the wicked, I am not one for taking it lightly as entertainment. 'Tis a sober and serious thing, a life taken. While I would attend to console a friend unjustly punished, to support him in his last moments before facing God as the great judge and law-giver of all ..."

"I don't want to miss it, O'Malley" Edwin replied, adamant. "I want to watch, as close as I can. I would watch him die, strangling slowly as the noose tightens, just as he and his friends murdered Mr. and Mrs. Padgett."

"Then you shall!" The bearlike miner clapped his own ragged cloth cap on his head, took Edwin by the shoulder, and bellowed to the crowd around. "Here – give way, give way! Here's a lad who's kin to the Padgetts of Pine Tree Diggings, come to see justice done, and a righteous sentence enacted on the guilty! Make way, make way!"

He was a large man, and a loud one. With Edwin's narrow shoulder in his grip, he shouldered ahead through the crowd like a fast clipper parting the ocean waves. O'Malley and Fredi followed in the bearlike miner's wake, little liking the prospect of witnessing a hanging at close quarters, but loath to abandon their young partner in a rowdy crowd gathered in the streets of a strange city. The crowd grew thicker and thicker in the street as they followed, into the heart of the city, and a wide cross-road which had been blocked to wagon traffic. There was a tall gallows there; a platform and a framework of heavy beams put up at the center-point, from which, ominously, the rope and noose dangled above a tall and narrow bench. In every window and from the top of every rooftop overlooking the crossroads there was as many crowing in – perhaps as many as thronged close to the gallows-foot.

All of this played out under a faultlessly-blue sky, lightly sprinkled with a few cotton-drift clouds, in the shade of poplar trees newly-trimmed with pale green leaves of spring, which trembled in the slightest breeze, a breeze which also blew pale tufts of poplar blossom everywhere. The bearlike miner delivered them to the very bottom of the set of steps leading to the gallows; here would the prisoner be led, close enough that they would see him, as close as they might touch him, if the hanging-party allowed, so close that the prisoner could look on them.

O'Malley, holding Nipper close in his arms, to spare the little dog from the press of many heavy feet, groaned under his breath, "Fredi-boyo, I like this not..." as the bearlike miner looked down on them all with an expression of satisfaction.

"There you are, lad. Enjoy the view. Pray for the bastard's soul if you must and for the souls of those so piteously slain at his hand, most definitely."

"I will," Edwin's voice retained that adamantine determination. "And thank you. Sir, may I know your name?"

"James Fennimore," the miner nodded, with an unexpectedly courtly turn of courtesy. "Some call me ol' Verginny Finny, on account of where I came from – Albemarle in the Old Dominion."

"There is no gentleman like a Southren gentleman," Fredi murmured, recalling the words of Mrs. Eberly, back in Galveston, but those words and any other which might have been said between them all were lost in a roar from the crowd, gathering and pressing closer, closer. Several men were determinedly forcing a way through the crowd, and in the press of it, Fredi and O'Malley were swept aside from Edwin and Ol' Verginny.

"Make a way, make a way!" came a stentorian call. As a way opened up, and remained open, Fredi found himself on one side of it, at the very foot of the stair to the gallows looking across at Edwin and Ol' Verginny on the other.

"Aye, they're doing it the way it was down in the Old Country," O'Malley observed to Fredi. He was taller, so that he could see over most of the crowd. "A foine thing, tradition. They're having him to ride on his coffin. Nothing like concentrating th' attention of the condemned on his fate. An' the consolation of divine writ, for all the good it may do an unrepentant sinner."

The man to be hanged, Wade who had murdered a family of gold-seekers on the Yuba, was a tall man, a real ruffian in appearance, sitting high atop his coffin, resting on the bed of a tumbrel-cart drawn by a single horse. The horse was led by a man who held a heavy fowling piece over his other arm. From the reaction of the crowd, Fredi was given to know this was the sheriff of Sacramento. Wade's arms were firmly bound by ropes at his back. He was coatless, with the collar of his shirt unbuttoned and loose around his throat. The prisoner was attended by an earnest-looking young man in clerical black and reading from a prayer book. Wade looked out on the crowd with a defiant sneer on his face, paying no attention to the minister with his book. Other men with well-polished weapons in their hands, or in holsters at their belts walked alongside the cart.

The horse drawing the cart halted at the foot of the stairs; the prisoner, with his hands behind him, stumbled in getting down from the cart, directly in front of Edwin and Ol' Verginny. One of his guards and the minister caught and set him on his feet. In that moment, Fredi saw Edwin's lips move. The boy was saying something to the condemned man, on a tone of voice too low to hear in the crowd; an exchange which likely no one else could hear, or would take note of in the boisterous gathering. Whatever was said had a galvanic effect on Wade. As he was led up those few steps, his head turned, looking back over his shoulder toward Edwin. Fredi could see that the sneer was entirely wiped from Wade's face, replaced with an expression of abject horror, as if he had suddenly seen the face of the Devil himself.

Now, the sheriff asked for silence. The clamor around the gallows died away to a murmur, as if of an ocean storm diminishing a gentle susurration of waves on the shore. No, the condemned man shook his head.

"No last words," O'Malley noted with mild regret. "I suppose it is because he is not a poet of an Irishman. All our love-songs are sad and all our last words are noble. Alas, he did not look as a man with very much to say of note. There they go, w' a sack over his head. I think they are not going to prolong this, Fredi-boyo, and I approve.

'Tis always been in my mind that Christians making a raree-show of a hanging is very like the blood-games in Roman times with the holy martyrs, or of when they burned witches and Jews alive."

"My father would agree with you," Fredi confessed. "I have no great liking for a spectacle either, but this is justice. If the laws of a country have it to hang a man for the crime of murder, then at least we should not be so squeamish as to look away, or insist that such punishments be done meanly and out of sight. That's the cowards' way of demanding a hard task without dirtying your own hands."

Fredi was thinking how curious it was, that the condemned man Wade was still looking in the direction of young Edwin, even after they put the sack over his head. Edwin's countenance reflected only a kind of grim satisfaction. Perhaps he had been to hangings before, Fredi reasoned, as the sheriff and his assistants half-lifted, half boosted Wade, unresisting, to stand upright on the tall bench, as they secured the rope on his neck and pulled it taut.

There was a gasp from the crowd, as the sheriff tipped over the bench with a mighty heave – so narrow that it toppled over at once. Wade dropped, kicking and writhing spasmodically, a struggle which diminished by degrees over the space of ten or fifteen minutes. The matter in his bowels and bladder dripped out onto the boards of the scaffold from his trouser-bottoms and then he hung there, limp and unmoving, a hooded scarecrow, swaying gently to and fro, while the crowd roared a final acclaim.

"Your justice is done, Fredi-boyo," O'Malley sounded as if he had been holding his breath. "And are you content with it?"

"I suppose that I am," Fredi admitted. He was not certain what to think of this; was O'Malley right in not wanting a spectacle of death for public amusement, or his father's implacable notion of justice being the right of every man to witness? The crowd began to wander away, although he supposed that the idlers among them, as well as those who had come some distance to watch the spectacle would remain long enough to witness the lifeless body being cut down and unceremoniously coffined. "Is this enough entertainment for us, O'Malley? I have suddenly found that my appetite is gone."

"Young Edwin's also," O'Malley remarked. It was true, for the younger boy had turned even paler in the face and he was vomiting at the foot of the gallows steps. Ol' Verginny the minor had already vanished back into the crowd from which he had sprung. "Are ye all right, boyo?"

"I'm fine," Edwin replied, wiping his mouth on the back of his hand; so pale that he looked green and still unwell. "Although I think that I will return to the boat. I am not really that hungry."

"There are some things that will take your appetite away," O'Malley replied. Quite astonishing to Fredi, he was much the cheerier of the three, not counting Nipper. "Now, take the little doggie with you, and guard our wagon. Count on us returning to the boat before dark, boyo. Perhaps you will have more of a liking for a good supper by then."

"Aye," Edwin answered, although he still looked shaky as he snapped his fingers and whistled to Nipper. The two of them were soon lost to sight in the scattering crowd, and O'Malley looked after them for along moment.

"For someone so keen to watch a hanging," Fredi ventured, as they walked along in the other direction, "He certainly had little stomach for it. I wonder why?"

"Aye, 'tis a puzzle," O'Malley replied, thrusting his hands deep into his pockets. "But I do not think the lad was so much keen on a hanging, as he was filled with hate for the man being hanged."

"I didn't see that," Fredi began and O'Malley shook his head.

"Ah, because you are yet an innocent in a world y'see as just and fair, for the most. Edwin now – I could see it in his face. He hated

Wade, with such passion as he would have volunteered to set the noose around his neck with his own hands. I canno' think why, unless it is that he was fonder of these Padgetts than he has let on … or that he might have been led into crime by Wade and his scurvy crew, and lived to repent of it. Ah, well; not our business, now that it is done. But mark my words, boyo, there may be more to this affair than we think."

Chapter 14 – Summer in the Diggings

Fredi and his two partners debarked at Yuba City after more than a week of poking along in the slow steamboat. The unsettling interval of the hanging at Sacramento had nearly faded from their minds in the excitement of approaching the fabled diggings after so long and arduous a journey. Edwin, recovering his spirits after witnessing the hanging, continued to enliven the journey with discourses on searching for gold, and on the most expeditious means of extracting it from wherever it might be – among river-gravel, or in the crevices of granite rocks.

"Likely there are many who would say that the North Fork is pretty well mined out, but Pa … Mr. Padgett thought it worth the trouble to winter over, to keep the claim, or to work a new one upstream, rather than just follow the rush to a new strike. He was pretty certain of it and so am I," Edwin said, when O'Malley questioned him closely about his intention of returning to the stretch of river at Pine Tree Diggings. "There was always enough and then some," he added, with touching earnestness. "At every likely bend. But we may have to pack in by mule beyond Downieville, if the road is no better … and it gets rougher, the farther we go."

The mountains loomed ahead of them; piling up in distant blue and lavender slopes, the very topmost still lightly touched the last winter snows. The scent of pine-woods breathed on every errant wind and to Fredi, every streamlet promised to be paved in gold.

"What are we to do with the wagon, then?" he asked.

As it turned out, Edwin was right about having to pack in all their supplies and gear, but O'Malley found an Irish storekeeper in Downieville, whom he had never met before but claimed to have come from Balleymena. The shopkeeper fell on O'Malley in voluble joy, the Irish coming out so thick in his speech that neither Fredi or Edwin could understand him.

"Likely that Con Reilly and I are cousins, several times removed through our mothers, for his sainted mother and mine were both Kellys from Castledown," O'Malley said, cheerful as a cricket. "He has struck a bargain with me on the strength of that relation; in exchange for the use of our wagon and mules during the summer, he will see that all our trash an' traps are packed entire to the Pine Tree Diggings, through the good offices of his friend in the mule-freighting concern … who is likely another cousin."

"Can you trust this man Reilly?" Fredi asked, warily.

O'Malley chuckled. "Of course, Fredi-boyo; Con's my cousin from Ballymena, and a good Catholic, as well."

Fredi sighed in deep exasperation and looked across at Edwin. "This is the man who unthinkingly accepts invitations to games of change with strangers in saloons. Is it no wonder he needs a keeper?"

Edwin grinned back, in delight – almost the first time that Fredi had observed a wholly unguarded expression on the boy's face. "We'll do, between us," Edwin replied, wholly confident. "And we are almost there." His face lost a certain degree of confidence, as O'Malley went to commiserate with his countrymen and arrange the disposition of the wagon and their own mules. Fredi briefly wondered why; and not for the first time. Edwin sometimes seemed as mysterious and unforthcoming as O'Malley did, when it came to background and personal experience. Was he himself the only honest and forthright person of the three in this partnership? Perhaps, Fredi concluded – but then, he was also the only one of them well-armed and a fair shot. The Colt made a considerable weight in the holster at his side, but not as much as the one looted from him by the bandits on the road from San Bernardino.

They set out from the ramble of a town that was Downieville – a town longer than wide, a ramble of stone-built, log and sawn lumber structures, all crammed into a narrow valley where two streams met, and overlooked by heights from which the trees had been removed, as if by some vast straight-razor. Some of the buildings were very new and fine, for apparently Downieville was of some years' existence, as towns in the gold country went, and possessed the additional honor of being the county seat. But the territory beyond was increasingly mountainous. Edwin was right; they could not have taken the wagon all the way to that stretch of the Yuba known as the Pine Tree Diggings. It was not, so O'Malley and Fredi were given to understand, a proper settlement, although if it proved rich enough, there was always that possibility. There was also the possibility of the road being improved, but until that day a pack-train of mules would make do. There were other hopeful Argonauts on the track toward the higher mountains; men in rough clothes; the poorest of them bearing only a heavy pack on their own bent backs. With a train of eight of Reilly's mules, every one so fully laden that more of their burden was visible than the mule itself, Fredi, O'Malley and Edwin counted as the most fortunate.

"We should be able to remain all summer, with what we have brought," Edwin promised. "And into fall – until the first snows fall."

"And by then, we will all be rich men," O'Malley promised expansively. Fredi thought again of how he would return to Texas, and pay Carl back the money for the cattle. This was a very agreeable contemplation and he relished his imagining for the remainder of that day. They camped that night in a small sheltered draw, picketing the mules by the waterside, lulled to sleep by a combination of weariness, the sound of running water, and the gentle tinkling of mule bells. Only Edwin seemed subdued, as if he moved under a private cloud of misery.

Toward the end of the second day, the mountains shouldered in on either side of the river. On the farther side of the ravine, the river described a gentle bend through a level meadow, which surrounded a small eminence which to Fredi somewhat looked like a kneeling woman with her skirts spread around her. A single tall pine tree, half-dead and gone silvery with weathering but still as straight as a ship's mast crowned the hill. Here the river spread into shallows, and the last of the afternoon sun sparkled upon the running water. A rough oblong of logs notched at the corners – the lower walls of a rough miner's cabin marked last year's diggings at Pine Tree. This ramshackle place had been roofed in some previous summer with canvas, which now hung from the rafters in tattered shreds.

"This is the place," Edwin said. Fredi noticed that Edwin looked very deliberately away from the ruined structure. "I b'lieve we have arrived in good time, so that we may stake our claim first of all and in the most promising part. This stretch was worked over pretty well last summer, so I doubt if there is much to be found, unless by digging into the hill. We should move a little farther and set up our camp just where the river bends north-east. Tomorrow, I'll see where color comes up strongest and that's where we'll set the cradle."

In the night – so dark a night that Fredi could barely see his hand before his face, he was wakened by Edwin; the boy cried out once, so loud that Fredi woke out of profound sleep. They had stretched their plain canvas shelter in a level place between a fallen tree, and a steep bank. It would not do for much longer than a night or two for they were in haste for some kind of shelter.

"Wake up," Fredi reached across and shook Edwin's shoulder. "You're having a bad dream. D'you want to frighten the mules?" He spoke in German at first, forgetting where he was, thinking he was a child again, and it was Johann with the bad dream. The younger boy woke with a gasp, and a choked cry of, "Don't touch me!" and struck out blindly at Fredi with the full force of his fist. That fist landed full on Fredi's face; it hurt. Fredi yelled as pain shot though his skull like a lightning-bolt.

"Stop that, you dummy!" Fredi shouted and launched from his own blankets onto the younger boy, pinning Edwin by the shoulders in his own bedroll with his own weight. Edwin fought him with frantic energy, hampered by the heavy quilts, and it turned into a blind tussle in the pitch-dark, Fredi shouting and Edwin sobbing, until O'Malley struck a patent Lucifer against his boot-sole and lit the single candle in an iron miner's candlestick driven into the earth bank.

"What's all this, then?" O'Malley demanded, while Nipper peeked out from under O'Malley's great-coat, piled at the foot of his bedroll, the dog's eyes gleaming in the dim candle-light.

"He was having a nightmare," Fredi replied, regardless of the blood streaming from his nose and Edwin thrashing about, even with Fredi's full weight braced against the younger boy's shoulders. "And when I tried waking him, he hit me!"

"Fredi-boyo, it's the nightmare speaking. Let him go," O'Malley urged him again, and Fredi sat back on his heels with a grunt.

"I didn't mean to," Edwin sobbed. "I'm sorry, Freddy! I dreamed that someone was trying to kill me."

"They say that if you want to wake a sleeper during a bad dream, you should shake their foot," O'Malley crooned. "Fredi-boyo, here's my handkerchief. Edwin, 'tis lucky you are, then, for our Fredi has a temper when he is roused. Say again that you are sorry; for wakening us all and frightening the poor little doggie. Go to sleep again, and dream of a river of gold – a lovely river, with water as clear as diamonds – and trees by that river, with trunks of ivory – yes, ivory branches, too, and leaves of emeralds …" Fredi, still simmering over the pain of his bleeding nose, took the handkerchief and crawled back into his disarrayed blankets, while Edwin sniffled in misery and

O'Malley blew out the candle. But O'Malley kept talking in the dark, weaving with his voice a spell of wonders and marvels, and Fredi drifted away into sleep, only a little rattled in knowing that he and O'Malley were about to spend a summer in the diggings, in the company of a boy who had nightmares about someone trying to kill him. "He hits me again," Fredi's last coherent thought before he dropped into billowy gray clouds of sleep, "And I might be tempted to kill him for real. But Nipper likes him, so I suppose that I won't."

The next morning proved to be the pattern for many another morning, through that long summer; Edwin went to the river-edge with the broad-brimmed pan, and scooped up a pan of river-gravel, sand and water. Crouching on his heels in the shallow water, he began agitating the pan so that the water and gravel swirled in a circle. He tilted the pan at the water's surface, as the water continued swirling, allowing water to sweep away a little of the gravel and sand. O'Malley and Fredi watched, breathless with anticipation.

"Gold is heavy," Edwin said, as earnest as a professor giving a lecture. "It will settle to the bottom of the pan. Don't ever slop the sand and gravel out; just let the water sweep it off, layer by layer. By the time you have a spoonful of sand left, you ought to see the gold – if there is any color in this stretch. I am bound and certain there is."

"How much can we claim of this riverbank?" Fredi asked anxiously.

"Only as much as we can work, the three of us," Edwin answered. "I think there was someone working this claim around mid-summer, but they abandoned it after a while, upon hearing stories of richer strikes. If you stop working a claim … then it's up for grabs. So … one of us must always be here on the claim."

"Aye, that's enough of a reason to take partners," O'Malley nodded sagely. "So – if this is promising enough, we set up camp and assemble the cradle?"

"That's the plan," Edwin dipped the pan under the water and let the slight motion scoop away all but a trifling smear of sand. "You see? There it is! Gold – enough to be worth setting up on this claim. I thought I might have to pan up and down this stretch for hours."

"You have the fortunate eye, boyo," O'Malley remarked, "And we'll be rich men, in the twinkling of an eye, that's for certain!" He and Fredi looked over the boy's shoulder, hardly daring to believe; but yes, gleaming in the dark sand in the water at the bottom of the pan were half a dozen bright globules, as bright and sunny as the edge of the sun, peeping just now over the shoulder of the hill to the east, and outlining the eldritch shape of the tall, half-dead pine tree upon it.

Edwin grinned at them in triumph and relief. "Perhaps not rich, but at least fortunate," he allowed. On that happy note, they went to mark their claim, set up a more permanent camp and assemble the rocker, in happy expectation of a fortune awaiting them, at the edge of a river running out of the mountains of California – where there was perhaps, a single great cliff of gold, crumbling into grains and pebbles of pure gold and scattering into the streams and rivers of California.

That single day would be one which Fredi would remember, long afterwards; remember for being a relatively pleasant one, the first day of a series of days in a summer spent performing back-breaking and rather boring labor, in all weather, much of it slopping about knee-deep in ice-cold river water, bringing shovelfuls of sand and river-gravel into the cradle, following that with bucket after bucket of water scooped from the same source, while one or the other of his partners gently rocked the cradle, back and forth and the other emptied out the top-sieve of gravel as it accumulated. Day after day of this, while the sun burned down on them, and their feet and legs grew chilled and numbed from the water. They tried water-proofing their boots with applications of beeswax against the water with only mixed success. Against the sun, they set up a length of canvas stretched between four poles cut from the spindly trees which remained on the hillside above, and labored on – from dawn to dusk, whenever it was bright enough to see the pure yellow gleam of gold, caught against the baffles of the cradle, and in the fold of canvas underneath. Even in the soaking rain they worked, pausing only for meals.

Edwin turned out to be the best cook of them all; which was fortunate, as they were continually hungry. The purchase of the square metal camp stove which O'Malley had championed in San Francisco and which Fredi had not thought necessary, proved to be a sensible and convenient provision in the end. It was often cold at night in the mountains, and carrying the heated stove into the shelter of their tent provided warmth as well as a means of cooking their simple meals, in which camp-bread, dried meat, beans, bacon, canned oysters and dried fruit pies figured heavily.

O'Malley insisted on a day of rest on Sundays, to which Edwin agreed readily and Fredi with some reluctance.

"The more that we work, the sooner we can leave here with our fortunes," he argued, and O'Malley shook his head.

"No, Fredi-boyo – we must take one day of rest in every seven, lest we become prisoners of our own ambition. It will kill us, to work every day from dark to dark."

"The gold will still be here," Edwin agreed. "It's not as if it is running away on legs, after all."

Fredi assented, although as the Sundays passed, he was not always averse to going down to the waterside and panning a round or two of gravel and sand on those days of designated rest, just to relieve the tedium. The finding of a few nuggets of gold – usually only the size of a pin-head, but now and again approximating a distorted pea – never palled. He tried hunting, but found eventually that all the game had been frightened away, especially as the Pine Tree Diggings filled with other gold-seekers. These men were as hard-working, even as obsessed as Fredi and his partners but also rowdy, much given to coarse language and even coarser amusements such as firing off their weaponry in the general direction of any wildlife seen moving, no matter how distant. No wonder everything but large birds soaring on the thermals high above the river canyon were frightened away.

O'Malley passed Sundays resting, and reading in the shade of the tent – whatever materiel came his way, from tattered novels, even more tattered magazines and newspapers diminished to the texture of tissue paper and visiting with other gold-seekers who set up claims on either side of the river, up and down. At midsummer, they were overtaken by horrific news; Mr. King was reported to have been shot down like a dog in the street by his mortal enemy, Mr. Casey. Fredi and Edwin were alike shaken by this news, which came to them through a much-thumbed copy of *The Alta California.* Mr. King had been carried to his home, and although attended by the best doctors, had died there of his wounds.

"I can't believe it!" Fredi exclaimed, and Edwin shook his head, saying, "I can. Mr. King riled up plenty of folk. He didn't believe in backing down." Edwin was reading faster than Fredi, his peaked face gone all somber. "He loved him a good fight – and was never happier than when he got it. And he hated the meanness and corruption, the way that there was one set of laws for Broderick and his friends, and another for everyone else."

"What did they do to Mr. Casey?" Fredi's outrage was undimmed. Mr. Casey had so many powerful friends it seemed likely that he would escape justice, just as the gambler Charles Cora had for shooting the marshal.

"They hung him," Edwin replied, and expression of awe dawning on his face. "Cora, too. After a fair trial by the Committee of Vigilance. Guess Cora's fancy woman couldn't do nothing with that jury. It says there that the Committee asked for a meeting the day after Mr. King was shot ... and so many men of good character signed on – they had hundreds armed and under military orders. There wasn't nothing the sheriff and the jailkeeper could do when the representatives of the committee showed up with four companies and a cannon pointed at the jailhouse door, and asked very politely for Casey and Cora to be handed over ..."

"What else?" Fredi lagged far behind Edwin in deciphering the tiny print of the *Alta California* very slowly, since it was only his second language and he had never been much of one for books anyway.

"They sent word out that certain other men had best leave San Francisco or face the same trial and noose. It seems that many took that warning to heart ... and San Francisco is suddenly quite peaceful... or it was, at the time of this issue." Edwin shook his head, and O'Malley puffed at his pipe and observed sagely,

"Ah, then – it was a good time to leave from that city when we did – especially as the animus of Mr. Casey might have spilled on the pair of you instead of poor Mr. King as it did."

"I'd like to think that I might have been able to protect him," Fredi protested, and O'Malley sighed.

"Fredi-boyo, a man's fate is already written in his stars – there is nothing that a poor mortal might do to revise it."

Fredi disagreed, but held his silence, and they did not speak of the matter again.

In general, Edwin avoided other company on a Sunday, preferring solitary hikes to the top of the bald hill with the towering half-dead pine atop it, although sometimes Nipper accompanied the boy. On a Sunday in early September, on one of his fruitless attempts to hunt, Fredi took that same path toward the top of the hill, appreciating when he reached it, the peerless view of the diggings below, although he did note that Edwin appeared a bit flustered, when he arrived, panting from the climb, with the shotgun from the wagon over his arm.

"Nice look-out!" he said to Edwin, who was sitting at the roots of the pine tree with Nipper curled at his feet. Nipper, dozing contentedly in the sunshine, looked at Fredi with sleepy eyes. Seeing a friend, he closed them and returned to whatever dog-dreams gave him contentment.

"Yes; you can see just about anything from up here," Edwin replied. The boy was sitting on a broad root, one of many which sank into the crest of that hill, gripping into the earth like a tick clinging to flesh. The dirt at his feet was tumbled, as if Edwin had been poking it with one of the long rusty iron rods from an abandoned cook-place along the played-out part of river. The other miners grumbled that the lower diggings had been picked clean of placer gold, although there was a party tunneling into the slopes across and above from the abandoned cabin which they had passed on first arriving at Pine Tree. The miners left holes that at this distance resembled prairie dog burrows. But no one among the new arrivals had claimed the ruined square of logs, not even as an impromptu saloon. The reason was that it had been where the Padgett family had been held hostage and murdered. A miner who had worked a claim farther up the river had let drop that information early in the season and word spread. Thereafter, everyone avoided the place as if it were haunted. Fredi would not have been surprised to learn that it was. Puffing from the exertion of the climb, Fredi sank down onto another root to rest.

Edwin left off prodding at the damp earth with that rusty iron rod and looked straight at Fredi, demanding, "Why did you follow me up here?"

"I'm not," Fredi replied, wondering why the boy seemed so edgy. "I was just curious. You come up here all the time on Sunday. There's no gold this far up the mountain, so you must be walking all this way to look at the view. I just wanted to see what you were looking at, that's all."

"It's none of your business," Edwin looked positively thunderous. He had exactly the same expression on his face that his sister Liesel's eldest daughter had when she pouted; which to be fair, didn't happen very often.

"It is, too," Fredi said, newly irked. "We're partners and why shouldn't I come and look at the view, if you think so much of it?" Just to bait the younger boy, Fredi set the shotgun aside, and made every appearance of taking his time and relishing the view of Pine Tree Diggings on a Sunday afternoon. "You can see every part of the diggings from here. Look, down by the river, there's O'Malley, washing his socks. And I could toss a pebble down into that old ..."

The certainty of the conviction that came to Fredi in that moment was like flash of lightning, a sudden burst of illumination. He knew it for a certainty, as certain as the sun coming up every morning in the east. "Your name isn't Blaine," he said, quietly after the moment of astonishment had passed. "It's Padgett. Your family lived in that place, not the family of your Pa's partner. They never died of the cholera, they were murdered by that Wade that we saw hanged in Sacramento. You lived there while your father worked his claim."

If Edwin had been as white as a linen sheet after watching the hanging, he was several degrees paler now. "How did you guess?" His voice trembled a little.

Fredi shrugged. "I just knew … and you've all but admitted it now." Fredi was rather proud of his newfound perspicuity. He had never been the one for brains, for seeing parts of a strange puzzle, putting them together, and making unerring deductions. That was more his father and his brother's aptitude.

"I guess I did," Edwin admitted, with a little sigh of relief, and they sat in silence for some moments, while Nipper twitched in his sleep as if he dreamed of chasing rabbits.

"How did you get away from Wade and all?" Fredi asked, genuinely curious.

From what he and O'Malley gathered from the talk in Sacramento after the hanging, Wade and four ruffians had come to the Padgett cabin when nearly all the other miners had departed ahead of winter storms. The gang he led were convinced Joss Padgett had taken a fortune from his claim over the summer and kept it somewhere close by. They took Padgett's wife and children hostage and tortured them, trying to force him into revealing where he had concealed it. The accounting of what they had done to Mrs. Padgett were told in whispers, by which Fredi deduced that they must have treated her in the same manner that Comanche raiders commonly treated white woman captives. That was ugly; in Fredi's opinion this alone justified hanging Wade. Wade's gang had also made a practice of waylaying miners heading home from the diggings to rob and murder. One of Wade's companions had confessed so on his deathbed, testimony that led Wade to the gallows.

"I wasn't here," Edwin explained, his peaky countenance shadowed by remembered grief and regret. "I was in Downieville. They sent me there. I was … one of the errands I was tasked with was to find additional lodgings for Ma and my little brother. Pa was planning to winter out on the claim with my brother John. There were supplies in plenty; Pa and John were accustomed to winter in the mountains. He was certain about the claim – didn't want to give it up through not working it. The trail was still open – not above six or ten inches of snow fallen, although there are storms which will bury a cabin in snow over the roof. I was to send one last pack-train of supplies to Pa, and on the return journey, they were to bring Ma and Sammy down to spend the winter in Downieville. Instead ..." Edwin gulped, although his eyes remained quite dry. "There was a party of miners, from the Reis mine away up the river from Pine Tree at Sierra City. They came down the river and stopped at our place. It was nearly night and a storm brewing. Wade ... well, he lied when they found him there, instead of at his place of business in Downieville. He lost his nerve once he saw they didn't believe him. Wade drew his pistol ..." Edwin gulped. "He couldn't stop them seeing what they saw ... He tried to get them to join in with him. They wouldn't, o'course. They were rough men, but decent – just as most of them are, in the mines. Wade boasted of what he could do to any Padgett kin, to make them tell him about Pa's grubstake. The miners from Sierra City ... they brought the bodies down to be buried decent, an' to prove what they said about Wade. Until then, everyone thought that Wade was a law-abiding man."

"What happened then?" Fredi seriously wanted to know. Yes, Mama had died on the bark *Apollo* – but he and Johann still had Vati, their sisters, and Liesel's husband. They had not been left suddenly alone and orphans in a chaotic world. "How did you finish up in San Francisco?"

"I was sent there by friends who feared for me," Edwin replied, with a small sideways grin, but amusement did not reach his eyes. "They had intended that I should take passage on the next packet-boat to go East, back to my kin in St. Louis, out of danger. But I had a different notion..."

"You wanted to come back to Pine Tree and work your father's claim." Fredi finished the thought, already leaping ahead, on the strength of his previous insight. "You couldn't do it by yourself, so you spun a tale to trick us into going along."

"Something like that," Edwin confessed, with something of a crestfallen expression. "It's a promising claim. We've pulled enough good color out of it, so you can't say I lied about that, Freddy. You and O'Malley are honest fellows. I was certain you would agree to be partners, and I needed your help. You were going to the mines anyway; it's not like I had to convince you. You could have gone anywhere else and done worse for yourselves without my help."

It sounded as if the boy was trying to justify himself, and Fredi wasn't going to have any of it. "You're right; we were going to the diggings. You didn't have to tell us a pack of lies, as if you didn't trust us at all."

"I wasn't certain if I could trust anyone," Edwin replied, his expression desolate. "Not even you. I had to come back here, not just for the claim, and I couldn't do it alone."

"What was worth telling us a pack of lies?" Fredi snapped. So angry at being fooled so readily, he would have left the Pine Tree claim right then and there. Edwin looked at him, suddenly solemn and penitent.

"Pa's cache of gold," he answered. "That Wade killed for. That's what I had to come back for, and not to let any know."

"Your father's grubstake?" Fredi felt as if he had fallen from a good height and had the breath knocked out of him. "Hidden somewhere in that old cabin?"

"No, of course not there," Edwin prodded the ground with the iron rod again. "Here. Pa buried it up here, secretly. He knew that any thief would search the cabin. Of course they would. It's here; been here all this time. Three big stoneware bottles of dust and nuggets, maybe four, if Pa had time to fill another while I was in Downieville."

"We've barely found enough gold here to fill a powder flask," Fredi exclaimed, with considerable resentment. "You said that this was a good claim!"

Edwin had the grace to flush, slightly. "Well, it is. We've done at least as well as anyone else, this summer. But the placer gold is about played-out, Freddy, at least here at Pine Tree. Pa struck it lucky last year, I guess. There's still plenty of gold; just harder to get at. Those fellows digging into the hillside down there? That's what it will take to get it. Pa was saying something of the sort, the last time I saw him alive. The easy gold is all gone. Now it's up to big combines and partnerships. Big machinery, and companies building flumes to wash away the hillside." He looked down at the holes that he had continued driving into the soft soil. "The fact is, Freddy, maybe we … maybe you ought to consider another digging before summer is over."

"You are going to break up the partnership, take your Pa's stake and leave us high and dry?" Fredi challenged the younger boy, who shook his head.

"No, we shook hands on it, you and I and O'Malley. We share and share alike, even in what Pa left here …"

"Absolutely not," Fredi rejoined, almost instantly, while a part of him stood apart and wondered where he had gotten to be such a tower of high moral principles. "We share in what we worked for, ourselves. Your inheritance from your father is yours alone. Nothing to do with me or O'Malley. So what are we to do now? Dig up those stone bottles and leave Pine Tree Diggings, now that your part is finished?"

"We should talk with O'Malley first," Edwin looked at him levelly and began scuffling over the numerous holes that he had made with the iron rod. "And see what he advises."

Chapter 15 – Leaving Lone Tree

Fredi broached the subject that very evening, as they ate a supper of beans, bacon and camp-bread and twilight fell in the mountain canyon of Pine Tree Diggings, although sunset still touched the half-dead pine tree, standing guardian over Padgett's trove. They made their customary seats from lengths of log, or rough chairs cobbled together from lengths of branch tied with soaked rawhide, and held tin plates in their lap. A raucous chorus drifted along the river, from where some of the other miners were holding a hurrah, and far off in the hills a coyote howled.

After a quick sideways glance at Edwin, Fredi said, "O'Malley, hasn't it seemed to you that we're just not finding all that much gold lately? Edwin thinks that the placer claim is almost played-out."

"Indade, it does seem lately that we have no' been taking as much out as we had at first," O'Malley nodded, agreeably. "Is this a cause for worry, Fredi-boyo?"

"It might become so," Fredi took a deep breath. "The whole point of this venture is that we must take out of it more than we spend to stay here, or what is the point? Edwin says that going farther for gold means digging out hillsides for it. I'm not at all certain that I want to live like a mole, digging in the dark, on the promise of a rich strike, maybe."

"I'm certain I do not," O'Malley allowed, with a keen look at Fredi and Edwin. "Since it has been harder work than I expected and not one for which I have any skill. But since it was a thing that you were set upon, and I had no other very certain plans."

"I thought that it was you, who were so set upon the mines," Fredi interjected. "And we might still go to another digging, one with more promise than this, if there is such…"

"That is still no good plan," Edwin had been listening intently. "It's as I was saying to you, Freddy; the gold left to be taken is only to be found through deep mining, or by means undertaken by those who have deep purses. There is still a living to be made here, but not through doing as we have been doing for three months."

But O'Malley was shaking his head, saying, "Noooo, lads ... 'tis been an interesting experience here, these last few months, but I agree with Edwin. There is no' much of a future in it. We earned more when I was playing the piano in the Headquarters Saloon and the Bella Union, and with much less toil. If we were to return to Downieville with our gold, and take up another business, I would no' be inclined against it. As it is, I am no' a young man anymore." O'Malley added, with a sigh of regret. Looking at him, Fredi realized that it was so; O'Malley looked tired and worn, as old as his own father.

"We might reclaim our mules and wagon, and return to teamstering," Fredi suggested. "There would be profit in the mines. Seeing what the cost of flour and salt-meat is, I'm certain of it."

Their education in the cost of groceries in places like Yuba City and Downieville; not to mention in San Francisco itself – had been abrupt and brutal, and the conviction that much of what they had panned from the icy water of the North Yuba would have to be spent on simple provender was a certainty which had begun to weigh very much on Fredi. Now he comprehended that Gil Fabreaux was correct; a fortune could be made, selling cattle at a hundred dollars a head to miners, but not if you were the miner who had to purchase a cutlet or a chop at that price.

"There is a gentleman I spoke with this very day," O'Malley said, in a meditative manner, "Who is buying up claims on behalf of a consortium. Should we choose to leave. he would offer a small sum for the rights to our claim. He and his friends propose a tremendous working to dam the river, and build a great flume, which would bring water to play with great force upon the hillsides, and retrieve much in the way of the gold buried within. It would be a marvel of the age – a very large enterprise indeed."

"Such as what I was speaking to you about earlier," Edwin murmured in an aside to Fredi, and he looked with great earnestness upon O'Malley. "If that is so, I do not have any objection. Placer-mining here is played-out. I'll come with you both, should you want to try another claim on another river … but I do not believe there are any more fortunes to be made from plucking gold nuggets from the side of a river, as if they were roses in a country garden."

"The gambling fraternity have an expression," O'Malley sighed, "About 'cutting our losses' – which, I believe would describe our situation in a fair way. Are we in agreement; now to practice another method of pursuing riches in the mines, other than standing knee-deep in ice-water, shoveling gravel into the maw of that contraption? I am for it. Although," He added, with a look around the diggings; the canyon itself, the distant mountains, gilded with the last of fading sunset, and a fond glance upon their camp establishment, "I have an affection for this situation, you understand. Not the boredom, and the labor, but the natural aspect. And the fact that we answered to no other in the conduct of our work."

Edwin nodded in assent and Fredi answered, "Yes," with a bit of a pang at doing so. He had pursued the dream of riches in the goldmines, worked toward that goal for more than a year. Now to walk away from it after barely a single season seemed dreadfully like a defeat. He had to acknowledge honestly that the claim was not as profitable as it had seemed at the first. Every day that they poured their energy into it and every day that their supplies diminished would leave them in rather poorer position. Fredi thought of some of those pitiful ragged maniacs in the streets of San Francisco, begging –

anything to put together a stake to return to the mines and perhaps strike it rich. Of that, they had as much of a chance as O'Malley did to win a huge pot at the gaming tables.

"I will talk to the gentleman who might purchase our interest in this claim," O'Malley looked at the last of his supper, already congealing on the tin plate in his lap, and put it down on the ground for Nipper to finish. "And we shall see about returning to Downieville and retrieving our wagon and mules ..."

"We might also consider selling the remainder of our supplies, the tent and the cradle before we depart," Edwin suggested. "If we are not to continue mining, then at least we may get back what we paid for them."

"An excellent notion," O'Malley agreed, but for a moment he also looked rather sad.

"There is one more thing," Fredi cleared his throat, and looked sideways at Edwin. "There is the matter of what Edwin's father left at Pine Tree ..."

To Fredi's mild chagrin, O'Malley didn't seem surprised at all – that Edwin was closer entangled in the matter of the Padgett claim, or the murder of that family by Wade's gang then they had both assumed. Like Fredi, O'Malley indignantly disavowed claiming any share of what had been left buried for Edwin between the roots of the tall pine tree.

In the end, the matter of departing the diggings turned out to be a fairly simple one; the man from the consortium handed over a small sum in notes for their signatures on a piece of paper. He also bought their tent and stove; the party digging in the hillside purchased the cradle and the remainder of their supplies. What they had left; coats and bedrolls, mostly, along with Fredi's cherished saddle – easily fit on the backs of two mules, at the tail end of a string returning from

Sierra City with empty packs. And so they made their way down-river, as autumn touched the first aspens on the high hillsides with gold, and frost in the mornings outlined every blade of grass, leaf and still puddle of water with a lacey fringe of ice, which crunched underfoot until the sun rose high enough.

Only Edwin seemed particularly cheered at departing from Pine Tree; O'Malley and Fredi looked back until the tall, silver-weathered tree was lost to sight, as the narrow canyon of the Yuba closed in on either side.

"What?" Fredi could hold on to his temper, but not his astonishment. "You said that you could trust that bastard of an Irishman! He was your cousin from Bally-oh-wherever! And now we find that he has sold his concern and skipped town with our wagon and our mules! O'Malley, this is a bad joke!"

"Fredi-boyo, we are not entirely without resources," O'Malley replied in a placating manner, which did nothing for Fredi's temper. They had walked all day, following the mule string, only to find that Con Reilly was gone entirely from Downieville. There was saloon where his establishment had been; a saloon of a more than palatial sort, built of planks rather than calico and canvas over a frame, and expanded to several times the original size. It contained a lavish bar with a mirror, and a small stage on the other side. No one could or would say how long Con Reilly had been gone, or to where. "The new owner; a soft-spoken gentleman, Mr. Craycraft – he is as generous as we would want – has offered me a situation, playing piano … and in a fortnight, a special show, for which a musician is truly required! A traveling revue with Miss Lotta Crabtree, the darlin' Faery Star of the diggings! Think o' that, me boys!"

"You'd think that she was the only child in California," Edwin remarked, somewhat sourly. Fredi, his attention diverted as well as relieved by the offer of employment for O'Malley, allowed, "Likely the only singing and dancing one. Well, I have no taste for washing glasses and tankards again, so I will see if I can find better employment. What about you, Edwin? Or do you have a taste for working over a dishpan?"

"I'll see what appeals," Edwin snapped. "In the meantime; where do we stay?"

"I have been offered a room behind the saloon as part of my wages," O'Malley replied, "Which is small but will save us some of our takings…"

"But meals …" Edwin began. O'Malley replied, "Oh, the use of their cook stove, surely. And they set out a marvelous free buffet daily."

"Over-salted, to ensure that the drinkers are thirsty," Fredi looked on the prospect with resignation. No; the summer in the mines should not be wasted through keeping themselves in room and board throughout the winter, although he did wonder why Edwin was continuing with the partnership, since he alone had the wherewithal now to take his inheritance East and be done with the gold-fields. But with winter coming, perhaps Edwin had second thoughts. The passes over the Sierra Nevada would be closed by heavy snow, impassable until spring. Of all the circumstances in the world which Fredi did not want to experience, stranded in the high mountains with diminishing food supplies ranked fairly high among them.

By the time that the Crabtree child arrived with her mother, riding in a high-packed packed mud-wagon along the road from Camptonville, Fredi had found work of a somewhat irregular sort. He rode for the express mail service of Everts & Wilson, twice a week, carrying letter mail between Downieville and Camptonville, more than twenty miles and a good day's journey, at a good gentle cantering pace. He would spend the night in Camptonville before returning the next day with saddle-bags full of mail brought by another express messenger from Yuba City on the steamboat from San Francisco. This work pleased him; being on horseback once again. And the mining towns were hospitable always, as the arrival of mail being looked for.

A small crowd gathered in front of Craycraft's saloon at a mid-afternoon to greet the much-vaunted infant performer's party; a bookish-looking and diffident man in his thirties who sported long hair like an Indian and a handsome woman of the same age in the front seat, handling the reins of the horse-team with brisk efficiency. The man had his arm in a sling; and moved as if he were in pain. Willing and eager hands assisted them both down from the mud-wagon, other hands secured the horses. A girl emerged from the back of the mud-wagon; a girl, somewhere between the age of eight and ten, if Fredi was any judge. The gathering in the street cheered, and the girl blew them impish kisses. She had red hair combed smooth under her bonnet, and snapping dark eyes in a rounded and still childish face.

"Lotta, Lotta – our darling Lotta!" To shouts and cheering, Lotta curtsied and blew more kisses, with the composure of a grown woman accustomed to praise; then took her mother's gloved hand with the shy gravity of a child. Her mother held a sturdy carpetbag in her other hand, and together the family climbed the few steps to the porch of Craycraft's saloon, where Mr. Craycraft and O'Malley waited for them.

At the door, Lotta turned around, calling out to the crowd, "Dear gentlemen, do come and watch me sing and dance tonight! But now – Mama says I must rest!"

Fredi shook his head, and walked on to the Wilson & Everts office. Tomorrow he would ride to Camptonville, a journey guaranteed to be a long and chilly one, especially if the sun never came from behind clouds. It was already turning to winter, this close to the mountains, and he was chilled to the bone in the short walk to confer with the express agent. He was glad to return to the shelter of the Craycraft's saloon kitchen, around in back where they shared the use of the stove for bachelor meals with Mr. Craycraft and that taciturn Chinaman who cooked those few dishes required for the free lunch spread in the saloon and heated water to wash the saloon glasses and tankards. Edwin was there, sitting on a wooden settee set in the warmest corner, feet tucked up out of the draft that crept across the floor when the wind keened against the outside door. He was writing a letter, it looked like; paper, ink-bottle and pen set on the bench. Fredi wondered who the orphaned lad had in the way of correspondents. Maybe those cousins in St. Louis?

"You had better wrap up warm tomorrow," Edwin courteously took up his letter, blowing several times across the paper, and setting his feet on the floor so that Fredi had room to sit down as well. "And take a pair of hot baked potatoes in your pockets, to warm your hands. That's what Ma always said to do, if we had to be out in the cold for a long while."

"That or half a brick," Fredi agreed, and Edwin snorted. "You can't eat half a brick, so settle for potatoes, I reckon."

"At least, I won't miss tonight's first night's show. Who's that letter for, then? I didn't think you had much in the way of kin … sorry, Ed. I spoke without thinking."

"No matter," Edwin replied, although his countenance appeared somewhat strained. "To my Aunt Sadie. It's a difficult letter to write, Fredi. I am telling her that I likely won't be leaving here until spring comes. And to let her know that I am still alive, of course."

Fredi mused, grateful for the warmth in the kitchen. The high mountain passes were, if not already blocked, soon to be. The highest peaks were already white with snow at midday, and a pale pink and gold at sunset. It was treacherous now, traveling very far into the mountains, much less venturing over them entirely ... unless one went by the southern route. It was in the newspapers, that a Mr. Butterfield and his company would be establishing a stage route, from San Francisco, to San Diego, around the southern mountains and through the deserts to Texas and beyond to St. Louis. But from what Fredi had gathered, all this was still being planned. There were no stagecoaches on the trail yet.

"It sounds like you're not really eager to go back East, after all," Fredi ventured, "You're just casting around for reasons that sound good to yourself."

The other boy nodded, shamefaced. "That, and I'm not feeling altogether right with lying to you and O'Malley," he confessed. "To get you to go with me to Pine Tree. That was under false pretenses, and my conscience has been bothering me something fearful, Freddy. You might have gone to some other diggings, and struck it rich there. But I talked you into Pine Tree on the Yuba, and it turned out to be all but played-out, and you haven't all that much to show for a summer, and I can't help thinking that was my fault. Ma and Pa raised me honest an' God-fearing. That was a wrong thing for me to do..." Edwin's voice wobbled perilously. Fredi, resenting how he and O'Malley had been so readily manipulated, now felt guilty in harboring that thought, for Edwin seemed on the edge of unmanly tears.

"Look, Edwin, it doesn't matter," Fredi fibbed; embarrassed because the other boy was being so girlish over something that was obviously true. He and O'Malley might just as well have struck it rich at some other digging. Or they might not. "It's all a matter of chance. Look – there was something that Ma'am Pleasant told me last winter;

she said that mostly, those who got rich in California – weren't the ones mining gold, they were those mining the miners."

Edwin seemed to have composed himself, and Fredi continued, more heartened by his own insight, an insight sharpened by experience of the last few months. "I didn't pay any mind when she said it, but now I think maybe she was right. She's a rich woman, and I don't believe she got herself that way, standing up to her knees in water, panning gravel … or in going onto her back and spreading her legs for a rich man to take his pleasure of her. *(Although, Fredi added silently to himself – she was fast enough to do that for her own pleasure.)* She's a clever one, indeed; she used her own good sense and hard work – mining the miners. Look, Edwin, maybe we might have struck it rich somewhere else, or maybe not, but this doesn't mean O'Malley and I are plumb flat-busted. We'll find a way."

"But I still owe you," Edwin's chin raised, in a resolute manner; mercifully to Fredi's way of seeing, the boy's previous distress was banished. "You and O'Malley are stout fellows, good friends. Pa would have done his best for you both. So, I will see you into a good situation, one way or another, and stay until I do."

"I thought that you hated California," Fredi said, as the music of a piano being played in the saloon itself began sifting into the far corners of the saloon.

"I do," Edwin replied, melancholy banished with resolution. "But there are some things here which are to my advantage if I remain. I'd still be under the authority of my kinfolk, you see. I do not relish the prospect of being treated like a child."

"How old are you, exactly?" Fredi ventured. He had always assumed Edwin to be about two years younger than himself, although he was sometimes puzzled over how the boy spoke with such authority on matters to deal with the mines, and of events which he recalled which made him seem older.

"Fifteen," Edwin replied, after a small hesitation. Fredi laughed. "Is that all? I should have guessed, since you have yet to give evidence of growing a single whisker ... but I would have thought you older. I guess it's the way of it, all along the frontier. My sister Magda's husband was a soldier before he was year older than you, and a Ranger in Captain Jack Hays' company when he was the same age as me! It sounds as if O'Malley is doing well on the piano here. Shall we go and listen? If you like and your letter is finished, give it to me and I'll take it with me to the Wilson & Everts tomorrow."

"I reckon I am," Edwin corked the ink-bottle, blotted his pen in a dirty handkerchief and blew on the final sheet of paper several times. There were several pages covered in elegant looping handwriting – very fine, Fredi noted, almost in passing.

"You write with a good fist," he said in mild admiration. "You could get work as a clerk, or writing letters for men without any education at all. At any rate, your penmanship is far better than mine."

"It's a thought," Edwin allowed, with an air of wistful consideration. "Now – playing a piano may be a better money-maker than placer-mining."

"If you were a girl who could sing and dance," Fredi chuckled, as they came out into the big saloon room, "That would prove to be the biggest money-maker of them all!"

In the middle of the simple stage, Lotta Crabtree was dancing – an energetic clog-dance, with O'Malley accompanying her on the piano which sat on stage to one side of the proscenium opening. The girl's feet, slippered in wood-soled clogs, were a blur of motion, tapping out a fast, rhythmic tattoo on the wooden stage, and she was smiling in triumph, although pink with exertion, and O'Malley – also somewhat pink in the face through the energy of his playing – likewise smiled. Mrs. Crabtree, as watchful as a turkey-vulture with a fresh kill in sight, sat on a chair below the stage with the carpetbag at her feet. She was a fresh-faced young woman, with the same red hair and dark eyes as her daughter, and an air of confidant authority about her. Mrs. Mary Anne Crabtree was every bit as formidable as Fredi's sister Magda – in taking to tour the mines in a small theatrical company, accompanied only by Mart Taylor and a single man to drive the wagon. Fredi thought on his sister with a twinge of nostalgia; he had gotten one single letter from his family, in all the months they had been in Pine Tree; a letter months-old by the time it was received. Now O'Malley struck one last triumphant chord, and Lotta stamped out a similar rhythm on the stage, and stood with her hands on her hips, laughing as if she had not a care in the world.

"You were off-rhythm a bit in the third measure," Mrs. Crabtree observed, with a mildly critical note in her voice. Lotta, still breathless from the dance, replied, "I know, Mama." The rebuke certainly had no other effect on the child. "I will be accustomed to Mr. O'Malley's playing by tonight. Now, we should go through *Banks of the Nile* once again. I shall mime cutting my hair and I thought to have a petticoat across my lap and a shawl over my shoulders, and begin by singing it as if I am sitting before a fire. What do you think, Mama? Can we contrive a sailor's jumper and trews before the curtain?"

"I'll see what I can do," replied Mrs. Crabtree, in a tone of voice which suggested that it was not all that much a challenge. "If not for here, then by the time we play in Grass Valley."

Lotta took a shawl from the stool which stood to one side of the stage, and with one hand, started dragging the stool toward center stage. At that moment, Edwin went up the three short steps from the main floor and lifted the stool, saying, "Where will you have it, Lotta?"

"In the very center," Lotta's dark eyes sparkled at the boy, and she thanked him very prettily. Mrs. Crabtree thanked Edwin also, appearing to take notice of him for the very first time. Meanwhile, O'Malley ran his fingers over the keyboard, drawing out a few experimental chords, complementing a tune that was unfamiliar to Fredi. It was a ballad in English and therefore not one which he knew well. Lotta perched on the stool, with the shawl drawn around her shoulders, looking expectantly at O'Malley, as he played the opening chords and nodded.

Lotta began to sing. She had a fair enough voice for a child, but somehow managed to imbue the lyrics with a curiously adult intelligence which Fredi found disconcerting, at the very least. She was a strange being, he thought; so completely polished and adult when performing, as she was now, but suddenly reverting to modestly childish manners when she was not. It was a credit to Mrs. Crabtree's skills for motherhood. It struck Fredi as somewhat unnatural, as if the girl was at these times not a small girl at all. The Faery Star, they called her in the mines – a miracle child.

"Oh, but I'll cut off my yellow hair, and I'll go along with you." Lotta sang, yearning and melancholy. "I'll dress myself in uniform, and I'll see Egypt too! I'll march beneath your banner while fortune it do smile, and we'll comfort one another on the banks of the Nile."

He listened to the lyrics with casual interest, but his attention was suddenly diverted to Mrs. Crabtree, not gazing on her daughter with her usual fierce intensity, but at Edwin, his hands in pockets and lounging against the arch where O'Malley bent over the piano keys, watching Lotta perform. Mrs. Crabtree had a most curious expression on her face; a kind of horrified curiosity, as if she had discovered some kind of slimy creature in her sewing basket, not knowing in the least of how it got there, or what to do about it.

But the moment passed, Lotta finished the song and the piano keys rippled a last refrain under O'Malley's nimble fingers. Mrs.

Crabtree's attention bent back toward her daughter, and Fredi thought nothing more of it.

The Craycraft Saloon was packed to the rafters that evening, excitement and expectancy crackling in the air like lightening. Fredi would not have been surprised at all, to see small lightening-bolts flashing in the haze of pipe-smoke which hung just below the ceiling. It seemed as if every shopkeeper, miner and teamster from Downieville and every camp within a ten-mile radius packed the floor of the saloon. The music of O'Malley's piano could barely be heard in the raucous crowd, when Mr. Craycraft mounted the stage and held up his hands, begging for quiet. Mart Taylor, who traveled with the Crabtrees was evidently going to be the opening act – he also could barely be heard; for the crowd wanted to see the star of the show. Singing, dancing, concertina-playing male performers were as common as mule-tracks in the streets of Downieville and the other mining towns. Mrs. Crabtree followed with a very credible dramatic recitation, to a murmur of acclimation. Then O'Malley favored them all with a dramatic piano solo, which he played with a lot of twiddling of scales and dramatic gestures. Fredi settled into a chair near the stage, possession of which he was prepared to defend with his knife and Colt revolver, if necessary. It appeared as if Edwin, having made himself useful at the afternoon rehearsal, had been nominated as a stage-hand, for Fredi caught a glimpse of the boy, pulling back the heavy ornamented curtain which was the saloon's main aping of a theater. He also caught a glimpse of Lotta's pale countenance, with an expression of frozen panic upon it, hesitating in the wings and then, Mrs. Crabtree, giving her daughter's narrow shoulders a vigorous shove, which propelled the child out into the middle of the stage, brilliantly lit by bright-burning footlights, with reflectors at stage-edge which magnified their light to an extraordinary degree. The little girl brought the house to a roar of acclaim, standing in the glow of the footlights, blowing kisses to the audience. She was dressed in trousers and a green jacket, with wooden clogs on her feet and gesturing with a tiny shillelagh … and for the next hour she held everyone's heart in her own small hands – singing and dancing, skipping across the boards of the Craycroft's narrow stage. Fredi couldn't recall the last time he had been so caught up in such a performance.

The curtain calls seemed endless – Lotta skipped out onto center stage, blowing kisses to the crowd on the fingertips of her tiny, childish hands. Even Nipper trotted out and briefly danced on his hind legs as an encore, to cheers crashing like waves on the seashore, and showers of gold-dust raining down; dust and a fine patter of nuggets. Lotta appeared to glow a thousand times more than the stage lights, as if that sudden attack of nerves when her mother pushed her out from the wings had never happened at all.

But the show was quite definitely over, now that Mrs. Mary Anne Crabtree was briefly seen, industriously sweeping up the golden harvest from the stage with a small hand-broom before the curtain ultimately swept closed. Fredi sighed, and vouchsafed his chair, knowing that he would have to rise very early in the morning, setting the potatoes to bake in the Craycraft kitchen stove for an hour, before he set off on that long cold ride in the morning. Business in the saloon was assured to be brisk for the next several hours. At least it wasn't him, but the resident Chinaman who would be relied upon to fire up the stove in the morning.

O'Malley and Edwin were in the kitchen, as Fredi passed through from the saloon; Edwin, so tense and quiet; the lad looked as if he were being reproved, as O'Malley demanded, "…Mother Mary, did y' think that no one would ever see the truth of it? And my reputation …" he broke off what he was saying, as Fredi opened the door. "Freddy-boyo, a private matter to discuss with young Edwin, d'y' mind?"

"Not at all," Fredi yawned. "I could care less – just don't shout it about, I have to ride to Camptonville in the morning." As he returned to the tiny room at the back of the saloon, closing the ill-fitting door after him, he wondered briefly why O'Malley looked so furious. O'Malley wasn't normally a man given to bad temper. No matter – it was private business, and frankly, Fredi was too tired to care very much; he unrolled his pallet in the corner farthest from the outside wall, a wall which radiated bone-chilling cold when the wind roared down the canyon. He was tired to the bone, and thought that O'Malley and Edwin should have been as well, what with all the excitement of Lotta's performance. He could hear their voices, though; but they spoke softly enough that he couldn't hear the words. Just before Fredi drifted away in sleep, he heard Edwin speaking for a long time, in pleading tones, and O'Malley sounding somewhat mollified.

Chapter 16 – Riding the Express

Wakened just before dawn by a distant rooster crowing in protest in the next street over from the saloon, Fredi crawled out from between his blankets. Pale light seeped through the gaps between the boards that made the lean-to shed appended to the back of the Craycraft Saloon. He pulled on his outer garments, noting with some surprise that Edwin and his bedroll were nowhere to be seen. From the foot of O'Malley's bedroll, Nipper looked out from beneath O'Malley's worn coachmen's overcoat with bright eyes, but declined to rouse himself. The dog abominated cold, as well as damp, a sentiment which Fredi shared, especially on this chill morning.

Fredi did wonder what had happened with Edwin. O'Malley gave every indication of being deep in slumber, and Fredi was loath to wake him and demand an explanation. Was it to do with the quarrel between the two on the night before? And where was Edwin? O'Malley would be playing the piano in the saloon tonight and for Lotta's second performance. It was his understanding that the Faery Star would perform twice more at the Craycraft Saloon, so he would have the opportunity to see the show at least one more time, after his journey with the mail and back.

The previous evening, he had importuned the Chinese cook, with gestures and very simple English, to put two potatoes to bake for him on the stove, when he banked the fires for the night; now the potatoes were done and hot. Fredi slipped them into the pockets of his coat, where they radiated warmth. He helped himself to coffee, from the pot already sat at the back of the stove; the coffee was also hot, and there was molasses to sweeten it, but no milk. The Chinaman came in from the outside, with an armload of wood for the stove. Fredi nodded to him, from courtesy. He didn't quite know what to make of the man, with his almond-shaped eyes, and long black queue snaking down his back; he didn't speak much English and no German. China was called the Celestial Kingdom, and was a long away across the Pacific Ocean. If Fredi had known much beyond that, he had forgotten it long since.

O'Malley was still gently snoring in his bedroll; Fredi pulled on his coat, wrapping a heavy muffler around his neck and mouth, and tiptoed more or less silently out of the back door of the saloon, still wondering where Edwin was, and what the dispute between the two had been.

It was light outside now; a faint pearly light sifting through the overcast. Frost crunched under his feet; either a heavy frost from last night, or a light snow-fall. The river was not yet frozen, although a substantial layer of ice rimmed the banks, those rocks in mid-stream and those places where the water lay still. The water itself was black, cold-looking, the river shriveled between its banks. Fredi walked along to the Wilson & Everts office, down a muddy street which even at the crack of dawn was full of lively activities; a few stores were already open, and the gambling hells really never closed.

The express office was no exception; Mr. Layton, who managed the office was a stickler for opening early. In the early days in Downieville, it cost a dollar a letter. Profits were still good enough, however – and the mail service was even faster. In the early days, before California was annexed and gold discovered, Fredi had been told it took six months or a year, for a letter to travel from the East.

"Morning, Dutch," Mitch Layton said, as Fredi came in. "Hope you dressed warm, today. It's gonna be cold enough to freeze the tail off a brass monkey, and worse tomorrow, if my bunions aren't lying."

"Two sets of flannel long-johns," Fredi replied, cheerfully. "And hot potatoes in my pockets."

"You'll need 'em today, Dutch. You gotta full pair of saddle-bags, and likely the same waiting for you in Camptonville. Keep your eyes wide open. There's been a couple of road-agents reported laying for the stage, last couple of weeks."

"Good thing I'm only carrying letters, then," Fredi patted the reassuring weight of the long-barreled Colt dragoon revolver, hanging from the belt under his coat. "Nothing worth getting shot over."

"You never know," Mitch Layton answered. "There are some damn-stupid sons of whores out there." He handed Fredi the packed pair of saddle-bags, bulging with mail, bound for Camptonville, San Francisco and the East. "Don't take any risks with 'em, if you do run into one. Especially with my horses."

"Safe as if a baby in the cradle," Fredi replied jauntily, slinging the saddle-bags over his shoulder. The horse was already bridled and saddled, tied to a hitching rail out in front, stamping impatiently and blowing out steamy breaths into the frigid air. Fredi flung the saddle-bags over, and mounted up, feeling as free as a bird soaring into the air. Mr. Layton's express horses were a very fine collection of horseflesh, Fredi thought to himself once more; fine-blooded, high-spirited stock rather than the small and nimble mustang cowponies of no particular breed that he had been accustomed to riding back in Texas and with Gil Fabreaux's outfit. Today's mount was a tall brown gelding with a slightly darker mane and tail; Mitch Layton said that this horse was named Brownie. Even at a trot, Brownie had a comfortable gait and his canter was a smooth as silk. There were some stretches when Fredi must rein him in, for Brownie loved to run when he was fresh – but it was a hard twenty miles and a little more to Camptonville, over a twisting, rutted road which had been established more by use and custom than any deliberate program of road-building.

No – Fredi was done with gold-seeking, if it meant standing knee-deep in ice-cold river water for most of a day, or grubbing a dark tunnel into a hillside, like a mole. It was only after giving up that notion of a fortune in gold to be had for a small labor that Fredi could see to the heart of the matter. Did this insight mean that he was closer to being a man; an admirable man, like Carl, or Captain Hays, or Gil? Riding for the express mail suited him better, although the work of it was no less arduous, and certainly no warmer.

"I'm just not cut out to be a miner, Brownie," Fredi confessed to his mount. Brownie's ears twitched, as if he was listening and sympathetic, even if Fredi was speaking German to him – that language of his childhood. Fredi had spent so much time of late speaking English that now he thought he had begun dreaming in English, too. "I can't stick staying in a single place. Maybe I will, some day. But this … always a fresh prospect over the horizon … something new and exciting. Vati used to say that you had to know yourself. Perhaps this is what he meant by that."

The sun was just peeping over the eastern horizon as he left the flats behind; a thin golden thread illuminating the mountaintops, but the valley of the Yuba Forks was still masked in blue shadow. Walk, trot, canter, all at a steady pace, intended to make all possible speed while conserving the strength of his mount.

Walk, trot, canter, matching pace to the condition of the road and the pitch of the slope in it; Brownie's steady, obedient hoof-beats ate up the miles, as the sun rose higher and higher at their backs, the mild midday warmth melting the frost on the trees, and at the edges of puddles.

"It's one of those things, Brownie," Fredi continued, in a confiding mode when they reached a slightly up-hill stretch of road. "Loyalty to a pard, like you and I. One for all, all for one. O'Malley and me – we're partners, too. And Edwin, too – even if I wonder what he has gotten up to? O'Malley sounded angry last night … What we do, we ought to do it together – a man needs good friends out here, and no mistake. There's men who wound up being knocked senseless in a tavern, send off on a ship to Shanghai, or dead in a ditch, if they didn't have friends looking out for them. O'Malley, now; if there was a man who needs a keeper. And Edwin is a babe in the woods, like that old story, for all that he says he isn't. If it weren't for them, I'd take my share of the gold from Pine Tree and go home to Texas. And that's the truth of it."

Brownie's ears twitched again, as if he understood perfectly. Walk, trot, canter, yet again. Pause to water him from the river, pause again for Fredi to dismount and stretch the kinks out of his legs and back, and eat his near-to-cold potatoes. Let Brownie graze briefly on a patch of winter-killed grass, and feed him a handful of oats, before resuming the journey. He saw only a handful of other travelers, all that way, for winter was closing in.

He reached Camptonville; brawling, sprawling, wood-smoke-shrouded Camptonville very late in the afternoon, Brownie, being a well-conditioned horse and accustomed to the regular long journey, still had sufficient energy to prance, as Fredi threaded through the outskirts to the Wilson & Everts office, and the stables behind. John Harvey, the express agent at Camptonville, came out to take charge of the saddle-bags. He was a very thin young man, a little older than Fredi, afflicted with a persistent racking cough that hinted at consumption. He had wrecked his health through laboring in the placer mines for three seasons.

"No problems?" he asked, as Fredi un-cinched his saddle girth. Brownie seemed to shiver with delight, and blew out his nostrils in a great sigh of relief.

"Not a whisper," Fredi shook his head. "Mitch said he had heard about a road agent setting up along the road, but I expect that he must be laying for the stage. I didn't see anyone the whole way who didn't look like he had a good reason for being there."

"It's too cold a day for any but an honest man," John replied, and coughed. "Well, when you get done with rubbing down Brownie, we'll go over to the Nevada House for supper. My treat, Dutch."

"Bring a full poke," Fredi replied, "I'm hungry enough to eat a whole beeve."

John Harvey laughed, shaking his head, and left Fredi to finish tending Brownie. The stable was unexpectedly warm; the bodies of the other four express horses and the milk cow stalled therein likely had a lot to do with it. Fredi filled the manger of the empty stall with dried hay, and a handful of oats, rubbed Brownie's long nose with affection, and went into the express office.

John Harvey lived there, in one of two little rooms behind the office; two lengths of dark red calico stretched from wall to wall and floor to ceiling formed the separating walls, Fredi would spend the night in the other, sleeping on a straw pallet, and head back to Downieville the next morning, with the mail dispatched from Yuba City which had arrived the day before. Fredi liked to think of that company of mail riders, moving up and down the tracks between San Francisco and the remotest of the gold camps; the saddle-bags of letters, moving by relay riders on twisting mountain tracks, and by steamboats plowing up and down the rivers. Perhaps he would be tired of this job soon enough, but at the moment – especially this moment, with his day-long journey over – he was supremely contented with it.

The next day he saddled another horse from the Wilson & Everts stable; a leggy roan called Whiskers, for the length of those wiry hairs adorning his muzzle, and set out to make the return journey to Downieville. Whiskers was not as well-mannered as Brownie, and a little more inclined to start at a sudden noise or motion. No day-dreaming in the saddle on this day, Fredi knew for certain. The day was not as cold as the day before; the clouds pressed close down upon the ridges lining the valley of the North Fork of the Yuba, clouds as gray as a dirty bar rag, and a slow penetrating drizzle fell intermittently from them. A fair number of the hillsides near Camptonville had already been stripped bare of wood; wood for fires, to build flumes and houses, and then those hillsides eroded down in search of gold, through massive water-workings. Fredi didn't care for the look of those stretches; as bare and barren as a desert. Farther up the canyon of the Yuba, stands of trees remained. Whenever Fredi paused to water or rest Whiskers, he could hear the quiet sound of water dripping from their branches. Such was the peculiarity of the atmosphere, that sounds carried quite far; he heard the sounds of a quarrel between two late-season placer-miners at Saint Joe Bar for quite some time before he came up on their claim. The hoof-beats of an approaching rider carried very well, over the quiet rustle of droplets falling from tree-branches; Fredi knew before he had gone-halfway toward Downieville that unless the weather worsened, or something like a tree suddenly falling across the track, that he would have good warning of any movement along the way.

"I should be hearing the stage, about now," he confided to Whiskers. He knew the hour that the regular stage would have departed from Downieville; Mr. Holladay's enterprise were famous for the strictness of their schedules. Three teams of horses, and the coach or a mud-wagon, would make a racket on the trail that he should be able to hear for miles. Given the timing of his departure from Camptonville, Fredi was pretty certain he would pass the coach well before he reached Goodyear's Bar ... yes, he thought he could hear the far-distant rumble of coach wheels, the hoof-thunder of fast-moving horses. If it was One-Eye Charley at the whip, the coach would be rolling at a fast clip. One-Eye Charley, a weathered and profane little man, had been pointed out to Fredi several times as one of the most accomplished stage-coach "whips" in the California diggings. It was said that he could flick a fly off the ear of one of his horses at a dead run with that whip, without even touching the horseflesh.

The sound of the coach teased him, as the trackway curved and bent, following the North Fork; now louder, now muffled. He thought nothing of it, until the noise of it ceased absolutely. No, that was not right. The hair on the back of Fredi's neck prickled. Mitch's warning about a road agent laying for the stage sprang into mind. That was it, Someone had waylaid the stage, around that blind turn just beyond. He knew this for an absolute certainty. They were being robbed, right this very minute: that's what that sudden silence meant. A sudden silence broken by the sound of a single shot, echoing and reverberating in the canyon of the North Yuba.

Recollecting it afterwards, Fredi wondered with a certain degree of horror what had gotten into him? The terror and indignity of being robbed by the bandit gang outside San Bernardino after departing from employment with Fauntly Bean was as fresh a memory as if it had happened yesterday, instead of months ago. That red insensate anger rose in him, an unstoppable tide, as he drew his Colt and kicked Whiskers into a gallop.

They thundered around that bend, Whisker's head held out straight before him, his flashing hooves throwing up globs of mud. Fredi shouted, a wordless cry of anger, when he saw the halted coach, the horses standing nervously in their traces, One-Eyed Charley Parkhurst with his hands raised and the fistful of reins loose at his feet; a strange and deadly tableau. A man with a dark kerchief wrapped around his lower face and a long shotgun in one hand, held the off-lead horses' headstall with the other. Three men also stood on the road with their hands raised, backed against the side of the coach. A fourth man lay crumpled on the ground, dead or merely wounded. A fifth with a revolver in each hand stood over him, one weapon still pointed down and smoking slightly, the other leveled at the three still standing. This man also had a dark kerchief pulled up to cover his mouth and nose, all but his eyes.

It seemed to happen at once very slowly and at the same time in the space of a single breath. Fredi saw the robber holding the shotgun, the sliver of his face visible between kerchief and hat pale with tension and nerves and One-Eyed Charley slowly lowering his hands, as the man with two revolvers turned swiftly toward Fredi. The robber's attitude was one of shock and surprise. With that cold and logical part of his mind, which seemed to be standing back and watching with clinical and unmoving judgment, Fredi wondered why he seemed … familiar.

Fredi crouched low over Whisker's neck, making himself as small a target as possible; for certain one or both bandits were going to shoot at him in the next seconds. The man with revolvers was already drawing a bead at him. Carl's voice whispered in his memory, Carl who had taught him to ride and shoot and kill a man if he had to. *"You'll have the advantage, Fredi – on a horse and moving fast – over a man standing on the ground and holding still. Don't waste it."* He and Whiskers were practically on top of the coach, the helpless passengers standing with their shocked faces and mouths agape. Icy-cold, in spite of that wave of insensate anger, Fredi took aim and shot – his Colt recoiling against his hand in familiar manner, for that was one of those things that Carl had made him practice, never telling Vati that he was being taught such soldierly skills. The bandit with the two revolvers spun backward, slammed by the force of Fredi's fair shot, as rider and horse flashed past. That icy-cold detached part of Fredi's mind noted, with mild surprise that Carl had been quite right. Fredi did command an overwhelming advantage of surprise as well as in mastery of a charging horse.

The bandit screamed a half-choked curse, "You dirty interfering bastard!" He stumbled, dropping one of his weapons as he fell more or less sideways off the track, before recovering his footing and running like a hare, clutching at his arm with his other hand.

In the next instant, One-Eyed Charley snatched up a shotgun from under his seat. The man with the shotgun dropped the headstall and ran toward where the other had stood, shouting a name. As soon as he was clear of the horses, One-Eyed Charley dropped him with a double-blast that sounded like a cannon going off; the second bandit fell, flopping like a rag doll into a boneless and bloody heap. Fredi felt bad about that, since it was the man with the pistols who had obviously shot that passenger. One-Eyed Charley's kill had done nothing, as far as Fredi could see, but to hold the horses. But he couldn't shake the feeling that he knew them and that they knew him, from somewhere.

Shaking like a wind-tossed poplar leaf with the aftermath of terror and exertion, Fredi reined in Whiskers, wrenching the reins one-handed with such force that Whiskers practically sat on his haunches like a dog. Hoping that no one could see that he trembled so, Fredi governed Whiskers to a walk, and approached the stage. The man on the ground was groaning most piteously; hurt but with sufficient life in him to be making an almighty fuss about it. Two passengers retrieved their own side-arms from where they had been either concealed or tossed by the bandits and belatedly fired after the fleeing robber, who was soon gone from sight, stumbling into the eroded gullies and sparse woods. They were cheering and shouting, as if they wished to forget how they had stood, cowed and helpless when Fredi came galloping around the bend.

One-Eyed Charley's weathered face contorted in an expression which might be mistaken for a broad grin by the imaginative. "Good shooting, boy!" he said. In contrast to his scarred appearance, he had a rather light voice. "And providential in your appearance, also!"

"It looks as if that one got away," Fredi reined in Whiskers by the side of the coach, so that he could stand in the stirrups and shake the hand that One-Eyed-Charley extended to him in warm appreciation. "I just winged him. Sorry about that – sorry for your trouble, Mr. Parkhurst. I have a great dislike of robbers and bandits, having once been robbed by Murrieta's gang myself. Friedrich Steinmetz, at your service. I am a mail rider for Everts & Wilson, the express mail company; most folk call me Dutch Freddy."

"Pleased for the acquaintance, Dutch. Can't say I have overmuch fondness for the bastards myself." One-Eyed-Charley spat – courteously over the far side of the coach, adding, "Well, now the poxy useless pricks are making themselves useful. Too damn late, now, and I'll have to make up time, no doubt about it. Take a look at that dead sonofabitch. Anybody recognize him?"

One-Eyed-Charley looked down on the bloody mess of the second robber, sprawled lifelessly in the track, with his lifeblood leaking into the mud from the mess that One-Eyed Charley's shotgun had made of his upper body. Fredi looked down on him likewise from Whiskers' back, as one of the passengers – nerve and manhood suddenly revived now that there was no real requirement for it – bent down and turned the body face up. The dead robbers' hat had fallen aside. The passenger pulled off the calico kerchief which had offered some brief disguise. Fredi looked again and his heart froze within him.

"I may know him," he said through stiff lips. "A man I came out from Texas with – two seasons ago. Eb Satterwaite; I reckon he fell in bad company."

"Well, California has got a plentitude of bad company on offer," One-Eyed-Charley replied, with a bald lack of sympathy. "He had a richness of choice in that respect. Look, you – tip his body to the side of the track. I gotta schedule to keep, and so has Dutch here. If anyone cares for this nutchless son of a bitch, they can come back here and bury him proper. Me, I'm not paid to care and neither is Dutch here."

"I'll pass the word in Goodyear's Bar," Fredi answered, now doubly shaken. He had held no real grudge against Eb, the responsible one of the Satterwaite brothers, but Zeke Satterwaite was another matter. He was certain now that Zeke was the other bandit; the one he had winged. Zeke sure as Hell had a grudge against him now, a grudge three times over. Fredi wondered if Zeke had recognized him in those brief, confused moments. With a sinking feeling at the pit of his stomach, he concluded that yes, Zeke undoubtedly had. It might have been almost two years since Gil Fabreaux's outfit trailed a herd of cattle overland but he and Zeke and Eb and the rest had been nearly eight months in constant company. If he could pick out and recognize one of their company at a distance on horseback, then any of the other boys could. And if by chance, Zeke hadn't recognized him, the near robbery of the Downieville to Yuba City stage would be the talk of the northern diggings and the name of the express rider who foiled it would be on everyone's lips.

Still shaken, he bade farewell to One-Eyed-Charley, and listened to the fulsome thanks of the coach passengers with a distracted mind. A vengeful Zeke Satterwaite, haunting the valley of the North Fork, and anyone would know that that the Wilson & Everts company express rider rode alone, twice weekly between Downieville and Camptonville – a road little traveled in winter. He could be ambushed and buried in a hundred different places along that road and no one would ever know. He would have to talk to O'Malley about trying their luck elsewhere.

Chapter 17 – Touring the Mines

Curiously, O'Malley appeared quite sanguine with Fredi's account of the ride from Camptonville, the encounter with the Satterwaites, and the personal danger which the surviving brother might pose. Fredi tracked him down at Craycraft's saloon as soon as he delivered the mail saddle-bags and Whiskers to Mitch at the Wilson & Everts office.

O'Malley was stirring a mess of eggs and canned oysters, in a small pot at the back of the Craycraft kitchen stove. The Chinese cook bustled about, sending looks of pure irritation at the two interlopers in his kitchen, while Fredi related his account of the attempted stage-robbery, and of his part in foiling it. The news would be all over the northern diggings, no doubt as soon as One-Eyed Charley and his passengers reached Camptonville. O'Malley listened, with sympathy – and some horror, when Fredi confessed to recognizing Eb and Zeke Satterwaite.

"Aye, poor lad," he said, shaking his head. "'Tis a tragedy indeed, for he was the sensible one. I knew the other was destined for a bad end; a pity that the judgment which should have fallen on him came to his brother, instead. You did very well, Freddy-boyo, very well and fearlessly, indade. And now you have a mortal enemy. Well, that is what it is to be a man, they say – knowing that you have stood for something, like the right of honest men to be traveling between here and there without fear of cutthroats. A righteous man should have enemies, it means that he has stood for something."

"I am thinking that perhaps we should leave Downieville, and the northern mines altogether," Fredi ventured.

O'Malley did not seem the slightest startled by that intelligence. Instead, he nodded soberly and replied, "Aye so. It is providential that I have this very day arranged with Mrs. Crabtree to join her touring company. Understand, Fredi-boyo; I once had a belly full of the life of a touring artist, in the capital cities and salons of Europe. But my skills at the keyboard are undiminished, or at least, not so far diminished that any audiences here will take note. I have no affection for the life and work of a solitary miner, so this is what must be."

Just as on the day they decided to give up the claim on the Pine Tree Diggings, O'Malley looked for a moment very old, and tired – worn to the bone, indeed. It was as if all the energy for living life had drained from him, and he looked as old as Vati. As old as Vati had appeared on that shattering day when Mutti's canvas-shrouded corpse was cast into the sea, on that fateful voyage from Hamburg.

"What of Edwin?" Fredi asked, for there was a third of their partnership to be considered. O'Malley chuckled, suddenly and most unexpectedly cheered, as if the black mood of a moment ago had never been.

"Oh, the lad has been taken on already. Mrs. Crabtree is a woman of inestimable worth and perception. She has seen how Edwin has made himself useful, and moreover, the dear little Faery Star has an affection for him. Edwin says that his own small brother was the same age when the lad was murdered by that blackguard Wade. And she and Nipper have already become fast friends! Now she is importuning me to have Nipper do a turn on the boards with her. Believe me when I say this, Fredi-boyo; she has the soul of a stubborn lady of many years, wrapped in the flesh and bones of a small child. And what I shall do … trading upon your swift work this day, is ask Mrs. Crabtree if she would hire you as a guard, you see." O'Malley laid his forefinger alongside his nose, looking very sly. "She does not trust the banks, not a bit of it. After the failure of Adams and Company, who may blame her? She gathers up the gold from every performance, after it falls on the stage … a fine and exacting housekeeper that she is, she sweeps with a fine broom … and then carries the gold in a carpetbag," O'Malley shook his head, in awe tinctured with slight disapproval. "After this turn in Downieville, she says she may have to substitute the carpetbag for a strong-box. Methinks it would be properly canny to hire a guard for it. What say ye to that, Freddy-boyo? It seems doubly fortuitous…"

"I would agree," Fredi answered, although he little liked the notion of appearing too much of a coward to continue his regular journeys with the mail. Still, employment with the Crabtree entourage offered a respectable-appearing alternative and would maintain the partnership with O'Malley and Edwin. Besides, the vision of showers of gold swept up from the stage by a careful housewife had considerable appeal. One might as well mine gold from the miners, as Ma'am Pleasant advised, rather than mine it at first hand. Yet even as he agreed, he was reminded of the quarrel between O'Malley and Edwin, the evening after Lotta's first performance in Downieville. "O'Malley … you and Edwin were having words, the night before last. I couldn't help overhearing, and you sounded terribly angry. Did that have anything to do with Edwin deciding to work for Mrs. Crabtree?"

"In a way, Fredi-boyo," O'Malley agreed, in a tone of voice which to Fredi sounded just a touch too hearty. "I had fair to lose my temper, and I spoke in anger … but it was between us, and nothing for you to concern yourself with."

And so was that Fredi entered on the next chapter of his life in California, throughout the spring and summer of 1857, little reckoning that it was to be the final one, although it had been dawning on him for some time that the gold mine adventure was not near what it had been reputed to be when he had embarked upon it. He was mildly saddened to depart from Downieville – but then, he had felt a similar emotion on departing from San Francisco, from San

Bernardino and before that from the hospitality of the Carrillos at Warner's. Where would the next night, the next week find him? This was a peripatetic life, a wandering player of no certain address, yet a certain degree of modest luxury through the association with the Faery Child. Mrs. Crabtree and Mart Taylor planned a tour of the mining camps in early spring and throughout summer, to return to a winter stay in San Francisco for the winter by the season's end.

It seemed to him, that as the Crabtree company traversed from camp to camp; from the north toward the south, and from the mountains into the flatlands, over muddy roads and the threat of uncertain weather – that they formed an odd and eccentric family. Mart Taylor was the father of it, of course, but pallid, indecisive, and always looking sideways to the authority of Mrs. Crabtree, as mother-in-command. After some thought along this line, Fredi decided that O'Malley was an uncle, or a brother to either of the two. He and Edwin were older sons, and Lotta, darling, impish Lotta, was the cherished small sister, upon whose' talents the entire enterprise rested. For the child was talented; there was no doubt of that at all. She lived for performing, often appearing to be only fully alive when on the stage, although sometimes her mother must prod her gently onto the stage, when she appeared overcome by momentary stage fright. A theater full of rowdy gold-miners, most often the worse for drink and boredom; Fredi himself wouldn't have set foot on a stage before them himself for all the gold-dust in all the placer mines of California. He contented himself by lurking attentively near Mrs. Crabtree and her heavy carpetbag, and if the crowd seemed most especially rowdy, casually resting one hand on the butt of the Colt in his belt.

Mart and O'Malley were mere supporting players and it seemed to Fredi, happy to be so. The audiences generally relished their turns – Mart singing, and O'Malley playing the piano, and showed their appreciation openly as well as profitably for the two men, but it was

Lotta whom the audience adored, no matter if it were a calico-walled saloon with an out-of-tune piano, or a lavish and purpose-built theater, adorned with gilt gimcrackery and crystal chandeliers brought at great expense from the East. But Fredi sensed that at the heart of it all, this was a fragile and ephemeral existence, this life of putting on a show, here and there. This was a life that dug no potatoes, butchered no cattle and built no houses; it was exhilarating in stretches, boring and uncomfortable in others ... and yes, the gold came easy, but Fredi didn't think that he was going to spend the remainder of his life this way, a way that depended upon the fleeting and facile butterfly favor of the crowd. Increasingly, he missed his blood family; Vati, Johann and his sisters, as well as the men they had married; quiet, competent Carl, solid and reliable Hansi.

"I suppose that it is possible to have enough of adventure," he mused aloud one afternoon late in summer. He and Edwin shared a narrow seat in the simple spring-wagon that was their method of transportation, with Lotta wedged between them and leaning with child-like confidence against Edwin. They were bound for a week-long engagement in Amador City, followed by a similar schedule in Mokelumne Hill and in the southern mines, as far as Mount Ophir. This lengthy period would allow a little more rest between nightly engagements. Perhaps, they might even find a laundry, and a decent meal or two. Mart, O'Malley and Mrs. Crabtree sat wedged together on the front seat: O'Malley had hardly room to move his elbows, as he drove.

"Never, Fredi-boyo," O'Malley answered over his shoulder, as buoyant as ever. "The road is always open, and calling to ye. Around every bend is a marvel of singular splendor, and new friends ye haven't yet met."

"I want to meet the crowned heads of Europe," Lotta announced, pert and self-assured. "Just as Miss Lola told me she had. I want to live in a castle and perform for kings and queens."

"Not in the way that Miss Lola did, for sure," Mart Taylor said, with a guffaw at his own wit as Mrs. Crabtree hissed at him to shush, and reproved her daughter. "Miss Lola was a woman of certain skills, Carlotta, dear, as well as necessary spirit of independence ..."

"I'll say she was," Mart chuckled again, "Certain skills most generally demonstrated in private to an audience of one. And mainly not the kind that a decent woman knows about, either – and not known by a woman whom a decent lady would admit to friendship with, even out here."

"Her finer qualities outweighed the others," Mrs. Crabtree insisted. "I do maintain that it is possible to perform on stage and still remain a respectable person ... it is just that such a condition becomes more of a challenge than just sitting doing needlework in one's own parlor. Crabtree is a man completely devoid of ambition necessary for our family to prosper. Starving in completely virtuous poverty has nothing to recommend it to a sensible female."

"And a heavy purse ensures respectability indeed, Mrs. C.," O'Malley remarked. "Indade, the heavier the purse, the greater the respectability – at least in the diggings. And I have played before the crowned heads ... or at least, some of those with coronets. To my mind, it's more rewarding, performing in the mines."

This was a far cry from what Fredi had envisioned, two years before, starting out from Indianola with a promise of employment from Gil Fabreaux. But as Carl would have confessed wryly, it was a living; what with his wages and his portion of the take from the Pine Tree Diggings claim, he wouldn't be returning to Texas entirely empty-handed, which was some consolation. He looked across at Edwin, a drowsy Lotta leaning against the boy's shoulder, and grinned. "We'll have some fine tales to regale the kinfolk with, won't we, Ed … hoping they are respectable, mind."

"I'm certain that they will be," Edwin replied. "If I am recalling her correctly, mind, Aunt Sadie is most primly respectable, for she married a wealthy man of St. Louis, connected to the Chouteaus by business partnerships. Ma … well, Ma often made mock of her, for that. Ma didn't have any pretense …" For a moment, Edwin's countenance reflected something of the same loss and grief that Fredi had felt, when the sailors wrapped Mutti in a canvas shroud aboard the *Apollo* – apologizing to Vati all the time, as they did it. But Mutti was gone from Fredi and Johann when they were seven years of age, and they had Magda and Liesel to look after them. Edwin had been a few years older, when the life of his mother, his father and close family were taken from him by the calculation of brutal men in an alien and lawless land – not the swift impersonal hand of ship-fever – and left him stranded alone in the world.

It was in Amador City that the first of those things happened; an occurrence which turned the whole enterprise upside down, from Fredi' view. They were rooming in Mr. Harrington's hotel, while Lotta, Mart and O'Malley made the rounds of performing in various Amador City saloons. Gold brought up from the vast Keystone mine made Amador City even richer than Camptonville had been; as Edwin explained once, there was no more gold to be got out through placer-mining. Now it came from deep-dug mines but the towns around the mines were just as rowdy and free-wheeling. The streets of Amador City were every bit as narrow and rambling as any other town laid out along narrow water-carved valleys. The wooden sidewalks along the storefronts rambled up and down in various states of repair, a step or two up or down at every twenty feet. O'Malley walked a little ahead on that afternoon, solicitously offering his arm to Mrs. Crabtree, with

Fredi, Edwin and Lotta following after, hand in hand. There was supposed to be a very fine general store, farther along and Mrs. Crabtree had declared herself in need of cloth to make another costume for Lotta who was growing like a vigorous weed, while Mart Taylor stood guard over the trunk which was their treasury now that it was beyond capacity of the carpetbag to contain.

Lotta chattered like a cheerful little bird, excited by anything and everything, especially by the attention that she attracted in a town where women of the respectable sort were rare and children even rarer.

Fredi didn't see what had distracted Edwin's attention, as they came to one of those uneven steps; but he turned at the sound of Lotta's cry of distress and caught Edwin as the boy fell forward, down two uneven steps, landing with almost full force against Fredi, who staggered backward and nearly fell himself. They stood frozen for that second, Edwin's body pressing fully against Fredi, whose arms went involuntarily around the younger, shorter boy.

There was something ... something not right. Fredi gaped in shocked astonishment.

"I am sorry," Edwin gasped. "I didn't see..." just as Lotta cried out again and Mrs. Crabtree and O'Malley turned around. "Are you all right – what happened?"

"I ... I missed my footing," Edwin insisted. "I might have fallen all the way, but for Fredi. I am all right, Mrs. C – not to worry."

Fredi silently dropped his arms from around Edwin's shoulders, struggling with the realization which had struck with the force of a thunderbolt, and damning himself for being a fool, all this last year. A lot of things made sense to his own mind now, starting with how Edwin talked older but appeared younger, how the boy had never stripped off his shirt or long-johns on the hottest days, or bathed naked in the river last summer, why his voice never seemed to break

… or how he had never grown a single whisker. *I'll cut off my yellow hair, and I'll go along with you,* Lotta had sung on that first time they watched her, in Downieville. *I'll dress myself in uniform, and I'll see Egypt too! I'll march beneath your banner while fortune it do smile, and we'll comfort one another on the banks of the Nile.* Fredi looked sideways at Edwin's profile, as they walked along. Oh, it was obvious now; seeing those features with eyes from which the scales had fallen. Everything he thought he knew about Edwin had been turned upside down, in just the space of ten seconds.

"I'll just bet that Mrs. C. knew right then, the night that Lotta sang Banks of the Nile in Craycrafts," Fredi mused silently. *"And that was why she hired Edwin, or whatever her name might be, to travel with them."*

When they came to the general store – which did indeed seem very well stocked, to the point of having bundles of goods hanging from pegs and nails set into the rafters overhead, Fredi detained O'Malley at the door, as Mrs. Crabtree, Lotta and Edwin went inside.

"A word, O'Malley," Fredi murmured, drawing O'Malley to a place by the shop-front where they might talk quietly and more or less confidentially. "In private, while the ladies are within. Am I the single one among us who never guessed that Edwin is really a girl?"

"Oh, is that the way of it, now?" O'Malley didn't seem surprised in the least. "How did you come to see what was before your own eyes, all this time?"

"When she fell full against me," Fredi answered, through his teeth. "I knew there were woman's breasts, under that shirt. Yes, I have engaged in congress with a woman, O'Malley, and I know the feel of a womanly body against my own … a woman is soft against the ribs. And everywhere else. There is a difference; I am not such a fool as I cannot note them when they are thrust on me as they were just now, although everyone else seems to think so!"

"Twill relieve your mind and your faith in your own perspicuity, I think, that Mr. Taylor does not know, or indeed take any particular interest, but he is accustomed to performing folk an' their own peculiar customs, to hear him tell. Myself, Fredi-boyo ... I did have some small suspicions early on, but they were soon alleviated, y'see. I thought to myself; the lad is just small, undersized for his age, and girlish in appearance. 'Tis a hardship enough, for any young lad to labor under, so I said nothing. A free country, is it indade. And the work of gold-miner; the very hardship of it and the roughness of the company, excepting ourselves, mind. What delicately-raised maiden would undertake it for more than a mere minute? And then, it was in Craycraft's, the evening of our darling Lotta's first performance in Downieville. Mrs. C. spoke to me after that first rehearsal. You were elsewhere at the time and I thought not to involve you. She was ..." and O'Malley looked as if he were close to shuddering in recollection of what the redoubtable Mrs. C. had said to him on that famous occasion. "...most irate, regarding my own eyesight and judgment. I attempted to reason with her, o' course, and related some of what I had learned of our companion during our association. Her name is really Elodie, by the way. The daughter whose body was never found, after the depredations of Wade's gang against her family. Because Elodie became Edwin, and vanished into the world of men. 'Tis a hard life for a woman without protectors, or indade, a woman without the inclination to throw herself on any protector at all, knowing that the character of many a man leads them to exploit their fragility." O'Malley sighed, deeply. Through the glass window of the general store, they could see Mrs. Crabtree, with her daughter and Edwin – Elodie – moving among the shelves piled high with random goods.

"Was that the cause of that fight between you that I overheard after Lotta's turn on the boards that night?" Fredi demanded, only a little mollified by O'Malley's confession. The older man nodded, with a deep sigh.

"Yes indade. I was horrified, just as you are now, at not seeing the obvious plain before your eyes! And at the trouble that it might have made for us and for Elodie, knowing that we had all been living in the same tent at the claim all summer. We could have been accused of debauching a helpless young girl, taking advantage of her innocence. Horsewhipping would have been the least part of punishment for that, and at the worst, hanging. They're altogether too fond of hanging in these parts, have ye not noticed?"

"I doubt very much that she is all that innocent save in actual bed-practice," Fredi observed, sourly. "Although neither of us has ever made advances to her, indecent or no. She has lived in the gold diggings and San Francisco for at least half of her life; if there is anyone in those places with the least shred of innocence about them, they are either a new-born babe or a complete imbecile."

"At any rate," O'Malley continued. "She insisted that she wished to continue the pretense of being a boy and declared that I should not to tell you. While you are a better prevaricator than you once were, you still do not govern your countenance, Fredi-boyo. What you think is writ too plain upon it. I think now that you have come to such realization, Elodie may be persuaded to put on womanly garments and leave off the masquerade, since Mrs. C. and Lotta would be her natural companions."

"It would be for the best," Fredi agreed, although with a certain pang. For all this time, Edwin – no, Elodie – had been as near to a brother as Johann, a sturdy companion, the expert when it came to mining and knowledge of California. Now knowing that she was a girl – no, very close to a woman – that shifted the whole matter in a manner unbearable to think about.

Eventually, Mrs. Crabtree, Lotta and Edwin – no, Elodie – emerged from the general store, laden with a muslin-wrapped bundle, and the storekeeper himself, fawning upon them in gratitude for their patronage of his establishment. O'Malley took the bundle, and offered Mrs. Crabtree his arm. They walked ahead with Lotta, hanging on her mother's hand while Fredi fell in behind with Elodie. He looked sideways at her, under the brim of his hat, and marveled again at what a blind and stupid idiot he had been, all this time.

He caught Elodie doing the same, and seeing that the others were some little way ahead and out of hearing, he said, "Well … is there anything else about you that I should have known?"

"There is," Elodie lifted her chin; a slight but completely feminine gesture. Again, Fredi berated himself for having been such an unseeing fool. "I hate eating blackberries, for the way that the seeds stick between my teeth. And I liked wearing my brother John's clothes. I always did, as it spared my best things when working at Pa's claim. It was …easy enough to pass as a boy. It was what I had to do. Mrs. C. understands."

"But did you have to lie to us, all this time?" Fredi demanded in exasperation and Elodie's face went obdurate.

"I didn't lie to you," she insisted, "I just didn't tell anyone that I was a girl. I simply put on boy's clothes and said my name was Edwin. Everyone looked at me, if they looked at me for very long at all, and took me at face value. There's no lie in that which I told."

"It was dishonest," Fredi insisted, exasperated at how coolly she twisted his words and her own actions, but Elodie remained unmoved.

"You can't lay the stupidity of everyone on me, Freddy – all but Mrs. C. believed from the first moment!" Now her voice changed, and it was as if tears were just hanging onto her eyelashes, waiting to fall. Fredi damned himself for a fool all over again, because he knew he was going to soften. Women about to cry always did that to him. "Freddy ... you and O'Malley can't be angry with me now, when it's your own selves you ought to be angry with. And you are, I'll bet anything. Because you're telling yourself that you should have seen, but didn't. You're angrier with me than you are with yourself – and that is just not fair! You and O'Malley are my friends, my pards! We all worked the Pine Tree claim! We may not have struck it really rich, but we were all for one and one for all, then and when we agreed to stick together in Camptonville. Why does the matter that I am really a girl make all that a mockery? I worked just as hard as you, I knew even more about mining than you two! Why does that now make so much of a difference that you won't even look at me straight?"

"You are playing with words," Fredi declared. "And whether you used words or not, you were still deceitful. I do not like having deceit practiced upon me."

"Then you had better become accustomed to it," Elodie retorted in blistering heat. "For a certain portion of the world will do it, whether you like it or no, like that devil Ward." Her peaked and big-eyed face reflected such an expression, it was as if saying the very name produced a vile taste in the mouth. "For he ... he pretended friendship with my father, and fatherly affection toward me, yet all the time, he was planning robbery and murder."

"How did that come about?" Fredi asked, at least as much to satisfy his own curiosity was it was to distract Elodie. "And how did you escape from him ... as he seemed so particularly set on stealing the takings from the Padgett claim..."

"I will tell you then," Elodie answered. "Because you honestly ought to know, for the salutary lesson that I learned, and which you ought to learn as well."

Chapter 18 – Hauntings

"It was said to us in Sacramento last year after the hanging," Fredi ventured, "That at first Wade was an honest, respectable man. He kept his store and his saloon orderly, and never turned away any in true need. But it was all a front, it came out later. His establishments were listening posts for his gang. When a miner was selling up on his claim and heading home with a full poke, all alone, Wade's gang would follow until he was gone beyond the reach of those who knew him for a friend ... then they would lay for him, commit murder and robbery, and dispose of the corpse where no one would ever know, or finding it, think that it was only some poor unlucky soul. Anyone hearing of the death of a miner, long after leaving the diggings, they would not connect it to someone they knew, or think it suspicious."

"Exactly," Elodie replied, although that delicately-boned owl-countenance still bore an expression of misery. "Because they had said their farewells, packed up their traps, and told everyone they were heading home. Back East, everyone would wonder for time, grieve for a bit, and think nothing more. And even if they did suspect foul play – why, it would be months, even years later before inquiries might be made!"

"He had a profitable criminal enterprise, then," Fredi nodded in grim acknowledgment of the very devilishness of Wade's designs for wholesale murder and robbery. "As well as his legitimate one. He might have continued in both for years, without raising suspicions among the folk in the mines."

"I think there may have been suspicions, toward the end," Elodie sighed, lost in memories. "Especially in Downieville. But not so much that he couldn't have ceased such plots and returned to honest respectability without exciting comment. I believe that he became inflamed by greed. Pa's claim proved to be very profitable, even if he did not boast of it to many outside a circle of trusted friends. But Wade knew to the very ounce how very profitable it was, since Pa purchased necessary supplies from him, over the space of two years and more. I have thought over this many times in the last year; Wade became greedy. Such greed overpowered his natural caution when he deduced that Papa must have hidden the greater part of his gold from the diggings. Once unmasked, he had no choice other than be the out-and-out villain."

"I wondered often how you had escaped from him," Fredi remarked. "Was that when you disguised yourself as a boy?"

Elodie shook her head. Although her expression was still strained, she seemed relieved that Fredi's initial anger had passed. "No, not right away. I was staying at the Palace Hotel in Downieville; not a hotel as they have it in San Francisco, or even very much of a palace, but a boarding house, kept by a very respectable couple, Mr. and Mrs. Enright. Sister Molly and Brother Paul – we called them that, as we were all friends. They were most especially friends of Ma's – Mormons, but still very kindly and respectable. They've gone to Deseret, as they had always planned to, else I would never dared show my face around Downieville. Most of the folk that Ma and I knew there to talk to, they have moved on as well. It's like that in the diggings, so you might have noted. Any roads, Ma and Sammy were supposed to come down from the claim, when the supply pack-train returned."

She looked away into the distance, at the hills rising above Amador City, the hills which concealed the treasures rapidly being taken from the vast Keystone mine. When she continued speaking, her voice shook only a very little. "Sister Molly and I were planning a special supper in celebration, that very afternoon. I was rolling out the crust for dried-apple pie, my hands all over with flour. Brother Paul came into the kitchen. I should have guessed from the look on his face. He said, 'sit you down, Sister Elodie, I'm afraid that I have very bad news,' He had just come from the livery stable where the miners from Sierra City had taken the Ma and Pa and my brother's bodies. I … I screamed and cried, I didn't believe him at first, and Molly held my hands, still covered with flour from the baking. I begged them to take me to see for myself, that I wouldn't believe until I saw, but Brother Paul shook his head. He sounded so sorrowful, and angry, too. He said that it was best that I not have such last memories in my head of them for all eternity. People will say that, you know. I didn't rightly comprehend, because I could think of worse pictures in my imagination. But over the last year, I came to see that he was right to do so." She drew a deep and shuddering sigh. Against his previous anger over how she had lied to him so readily and he had been fool enough to fall for it Fredi felt considerable pangs of sympathy. It was bad enough for a boy to find out of a sudden that all his family had been cruelly murdered; doubly bad for a young girl, innocent and defenseless in a wicked world. But then, this was Elodie; not all that innocent and assuredly not without friends as well as defenders. Still, he couldn't help feeling that it was given to him to protect her, little as she seemed to need it.

"So what happened, then?"

"Brother Paul and Sister Molly; they both were worried. Because of what he had heard what the men from Sierra City were saying. About Ward swearing in a frenzy that he would track down the Padgetts, every last one, and torture the secret of Pa's cache of gold out of them. That meant me, of course. No one could say for certain about who was in Wade's gang, you see, in Downieville or anywhere else in the nearby diggings. How many of them might still be laying low, and waiting his chance? They were frantic with fear for me, because of this. They had been Mormons in Missouri. They knew how it was, when neighbors and acquaintances turned to deathly enemies overnight. Brother Paul first had the notion, of us going to the fellowship and asking that I be sealed to him formally as a wife, and that we make our way to Deseret immediately, in spite of winter coming on. That way, I would be under his protection and that of their community. I could not countenance that. Such would require me to make a pretense of conversion to that sect," Elodie shuddered. "I found that prospect abhorrent; a mockery of honest belief and devotion. I could not swear an oath before God, that I honestly believed in their God and their rules, taking them for my own, even to save my own life. Sister Molly upheld me in this. She is a godly and God-fearing woman, with no toleration for cant and swearing falsely. She and Brother Paul then suggested that I should put on my brother's clothes and that he would escort me as far as Yuba City, for the steamboat to San Francisco and there I should take passage and return to my kin in St. Louis. He and Sister Molly should say to one and all that I had never been to their place. I had only been a day or so in residence there and not in the public rooms and if anyone made note, then they would say that I was a cousin visiting. Meanwhile, they should advance their plans for leaving also. I know that Brother Paul was worried regarding my safety after departing from Yuba City – but he had his own family to think about."

"What of your father's cache of gold?" Fredi asked. Elodie sighed again.

"There was no chance of retrieving it, Freddy, with winter coming on and all. There were few enough living who even knew of it and only one – me – who knew exactly where Papa had concealed it. I thought it best to take Brother Paul's advice and seek shelter in San Francisco, until all the furor died down. A gamble, of course, but hasn't O'Malley said often enough that existence itself is a gamble?"

"That was very clever and level-headed of you," Fredi commented, in grudging approval. "But now that everyone but Mart

Taylor knows that you are a girl, and you have your father's fortune in your hands once again, what are you going to do? I say that you should do as your friends urged you; return East to your kin. O'Malley is well-situated with the touring company of our dear little Faery Child and I have it in mind already to go back to Texas as soon as the season allows it. There's no need for you to stay on out of concern for us, as your trusty pards ... especially not, since now we both know your true identity. There's no earthly need for you to wear those duds, or stay in California, just because you feel guilty about suckering both of us unto going with you and setting up a claim at the Lone Pine Diggings. Give it up, Elodie. It's all done. That's what I would say. I don't need a keeper, neither does O'Malley ... although," Fredi added, in the spirit of absolute honesty. "He does give the appearance of it. But he got along before I made a partnership with him, he'll get along without it now. Go home to your family, Ed – Elodie. This is no place for one such as you."

"I suppose that I should," Elodie agreed, with some reluctance. "And Mrs. C. is after me to put on proper women's clothing again. She found me a dress and some petticoats, and bought me a proper corset. She says there has been no need for me passing as boy for months. I say that it just makes it easier to get along. No one notices another boy but everyone takes notice of a woman, especially one all by herself. She must be no better than she ought to be, and without a man protecting her. You know, they hanged a Mexican woman in Downieville a couple of years ago? She stabbed a man who was bothering her when he didn't take no for an answer and folk got real riled over it."

"You're not by yourself now," Fredi pointed out. "You're with us and Mrs. C. – you shouldn't have to pretend any more, anyway."

"You are right," Elodie agreed. She didn't look particularly happy at the prospect although it may just have been the thought of the corset.

The very next morning, on their departure from Amador City in the spring-wagon, Elodie appeared, in shy companionship, holding Lotta's hand as they came down from their rooms at the hotel. She wore a dress of sprigged red and dark blue calico which came all the way to her boot-toes, the woolen round jacket that was her customary winter over-garment, and her hat was the same battered straw that she had always worn as Edwin. Fredi damned himself once more for his own lack of eyesight. How could anyone have ever thought her a boy, unless one of ten or twelve? Somewhat to Fredi's chagrin, not even Mart Taylor turned a hair.

"So you never even wondered?" Fredi hissed at him, as the two of them loaded Mrs. C.'s iron-strapped treasury trunk into the back of the wagon, and Mart Taylor shrugged and spat into the mud at their feet.

"I mind my own business, Dutch," he replied with a broad grin, "As long as they keep their noses out of mine, I keep mine outta theirs. Your pard turns out to be as pretty a girl as ever turned heads along Montgomery Street? None of my business. Heck fire, little Lotta dresses up like a boy for singing and dancing. Some bit of fluff does it for real, they got their own good reasons. Reasons which are no skin off my arse, or so I figger. You wanna bend my ear about it, feel free. Other than that; none of my business. Now, we gotta be in Mokelumne Hill by nightfall. You gonna fasten up your end of the tailgate or look at it like you never seen any such thing before?"

Fredi told Mart what he could do with himself at that; Mart only grinned even more broadly. They hit the trail south for Mokelumne Hill, which had been such a very rich digging in the early days that miners might rightfully claim only sixteen square feet – and yet from those small claims, Fredi heard tell that many of them had made incredible fortunes from them. He was becoming rather tired of hearing at third and fourth-hand about how so and so had struck it rich when only one man that he knew of personally – Elodie's father – had managed that miracle. In the last few months, he had come to the sour conclusion that all of those telling marvelous stories of the riches in the mines must somehow be related to those nobles and princes back in Germany when he was a small boy, who told marvelous tales of the beauties and bountiful opportunities to be found in Texas.

"It's as rich a place as Amador City," Mart Taylor slapped his reins on the back of the two teams of mules pulling the wagon, "And with the scum of the earth from every nation, they say that the bandit Murietta preferred the gambling hells there over any other in the southern mines. But the respectable citizens finally formed a vigilance committee, just as they did in San Francisco, and everyone has minded their manners pretty much ever since then. Although the place has burned almost to the ground at least once, since being established."

"Indade, has not every town of substance in the diggings burned at least once, even without a visit from Edwin Booth, the Fiery Star?" O'Malley scratched his jaw and Elodie giggled. It was a common jest among the mining towns; the formidable Shakespearean actor had toured among them for most of a year with near-catastrophic fires following in his footsteps across the stages of many a town where he performed. "Ah, well, until it is a mandate that buildings be made of stone and brick, rather than basketwork and calico, then towns will burn. And for how long will we remain in the splendid metropolis of Mokelumne Hill?"

"At least a week," Mrs. Crabtree answered, brisk and decisive, as usual. "There is, if I remember well, a very fine hotel there, run by a French gentleman named Léger."

"A Frenchie, aye?" O'Malley sounded interested, and approving. "Then at least, the food will be of a superior quality."

"And I hope the beds are soft, and with clean sheets," Elodie added. "We have been spoiled with luxury, these last few months."

Fredi kept his thoughts to himself; which was that if he were tired enough, he could sleep comfortably on a rock slab.

Mokelumne Hill proved to be a town which geography had favored with a considerably less precipitous setting; an open but slightly sloping site, a tangle of streets wandering through it as they willed, freed from the constraints of river-threaded canyon which restrained so many of the other major diggings; all set about with gentle hills covered in patches of chamisa scrub and dotted with dark green oak trees. The town itself presented the very picture of well-established prosperity, and an urban variety among the various nationalities in its streets and businesses that Fredi had only noted back in San Francisco; Chinese and Chileans, Americans of every degree between prim, black-frock-coated Yankees and Southerners in flannel shirts with their belts stuck full of knives and pistols, dapper Frenchmen and swaggering Australians, Englishmen who drawled and brandished their elegant walking sticks, solid Bavarians and Prussians speaking in accents familiar to his own ears. There even appeared to be a brewery in town, if Fredi's sense of smell was any judge, perfuming the air with the scent of hops and crushed wheat as they fermented away.

There was the expected warm welcome at M. Léger's establishment in the late afternoon; Mrs. C. and Elodie pled exhaustion from the journey and took Lotta with gentle firmness to their room, although Lotta stubbornly insisted that she was so not tired, and she wanted to walk out with Fredi and O'Malley and Mart, to explore the streets of Mokelumne Hill. O'Malley coaxed her obedience by snapping his fingers and bidding Nipper to remain with her, as a diversion, for which Mrs. C. tendered them a brief look of approval. They walked out to the main street of town, amiably disputing over which way they preferred to wander. Fredi wished to locate the brewery, and ascertain if they had a beer-garden, as would be proper; tables set out among trees and arbors, under a clear blue sky – for it was a mild day indeed for autumn.

"No," said Mart Tayler, "We can walk down through China Gulch, and marvel at the strange customs of the Celestials."

"Let us stretch our legs, after today in the wagon," O'Malley demurred. "And leave the Celestials to their suppers, undisturbed. 'Tis not agreeable to me, to stare at others, as if they were exhibits in a zoo, or in Mr. Barnum's museum of curiosities. And when we have stretched our legs, return to the hotel for a light supper."

Fredi agreed, although he was still wondering about the chances of spending some agreeable minutes in a beer-garden, on such a temperate afternoon. Mokelumne Hill appeared to be a town stocked full of every amusement for the wandering miner, and of every possible taste from the sordid and base through the elevated and gentlemanly.

"I would not say no to a drink of the celebrated water of life," O'Malley added, with a note of appreciation in his voice, as the three of them passed the door of a more-than-well-appointed saloon, just across from the hotel. This early in the evening, the place appeared only partly-filled with customers still convivial, and well-behaved.

"I am agreeable to that," Mart replied, and they both looked back at Fredi, with expectant expressions on their faces. Fredi sighed;

saloons were all very well – and this one appeared to be one of the better on offer in a mining town.

"No more than three rounds," he said, "For we will be joining the ladies for supper and I think it rude to have too much of the stink of a saloon on our breath and on our person."

"Grand," O'Malley agreed, with a blinding smile.

Ever afterwards, Fredi recalled that moment, as if preserved in a species of clear amber; O'Malley smiling, without a care in the world, Mart Taylor already shouldering through the open door of the saloon – the sky above, already fading from blue into the oyster-shell of early evening, the tawny and mottled dark green shoulders of the California hills rising above the jumbled rooftops of a town, a town like so many others in the diggings. The voices of men in animated conversation and the clinking of glasses and bottles on the heavy Circassian walnut bar drifted out through the open door upon a whiff of tobacco smoke. He wondered if the chances of a simple beer would be good enough, and blinked in the comparative dimness as he stepped over the threshold after his companions, momentarily blinded after the bright afternoon outside.

As they walked toward the bar, a man sitting alone at the first table they passed, seemed to take startled note of their presence. Fredi saw him only as a vague shape, but the voice was dire and familiar; Zeke Satterwaite.

"You dirty murdering Dutch bastard!" Zeke Satterwaite exclaimed, insensate with fury and likely too much whiskey. He launched himself at Fredi, a gleam of daylight flashing across the long hunting knife in his hand, his chair clattering against the floor behind him. Fredi's hand went to the butt of his own Colt. For a long time after the stage-robbery on the road to Camptonville, he had walked warily in half-expectation of an encounter such as this, but he had relaxed his guard, as the weeks went by without any such incident.

"Boys, there's no need ..." O'Malley stepped between the two, making a fruitless, conciliary gesture. Zeke Satterwaite's knife went into O'Malley's chest – to the left, striking upwards a little below the line of O'Malley's ribs. And that was also another of those moments preserved in clear amber; the little grunt of pained astonishment that O'Malley made as he fell backward into Fredi's arms, the knife stuck fast in his chest nearly to the hilt, the widening expression of horror on Zeke Satterwaite's indifferently-whiskered countenance as he stood, empty-handed, the curiously small dark stain widening on O'Malley's garish brocade waistcoat.

"Fredi-boyo," O'Malley said, very clear and distinct. "I fear that he has murdered me. Send for a priest, as has been some little time since I made Confession."

"Lie still," Fredi pleaded, as he lowered the weight of his friend to the floor, and Mart Taylor bellowed, "Fetch a doctor! Is anyone here a practitioner of medicine!" The peaceful atmosphere in the saloon shattered, shattered as if a brick had been thrown into the mirror behind the back-bar, but Fredi was hardly aware of it, kneeling on the plank floor of the saloon, with O'Malley's head and shoulders resting against his knees. The two of them were a quiet island, at the middle of a storm, a storm that howled around them. He was barely aware that two or three other men had tackled Zeke Satterwaite, as the latter broke out of his momentary paralysis and dashed for the door to the outside. A circle of faces surrounded them. Fredi was put in mind of a herd of curious sheep; only these were men, and their expressions reflected horror, concern, or just plain curiosity.

"I have no need of a medical man," O'Malley insisted, in perfect tranquility, as he looked up at Fredi. "Fredi-boyo, 'tis sorry I am, to miss tomorrow's performance. I've never made a habit of disappointing the audience, y'see."

"Don't worry about it," Fredi encouraged him, inwardly quashing the panic in his own mind, seeing Zeke's hunting knife sunk nearly to the hilt in O'Malley's midsection. At his back, someone murmured, "Fetch Father Bobard, quickly!"

A patter of quick footsteps, and that was Elodie with Nipper running at her feet, heedless of the skirts of her dress and petticoats pooling around her as she went to her knees on the filthy saloon floor at O'Malley's side. There came Mrs. C., slightly slower, as pale as a sheet as Elodie cried, "My God, O'Malley – you are hurt!"

"But not yet slain," O'Malley replied, with a glint of his customary humor. "I'm lying down a while to bleed, then up and play the piano again."

"You should have a doctor!" Elodie cried. Tears began falling down her cheeks and spotting the bodice of her dark calico dress. She took one of O'Malley's hands in both of hers. "Oh, help him, please – bring a doctor at once!"

"By my faith," O'Malley said to Fredi with perfect composure, but with a catch in his breathing which boded ill to Fredi, "Here's a scene to gladden the heart of any dramatist. Another weeping queen and a boat to bear me off to fair Avalon, where I might be healed of this grievous wound …"

"A doctor … did someone call for a doctor?" A man came through the saloon door at their backs, and elbowed his way through the crowd. "I'm a doct … oh, dear."

He was a middle-aged man, somewhat weathered in the face, but he was clad in a townsman's dark claw-hammer coat, carrying a satchel of the kind that Fredi was accustomed to associate with those who practiced a medical trade. He knelt with a grunt of discomfort at O'Malley's other side and opened the bag as if more to reassure himself and the interested crowd gathered around.

"Move you all back, give him as much air as possible," the doctor commanded, but the expression of despair on his countenance belied the authority in his voice. "Is this a show in Mr. Barnum's exhibition of curiosities? A bit of decency, I beg of you all. My dear sir," he turned now to O'Malley, that curious instrument for listening to heartbeats already in his hand, "I am Dr. Alfred Bowman, late of the University of Knoxville school of medicine. I see that you have a knife in your chest ..."

O'Malley grimaced. "Polydore Aloysius O'Malley, once the Irish Infant Piano Prodigy, and pleased to make your acquaintance, sir, under any but these circumstances. Indeed, my diagnosis agrees with your own, in every respect. If I may be so bold to ask of your recommended course of treatment?"

Dr. Bowman sat back a little on his heels. "I would suggest surgical intervention, of course – removing the instrument, but preferably at my place of business. But there is some ... risk involved in transporting you there, so I am well-prepared to begin treatment here, for whatever relief may be obtained by it. I cannot hold out much hope for survival, Mr. O'Malley."

"Aye well," O'Malley coughed a little, and to Fredi's horror, a line of bright blood appeared on his lips, stark against his face ... which now seemed to have gone gray and drawn. "You ... may do as you think best ... but I would wish for the proper rites first, while I am able to confess those of my sins ..."

"Here is Father Bobard!" exclaimed someone on the outskirts of the crowd. In the next instant men made way for a man in priestly black, who like Doctor Bowman, also carried a business-like satchel. O'Malley's face brightened, as if he were seeing a friend.

"We dare not move him," Dr. Bowman said, in an undertone. Father Bobard nodded, and held out the crucifix which hung on a long chord around his neck so that O'Malley could kiss it with appropriate reverence.

"Peace to this house," he said, although with a gently ironic look on his face as he said it. There were obviously some of O'Malley's coreligionists in the saloon, for there came a responding murmur, "And on all who dwell within," and a rustle of clothing as they crossed themselves. The priest brought out a sprig of green pine and a clear glass vial of water. Fredi knew that it must be holy water – something that meant much to those devout Catholics of his acquaintance.

"You'd best make it short, Father," said Dr. Bowman in an undertone, and Fredi felt as if he himself had been stabbed through the heart as well. Elodie wept silently, clasping O'Malley's hand between hers. The pallor of O'Malley's face was even more pronounced, as well as the spreading red stain around the knife. Father Bobard hurriedly sprinkled the holy water, dashing drops in a small circle, as he intoned the ritual prayers and laid out a white cloth on the seat of a chair within O'Malley's eyesight – the very same chair, Fredi thought, which Zeke Satterwaite had been sitting upon. Upon the cloth went certain things which the priest brought from his satchel – a smaller vial of yellow oil, the Communion wine and bread – the body and blood of Christ, as Fredi's somewhat erratic education had it, although why this should be so, was something his education had not included, since Vati was a free-thinker anyway. But O'Malley believed, although his voice failed in strength as he repeated the words. Father Bobard hastily anointed O'Malley with the oil, pronounced the final blessing, looked across at Dr. Bowman and nodded. O'Malley's countenance, as pale as it was, bore an expression of beatific happiness. Nipper, all but hidden in Elodie's skirts whined almost soundlessly.

"Look to Elodie, Fredi-boyo," he whispered. "Take her home to her kin, once our partnership is sundered. Promise me you will do that. See to the little doggie. But stay with me for now, 'til it is done."

"I will do that," Fredi promised, numb and unthinking, as O'Malley's eyes went toward the doctor.

"Do what you must, now," his voice now without any strength at all. The doctor brought out from his bag a wad of cloth dressing in one hand, while with the other, he took firm hold of the knife hilt and pulled.

It came out from O'Malley's chest readily enough – slid out in a fountain-gush of blood, which Dr. Bowman pressed the cloth upon, although the cloth, his hands and even his shirt-cuffs were reddened, saturated in an instant.

"Better," O'Malley said, with a stronger voice than he had spoken in for some few minutes. Looking down at O'Malley's eyes – his head still resting on Fredi's knees – Fredi noted the exact moment when the spark of life that was the essential spirt of the man was extinguished, a body only, laying slack and lifeless on the saloon floor. Nipper whined on a louder, more frantic note, Father Bobard crossed himself and Elodie sobbed in earnest.

Chapter 19 – Ashes, Ashes

The body of O'Malley was buried in the Catholic cemetery, out on the eastern fringes of Mokelumne Hill, three days later, as a winter chill breathed ice-cold from the high mountains. Zeke Satterwaite was hanged on that same day, very early in the morning. Dazed by grief and the speed at which it all seemed to have happened, Fredi felt no inclination to watch the hanging, although it seemed the folk of Mokelumne Hill were about equally interested in attending on both, if the brief trial were anything to go by.

Fredi was summoned to testify at the trial. But even earlier, on the morning after the murder he was asked to verify what he knew of O'Malley for the records of the county coroner making a record of the death; a gentleman of middle years, who spoke with the accents that Fredi had come to associate with Englishmen, and the way which Mrs. Crabtree spoke the language.

"Polydore Aloysius O'Malley," he said, around a lump in his throat. "He came from Ballymena, in Ireland. About forty years of age. I do not believe he was married, ever, although he did have a brother and a sister, too – but they are dead. I believe that he spoke of a father, living – and he was the only living support. If he has other living kin, I just do not know their names. He … had toured the capitols of Europe, playing the piano, some time ago. I reckon it must have been at least thirty years since. He said that he was billed as the Infant Piano Prodigy of Ireland, and performed before the crowned heads of Europe – but that is only what he said of himself."

"He told me that he was from Ballycastle," Elodie ventured. She had recovered her composure. She, along with Fredi, Mrs. Crabtree and Mart were meeting privately in the parlor of the Léger Hotel. Nipper the dog continued on his devotion to the coffin which held his late master, laying on the floor nearby, curled in a tight brindle circle and silent in his canine misery. The well-dressed gentleman from some civic authority in Mokelumne Hill, charged with responsibility for public records, looked between them with some understandable bafflement.

"He said once, when someone tasked him about that ... that he had gone to school in one, after being born in the other, and all of them were within five miles of each other anyway." Fredi ventured at last. The gentleman nodded, dipped his pen into the inkwell set into the top of his portable writing desk, and scribbled away. The pen made a faint scratching sound in the silent parlor.

"Still, it is curious," the gentleman remarked, as he dried his pen nib and corked up the ink-bottle. "I myself have long been a devotee of the terpsichorean muse and I attended ever so many performances – in London, mostly."

"He means," hissed Mart Taylor in Fredi's ear, noting Fredi's obvious bafflement, "That he liked music. Of the uplifting sort – a lot."

"I had never heard of such a prodigy of Ireland," the official continued. "Infant or of any other condition. I am certain that I would have, such was my degree of devotion to performers of note in my younger days. Still and all, the gentleman was a most accomplished and welcome performer to Moke Hill. I extend my condolences to you all. We are sadly deprived, so you must also be deprived to an unimaginable degree by the loss of his friendship and camaraderie."

"Thank you," Mrs. Crabtree said, with commendable resolution. "For your sympathy and consideration. Mr. O'Malley was a dear and charming companion; we feel his loss very deeply." The official bowed over her hand, the writing desk under his other arm, and took his departure. She looked then at Mart and Fredi, her expression still pale with grief. "I suppose we must remain long enough for the final rites; Lotta is distraught and has no stomach for performing. I have every intention of returning to San Francisco for the winter, since this was to be our last stop anyway."

"We ought to do one last show," Mart suggested. "An abbreviated program, to benefit Mr. O'Malley's kin in Ireland, wherever they be found. He did speak once or twice of aged parents, and of being their only means of support…"

"Can we find them?" Elodie's eyelids were pink with sorrow and sleeplessness. "I went through all of his carpetbag of things, to find something decent for him to buried in. There are no letters or mementos. I am certain from the way he spoke of Bally-whatever that it was a small town. Everyone knows everything, in small towns."

"I …" Fredi began, and was struck by a sudden thought, and the recollection of how he and O'Malley were robbed after departing from the Bean establishment in San Bernardino. The bandits took his revolver, and O'Malley's watch and fob, but not the largest portion of their stake, which had been sewn into the hems of O'Malley's thick and many-caped coachman's overcoat. "Mrs. C., may I use your sewing scissors? I have an idea about where O'Malley may have carried his most valued small possessions."

"Certainly," Mrs. Crabtree replied; she produced them at once from the little chatelaine purse which hung from the waist of her day dress. Fredi ran upstairs, to that room which he and Mart had shared with O'Malley. The coachman's overcoat hung from the hook where O'Malley had hung after their journey from Amador City. Fredi bundled it into his arms, and returned to the parlor.

"He sewed our stake into the hems of this coat," he explained, and turning up the first cape, began carefully unpicking the hem. "To conceal it from robbers. It occurs to me, that he must have done it before – it's a very good means of keeping small things hidden and close at hand when traveling."

Silently, Elodie began to help him unravel the hems, as Mrs. C. produced a small button-hook. Fredi's intuition was rewarded almost at once; a handful of coins and notes, a plain watch-fob made in the form of a seal with the initials JH. In the second hem, Elodie unearthed an envelope without any letter in it, addressed to Jos. Hurley, c/o Galgorm Castle Lodge, Ballymena, but a continued search turned up several folded pieces of newsprint, much abraded about the edges. Fredi unfolded them with the greatest care; some of them bore the date of May, 1849, and concerned an assassination attempt on the life of the Queen, while riding through Green Park in an open carriage, on the part of an unnamed Irishman, and the fruitless search for the unsuccessful assassin, now a fugitive at large. One clipping included a drawing rendered by an artist from the descriptions provided by eyewitnesses.

"I cannot say with any honesty that this resembles Mr. O'Malley," Mrs. Crabtree said at last. "I recall the fuss over it, though I was but a girl at the time. There were always madmen and Fenians shooting at our very dear Queen. It was her good fortune and ours, together with the vigilance of our police and the affection of her subjects, that such malicious brigands had the most appalling aim." She fetched up a deep sigh. "I don't suppose that we shall ever know the real truth of O'Malley, but I cannot believe that he was ever so wicked a man as to plot the assassination of a woman."

"I cannot say that I knew him well," Elodie began, her eyes sparkling with unshed tears, and Mart interjected, "That's the truth of it; none of us really did. Save that he was damned good – sorry, Mrs. C. – at tickling those ivory keys."

"I was his pard in this country for two years," Fredi admitted, "And I cannot swear with absolute confidence that anything he ever told me was the truth."

"But he was a good man," Elodie insisted, passionately. "He was kind and wise, and brave and he kept my secrets and protected me as if I were his daughter. He worked without complaint at our claim and at playing the piano, even if that duty was distasteful to him. If he had secrets, they are his to keep. We should bury him with honor, and recall our memories of him with the utmost affection."

"That is a matter I will not dispute," Fredi agreed, without hesitation. "And that I intend to honor his last words and escort you back to your kinfolk in St. Louis. I am done with California and gold. I intend to return to my own family, having only this last duty laid upon me to fulfill."

"There is no more excuse for you to remain, Elodie my dear," Mrs. Crabtree said, in a most stern voice. "I know that you have long relished the freedom that this life affords you, but you are still so very young. You must have the support and shelter of a family – a family of your blood. Mr. Steinmetz is a most able protector. When we return to San Francisco, we will consider most carefully the safest and most expeditious means of conveying you to that refuge."

Fredi thought that Elodie looked as if she wished to argue, but to his relief, the girl merely nodded a sad assent. She ran her fingers over the last unpicked hem, stroking the heavy wool as if she were petting Nipper, before folding up the coat.

They all attended the burying as chief mourners, the women clad in hastily-assembled black, although Fredi and Mart Taylor had to make do with bands of crepe on their coat sleeves. There were a fair gathering of townsfolk; Fredi wondered what on earth this could mean for them, all who didn't know O'Malley form Adam's off ox. Mokelumne Hill was a town well-equipped with cemeteries and people who went to funerals out of boredom. The burial took place on a low hill to the east of town; the cemetery dedicated to the Catholic church named for St. Thomas Aquinas. All morning it threatened rain, lead-colored clouds pressing close on the hills, which only added to Fredi's sense of oppressive grief.

"I would have wanted to bury O'Malley on a bright sunny day, with flowers blooming everywhere," he admitted quietly to Elodie. "I don't know why. But it wouldn't have felt so … so final."

"I know," Elodie's countenance was drawn and pale. She looked nearly as lost and young as Lotta, standing between them, Nipper at her feet with a black ribbon tied around his neck, as Father Bobard made the final blessing and bade farewell to the handful of mourners, and gestured to a pair of roughly-clad laborers to begin filling in the grave as a splatter of rain began to fall. Nipper whined in abject misery as the rain fell, heavier and heavier, turning the bare earth to mud, puddling in the trodden footsteps of the mourners,

"We should go now," Mart suggested, but Nipper wouldn't come, although he was soon soaked to the roots of his coarse fur, and shivering in the chill. He snapped at Elodie when she bent down to pick him up.

"Oh, for the love of God," Fredi exclaimed in exasperation. "You stupid animal, we should let you stay here and starve!"

In spite of his heated words, spoken of impatient worry mixed with sorrow, he went to their wagon, standing on the cemetery road behind the empty hearse, and fetched O'Malley's old coat. Meanwhile, Elodie attempted to coax a reluctant Nipper away from the new grave. The dog was taking one or two steps toward her … and then looking over his shoulder at the high-piled fresh earth, new-dimpled by rain, and moving away again. Fredi shook out the coat, and swooped Nipper up in those generous folds. The dog struggled briefly, but Fredi wrapped him fast in it, as he had on that other occasion and carried him away.

When they departed Mokelumne Hill on the following morning, Nipper traveled still wrapped in the coat, in Lotta's arms. The dog was still the picture of misery, but he didn't give any sign of wanting to escape and return to that lonely vigil in the graveyard, either at the time of their departure or at any point in their sad and winter-harried journey to San Francisco.

"He has transferred his affection to Lotta," Mrs. C. observed with some relief, as they waited at Stockton for the regular packet steamboat to San Francisco. "Poor simple creature! Well, she has always wanted pets, so that I suppose I can allow this."

"He can dance to the penny-whistle, if Lotta can learn to play it," Fredi said. He and Elodie had talked over the means of their return to the East. It was too late in the year to attempt the northern trail, and without Elodie resuming her boy-disguise again, there was no practical means of them working their way east through hiring on as teamsters, as had been Fredi's initial thought. Whenever he regarded Elodie, he knew that she would never be able to put on the pretense of being a boy for long, especially in the close company of teamsters over the months that it would take to work their way east. She was too tall to pass as a boy of twelve or thirteen, her features and womanly frame altogether too fine, too delicate to convince any but the blind that she was an older lad.

"Mr. Butterfield's company has a contract to convey the mails over the southern route," Mart Taylor suggested, finally. "They have been sending a regular stage, twice weekly from San Francisco to St. Louis for over a month now. It's expensive; $200, I believe – but safer than a journey across Panama and being stranded waiting a ship – and shorter than going around the horn. They're guaranteed to make the journey in twenty-five days."

"Given the cost of passage by ship, plus lodging and victuals, I'd say that sounds very much a bargain," Mrs. Crabtree allowed. "And you would have the security of traveling with a well-established company, as well."

"Twenty-five days," Elodie shook her head in wonderment. "Truly? It was … near to eight months by wagon, when Pa first brought us out to California. It seemed then as if it took a year, longer even, and it cost near everything we had, to buy stock, and fit out the wagon, buy supplies. I suppose that we should go to the express office as soon as we can. I am certain that there must be a great jostle for seats, too."

"You may have to wait several weeks, my dear," Mrs. Crabtree agreed. "But that will allow time for you to rest, and procure a better wardrobe for travel – and I don't think that you want to be welcomed back to the bosom of your mother's kinfolk in rags."

"No, I think not," Elodie agreed.

It turned out to not be such a long a wait as all that, for two seats on Butterfield's Overland Mail Company coach to open up. Elodie and Fredi shared the Crabtree family's rented house for little more than a week, during which time Fredi assembled his few possessions – chiefly his saddle, and for a souvenir of the gold mines, one of the gold-washing pans from the summer in the Pine Tree Diggings. He did purchase a particularly fine suit and waistcoat from a pawnbroker in Portsmouth Square who had it from a member of the gambling fraternity who had experienced a sudden streak of abysmally bad luck, and arrange to have it altered to fit him. But otherwise, all of his luggage, including a pair of thick blankets and his revolver fitted into a single large carpetbag which was what the Overland Mail allowed.

"I may as well look as if I struck it rich, once I get home," he allowed to Elodie on the very morning they departed from the Express office on the Main Plaza. It was just about sunrise, and San Francisco was wrapped in winter fog. Lotta had given a sparkling performance at the American Theater that very evening before, and the Crabtrees had treated the two travelers to a magnificent supper, saying with much foreboding that likely it would be the very last good meal they would have for the next three weeks and a bit. Elodie giggled. "You look magnificent, Fredi – quite the city dandy."

"And you look mighty fine yourself," Fredi replied, for she did; unexpectedly elegant in a plain dark broadcloth traveling dress which closed with line of covered buttons marching up the front to a high collar just underneath her chin, where the ribbons of a simple straw bonnet tied in a bow. She and Mrs. C. had planned the disposition of Elodie's money, since they could not transport a fortune in gold on the Overland Mail. A portion was made over in notes, sewn into the bottoms of their carpetbags, the rest deposited in the care of the Wells-Fargo Express company, to be transported in security to a St. Louis establishment. Upon returning from Mokelumne Hill, Elodie had sent a letter to her Aunt Sadie, a letter which hopefully, would be received in St. Louis in a timely fashion before their own arrival.

"What will you do with yourself, once you have seen me back to my aunt's?" she asked, and Fredi grinned, suddenly light at heart.

The world was bright and fair, and full of promise, as he saw it. "I have enough saved from my share of Pine Tree to repay my brother-in-law, and then a little bit left over. I suppose that I shall just find another job. I'll look up Gil Fabreaux and see if he needs another hand, or see if Jack Slade is still hiring teamsters. There's always something, Elodie."

"I wish that you had let me pay for your seat in the coach," Elodie said, for the fare had taken a substantial portion of his own takings from the last two years.

"I'd never take money from a woman," Fredi insisted. "It's not right. I promised O'Malley on his deathbed that I would see you home. And home we will be, after seeing the elephant, that's for certain."

"I don't know about that," Elodie said, as the Overland Mail coach appeared from the direction of the central post office. It was painted bright red, with the letters Overland Mail Company limned in gold on the sides. The bags of mail intended to be delivered to the east already weighed down the luggage boot. The crowd awaiting – either passengers and their friends to see them off, or just idlers with nothing better to do – chorused their awe and admiration. *Such a magnificent sight! And in a journey of less than a month to cross half the continent!*

In the decades afterwards *(and Fredi lived to see the first years of a new century, long enough to sample many of the advances made during those years, and every one of them unthinkably luxurious in comparison)* the memory of that epic journey by coach seemed sometimes like an extended and surreal bad dream. For it was a journey of three and a half weeks, of constant motion and turning wheels, galloping horses and sometimes mules, a relentless passage through day and night, with perhaps twenty minutes of erratic rest while the horses, or coach and driver were changed. It was a nightmare epic of dust and cold, of bad food and little of it, hurriedly-snatched at a dirty table and from cracked and nasty china and tin, of jolting over ruts, and sleeping fitfully, leaning against the back of a hard wooden bench, Elodie leaning against his shoulder, or with her head and shoulders resting in his lap, the two of them swathed in one of their blankets against the cold of passage across the mountain passes. The coach was very shortly traded in for a celerity wagon, a light spring-wagon with a light canvas cover and sides which could be rolled down as a fragile defense against inclement weather. Even so, it still was winter across the southern trail traced by Mr. Butterfield's overland mail company, and the cold and blowing dust were barely slowed by the canvas coverings, or by their own blankets.

A bare three or four days – Fredi was not certain at all of how much time had passed, they passed briefly through Warner's – and the home of Dona Vincenta and Don Jose-Ramon. Part of their establishment was now a stage stop and a small general store and post office, to his astonishment. He stumbled blearily from the stage while the horses were being changed, weary and aching in every limb, hoping to purchase some small edibles while Elodie looked for a place to decently relieve herself. He thought that he recognized young Jose Antonio in the back of the general stores, as he purchased some oranges, some pieces of sweet ribbon candy, and half a dozen pieces of hard-tack. He also filled up their water bottles at the well, saying wearily to Elodie as he did so, "Just close your eyes and think of the weevils and bugs as additional nourishment."

"Quick, go piss while you have the time," Elodie returned, as she took the bottles from him. Fredi sighed; never would be become accustomed to a woman speaking so frankly of the lower functions.

Dust and cold, the ceaseless beat of hooves, the jehu's cracking whip, the endless maddening swaying of the celerity, cold stars dancing the black sky overhead, wakening from a dazed slumber when a wheel clipped a large rock or a particularly deep pot-hole, sleeping all crammed together like salt cod packed into a box. It was fortunate along some stretches that they shared the celerity with only two or three others, for then there might be sufficient room to let down the seat-backs and sleep laying down. That fitful sleep was a far-distant cousin several times removed from a good night on a soft featherbed, or even under the open sky on a thick bedroll, but was still an improvement on the hideous discomfort of trying to sleep while sitting upright. Fredi awoke on one occasion about halfway through the journey to look up and see the massive, tip-tilted rock formations which sheltered Hueco Tanks. For no little time in that passage, the past and present merged in his mind. *Was he carried along in the Butterfield celerity wagon, or slumped in Fleck's saddle on that last long night drive, urging the thirsty, suffering cattle ever westward?* That vision passed as in a dream, although he did wonder later, if that was that Gil Fabreaux riding point on a dark, shadowy herd of longhorns which he saw – or thought that he saw on one night when the Butterfield Overland passed through – around – between a herd of cattle. Ghosts or real? Fredi could not decide if it was a true-seeing, a dream, or only an exhaustion-fueled nightmare, as when the stagecoach passed through the vast and desert New Mexico Territory. *Was it at Mesilla?* He thought he saw Fauntly Bean in his flamboyant Mexican suit, adorned with a constellation of silver buttons and a red silk sash about his waist.

At Fort Belknap, some days later; that was no dream-seeing, when the stage-wagon pulled in. The relief horse teams were ready to go, restrained by the hands of the station grooms. This was a station where they had a bare twenty minutes' pause. Fredi stumbled down from the celerity in a mild daze, wearied and aching in every limb. No, there was no meal at this place that he wanted to eat; but he and Elodie did wish to refresh their canteens.

He was doing so at the well, when a familiar voice observed, "Dutch Fred, that is you? You must have prospered in California!"

Through the haze of weariness and dislocation, Fredi peered up at his interlocutor. "Charlie!" he cried. It was indeed Charlie Goodnight, his friend from the Fabreaux drive, who had counseled him to guard his temper. "It is good to see you indeed! No, alas that I did not prosper in California – not to the extent that I had hoped. O'Malley and I had a claim for a while, and then we did some other work in the mining camps, until O'Malley was knifed and murdered. You remember the Satterwaites, Charlie? They both came to a bad end, for all that Eb tried to keep Zeke from trouble. Eb was killed trying to rob the Camptonville stage, and Zeke got himself hung in Moke Hill. He was the one who knifed O'Malley, you see. I think he regretted it, for it was me he was going for…"

"Damn," Charlie looked somber. "I hate to hear that, Dutch. Damn shame, I liked Eb. Bet that Zeke talked him into it. And O'Malley, too … crazy old coot. Did you ever get a straight answer as to where he came from, and what his real name was?"

"Never did," Fredi answered. "But I'm pretty certain it wasn't O'Malley … may have been Hurley, Joseph Hurley."

"Slippery to the last," Charley shook his head, and added, with a laugh. "At least you got out of it enough to buy passage on the Overland Mail! You were rewarded in some sense. Did you get hitched in California? That is some pretty lady, Dutch."

"Not a wife," Fredi acknowledged, with some mild regret, for he was quite fond of Elodie. "I'm still a rolling stone, can barely support myself. Miss Elodie Padgett is among my circle of friends. I am charged with escorting her safely to her family in St. Louis."

"Oh, that's the way of it," Charlie nodded. For himself he looked about as he had during the Fabreaux drive; a little more weathered, a little less of a lanky boy. "The both of you look tired, and hungry, too

"We have not eaten well since we left San Francisco," Fredi admitted, with regrets. "The food at the road ranches is vile beyond belief. If it were not for what we have could buy … Remember the Carillos, at Warner Springs? I bought some oranges there; we made them last for a day and a half. When we get to St. Louis, I think that I shall sleep like the dead for about a week … but you – do you have that fine ranch yet?"

"Working on it," Charlie grinned. "My step-brother and I are running cattle 'bout sixty miles southeast of here. Ain't made a fortune on it yet, but I'm aiming to be there before I'm thirty. I'm here buying supplies for the winter. But I ain't got such a long trip before me as you have. I don't envy you none."

They talked for a while, while the horses were changed out; with the better road, their journey was continuing in a fine Concord coach, which swayed like a cradle and afforded a little more shelter from the elements than the celerity wagon. Otherwise, it was merely a little less uncomfortable. But then the coach was ready to leave; Fredi and Charlie slapped each other' shoulders and promised to write. Then the jehu took up his reins and whip and it was time to hand Elodie up into the stage.

Before they had gotten three or four miles east of Fort Belknap, as Fredi sank into a weary doze, his stomach grumbling so loud that he was afraid that Elodie would hear it and make comment, there came a shout from behind the coach. They were being chased by a horseman, who drew up, and level with them. Fredi stood, leaning from the coach door; Charlie, standing in the stirrups as his horse galloped along, matching the speed of the coach and holding up a basket tied around several times with a vast calico tablecloth.

"Brought you some supper!" He shouted, as Fredi's fingers closed around the basket handle. "Be safe on your journey, Dutch – you and Miss Elodie!"

With a final wave, Charlie's horse slowed, and he was a figure dimly seen and veiled in dust, vanishing in the distance and the overland stage rolled on. The basket contained cold fried chicken, a slab of dried-apple pie, a handful of shelled pecans, half of a loaf of sourdough bread and a stoneware bottle filled with vinegar shrub. Fredi and Elodie ate ravenously of every bite, thanking Charlie for it every time they paused to wipe their fingers and lips.

Chapter 20 – A Parting in St. Louis

To Fredi's vague astonishment – and he was too wearied by the rigors of the journey to be particularly excited about the new experience – the very last leg of their journey to St. Louis was undertaken by train; the fabled iron horse, of which he had read, but never in the flesh laid eyes upon or experienced. He and Elodie, filthy dirty, stumbling with exhaustion and aching in every bone from the rigors of the journey, carried their meager luggage to the wooden passenger car hitched behind a smoke-belching iron beast with a towering chimney-stack.

"We're almost there," he said, to a wearily drooping Elodie. She had only the energy to nod and fall asleep leaning on his shoulder in the comfortless rail car. Iit was not nearly as easy a passage as the gently-swaying Concord coach had been; but a noisy, clattering, bumpy ride, screeching steel wheels on the rails and smoke and hot cinders blowing in, until Fredi finally wrenched the nearest open window closed. Smoke still seeped in through gaps around the ill-fitting windows and doors. If this was the modern age of travel, Fredi told himself, the modern age of travel could stuff all that into his saddle-bags. He would ride a horse and sleep on a blanket on the soft grass under the nearest hedge. He and Elodie were so desperately exhausted that they did fall into a fitful and unrefreshing slumber – until they reached St. Louis, half a day later. The train halted with a crash and a terrific jolt which would have wakened the dead.

"I don't know if my aunt received my letter," Elodie looked as if she were about to weep from exhaustion and over-jangled nerves. Fredi felt as if he had been thoroughly beaten with Indian clubs. Not even after the horrific storm at sea, on the ship coming over from Germany had he felt that awful. But he picked up both of their carpetbags in one hand, and supported Elodie with his other arm around her waist, and helped her to the platform, where they stood alone in the scattering of other departing travelers. No one seemed to take any interest in them, at first. Fredi set down the bags, uncertain of what to do next, should Elodie's kin not be there to meet them.

"I suppose that we can hire a driver with a carriage to take us to her house," he suggested. "You do know the address…"

"I do, but I don't know the town, at all," Elodie replied. "And how can we find a trusty driver when we are strangers here? I am so tired, Fredi. My mind is gone all foggy with wanting to sleep and sleep…"

"We'll walk out to the front of the station," Fredi said, with considerable firmness, considering that his own mind was also fogged with exhaustion. "And ask the stationmaster for a reference." He picked up the heavy carpetbags again, feeling as if his arm was about to be dragged from his shoulder, but at that moment he noted an older woman on the platform, attended by several young men and a girl of about Elodie's age. The women were fashionably turned out, and the older woman's bonnet was a magnificent confection of lace, feather plumes and flowers. She was looking about anxiously, searching for someone … then Fredi observed when her eyes fell on their own bedraggled selves, and the expression on her countenance instantly turned to joyful recognition.

"Elodie! My darling!" the older lady shrieked, as she rushed toward them in a most unladylike manner. "You are here at last – we have met the train from Tipton every day since we received your letter! My dear child, how you have grown! And the very image of your mother!"

"Aunt Sadie?" At that, Elodie burst into tears, as her aunt enveloped her in a fond and ruffle-trimmed embrace, her generous hoopskirt swaying from side to side. "It's been so long," Elodie gasped, between tears, "And the journey has been … horrible, Auntie – rapid, but horrible."

"Never mind that, my dear," Aunt Sadie kissed her niece with marked affection. "All the way from California! We have read in the newspaper of the progress of the Overland Mail – how you dared that journey all alone..."

"Not alone, Auntie," Elodie gulped. "This is Mr. Steinmetz. You should know that he was tasked by my friends in California with being my escort and protector. He is my dear friend and perfect gentleman for all that."

"You wrote so in your letter, child," Aunt Sadie replied, eyeing Fredi from boots to head. For a moment, things went rather gray for Fredi himself, as Aunt Sadie continued. "My dear, from your letters, I was expecting a rather older and more respectable gentleman ..."

"Mr. O'Malley," Fredi recovered something of composure, and his voice – along with no little horror at realizing that things had been different in California. "He was my partner in our business in the mines. He took unto himself the protection of your niece, and it was his dying charge to me that I return her to her kin. I am Frederick Steinmetz, at your service ..."

"A foreigner, are you?" Aunt Sadie held up her hand for Fredi's respectful salutation. "Well, never mind that – you are a dear lad, for seeing my sister's girl all this way. Our hospitality is yours, for as long as you wish to remain, before returning to your home..."

"Welcome it is," Fredi answered, and from exhaustion, his tone of voice was much more reproving than would have been otherwise. "Thank you for extending it to me but I am not a foreigner, madam. I have lived in Texas since I was a small child. I intend to return there, as soon as I have rested and recovered from the rigors of travel..."

"You are welcome, indeed, Mr. Steinmetz," Aunt Sadie took the reproof with only a slight frown, before snapping to the two young gentlemen accompanying her to take up the carpetbags. It seemed that they were nephews; Fredi was too entirely exhausted to catch their names, and indeed, the remainder of that day remained in his memory ever afterward as a blur of faces, and a short journey to a quiet, substantial neighborhood of terraced houses fringing a pleasant fenced square, adorned with many trees, shrubs and graveled paths. Aunt Sadie, sadly a widow now, lived there with her daughter, and one of her married sons with his wife and children.

Elodie insisted several days later that they had been treated to a splendid supper, and Aunt Sadie and the cousins were most intensely curious regarding California and the marvel of that long journey; for himself, Fredi could not call to mind any of it.

"You were most entertaining and gracious," Elodie insisted.

Fredi only shook his head in wonder. "The only part that I cared for was being able to put off my clothes and fall into a nice warm bed," he replied. "And that the room and the bed in it weren't crashing and bouncing all over the place."

He slept for two days straight through and awakened, almost completely recovered on the morning of the third day. Elodie complained of feeling ill for several more days, to the hovering worry of Aunt Sadie, who had the doctor who attended on her family come to the house every day, until Elodie was pronounced recovered from the rigors of their journey.

"So what did you do with yourself, these last few days?" Elodie asked. They were sitting in the parlor with Aunt Sadie's daughter Clara, a pretty girl of sixteen or so. Aunt Sadie herself bustled in and out of the parlor, attending to household matters, while Clara attended to her needlework and Elodie tried to.

"I went looking for work," Fredi answered, readily. "Work that will return me to Texas."

"What kind of work?" young Clara asked, with shy curiosity, just as Elodie asked, "Did you find anything yet?"

Fredi had become reluctantly aware that Clara looked on him with an admiration not wholly unromantic. He was certain that Aunt Sadie was aware of it also and did not look on this with favor. If he read the situation right, Elodie's aunt would not evict him from her household, but neither would she encourage him to remain any longer than strictly necessary.

"Any kind which takes me home to Texas, Miss Clara," Fredi answered. "But I have word of a friend of mine, who works as a wagon-master for Hockaday and Chorpening. If he is in town, perhaps he will see me to a job, or refer me to a friend who will. I am going to go to the freight offices this afternoon to see if he is in."

"I wish that you could remain in St. Louis," Clara's eyes shown with girlish affection. As Fredi opened his mouth to explain why he could not, Elodie's needle went into her thumb and she swore a sudden and manly oath. Unfortunately, she spoke it just at the moment that Aunt Sadie returned to the parlor.

"Elodie, my dear! Such coarse and unladylike language! What that says of the coarse company you have been keeping …"

Elodie burst into tears and flung the embroidery hoop aside. She ran from the parlor, leaving Clara and Fredi astonished and Aunt Sadie purse-faced with outrage. Fredi thought it wise that he also make an excuse to leave, on the grounds of his looking for news of Jack Slade at the Hockaday and Chorpening office, before Aunt Sadie recollected that he had been a portion of that coarse company that Elodie had been associating with over the last year.

He was wearing his good city clothes – the suit formerly the property of the unfortunate gambler. At the very least, Jack would think that he had prospered in California. The offices of Hockaday and Chorpening's agent in St. Louis were near the waterfront; where the wide brown Mississippi slashed across the land, as wide as the bay at San Francisco and even busier. St. Louis was tidier, an orderly place of red-brick buildings and well-drained streets, not the mad hugger-mugger of San Francisco's jumble of hills and waterfront. The bustle of the waterfront drew him irresistibly; so many splendid steamboats, the finest of them got up like massive floating layer-cakes, trimmed with carved wooden lace. Their tall ornate smoke-stacks reached almost to the sky, it seemed to Fredi, spewing clouds of dark smoke into the air. The wheels at side or stern which impelled them were massive things, unimaginably powerful. Floating palaces they were, adorned with bright brass, gold paint. There were other, more prosaic conveyances, as well; plain workaday barges with their decks crowded with cattle, or freight wagons – it was too yearly in the year for emigrant trains bound for Oregon and California to assemble, Fredi knew. But there was talk of rich gold strikes at Pike's Peake in the headwaters of the North Platte river, away up on the nearer side of the Rocky Mountains. Fredi didn't doubt that there would be gold-seekers wending their way up-river and into the mountains, as soon as the trail season opened in early spring, and maybe even before then.

He found a balk of cotton bales to sit upon, tight-packed in their wrappings. Cotton ruled the South, indeed; cotton to feed the mills of England. He might as well relish the view of the waterfront; nothing quite so enjoyable as watching other people do work that he didn't have to do himself. A little way down the waterfront, close enough to speak to without raising his voice, a bearded and lugubrious-faced man of middle age drove up with a wagon piled high with cut wood, cut and cured for the fires, the fires of homes and those which burned in the boilers and heated the steam which turned the wheels that carried the weight of commerce on the broad bosom of the Mississippi. Fredi nodded to the man, who was accompanied by a Negro servant, as roughly-clad as his master.

"For a nickel, I would help you unload the wood, save that I am wearing my best clothes," he said, and the man chuckled, without any humor at all in it at all.

"Just as well," the man replied, "For I can't afford a nickel to pay you. You're looking for work; I take it?"

"Yes," Fredi nodded. In one of those flash insights, he saw this man as one of those trusty ones, like Gil Fabreaux. The ancient expression of tragedy in his eyes – Fredi was hard-put to see that insight into words. This was a sad man, one who bore the weight of the world on his shoulders, or maybe it was only the weight of desperate poverty and responsibility. His team animals looked to be in prime condition, well-kept, almost better than their owner. "Friedrich Steinmetz. Most folk call me Dutch."

"My friends call me Sam," his new acquaintance ventured, after some moments. "Sam Grant. So you are looking for work? Hard enough to find, after the panic of last year."

There was a steamboat, a very flash and splendid one, approaching the wharf where they sat and waited, as if there was all the time in the world. But poor men must wait on the convenience of others; Fredi knew that, well enough. Likely the load of wood was intended for the boilers of that very boat.

"I'm really looking for work that will take me home to Texas," he confessed, after some moments. This was a strange, random confidence with a complete stranger, but after three weeks of rolling torment on the Overland Express and a week of uncomfortable social obligation to Elodie's Aunt Sadie, he would take his comfort where he found it, grateful that it was in conversation with this stranger in the open air of the St. Louis dockside, and not in a saloon, where someone might come at him with a knife and kill a friend in error. "I've been in the gold mines of California – near two years, now. I didn't strike it rich, so now I am going home after completing a task obligated of me through honor."

"California," the other man nodded. "Been there myself. I didn't strike it rich either; bad luck or intemperance in habits, I don't know which. But honor and duty … A burden – a heavy one, indeed. But some are meant to bear such burdens and grateful for the opportunity."

"You are right about that, Sam," Fredi agreed, acknowledging to himself that he had become fond of Elodie, as fond as a sister, in the same degree of affection as he had felt for Lotta, the Faery Star. Seeing her safely bestowed with her family was no mean accomplishment. "I could not look at myself in a mirror, if I chose to turn aside."

"If such tasks were lightly accomplished," Sam mused, "They would be commonplace qualities and men would not value them so highly."

"You sound like my father and his friends," Fredi answered. "They all have a taste for those matters. I don't. Vati makes clocks and mechanical toys for children. Philosophy is just his amusement."

"Philosophers," Sam scratched his bristly chin. "I can't claim to be one myself. I'm a farmer and not all that good at it. I did some soldiering, for a while. Maybe I should take up philosophy. It sure couldn't pay any worse. Ah, well; here's to the sale of a load of wood."

"I have a friend who works for Hockaday and Chorpening," Fredi allowed. "I am hoping to see him today and find work through him. Driving a wagon, I hope – and going in the direction of Texas."

"I wish you good luck with finding work, Friedrich – and a safe journey."

"Thank you, sir." On impulse, Fredi stuck out his hand, and Sam shook it gravely. "The best of luck with your wood ... and your farming, too."

There was not to be a meeting with Jack – it seemed that he was on the trail, fighting his way east against bitter winter storms with one last returning wagon company, but there was work for Fredi; the company had a supply train of six wagons going to Fort Belknap the next week, and there was a place for him in it, since one of the other teamsters had broken his ankle falling from his wagon that very morning.

The clerk at the freight company exclaimed in great good humor. "Providential – are you certain that you didn't push him yourself? I just now got word that he can't work for weeks, and I haven't even started to ask after a replacement!"

Fredi counted it as fortunate that the freight wagon company was set to depart St. Louis for Fort Belknap just as Aunt Sadie's welcome for him had worn thin. Young Clara had too obviously set her cap at him; mildly embarrassing for Fredi and a matter of considerable distress to Aunt Sadie. With relief, he set aside his good suit, put on workaday garments, packed his carpetbag and saddle, and departed the house on Lafayette Square for the teamster's encampment on the outskirts south of town. He did promise to pay a farewell call on Elodie, before they departed, but in the rush of work to pack the goods wagons, and assemble the necessary stock for the journey – he let it go until the very day they were to roll out.

"We're waiting on one last shipment," the wagon-master told Fredi over a hasty breakfast at a nearby boarding house. "You will have about two hours to finish your courting. If you aren't here at ten of the clock, then you better find yourself another employer."

"I'll be here," Fredi promised, with somewhat of a sinking feeling in his heart. Elodie was the last of his California friends; it somehow didn't seem right that he could have put her out of mind for most of a week. He hurried through the busy streets, rehearsing in his mind what he was going to say to her in farewell, and breathless, rang the bell at Aunt Sadie's house.

He should have saved himself the worry. The Negro housemaid who answered the door said that Miss Padgett was not at home and not expected to return until afternoon.

"But she lef' you dis letter," the girl said, consolingly. "She say to me – if'n he come to visit – he is to have dis."

"Thank you," Fredi gasped. There was no time to write and leave a message of his own. "Tell her ... that I wish her the very best. I will write to her as soon as I can. But there is no time now – we are leaving within the hour for Texas."

"I surely will do dat," she promised, and that was that. Fredi put the letter into the pocket of his jacket without looking at it; he would just about have time to get back to the wagon-park, on the banks of the river south of town.

To his relief, the wagon company was still there when he came panting along the riverbank, appearing no closer to rolling out than when he had hared off to say goodbye to Elodie. He slowed his footsteps on the muddy path, and looked out at the river, where an especially large stern-wheel steamboat was threshing down-river at speed, aided by the swift current. The river here ran deep as well as swift – not like in Texas, where it was said of those relatively shallow streams that one could break open a cask of beer and coast on the foam for a mile or two. This river was one fit to bind the continent, next to which most other rivers were mere streams in comparison. The steamboat was passing a bare stone's throw from the bank, close to where Fredi stood. He couldn't help but stop and admire the

manifestation of what his father claimed was a miracle of the age –
the steam engine. The only thing to top steam-driven ships and
locomotives, Vati said, would be when some clever engineer worked
out how to make steam-powered flying machines.

A handful of passengers stood on the tiered decks of the
steamboat, most of them looking out toward the shore; a handful of
ladies in bell-shaped crinolines, their bonnet-ribbons streaming in the
light breeze, and a slender boy whose jacket reminded Fredi of Elodie
when she dressed as Edwin. The boy turned, his gaze falling on Fredi
– he waved, just the once and Fredi stood thunderstruck. It was
Edwin, as he had first known him in San Francisco, selling
newspapers side-by-side on Montgomery Street. In the moment of
that realization, the steamboat passed on down the river, the figure of
Elodie in her boy's clothing merely a dark figure against the gleaming
white superstructure.

He fumbled for the envelope in his pocket, ripped it open with
shaky fingers. A single sheet of notepaper folded around a quantity of
notes, the notepaper marked with Elodie's neat script.

My dear friend & brother Frederick:

I suppose that I may call you my friend and brother, given how
generously you have treated me throughout our association, especially
as I began that association with you and Mr. O'Malley in telling you
both a number of deliberate untruths. While you were both the soul of
Christian forgiveness when I confessed them, my conscience still
continues to torment me with regret over how I deceived you and
traded upon yours and Mr. O'Malley's good will – for my own
advantage, and to your own disadvantage. Indeed, you spent a large
part of your own gains in California in carrying out Mr. O'Malley's
dying request to see me safe to Aunt Sadie's house. Your gallant
service was in vain – alas! I came to realize over the last few days that

I have become accustomed to a certain degree of freedom in conducting my life. I am unfitted for the restricted life which my aunt expects of a lady of good family and a substantial heiress in St. Louis. I simply cannot submit tamely to having my wings clipped; no more than a wild hawk can endure the gilded existence of a songbird in a pretty cage. During our association with Mrs. Crabtree, she favored me with much good advice in regards to establishing myself as an independent woman of means.

I am attempting to make good use of her counsel, in representing myself to be a spinster of independent fortune and legal age with regard to my father's fortune. By the time you read this – and I have no doubt that you will return for a farewell visit before departing to Texas – I will be well on the way to New Orleans, and thence to New York. I intend to travel to Ireland, and make inquiry there into Mr. O'Malley's surviving family, and ensure myself of their security and comfort in their advanced age. I have no other firm plans, but I think it likely that I will remain in foreign lands. I have always wanted to travel, and see the various marvels of which I have only read in books and such publications as were available to us in the mines.

For yourself – I know that you are proud and stubborn and would reject any such portion of unearned largess. You would not accept my purchase of your passage on the Overland Mail, insisting that such was your obligation alone. I enclose an amount in American banknotes sufficient to recompense you for your expenses, and trust that you will not only accept them now in good heart, and with my most profound thanks, but make use of them to your advantage.

In affection and with gratitude, I remain

Elodie Amelia Padgett

Fredi read the letter over twice, stuffing the notes safely away in his pocket. By the time that he had done, the steamboat was nearly out of sight around the next wide bend of the Mississippi. He was not even altogether certain now that the boy he had seen so briefly was Elodie. Not that it really mattered – if she meant what she had written in the letter, then she was gone, likely never to return.

When he had a moment, he would do as O'Malley had done – take a needle and thread, and sew them securely into the hem of his heavy round jacket. No, he would not suffer again a theft such as the one which sent him on this golden road almost three years ago. And in two months, he would be home, and repay Carl. Although, he thought – perhaps he would stop and visit Charlie – and buy a good horse from him. After all, he had his pride as a Texas drover.

On a chilly day in early March, Fredi rode up the river track from Comfort, noting with approval that new grass had already begun showing, long, lush and green, starred with wildflowers. Cattle grazed along the sheltered places on the riverbank, gathered in the thin shade of the oak trees that dotted the rolling hills around the Becker place. He paused long enough in his journey to speak to Carl's nearest neighbors, the Browns, who also ran cattle and farmed a patch, around their ramshackle cabin.

"Why ever it's young Fred!" Mrs. Brown – near toothless and slatternly in her faded calico dress – exclaimed. She dashed a basin of dishwater over the edge of the sagging porch, onto a disgruntled pig, who squealed and moved grudgingly perhaps three or four feet, before collapsing with a grunt. "Where you come from, you scamp! Carl tol' us you were out in Callyfornia, looking for gold!"

"I was," Fredi replied – he did not dismount from the horse he had bought from Charlie Goodnight. He was almost to home, and did not want to the be object of lavish welcome at the Browns, since it was likely that courtesy would require him to remain for at least an hour – and he was tired and longing to ride up to the Becker homestead – the tall stone house on a rocky knoll overlooking the river valley below, the house with the bird on a nest in a branch of an apple tree carved over the door, the date of the house building carved below. "But now I'm done, and home again."

"And about time, too," Mrs. Brown replied. "Brown and Carl are looking to hold the spring round-up next week!" She shook her head, adding, "Well, I should like to hear of your adventures, young Fred – but you are longing for home, and I dessay that we will hear of all your tales soon enough. Welcome home, Fred!"

"Thank you, dear Mrs. Brown," Fredi replied. Yes, the Browns and all of Carl's neighbors would be agog to hear of what he had seen in California. But he was struck by the sudden sure conviction that very few would believe him, and perhaps he should let it all go. Although those that knew of Colonel Jack Hays would likely credit what Fredi told of encountering him on the waterfront, after having rowed a small boat across the bay from Oakland Township. But all the rest; bandits, and robbers, gold in the riverbanks, murder in the streets of San Francisco and the saloons of Moke Hill, of Ma'am Pleasant's erotic wiles, of girls dressed as boys, an amazingly rich cache of gold under a half-dead pine tree on the North Fork, of Mormons and gold-miners, fugitive Fenians, and the Faery Star dancing under a glittering golden rain thrown on stage … likely Carl's neighbors would never believe a single word of it.

And Fredi had no intent of telling them anyway. He took his courteous leave of Mrs. Brown and her pig, and rode on up the valley, seeing the yellowed ivory limestone of the Becker homestead appearing coyly through the trees as he neared the place. When he came up the track that curved around the walled orchard and led to the farmyard, he met Carl, leading the old horse, Three Socks, hitched to a cart full of well-rotted muck down from the pile beside the barn to dig into the earth around his precious apple trees. His brother-in-law stopped the cart, and grinned, quite unsurprised.

"So you're back," he remarked in German. "Nice horse. Did you buy it in California?" Carl was as incapable of being surprised as anyone on this side of the grave, Fredi reflected. It was nice to speak German again, as good as putting on an accustomed and comfortably shabby garment.

"From a friend at Fort Belknap," Fredi answered. "Who swore that he has the blood of champion trotters in him."

"If he was a good friend, he might even have told you true," Carl nodded. "Good that you're back, since we're planning on rounding up and branding the spring calves next week. Did you strike it rich in California?"

"Not so much," Fredi replied. "I really didn't spend all that much time in the mines."

"Tell us all about it over dinner," Carl said, and Fredi shrugged.

"Not all that much to tell – it was all pretty silly, at that."

Notes for *The Golden Road*

This Western adventure has been planned for almost seven years, ever since the completion of the *Adelsverein Trilogy*. I had originally sketched out another trilogy with the theme of the western trails; the first of which would follow the life of Margaret Becker in Texas, and serve as a kind of prelude. Eventually that became two books; *Daughter of Texas* and *Deep in the Heart*. The other two in that set would be *The Quivera Trail* – the story of Dolph Becker and his English bride and this volume – the adventures of a wide-eyed teenage Fredi Steinmetz in Gold Rush era California, slotted into sequence in the Trilogy between *The Gathering*, and *The Sowing*. That he had been to California and back, hunting for gold and never finding much of it was mentioned very briefly in *The Sowing*. I had always wanted to write a picaresque Gold Rush adventure ... the mystery is why it took me so darned long to finish this one.

I wrote those first elements of what I had begun to call the Western Barsetshire Cycle, and sketched out the first chapter or two ... and then got distracted; first by the prospect of rebooting the Lone Ranger mythos, as a historically accurate YA adventure set in the time of the Republic of Texas, and then the prospect of wrapping up the story-line suggested in *Daughter of Texas/Deep in the Heart,* with a young woman coming west and discovering an old family scandal. *Sunset and Steel Rails* was inspired by reading about the Fred Harvey Company, and nothing would do but to drop other projects to work on that one. That book did have a bearing on this one; in that Fredi Steinmetz appears as a character; late in middle age, still a man of action, very much at home in the late 19th century west. How did he get that way? Cattle drover, gold-miner, mail express rider, newspaper seller, soldier, stage hand, and bottle-washer, trail boss and rescuer of ladies in distress ... it became quite a story on its own.

On the way, he encountered a good many other interesting people, some of whom later became very, very well known, one way or another. This adventure encompasses nearly as many historical characters as *Daughter of Texas/Deep in the Heart,* which was practically a Who's Who of the Republic of Texas. It was of mind-boggling, realizing how many later-to-be-famous people were in California in 1856-58 – and working out a creative means of having Fredi encounter them.

In this book his adventures begin in Texas; the Yankee brothers whom he meets at the start of his journey – whose name he hears as "Homestead" are the writer and urban park designer Frederick Law Olmstead and his brother – who as fortune had it, were traveling through Texas and the south during those years, writing and reporting on what he found there. Angelina Eberly – who appeared in *Deep in the Heart* – had moved to first Port Lavaca in 1847, and the following year to Indianola, to run a very well-appointed hotel; the American House. The teamster, Joseph Alfred "Jack" Slade who befriends and hires Fredi appears to have been working at that time in Texas as a freighter or stage-coach driver. He was described by Mark Twain some years later; *"He was so friendly and so gentle-spoken that I warmed to him in spite of his awful history. It was hardly possible to realize that this pleasant person was the pitiless scourge of the outlaws, the raw-head-and-bloody- bones the nursing mothers of the mountains terrified their children with."* As mentioned, Jack Slade began a career in the west, as an Army teamster, driving military freight wagons during the Mexican War. Eventually he achieved achieving the dignity of a job as wagon-master for a Salt Lake City-based freighting concern on the Overland Trail, and then fame as section superintendent, overseeing the doings of the all-important stage line on the Central Overland trail. He was one of those instrumental in establishing the Pony Express in 1860. But the soft-spoken and polite aspect of Jack Slade's personality utterly vanished when he drank. He became as dangerous and as uncontrollable as a coiled rattlesnake. Repeated drinking binges followed by violent outbursts cost him his job with the Central Overland, and eventually his life. He was hanged in public in Virginia City, Wyoming, in March, 1864.

The horse-trading Sally Doyle was likewise a real person with an outsized reputation. Rancher, freight-boss and horse trader in the years before the Civil War, Sally Doyle is still popularly known as Sally Skull to local historians. There were many legends attached to her life, some of them even backed up by public records. Her full given name was Sarah Jane Newman Robinson Scull Doyle Wadkins Horsdorff. She married – or at least co-habited – five times, the first time at barely the age of sixteen to a fellow early settler in Texas, Jesse Robinson. She rode spirited horses, and astride – not with a lady-like side-saddle. She tamed horses, raised cattle, managed a bullwhip and a lariat, spoke Spanish fluently and was a dead shot with a revolver. There are no daguerreotypes or any sketches from life of Sally, only brief descriptions by those who met her and took note. *"...Superbly mounted, wearing a black dress and sunbonnet, sitting as erect as a cavalry officer, with a six-shooter hanging at her belt, complexion once fair but now swarthy from exposure to the sun and weather, with steel-blue eyes that seemed to penetrate the innermost recesses of the soul..."* was the testimony of one obviously shaken individual. Her first husband sued for divorce, claiming abandonment, among other charges. Two weeks after the divorce was granted, Sally married a gunsmith named George Scull. Although she married three times more, it was an alternation of his surname that she would bear in folklore. Jesse Robinson is on record as surviving marriage with Sally, which cannot be said with assurance of one and possibly two subsequent husbands.

By the time of the 1850 US Census, Sally and George Scull were no longer a couple. In land sale records, she declared herself as a single woman and George to be deceased. She also acquired a ranch of her own, at Banquete Creek, some twenty miles west of Corpus Christi. There she conducted profitable horse-trading and cattle-ranching enterprises, and acquired another husband, one John Cook. Sally bought horses from as far away as Mexico, selling them up and down the Gulf Coast as far as New Orleans. She paid in gold – carrying her funds in a nosebag hanging from the horn of her saddle, just as described here. She already had a reputation as a woman not to be tangled with. No one messed with Sally; like many another old west gunslinger, a ferocious reputation was as much an effective defense as was her bullwhip, six-shooters, bowie-knife … and another pair of hideaway pistols concealed in the folds of her split-skirt riding costume.

An abiding element in Sally's legend is that she killed one of her husbands, or contributed to his drowning at a river crossing. Scull or Doyle are the likeliest candidates, as the other three appeared in public records long after their turn in the marital barrel with Sally. Sally's next essay in matrimony, with one Isaiah Wadkins, was brief and disastrous. She filed for divorce, accusing him of not only beating her and dragging her bodily a good distance, but also of living in open adultery with another woman in Rio Grande City. The case of adultery was so open that Sally was readily granted a divorce and the grand jury charged Isaiah. Finally, on the eve of the Civil War, Sally took up with one Christoph Horsdorff, a man about half her age.

The Union blockade of the South changed everything for Sally. The U.S. Navy's blockade of Southern ports and commercial shipping held a noose strangle-tight on the Confederacy … but there was a single, significant work-around to that noose: Mexico. The cotton-wealth of Texas flowed across the border at Matamoros and from there out to the wider world. Sally with her years of local business experience, her horses and wagons had a vital part in this. But when the war ended, Sally Scull vanished. No one reported any memorable encounters with the fearless, hard-riding, pistol-packing horse-trading Sally. Fires in the courthouses in localities where she lived or did business erased Sally from the public records. There is no record of her death and no known grave, only a story to the effect that she and Christoph Horsdorff went out for a ride one day from the Banquete ranch, and he came back alone ... but nothing conclusive or known for certain. Horsdorff went north, and married another woman in 1868. A tradition persists that she went farther west, to live with kin. She would have been in her fifties or sixties, and decades of hard living and hard work in the out-of-doors would have told on the strongest physique.

Of Fredi's friends in the early chapters of this book, Polydore Aloysius O'Malley is a whole creation. So is Gil Fabreaux, although the journey to California with a herd of cattle is based on reminiscences recorded in J. Martin Hunter's *Trail Drivers of Texas*. Until reading that materiel as part of my research for the *Trilogy*, I had not been aware of pre-Civil War long trail cattle drives, especially not over the southern trail to California. Charlie Goodnight – although a real and significant character, and one better known than Jack Slade or Sally Skull – is not known to have been involved in a long trail drive to California, although from the biography that I have of him, by J. Evetts Haley he was briefly interested in making such a journey, and spent a number of years in his late teens "messing about" on the unsettled frontier. It is not entirely out of character to have included him in Gil Fabreaux's venture.

On to California, which marked the high tide-line of the Spanish empire in the New World. Which was a quiet backwater until gold was discovered in late 1848 at Coloma, by the employees of Captain

Sutter – who, for his various enterprises, was desirous of building a sawmill in the foothills of the Sierra Nevada. Fate would have it that his business plan encompassed his own eventual ruin … and the ruin of those Hispanic property-owners who had vast estates on that far-flung fringe of empire. Theirs was a rural society presided over by an aristocracy of landowners who had been granted their holdings by the king or civil government. Their names still mark the land in the names of towns, roads and natural features; Carrillo, Sepulveda, Verdugo, Vallejo, Dominguez, Pico, Castro, Figueroa, and Feliz, among many others. They ran cattle or sheep on their leagues. The hard work was mostly performed by native Californian Indians; those who had survived such epidemics as were brought inadvertently by Europeans and who were amenable to being trained in useful agricultural skills. Their estates produced hides, wool and tallow; their owners lived lives of comfort, if no very great luxury. From all accounts, they were openhandedly generous, amazingly hospitable, devout and a little touchy about personal insult and apt to fight duels over it, but that could be said of most men of the 18th and early 19th centuries.

One of those tracts was at present-day Warner Hot Springs. A fine property on the main southern trail, it was the object of considerable legal wrangling, as it was inadvertently granted to two different claimants; Silvestre de la Portila in 1836, and transplanted Yankee, John Joseph 'Juan Jose' Warner eight years later. Juan Jose Warner built an adobe house on the property, and conducted ranching and trading operations until an uprising by local Indians drive him out in 1851. In the meantime, Silvestre de la Portila left the property to Vincenta Sepulveda, the daughter of a long-established local family. The powers that be decided in favor of Dona Vincenta, who at the age of 21 had married another scion of a well-to-do ranch family, Tomas Antonio Yorba, who was more than twice her age. After ten years of productive and apparently happy marriage Tomas Yorba died, leaving his wife the residence, large herds of sheep and cattle, considerable jewelry and the care of their four surviving children. She continued managing the property, her household and her business; a wealthy, attractive and capable woman. After a decent interval, she married Jose Ramon Carrillo. Romantically, they met at the wedding of Dona Vincenta's niece to an office of the Mexican Army. Jose Ramon Carrillo had a reputation for physical courage, which was not based solely on his experiences as a soldier. *(He had engaged in several skirmishes between Californios and the Anglo members of the Bear Flag party, or during the Mexican War and in fighting with hostile local Indians, which was pretty much what had been expected of a man of his age and class.)* The story that he told of his fight with a bear is taken from historical records, as is the debacle of his second encounter with a bear, witnessed by Fredi and O'Malley. During the Civil War, he also served as a spy and scout for the Union Army in the Sonora. There were shadows falling on him, however; a political and business rival was found dead, shot in the back by person or persons unknown late in 1862. Two years later, Don Ramon also fell to an assassin's ambush. The murderer was never identified. Dona Vincenta continued to manage the ranch, with the aid of her grown son for another five or six years, before moving to Anaheim, and a long retirement in the house of her married daughter; Dona Vincenta lived to the age of 94. The Warner Hot Springs property was sold in the 1870s, continuing as a profitable sheep ranch for the remainder of the century and into the next. The house is now a museum, and open to the public.

Fauntleroy "Roy" Bean, later "Judge Roy Bean, the only law west of the Pecos" managed by some miracle to live a long and eccentric life. There were so many legends attached to his name – many of which he encouraged himself – that it is sometimes difficult to be certain which are truth and which are exaggerations. I have chosen to go with some of the more entertaining stories, specifically the affair with a local belle, the duel and the almost-hanging. He was a Kentuckian who gravitated down river to New Orleans in his mid-teens, got into trouble with authorities there, and migrated to San Antonio to work with Sam Bean, an older brother who had worked up a nice business hauling freight – just as Jack Slade had done – after Army service in the Mexican War. The brothers Bean; Roy and Joshua, followed the Gold Rush to California. Cannily, they did not waste time and energy hunting for gold. Fauntleroy fought a legendary horseback duel with another man in the streets of San Diego; both wounded each other, and startled the town considerably. Fauntleroy was arrested, and confined in San Diego's first proper stone-built jail; the first prisoner confined there and the first to escape from it, with the aid of a pair of knives smuggled into him, supposedly concealed in the gift of some tamales from one of his lady admirers.

Joshua set up a saloon in San Diego, and eventually another one in San Bernardino – but Fauntleroy continued to be the scapegrace little brother, eternally bailed out of trouble by his older brothers. I have slightly altered the sequence of events, regarding Fauntleroy's exodus from San Diego, and Josh Bean's murder in San Bernardino. It does not appear that Fauntleroy Bean lingered in San Bernardino for very long. He joined his other brother Sam, in running a saloon and grocery store in a hamlet near Silver City, New Mexico. During the last years of the Civil War, he was working as a teamster again, in San Antonio, hauling cotton to Matamoros, Mexico, to evade the Union blockade. The post-war years saw him remaining in San Antonio, varying his career by keeping a saloon and retailing firewood, beef and milk to the good housewives of the area. Alas, the firewood was cut from a neighbors' wood-lot, the beef also rustled from neighbors; and the milk was adulterated with creek water.

Fauntleroy Bean is mentioned briefly in *The Quivera Trail*, as "that awful Bean person" when Jane Becker is warned against purchasing milk from him.

The notorious outlaw Juaquin Murietta – known as the Robin Hood of Gold Rush-era California is a figure swathed in even more mystery than the original Robin Hood. He is supposed to have been a gold-seeker who came to California from Hermosillo, Mexico as a '49er, clashed with American Argonauts, and thereafter turned to what was quaintly called "a life of crime." His motivation, experiences and the deeds of his gang are all a matter of conjecture, most of it of the sensational created-out-of-whole-cloth sort. There may have been several Mexican outlaws operating under that *nom-du-guerre*, as it were. Juaquin Murietta and one of his outlaws, Manuel "Three-Finger Jack" Garcia may have been killed by a detachment of California Rangers near Coalinga in 1853. The supposed head of Murietta and Garcia's hand were displayed, preserved in jars of alcohol up and down towns in the gold fields … or it might not have been the right head and hand at all. (*Juaquin Murrietta's nephew, variously known as Tomaso Rodendo, Tomas Procopio Bustamante, and half a dozen other aliases was a bandit of equal or greater renown in the 1860s through 1880s, as an associate of Tiburcio Vasquez, and is supposed to have been the inspiration for the character of Zorro.*)

Which brings us to San Francisco of the 1850s. Responsible citizens had once before resorted to a Committee of Vigilance, in response to a riot instigated by a criminal element known as the 'Hounds' in 1851. The Hounds were housebroken, following a judicious culling of the most notorious ring-leaders – either hung or exiled, but that was only a temporary solution. Five years, later the situation degenerated to a point beyond the toleration of honest and civic-minded citizens. By 1856, it was more than just a situation of sober citizens faced with obstreperous criminals – by 1856 it was sober citizens arrayed against a corrupt, criminal-allied, and crony-capitalist big-city machine. A local and trusted financial and express firm failed the year before, sending shockwaves through the business community. Company assets were taken over in what was suspected to be shady means which benefitted those most closely allied with the political machine. James King of William was one of the most vocal crusaders against the endemic corruption. The *Daily Evening Bulletin* riveted and titillated the reading public with his editorials and straight news stories as thoroughly as he angered those whom he targeted. The shooting of the federal marshal by the gambler Charles Cora happened as outlined here, as did the murder of King himself by James Casey, the man he had outed as a convicted felon. Both Casey and Cora were charged, tried and hanged by the Committee – but this was a storm that was building slowly, and that would have been obvious to anyone paying attention.

William T. Sherman, later famous for (among other things) an armed jaunt through the Georgia countryside in the last year of the Civil War, was in San Francisco at that time – a civilian bank manager for Lucas, Turner & Co, whose bank building still stands. He also briefly served as commander of the California militia – but resigned during the period that the Vigilance Committee held all the cards. The governor of California wanted to put down the organization, calling it an insurrection, but the local Army commander refused absolutely to supply the militia from the military armory, and that was the point when Sherman resigned. Ulysses S. Grant also served in California, along with Sherman – his eventual commander and good friend. But the loneliness and boredom of frontier service at that time got to Grant, and he resigned from the Army and returned East ... living in striated circumstances on a hardscrabble farm outside St. Louis, where Fredi meets him, waiting to sell a load of wood at dockside. John Coffee Hays, the famed former Texas Ranger commander had also settled for good in California by this time – in Oakland, across the bay from San Francisco. He was named the US surveyor-genera for the State of California, and amassed a substantial income from real estate and ranching. He was often observed, in a small rowboat, commuting across the neck of the bay from his home in Oakland to attend to business in San Francisco, as Fredi observed.

And that brings me to the mysterious and controversial Mary Ellen Pleasant, the woman of a thousand stories and about as many aspects; so many of them that even she may not have been entirely certain which of them were true by the end of her life. White or black, good Quaker or voodooienne, shrewd Yankee, languid New Orleans charmer, a good friend to women and escaped slaves, or a procurer, extortionist or merely a good businesswoman, a financial supporter of John Brown's uprising ... all that can be said for certain is that she arrived early in the 1850s in San Francisco, identifying racially as white, a skilled cook, and took employment running exclusive boarding and restaurant establishments. She partnered in investments with Thomas Bell, and amassed a considerable fortune. After the Civil War, she changed her race to black in the City Directory ... and eventually engaged in a lawsuit which resulted in the desegregation of the city's streetcar system.

Like many performers who achieved super-star status by performing before audiences in California, Charlotte Mignon "Lotta" Crabtree arrived from somewhere else – in this case, New York. Her parents, John Ashworth Crabtree and Mary Ann Livesey Crabtree emigrated from the British Isles sometime in the 1840s. John, seeking adventure and a fortune in the Gold Rush, went by ship ahead of his family; his wife and daughter followed in 1852. Legend has it that he was not on the docks to meet them when they arrived in San

Francisco. Eventually a message arrived from John, directing them to the boom-town of Grass Valley, in the foothills of the Sierra Nevada, where he had given up on mining gold and settled on running a boarding house. In the biographies of Lotta Crabtree that I can locate, this marks the last life-significant decision he made regarding his family. Thereafter, Mary Ann ruled Lotta's life and career choices. She encouraged her daughter in performing long sentimental ballads, playing the old-fashioned minstrel-show banjo and enlarging on a repertoire of dance moves; Irish jigs, a little ballet, fandangos and soft-shoe, Highland flings and reels. The child was a born entertainer, and encouraged by a neighbor, the notorious Lola Montez – born Eliza Gilbert, fresh from a turn as the official mistress of the mad King Ludwig of Bavaria, and eventually to travel on to Australia to perform in gold camps there. Mary Ann, the soul of stubborn practicality, had no reservations about her child performing in public, although she nixed the Australia notion. The Crabtree family moved to another gold camp, Rabbit Creek, where tavern-keeper Mart Taylor, often hosted traveling dramatic groups, singers and musicians at his business. Lotta Crabtree made her professional debut there at the age of six, dressed in in a green long-tailed coat, knee-britches, a green top-hat and brandishing a miniature shillelagh. She sang and danced an Irish jig … this brought down the house, and a rain of coin and gold nuggets. For two or three years, Lotta and her mother toured the gold camps; a kind of 19th century Shirley Temple and every bit as popular. Mary Ann turned out to be a scrupulously careful manager of her daughter's fame and money. By the end of the decade, the family had moved back to San Francisco – a base from which Lotta continued touring and performing. Eventually, Lotta and her family returned East, where Lotta continued to perform to rapturous applause and tour with her own company. She performed in roles especially written for her; lively, petite, given to performing in male clothing and daring to smoke slender black cigars. By any standards she was attractive, had many admirers and brief romances, but never married. Mary Ann invested the takings from Lotta's theatrical performances in bonds and real estate which generated sufficient income to support the family when Lotta retired from performing at the age of 45. She spent the rest of her life in comfort and mild luxury, dabbling in painting, charitable work and foreign travel. Lotta Crabtree left a fortune estimated at 4 million dollars when she died in 1924. The bulk of it was in a charitable trust to benefit aging actors, animals and veterans.